The Ulysses Man

A Novel

Shane Joseph

Other Books by Shane Joseph

Novels

Redemption in Paradise

After the Flood

Short Stories

Fringe Dwellers

The Ulysses Man

A Novel

Shane Joseph

This is a work of fiction. Any resemblance to events, or to people living
or dead, is entirely co-incidental and beyond the intent of the author or
the publisher.

First Edition

Cover Design—Joanna Joseph

Typeset in Garamond

Library and Archives Canada Cataloguing in Publication

Joseph, Shane, 1955-
The Ulysses man : a novel / Shane Joseph.

ISBN 978-0-9869528-0-7

I. Title.

PS8619.O846U49 2011   C813'.6   C2011-905324-1

This book is dedicated to my parents, Sherman and Gladys, who gave me my first home.

- Shane Joseph

My home for the first six years of my life as an only child was idyllic and nestled in the loving care of my father and mother. I was cocooned from the outside world and from the dramatic events of change taking place in my newly independent post-colonial homeland, Ceylon. Then my brother Paul was born and everything changed. The home I thought I had disappeared. This is my story about how I re-discovered home...

- Martin James

Part 1 - Escaping Home

"It is equally wrong to speed a guest who does not want to go, and to keep one back who is eager. You ought to make welcome the present guest, and send forth the one who wishes to go" – Homer

1. Do They Shoot Dogs in Canada?

Martin James's brother Paul was born two days after Easter in 1961. Martin remembered the strange antiseptic smell of the hospital when they visited Mum and the baby; and the smell hovered over the infant even when Paul was brought home, despite the talcum powder and lotions they poured over him. Paul's arrival saw his parents shift focus from Martin, until then, their only child; they looked distracted, for the baby was colicky at night. They quarrelled. Dad slept in the spare room as he had to go to work the next day, and Mum cried often as she lulled Paul to sleep and stuck a sucked out breast in the little bugger's mouth. Martin didn't like Paul much and couldn't understand why everyone fussed over him. Dad stopped reading Martin his favourite western comics at bedtime. Dad had stopped reading comics altogether—his one pastime. Dad was so busy.

When they took the baby over to Grandma's for the official "showing" after the Christening, Jess, the mixed Alsatian, had just littered again. Jess's litters varied, as different dogs crept over the fence to mate during her heat periods. The pups were golden hued this time, and one lively fellow caught Martin's attention.

"I want to take him home," Martin cradled the pup and announced firmly to the shrinking pool of aunts and uncles who were cooing over Paul and passing him around like a rare commodity. Many extended family members who had already emigrated to Australia or Canada would never see Paul, and others in the room—but "in process,"—would probably see him just this once.

Dad looked up, embarrassed, and stared at his older son. "Let's talk about it later."

"No, I want him today," Martin said, barely holding back his tears.

Grandma stepped into the fray. "Oh, let him have one, child. I was going to put those creatures to sleep anyway. Jess is a puppy factory. The pups grow up and come back to mate with her and it goes on and on…"

So, as Mum and Dad coddled Paul in the taxi, Martin petted the little pup in his arms, naming it Goldie before they got home.

Goldie grew up fast. It ran everywhere, and followed Martin all the time, at first not quickly enough to keep pace, but catching up by the day. The Jameses lived in the Buddhist temple town of Kelaniya, a few miles outside the capital city Colombo. Their home was a townhouse in Perera Gardens, a large estate thick with tropical vegetation. Fifteen rental units occupied the estate: small two and three-bedroom bungalows. The road running through Perera Gardens was sandy and the houses ringed lawns on which large coconut trees sprouted. This was Martin's, and now Goldie's, stomping ground.

During the dry season, Martin took his bicycle rim out daily, propelling it with a well-worn stick lodged into the crevice running through its circumference. He ran through the estate, weaving in and out of the trees. The trick was not to let the rim run away or fall down, despite the twigs, cow dung and stones littering the route. With the wind flapping behind him, the familiar confines of the estate were comforting: amused glances from neighbours going about their household chores, smells of curry as he neared kitchens or of smoke when someone was incinerating garbage. As a six-year-old, he could roam about freely and so it didn't bother him, as it did his parents, to be a Christian in a garden full of non-Christians. This became his and Goldie's routine for the next six months.

Martin ignored Paul and Seetha the ayah, who carried the baby whenever she was through with her housework. Seetha was an "old maid," and had no children of her own. Paul had suddenly become "her child" and she would shoo Martin away from the baby.

Martin yearned for the long walks he used to take with his mother before Paul arrived, for the stories she read him on those walks when they would sit in the shade of the coconut grove where the river skirted the southern end of Perera Gardens. She had been an English teacher briefly, before she married and then stayed home to raise Martin. Her favourite books were Homer's *Iliad* and *Odyssey*; Martin was captivated by the courage of Hector and Paris, but Odysseus, or Ulysses as he was otherwise known, was his real hero; not only was he brave, Odysseus was also cunning. Martin missed laying back in the grass and looking up at the sky between the waving coconut fronds, listening to his mother's animated voice conjure up scenes of chariots and swordfights and monsters, hearing the yells of men locked in mortal combat, feeling the gush of blood, and smelling the sweat of human endeavour.

One day, when Seetha was out in the garden watering the cannas, keeping an eye on Paul who was kicking and sucking his rattle on the blanket spread on the lawn, Goldie ambled over. The dog sniffed and drooled on the baby. Seetha dropped the hose and screamed at the animal. She threw a twig at it; Goldie snapped at her viciously. Part of her frustration, Martin realized, was that the dog had been active in the garden recently and had pissed on the plants several times. The *ayah* then kicked the animal, spewing her broken English. "*Ayyo!* What happened this dog? Biting now, hah?"

Martin quickly sprang to Goldie's aid, fearing that Seetha might stone it next, like she had done with Gunadasa's dog, when the old widowed accountant had watched Seetha bathing at the well in her *diyareddah* one day. On that occasion, Martin stumbled on her soaping herself slowly and deliberately under the wet cloth, while the accountant grinned by the fence and his dog barked as if in heat. Upon seeing Martin, Seetha quickly retrieved her hands from their sensual self-ministrations, picked up a stone and hurled it at Gunadasa's dog, shouting, "*Para Balla!*" while the accountant shuffled off, smiling.

Now, as Martin pulled Goldie away from Seetha, he sensed the agitation in the animal. It roared and snarled, and the dribble was thick on its tongue. That night it barked a lot and Dad got up several times shouting "That bloody dog! What the hell has got into it?"

The next morning, Martin found Goldie with a thick ring of foam around its mouth. It had run about the house in the night drooling on everything. Seetha rushed out of the kitchen where she slept on her mat at night, shouting, "*Aney—pissu balla!*"

"My dog isn't mad!" Martin protested, but Mum had an alarmed look on her face and locked Paul up in the master bedroom. Goldie was tied to the coconut tree by the well in the back garden for the rest of the day, where it howled and frothed even more.

That evening, the neighbours, led by old Gunadasa himself, came in procession to the James house to say that they couldn't put up with a mad dog in the estate, and could the Jameses "Please do something about it."

"What the hell do you want me to do, Gune?" Dad yelled. He'd just cycled home from another gruelling day at his job as a clerk in the city, after scouring the shops for a particular brand of powdered milk for Paul, the only kind the infant could digest.

"Must put it to sleep or take to the vet or something, no?" Gunadasa turned to the rest of the sombre-looking neighbours who nodded in unison.

"There is no vet in Kelaniya. I'll have to take the animal into Colombo. Can you give me a lift in your car?"

"Are you mad, James—with a mad dog inside?"

"Then you'll have to wait until I have the time to do this. I've got other priorities—like finding milk for the baby. There was only one tin available today. This bloody country is going to the dogs with all this import control bullshit."

"Well, we've warned you."

The neighbours nodded sadly.

The next morning a dead rat was found floating in the James's well and the water was undrinkable.

"Bloody cowards!" said Dad.

"They are trying to tell us something, Victor," Mum said.

"I suppose I'll have to wring that dog's neck and give them the carcass as proof."

"No, don't hurt Goldie," Martin interrupted, choking on his jam sandwich. "Goldie is sick. You take Paul to the doctor all the time, why not Goldie?"

"Because animals are not equal to humans," Dad said, and shut off further discussion.

Goldie's condition worsened. At night, Martin stole in with food for the animal, now moved into the spare room and chained to the bed in deference to the neighbours. There was frothy spittle, urine and feces all over, as the animal had no way to "go outside." And a terrible smell like meat rotting in the open-air market in town at the end of a hot day. Seeing its master, Goldie stopped barking and took on a plaintive look that convinced Martin the animal was not mad; perhaps ill, just like Paul was with his periodic colic.

Things got serious when Seetha's mother, Kodagamage Margaret Nona arrived on the scene. Martin did not like Margaret, with her blood-red mouth and missing teeth; she chewed betel incessantly and spewed forth indiscriminate streams of crimson spit wherever she settled. Therefore, Mum never invited her into the house. Margaret would sit by the well and boast about how well her seven daughters were doing, employed as domestics in various homes, and how she visited each one monthly to check on working conditions. "I guarantee my daughters will not have illicit love affairs, unwanted pregnancies—none of that," Margaret constantly reminded Mum. Today, however, she was in a different mood, Martin observed while hovering in the vicinity.

"My daughter will need twenty-one injections in the stomach," Margaret said with finality, raising her sari and squatting on the back porch after listening to Seetha's recounting of recent events. She spoke in Sinhala, placing Mum, with her comfort for speaking in the patois English of the Dutch Burghers, at an immediate disadvantage in the discussion.

"The dog is not mad. At least, we have no proof yet," Mum said, in halting Sinhala.

"Then you must find out. Soon. Or I will have to find another place for my daughter. Think of it, even your baby will need injections now."

"What do you want us to do?"

"There are ways. Poison."

"No!" Mum was furious at the suggestion. "I thought you people didn't kill animals?" Martin hugged the hem of her skirt, trying to shut out these diabolic plans.

"We can always go to the temple afterwards and do *pooja*. I can arrange for a man to come and dispose of the animal."

"You will have to talk to my husband before you do anything." Mum went indoors dragging Martin with her.

That evening Mum and Dad talked in whispers for a long time on the back porch.

From scraps of the hushed conversation that Martin picked up, it became clear that the animal couldn't just be disposed of. It had to be analysed for rabies at the dog pound laboratory in Borella.

"And they only want the head at the laboratory!" Dad hissed.

"Shh!" Mum countered.

"I wish you would make up your mind and get your sister to sponsor us," Dad said. "Ever since Independence, I've become more of a stranger here. Very soon there will be no Burghers left in Ceylon."

"Where is this coming from? Every time you face a challenge, you want to Burgher-off somewhere."

They were silent for awhile. Dad slapped his thigh and swore, "Bloody mosquitoes."

Mum spoke in a pre-occupied tone. "Canada is not easy either. It's a lot of hard work over there. No servants. And it's cold."

Martin was forbidden from going into the spare room, and food for the room's four legged occupant was now dropped in from the outside window. Martin would peer in through the bars of the window at Goldie, who though weakening, summoned the courage to bark whenever anyone came by, disgorging clumps of brownish-yellow phlegm. Its eyes poured over Martin, seemingly to imply, "Why?" And Martin had to avert his gaze each time. The sick dog was like a judge condemning him to eternal damnation.

The "problem solver" arrived on a Sunday, three days after Poya, the day of the full moon. He carried a single-barrel shotgun that looked like it had last seen action in WWI. He was thin and tall, and wore a white sarong and banyan. He looked through the window and wrinkled his nose. "Can't take him out, *mahattaya.*"

"What do you mean?" Dad had taken two shots of arrack before the shotgun man arrived. It was early in the day, but Dad had cut his toe working with the mammoty in the back garden and had needed a pain killer. Martin guessed that Dad had been distracted during his labours. Dad had been distracted all week.

"This dog is too far gone," the man replied. "We'll have to shoot it through the window."

Dad downed his glass but did not say anything. He looked beaten.

"I guess I'll have to say goodbye to the clothes in the spare room," Mum said in resignation.

"But Buddhists don't kill," Martin said. "Isn't that why you asked me not to shoot birds in the paddy field with my pellet gun? Because of what people would say?"

"This is different son," Dad said putting his arm around Martin. The logic still did not add up for Martin, and he struggled for other arguments.

"Why can't we get the vet to come, instead of this man?"

"Vets don't make house calls. Animals are not important," Dad said. Then, turning to the man, he said, "The laboratory needs the head."

Martin took his favourite book, *The Call of the Wild,* and forced himself to stare at the pages at the other end of the house. When the shot rang out, echoing like cannon fire, he dropped the book and ran around to the back where Mum was throwing up by the well.

Martin was torn between hugging his mother—partly for his own protection—and being riveted by the cordite fumes hovering around the spare room window, behind which he knew something horrible had just taken place. Thus he remained frozen in horror as the adults began to stir from their own immobility, each silently shrugging off their shock from the gun fire. He never hugged his mother in the end. Nobody hugged anybody it seemed, for they were each cocooned in their own loss.

They later cleaned up the spare room: bloodied clothes, furniture and knick-knacks, piled up by the trash heap for burning. Every time Mum, Dad or Seetha came out of the room, their faces took on ever-lightening ashen shades that even the bright sunlight failed to rejuvenate. Margaret had suddenly shown up and was carrying Paul, who was howling worse than Goldie ever had, but everyone was too distracted to pay attention. Margaret directed mopping-up operations, while Paul bawled away.

Martin stomped over to Margaret and Paul. "I HATE YOU!"

The gunman sat under the guava tree chewing betel until Dad stopped what he was doing and gave the man some money. The man got up, hauling his heavy weapon, joined his hands in a "thank you," bowed, and left. Dad finally brought out a rug with something wrapped inside it. He took it over to the communal latrines located about fifty yards from their row of attached houses.

The James's designated lavatory was at the far corner of "latrine alley" where the jungle encroached on the southern end of Perera Gardens. Martin followed in a daze. Approaching, he heard cursing. Dad was muttering to himself with the rug open on a block of concrete. Goldie's head looked intact, but its stomach had exploded and hung in place by skin and bloody entrails. And those pathetic but accusing eyes were angled at Martin again, this time in a fixed stare. Martin suppressed an involuntary sob; he did not want to cry in front of his father.

Dad swung the axe to chop off the head. After several swings, his cursing started again.

"Martin, go and get the kitchen knife. This skin is too thick for the axe," Dad barked.

Martin remained frozen.

"Damn you, child! You and your bloody pets." Dad limped back to the house, the bandage on his foot turning brown in the sand. He emerged a few moments later with the knife in his hand. Martin suddenly got life into his legs and ran, not toward the house but through the garden and out into the estate. He wished for his bicycle rim and that he could sail away from all of this with the wind on his tail. But his rim had been in the spare room and was now on the trash heap.

Martin gathered stones and pelted them at the coconut trees— one tree per neighbour. He reserved a tree each for Margaret, Seetha and the gunman—and they got a double whamming. Sobbing interfered with his aim and a few stray shots landed on Gunadasa's roof. After Martin had exhausted himself, he wound his way back to the house. Dad was mounting his bicycle, a travel bag slung over his shoulder. He had changed into his work clothes but hadn't shaved. He wore only one shoe; his other foot, quite swollen, was wrapped in a fresh bandage.

"Can you cycle all the way, dear?" Mum looked worried. She now had Paul in her arms. Margaret and Seetha were nowhere to be seen.

"Do I have any choice?" Dad growled and pushed off. The bike wobbled every time he pressed down on the pedal with his injured foot. It would take him three hours to get to the laboratory. And three hours back.

Goldie did not get a funeral, but received a cremation instead. At least, that's how Martin remembered it. As the pyre of bloodied contents from the spare room blazed that evening on the dirt heap, Goldie's headless cadaver reposed on top. Martin's eyes were riveted on the burning flesh, even though Mum said that he should not look.

Dad returned home late that night and had a high fever for the next three days, having to call in sick for a week until the swelling in his foot subsided and allowed him to ride his bicycle to work again. Just as he was mending, a letter arrived from the laboratory.

"Those assholes!" said Dad, waving the note wildly. "The dog had distemper!" He spent the rest of the day burying the implements used to dispose of Goldie: the knife, the travel bag, the rug, the axe, even the clothes he had been wearing that day. He looked like a reluctant murderer trying to rid himself of anything that reminded him of his wasteful act and of his victim. Dad looked like he wanted to forget that day had ever happened, just like Martin did.

The next day Mum gave Seetha notice. "I'll look after my children myself," she said, wiping back tears and hugging Paul closer to her.

That afternoon Martin caught her writing a letter. "I'm asking my sister to sponsor us to Canada. Do you remember the pictures she sent? Churches with tall spires, Niagara Falls and all that?"

"Do they shoot dogs in Canada?"

"No. At least, I don't think so," she said, as she continued to write; but her face now wore a frown.

Martin went outside. A new bicycle rim leaned against the wall by the well, compensation from his father for the trials they had just gone through. Very soon, he was wheeling it faster and faster through Perera Gardens. Instead of coconut palms, he imagined leafless trees and a white landscape, seeing a golden retriever running ahead, turning back from time to time to bark gloriously into the morning sunshine glinting off the snow.

2. **School for Majorities**

The first time Martin felt a stranger in the land of his birth, was the day he entered school. They put him in the Sinhala class because English was being dried up in the school system, or so Dad said. Martin's understanding of Sinhala was colloquial, only what he had picked up from Seetha the maid and from other children in Perera Gardens where he had lived all his life. He spoke English, or more appropriately Burgher—a patois English—at home. He had learned from his parents that Burghers (or *Lansiyas* as they were called by the locals), whether of Dutch or Portuguese extraction, spoke English at home, given their privileged status in the civil service and mercantile trades under the last colonial occupation by Great Britain. All that had ended with Independence fourteen years ago in 1948; English was being phased out in education with the advent of Sinhala as the official language of government.

That first day at St. Bernard's Christian Boys' School, the nuns in their white and brown habits were everywhere: one at the entrance archway handing out forms, and another in the quadrangle barking instructions to the white uniformed boys being shepherded by her colleagues into four distinct columns. "Peter House here, Andrew House here, Anthony House here and James House here."

The allocation was arbitrary, depending on when the students arrived in the quadrangle that day. Upon assignment, students were to remain loyal to their respective houses for the rest of their primary school days, competing against each other in athletic meets, and at cricket and soccer matches. Martin landed in Peter House. Dad later explained that these house names dated back to colonial times and were part of the school's tradition, too deeply rooted to be changed. Dad laughed when Mum wanted to know—now that everything was going Sinhala—would the houses be re-named Peduru, Andare, Anthonis and Jamis respectively?

When the new students were assembled, Brother Anselm, the principal, took the stand on the raised stage in front of them. He was a short man from Belgium, who had arrived in Ceylon twenty-five years earlier as a newly ordained Christian Brother, and who had risen in the ranks to become principal of the primary school at St. Bernard's, or so Dad had said reverently. "He was a young tyrant, when I was in school. A thorough disciplinarian."

Brother Anselm's hair was thinning and grey and his jowls burst over the tight white cassock. He constantly blew into a soggy handkerchief, and his nose was a bright red.

"My dear boys," he said, and paused for another nasal clearing. "Welcome. Today you continue a noble tradition at St. Bernard's. We have been an institution for 110 years and have weathered the storms of war, independence and nationalization. Thanks to the generous contributions from your parents…" He paused to look at the anxious mothers standing at the rear (Martin noticed that there were no fathers at this opening ceremony), gazing anxiously at their dear little ones as if they were entering some kind of institution for the damned, "… we are able to continue to educate you in our tradition.

"Sister Bernadine here…, " Brother Anselm nodded reverently towards the tall hawkish nun standing a step behind him, who in turn bowed adoringly in his direction before returning her fixed stare at the columns of boys, sending a shiver down Martin's spine, "…and I, along with all the teachers and nuns, will be responsible for your education. Sister, do you want to say something?" Brother Anselm seemed eager to give her the spotlight, as he turned his back on the audience and blew his nose so hard the boys in the front started giggling.

"Yes. I do." The nun preened in front of the gathering, her steely eyes running down the four lines of cherubic studentdom that had become a trifle misaligned following the trumpeting of Brother Anselm's nose. The lines straightened the moment her glare fell upon them. Even Brother Anselm stopped blowing his nose and looked nervously at her.

"Boys, from now on there will be discipline in your lives," Sister Bernadine announced. She levelled a scornful stare at the parents. "School starts at 8:30 a.m. sharp. Late-comers will stand in full view of everyone in the classrooms until the next period and get extra homework. No fighting is allowed in the quadrangle or in the classrooms at any time– in fact, no fighting anywhere. Do you see this cane? Malacca, the very best." She brandished a thin, polished, four foot long rattan cane and swished it in the air a couple of times. "I rarely have to use it. Remember that. Now, you will all go to your classes." And with that she strode off, her head in the air and to one side. Brother Anselm nodded benevolently at his new pupils and hurried after her.

There *were* fights. After the first public canings, Martin realized that the clergy were super-powerful and God's messengers after all – no one complained, not even the parents. After a while, the students got smart and figured out how to slug it out in between the nuns' "patrols." This sometimes meant that a fight would go on for days because of the breaks between punches, and it had come to a point that students would memorize who owed whom the next punch when fighting resumed.

Reality hit Martin when he entered his classroom of forty students on that first day: there was not a letter in English anywhere—everything was in Sinhala, from the exercise book to the text books on his desk. If this was the drill, why had Brother Anselm and Sister Bernadine addressed everyone in English? "Tradition," Dad explained later. "They are the last of the old brigade. When they retire, that tradition will also die."

The moment he sat down at his assigned desk—an old chiselled monstrosity that creaked and appeared to have the school history engraved on it—Martin got shot in the back with a "pee fruit." He felt the wetness and smelt the urine-like odour trailing down his clean white shirt and between his shoulders. He swung around and was about to hit the giggling kid who had sprayed him, when the teacher walked into the class. "Another tradition," Dad explained. "We all shot, and got shot, with those messy things—they grow all over the school grounds."

Mrs. Silva, the class teacher, looked kindly but haggard. She was accommodating to the kids, knowing that some of them did not speak Sinhala at home. Martin struggled with his books that first day but a competitive impatience got hold of him whenever he peered over at his Sinhala colleagues who seemed to be sailing through the lesson. He did not want to be left behind. Ranjith, his neighbour, looked jubilant and self-satisfied at Martin's discomfort.

"Now you will have to learn like us," Ranjith said, striking a superior pose. "It will be hard for you."

"Why are you so happy that I am having difficulty?"

"Because Burghers think they are smart. *Thatha* says that you people have all the good jobs because you speak English at home—and now with Sinhala coming in—you fellows will have to go away and let us move up."

Later, seeing the frustration on his face, Mrs. Silva called Martin aside. "In Sinhala, it's easier—remember that—you spell as you pronounce, not like in English. For example, island will be spelled 'I land'" Then the light bulb went on for him. *You spell as you pronounce.* Soon he was getting the hang of his writing assignment.

At the end of that first week, Mrs. Silva playfully ruffled Martin's hair and told his mother, who had called in to check on her son's progress, "Martin is a bright boy, just a little anxious. But he learns fast. He'll not only do fine, he'll excel."

The playing field, or more appropriately the quadrangle around which the classrooms were situated, was another test of courage. Nihal and Balan were two bullies whose role in life was to harass the new students. These boys were in grade three when Martin entered grade one. Obeisance had to be paid at every level of the pecking order of primary school, culminating at grade five.

New recruits from grade one had to run around the stone quadrangle barefooted before they were allowed on any team. Mothers who accompanied their little charges to school every day, because of distance, or the need to provide care, or because they were not working and had nothing else to do at home, were ensconced in the shed at the back of the school, spending their time chatting or knitting and occasionally glancing at the little figures at play, unaware that none of their children could tell on the bully for fear of reprisal. As for the victims, well, boys did not cry—their fathers had drilled it into them—so the bullies got away with their "treatments."

Nihal picked on Martin almost immediately, who, given his European roots, was taller and broader than most of the grade-ones, or even some of the grade-three kids, like his tormentor.

"Hey you, *Lansiya,* take the ball and run. Ten times for you."

Martin looked at his mates who had started running around the quadrangle, shook his head in disbelief, yet got on with the program. When the others stopped at lap five, Martin stopped too.

"Why are you stopping?" Nihal came out staring right into Martin's face.

"Because I finished, like everyone else." Martin replied, panting.

There was a tittering among the boys, and Balan laughed. "Give him the works, *machang*." Balan shrugged and turned to the rest. "You don't obey, you get the works."

Balan threw the ball angrily on the ground and it hit a stone and bounced away. He pointed to one of the smaller boys. "What are you standing there for? Go and get it before I give you a smack." The smaller boy scampered after the ball.

"You will run ten laps because *I tell you*," Nihal said to Martin, looking around smugly. Martin held his ground trying to get his breath back. There was no way he was going to do another five laps. A stone had smashed his sole, and he felt the numbness that preceded a giant bruise underfoot, the classic "*gal thaluma*".

"I can't," Martin protested as Nihal pushed him. Balan who had come from behind went on all fours so that Martin keeled right over the crawling older boy. The children laughed nervously. Martin hit his shoulder on the hard ground as he fell on his back. He looked up helplessly. *Would someone come over and stop this?* But the nuns, who were always around, seemed to have disappeared somewhere. Ironically, as Martin found out later, Sister Bernadine had called an emergency staff meeting just about then to discuss escalating rowdiness in the playgrounds during the intervals. And the dear mothers in the shed were looking occupied as usual; even the ones glancing over periodically appeared smug over the fact that the children seemed to be having such a good time in the playground. *Look over here, come and stop this!* He wished his mother was in the shed, but she never accompanied him to school, wanting him to be independent from an early age. Besides, she had her hands full with Paul back home.

Nihal threw the ball at Martin's exposed stomach. Martin rolled over in pain, throwing up his lunch. That's when the lights in his brain started to take on a reddish tinge. Why the hell was everyone trying to be better than him, when they were not? *If I don't help myself, I'm finished.*

As Nihal stepped forward to punch the *Lansiya*, the said *Lansiya* himself shot up screaming and whacked the bully in the neck, leaving him gurgling for breath. Balan was just getting up from his prone position when he received a kick on the behind from the crazed Martin that sent him sprawling back in the dirt. As Balan tried to get up again, Martin jumped on his back and pummelled his head. Then the "maniacal *Lansiya*" stepped across to Nihal and gave him a smack on the cheek that sounded like a thunder clap. Martin was having difficulty keeping his unleashed rage under control. Suddenly he wanted to kick the shit out of these two cowards, for that's what they were—cowards. He was scared to stop, lest he lose this new-found energy as the rage dissipated.

Mercifully, Sister Bernadine—her meeting over—was cutting through the throng of boys, cane raised in the air like Moses' staff over the Red Sea.

Punishment was swift. Nihal, Balan and Martin bent over in the principal's office where Sister Bernadine applied the Malacca cane with precision. Martin suppressed tears; he was not going to wilt in front of the bullies. Balan begged for mercy and howled when he got no clemency. Nihal wailed from the first strike. A clutch of startled mothers hung outside the principal's office, hugging each other for emotional support. "And we didn't even know those children were fighting, no?"

That night, after Paul was put to bed, his mother applied balm on Martin's pink and puffy bum. Martin stared at the wall in anger, hurt, and embarrassment. She then read him the tale of the Cyclops from Homer's *Odyssey,* one of Martin's favourites.

"Darling, you must be strong, like Odysseus. One day you will rise above all this." He felt protected, ensconced in her warm, earthy smell. He wanted to remain there, but he knew that moments like this would be fewer and fewer as he grew older, for Paul could wake up at any time and command his mother's attention. In his mind's eye, he saw Nihal as the Cyclops and the nuns as the Sirens, and he clung closer to his mother, whose voice carried on softly like the waters of that fabled Aegean Sea.

His mother stroked his head and continued, "When we were growing up, it was a different world. The British ran everything. We studied in English and read the classics—Shakespeare and Homer. Things were much easier, other than for during those few WWII years.

Everyone had a role and place in society. Your world is harder. It's changing. You must be brave. You must be resilient. You must never give in."

He did not know what the word 'resilient' meant. Right then, he didn't care; he was feeling very sleepy and safe. Then a thought flashed through his mind: he had been thrown into a new world, a more hostile one than the familiar confines of Perera Gardens, and there was no going back. The thought transformed into a swell of sadness at something lost. He wanted to cry, but held back. He remained silent, just gritted his teeth when his mother kissed him on the cheek and bid him goodnight. He had to become like Odysseus—that would take care of things.

3. **And Finally, a Sister**

Martin's eleventh year was etched deeply in his memory. It was the year, when least expected, the first cracks appeared in his family.

Martin had remained an only child until he was six. Then Paul was born, followed by a second brother, Barney, two years later. After the last arrival, Victor James, for the first time, gave up on his dream of immigrating to Canada. Every time the family had applied, they were turned down—three years in a row. First, it was because their European ancestry was a little cloudy. But most Burgher families had dark secrets that involved cohabiting and procreating with the natives, Victor had rationalized. The second time they were turned down because Victor's skills were not in demand. The third time, he just burst out in anger and stormed out of the interview when the pompous Second Secretary asked, "So why do you *really* want to go to Canada?" followed by, "You're not really of European descent are you? How come you are so dark-skinned?"

"Don't those bastards know anything about gene-skipping? All it takes is one darkie in the family tree to fuck me up." Victor brooded all the way home from the last interview.

The Jameses would have gone on reproducing had Martin's mother, Carmen, not suffered a prolapsed uterus; Victor was advised to cool it after the last child. Carmen had her hands full with Barney, the sickly one, so Martin was packed off to the boarding at St. Bernard's and only allowed to come home on occasional weekends and during the term holidays.

"But I don't want to go," Martin protested all the way to the boarding, to no avail. He was left with a suitcase of clothes, a satchel of books, and the stern faces of the Christian Brothers who ran the establishment.

Life in the boarding was one of strict time tables: waking at six o'clock and making one's bed, then into the communal showers, off to church for prayer and into the common hall for breakfast. A half-hour was spent preparing for school. Regular classes ran until 3:30 p.m., after which Martin, who had developed a keen interest in cricket, went to practice for the under-12 team. When he got back to the boarding at

5:30, it was study time in the library. Silence was an absolute must, with Brother Joachim, head of the boarding, patrolling the halls, until the bell sounded for dinner. Night prayers took place in the chapel and the boys were finally free at nine o'clock to goof around for 30 minutes before the last bell sounded for bed.

This routine continued for the first three months of Martin's boarding life. He missed home and wrote letters to his mother, enquiring how his brothers were, sometimes biting back the urge to accuse them of being the cause of his exile. The replies were infrequent but evoked tears when they arrived: his mother always wanted to know if he was taking his Vitamin B and cod liver oil capsules that she swore by. Dad never wrote; in fact, Victor had gone into a deep silence following the last immigration interview. He rarely carried Barney or played with Paul, let alone spoke to Martin when he was back for the holidays.

Buddy Gomez was Martin's mate in boarding school. Buddy, a boarder for life, was an orphan taken on by the largesse of the school. Buddy never went home for holidays or on weekends, unless one of the other boys invited him over. He spent most of his time working at the school office and helping the clerics with their chores. Buddy knew when to protest about poor conditions and when not to. When Martin complained about the soup, Buddy had advised him to shut up. Instead, Martin went without dinner for three days before caving in and apologising to Brother Joachim. One day, when Martin was late after cricket practice, Buddy told him to go and say he was sorry to Brother Joachim. Martin did not; after all, he reasoned, it was the cricket coach who had delayed him, and they all worked for the same school, did they not? Martin got yard duty, which meant he was made to sweep the yard at 5:30 in the morning with the ekel broom; and to make matters worse, Brother Joachim's instructions were that the lines left in the sand by the broom had to be in perfect symmetry to indicate that it had been swept thoroughly. Because of the tougher life, Martin found that he was missing his family less, crying less at night, and developing the inner strength to strike back. There was no way to hit out overtly—he would be punished—but there were covert ways to restore the balance of power.

Opportunity came unexpectedly in the form of Brother Joachim's night summons to Buddy. When Brother Joachim did his night rounds, he'd often touch one of the boys on the shoulder. He never touched Martin, who was still classified as a rebellious youth needing regular caning and other punishments. Brother Joachim touched Buddy frequently. On those nights, when Martin rolled over in bed, he noticed that Buddy's adjoining bed was empty. One night, he heard sobbing. As boys—especially the boarders—were never supposed to cry, Martin rose, opening his eyes wide. Buddy was standing by the edge of his bed. He then sank to his knees and started the Lord's Prayer, repeating, "Deliver us from evil" a few times, before crawling into bed and lying there sobbing, without pulling the sheet over him.

"Where were you last night?" Martin asked the next morning after breakfast, on the way to class.

They paused by the huge banyan tree. Buddy was silent for a while. Then he spoke in a flat monotone, "I got my ass fucked."

"What!"

Buddy did not make eye contact. He looked resigned. "You don't know what's going on? Normally he puts it between my thighs and it's over soon. Yesterday, he was in a bad mood. It hurts."

"Puts what?" Martin did not know a lot about sex. He knew that his mother and father did something together; he'd heard his father's groans and his mother's "sh's", and he knew that babies were born because of what parents did, but he hadn't yet discovered the details. That day under the banyan tree, Martin got the facts of life from Buddy in all their warped packaging.

"Don't worry, your turn will come," Buddy said, heading off to his class.

Martin was on guard from that day on, averting his gaze whenever Brother Joachim looked his way, making sure never to cross swords with the head of the boarding, nor any of the other assistant brothers, wrapping the bed sheets around him tight at night so nothing, or nobody, could get through to his body. Going home on weekends was a relief, an escape from a very tense situation. Returning on Monday was hard.

One day, when Martin returned home, he saw his mother by the well drawing water. She was dressed in a housecoat and labouring at drawing the bucket from the deep below.

"Mum, I'm home. Water cuts again?" he asked. As she turned around, he noticed her belly was swollen. There were tears in her eyes.

"Oh, Martin, I missed you." She let the bucket go and it sped down into the waters below and the rope whipped her back in its rush. She did not seem to notice and embraced Martin with an ardour that surprised him.

"You're going to have another baby?"

She puckered her lips and squeezed in her cheeks, eyes streaming tears, and nodded. She hugged him again.

"Why are you crying then?"

She started wiping her eyes and tried to regain composure. "Your daddy wants a girl now."

"But you can hardly look after Paul and Barney."

"I have to please your daddy. He is not well. He's depressed. Ever since the interviews."

Martin wanted to shout at his father, hit him even. Instead he said. "When is the baby due?"

"Christmas," She brightened, expecting him to be happy at this joyous event that would coincide with the coming of that other divine child.

"Oh, no!" That meant she would be gone to the hospital just like the other times when Paul and Barney were born, and the house would be bedlam after she returned. Dad would be too distracted to buy fireworks that were so a part of the Yuletide celebrations—he'd be drinking every night. There'd be lots of people fussing about the place telling his mother what to do and what not to do. Paul and Barney would try to tear the baby's eyes out because they would be feeling neglected. Paul had tried to do that when Barney was born. Managing Paul and his jealousy had been tough enough; now both of them would be at it, and Martin knew he'd be expected to keep an eye on his younger brothers.

Over the next several months Martin dodged Brother Joachim and Buddy became increasingly despondent. Martin came upon Buddy by the banyan tree one morning to catch him staring into the distance, tears streaming down his face.

"What's up?" Martin asked, jerking him on the shoulder.

Buddy remained silent and did not protest the rough handling. The pile of books on his knee slid off and spewed the ground. Martin scooped them up and as he made to hand them back he looked into Buddy's eyes and gasped. It was as if he were looking at the dead Goldie spread out under his father's axe on that dreadful day years ago. In panic, he shook Buddy more vigorously.

"Wake up, *machang*. What's going on?"

Buddy sighed, picked up the books and rose, his shoulders stooped like a hunchback. "I wish I could go home." The he began sobbing. "If I had one."

"You can come to mine this weekend," Martin said.

Buddy shook his head. "It's not the same. People are usually kind when I am there. I want to know what a real home is like, where I can be who I want to be."

"Real homes are not always happy either."

"Still..." Buddy looked like an old man as headed back to class. Martin kept pace with him but did not know what else to say.

The following day Buddy disappeared. He just did not show up for classes. Brother Joachim looked very upset and was seen pacing the halls as if trying to find Buddy in any nook the boy could possibly be hiding in. A rumour began that Buddy had been used as a "bili", a sacrifice, to the giant office tower being built on a part of the school's property, sold by the St. Bernard's to weather tough economic times as government support for Christian schools had been eliminated. Concrete for the foundations was being poured, and the story went that Buddy lay beneath it—a human sacrifice to appease the Gods and ensure a long life for the building. Martin spent evenings staring at the construction workers at the site, against the pleadings of his fellow-boarders, lest he too end up under the concrete. Something didn't add up for him. *Builders don't kill children. Dad would have told me.*

The brothers posted notices around the school to dispel rumours, asking for any information on Buddy's whereabouts. A mass was offered for his safe return, and every boarder was forced to attend. Brother Joachim stood at the entrance ensuring a 100 percent attendance, but one had only to turn around to see the man aging before everyone's eyes.

A week later, the body of a student was found in Wellawatte, knocked down by the express train bound for Kandy. The driver said that he had seen a boy running by the tracks, trying to jump aboard. When the train went around a bend, the driver lost sight of the would-be passenger, still trying to hop an illegal ride. Buddy was identified at the morgue by a tearful Brother Joachim and the principal, Brother Anselm. Another mass was held for Buddy's soul. Martin was numb during the entire service. He was kicking himself for not seeing the danger signals written all over his friend's face and for not warning anyone. But what could he say? That Buddy was missing home? Everyone was missing home. That Brother Joachim was buggering Buddy? Who would believe him? One thing was for sure, he didn't have to dodge Brother Joachim any more—his nemesis had become a pathetic wreck, spending most of his evenings in the boarding chapel praying feverishly.

A week after Buddy's funeral, Martin sneaked into the chapel to reflect and remember his dead friend because he could never concentrate during the numerous group prayer sessions that the brothers had organized ever since the boy had gone missing. Despite all the stuff they fed him at Religious Knowledge class, he had difficulty believing in the Hereafter with its cherubim and seraphim, especially when God's ministers on earth were such devils, but he found the chapel comforting and a place that he felt, that if he concentrated enough, he could connect with his dead friend, for surely Buddy's spirit must be around and his ghost would not be the frightening kind, instead perhaps a frightened kind. Try as he might though, he saw no ghosts. But he saw someone else.

Brother Joachim was in the front row, rosary gripped between clenched palms, a rivulet of sweat making is way down his forehead, swaying backward and forwards like he was in some kind of a spasm or trance. Martin decided to leave and rose. The brother swung around the moment Martin's cleats scraped the stone floor. In the dim light, Martin saw Brother Joachim rear to his feet, his mouth agape in a scream of silent horror and then the man took off, scurrying like a scared mouse through the rear sacristy door. Martin scratched his head in puzzlement. *Do I remind him that much of Buddy?*

After that encounter, vengefulness seized Martin and he took great delight in slipping notes under Brother Joachim's door, forging Buddy's handwriting from his friend's school books that still lay in the locker next to his bed. Cryptic notes like "I'm going to get you!" or, "Tonight, I am coming to you." The notes helped Martin come to terms with the empty bed he slept next to each night, and the sobbing that still seemed to emanate from it. Perhaps Buddy had spoken to him after all and instructed him to write these notes. Brother Joachim continued to wither.

The following month, Brother Joachim was transferred from St. Bernard's and was never heard of again.

Martin's mother started to get bigger and more tired and an *ayah* was again hired to help. The servant, Kamala, was an older woman with rotting teeth, who chewed betel incessantly—Carmen James had not had the time to do a proper screening this time. Whenever Martin visited, he found his two siblings playing in the garden, their clothes dirty, and sand all over their bodies, the *ayah* looking busy in the kitchen with the cooking, and his mother lying in bed, snoring gently. His father took a few more drinks than normal and went out frequently at night to the bookie at the top of the road to check the odds on the horses. Victor James was a regular punter on the English horse races that were broadcast in the former colonies via BBC Radio.

During his mother's seventh month of pregnancy, when Martin returned home one weekend, the house was deathly quiet. He thought that Kamala had taken the kids for a walk, and went straight to his mother's bedroom. He heard groaning as he neared. His mother was vomiting into a basin by her bed. Her cough was hollow. She did not see him in the doorway. She lay back and placed her legs on a pile of pillows under her feet.

When she saw him, she held out her arms silently and he ran over and hugged her. She smelt stale as if she had not taken a bath in a week.

"What's the matter Mum?"

"It's this baby—she's a tough one."

"Do you know that she is a girl?"

"I can feel it. She's different from all of you. Don't tell your father. I want to surprise him."

"I hope he will stop asking you to have more babies after this."

"Doctor says I have to take bed rest from now until she is born. Keep my feet up too. Such a waste of time. I could be getting so much done. Christmas is around the corner. How are you?"

He just hugged his mother again. That whole weekend, he hung about her bedside, ordering Kamala to bring his mother soup and nourishments continuously. He went into Paul and Barney's shared bedroom and said, "If I hear a peep from you this weekend, I'll slap your backsides." He'd had a lot of personal experience with Sister Bernadine's Malacca cane. Even little Barney got the message.

On the Sunday afternoon, when his father was on the back porch, reading the newspaper with a glass of arrack in hand, Martin got ready to take the bus back to the boarding. He came out on to the porch to wish his father goodbye.

"Going back are you?" Victor did not look up from the newspaper. Martin had never been apprehensive in his father's presence in the past. In his mind, Dad was a kind and compassionate person, especially when he told stories, and had taken Martin to the movies. Yes, Victor did get mad, but when he did, he ranted at circumstances, not at Martin. In more recent times however, Dad had become distant and harsh. He seemed no different from those taciturn and unemotional brothers in the boarding.

"Mum needs your help," Martin said.

"She's just griping because of the pregnancy. She'll be okay. Women get that way when they get close to delivering."

"You're not listening, Dad – she needs help. It's different this time."

A page turned. "Hmm?"

Then Martin dashed over to his father, took the glass of arrack and threw the contents into the garden. The newspaper came down. Victor's face looked incredulous, uncertain.

"She needs your help! And she doesn't need any more babies. And when I come back home this Christmas, I am not going back to that bloody boarding again!" Then he was running, picking up his bag and running up the garden and down to the bus stop. He wanted to keep moving, fearing that his father would catch him and beat him for being disrespectful. When he finally slowed down, out of breath, there was no one pursuing him.

The bus was not due for another fifteen minutes and, as they never operated on time anyway, Martin retraced his steps tentatively. From the top of Perera Gardens he could see Victor standing on the back porch scratching his head and staring down at what was now an empty glass. Then he kicked the glass with a ferocity that surprised Martin and stalked off indoors.

He dreaded coming home the next weekend, but when he did, his father did not mention their altercation. In fact, his father had bought some prescriptions for his mother, and she was sitting up in bed, the colour returning to her cheeks. His brothers, who were playing noisily under the papaw tree when Martin arrived, ran into their room and played Snakes and Ladders for the rest of the day, peeping out of their door from time to time and scurrying inside the moment he passed by. Occasionally Barney would bawl out as he couldn't count and Paul usually cheated, but even the little guy's crying was muted.

"I'll be so happy when this baby is born—it's got to be the last one. I'm going to ask the doctor to make sure about it," Mum said.

Martin was sitting by her bedside, he was reading her a story from Grimm's fairy tales – his mother's other favourite, after Homer. He paused at his mother's comments and looked up puzzled. "Can they do that? Make you not have babies?"

"Well, they are going to have to. These days they say they can do something to my tubes or my womb so it won't hold a baby."

This was all a bit much for Martin. His palms broke out in a sweat. He continued reading the fairy tale out aloud, but his mind was no longer with the brothers Grimm. He was astounded by his mother's frankness, but pleased and excited too. He seemed to have crossed a threshold with her that he was sure even his father had not stepped over. Martin didn't know anything about "tubes," but nodded gravely.

When school closed for the Christmas holidays, Martin came home expecting to see changes. Sure enough, the plastic Christmas tree, bought at Cargill's department store several years ago, had not made its annual reappearance from the tool cupboard this year. His mother, being propped up in bed, could not decorate it, and Kamala, a Buddhist, knew nothing about Christmas trees. His father was pre-occupied as usual: Victor had a sheaf of old racing sheets and was studying "form." His mother explained that this was his latest recreation—no more blind bets—he analyzed every horse for its past accomplishments, checking weight, distance and jockey, to come up with a surer chance of a win. But the winnings were still to pan out.

And the fireworks that Dad always bought the week before Christmas did not happen either. "Got to prepare for the doctor's bills," he muttered.

"If you were not putting all your money on the horses, there would have been some to spare. *Aney,* what are these boys going to do without fireworks?" his mother groaned from her room.

Sunil, the next door neighbour, visited and gave Martin an idea. Why not make a kerosene cannon, like the ones they made to celebrate the Vesak festival? Sunil too was missing the fireworks at the James residence; being a Buddhist and not celebrating Christmas, he still got to light some every year under Martin's largesse.

The first step in the art of making a kerosene cannon was to find a long bamboo shoot about three inches in diameter, clean out the inside to render a hollow pipe with one end still closed. An opening was made about a quarter of the distance from the closed end. The cannon was tipped up on several bricks with the closed end resting on the ground and the other end hoisted up at about a 60 degree angle. Kerosene oil was poured in from the raised opening and it trickled down and nestled at the base of the cannon, against the closed end. Sunil explained all this to Martin in painstaking detail as they proceeded to construct the device.

"Do you need gun powder to make it fire?" Martin enquired, peering at the shaky contraption.

"No, no." replied Sunil. "You stick the *pandama* into the hole and blow!"

Sunil did not elaborate on the fact that a quick withdrawal of all body parts is necessary, because the combustion caused by the inserted taper, or *pandama*, expands and blows through the open end of the cannon with a huge blast. The explosion also extinguishes the fire inside, and the cannon is automatically readied to repeat the action and produce the next shot.

Martin and Sunil got involved in getting the cannon operational. It was a bit of a challenge as kerosene oil had to be "procured" from their respective kitchens, and that was proving impossible until Sunil's mum went on her daily errand to the market and Kamala got busy with Paul and Barney. Martin and Sunil had just rendezvoused back at the cannon after a round of procurement, when Kamala came running out of the front door screaming, "Baby, baby – *Missie* is dying!"

Martin ran into the house. His mother was writhing on the bed, the bed sheets all over the floor. Yet, she was still issuing orders, "Call your father from Mrs. Gunawardene's telephone. And get the taxi to come." She clutched the bed frame and squirmed, blowing through her mouth.

Martin knew the drill: Mrs. Gunawardene had the only reliable telephone in the neighbourhood. Victor had to bicycle all the way from the Fort, and that would take more than an hour. The local taxi driver at the junction had been put on standby and, providing he was not out on a fare, would transport his mother to the hospital. Martin ran to Mrs. Gunawardene's house and shouted, "Call my dad, Mum is having the baby!" Leaving Mrs. Gunawardene, who had performed this routine twice before and would execute again with flair, Martin ran bare-footed to the junction, about half a mile away. Pediris, the taxi driver, was sitting by his old Morris Minor, chewing betel and looking bored. His eyes brightened when he saw Martin's distress. "Ah, *baby mahattaya*, is it time? Okay let's go, get in."

While Kamala held the two teary-eyed younger siblings, Martin and old Mrs. Gunawardene helped Carmen into the taxi. Mrs. G. was smiling. "Don't worry child, everything will be okay. Here, Martin, you go along with your mother. We will look after the home."

Just as the taxi was pulling out, a loud bang went off. A blackened Sunil came running around the corner, beaming and coughing at the same time. "It's working! The cannon's working." And as if to herald them on their way, Sunil re-loaded and blew once more and the cannon bucked and the stench of kerosene wafted in through the taxi's open windows.

When they arrived at the hospital, Carmen James, despite her condition, issued further orders to the nurses and orderlies who took charge of her. As she was wheeled away, she managed one more instruction to Pediris, "*Mahattaya* will settle your bill, take my son home now."

"But Mum, I want to stay. At least until Dad comes," Martin pleaded.

"No, this is not a place for you to stay alone. I will be okay."

Her pale face and drawn features told him not to argue, but once she had disappeared from sight, Martin told Pediris to go home without him.

"*Aney, baby mahattaya*, how to do that? Your father will never pay me. And your mother—she will kill me!"

"I am not leaving until my father comes."

"Then I will also stay. My meter will be ticking and your father will have to pay extra."

His father's impending wrath over the inflated taxi bill took second place to Martin's anxiety over his mother. Martin decided to stay. Pediris drove the taxi off to the parking lot and took out his betel pouch in preparation for a long chew.

Martin paced the antiseptic-smelling hallways, not knowing where they had taken his mother. Nurses walked by, talking among themselves in hushed whispers. The hospital smell was everywhere, comforting as well as sickening. He went to the office and asked what room his mother would be in. Because they were full and the duration of her labour unpredictable, he was told that a room would be assigned only after the birth. For now, his mother was in the confines of the delivery room "where no visitors, including relatives, are allowed."

He was hungry and had no money. He went back to the taxi and asked Pediris to give him a rupee and put it on the meter. "No problem *baby mahattaya*. What is one rupee after all? The bill is now over seventy-five rupees and counting," Pediris reminded him slyly.

Martin went to the Indian restaurant across the road and bought five *masala vaddehs* and heartily dug into them. They tasted so good today.

When he returned, his father, whose bike lay against the entrance parapet, was arguing with Pediris. Martin hung back, not wanting to be the reason for the tariff hike. Finally, his father stomped his foot, took out a sheaf of bills from his shirt pocket, counted several, and shoved them at Pediris. Then he chained his bike to a post and stormed off into the hospital. When Martin followed gingerly, Pediris pulled around in the taxi and called out from the window, "Don't go near your father now—he's mad at you!" With a smug grin that suggested he was taking the next couple of days off to hit the arrack tavern, Pediris gunned his aging Morris, which chugged through the hospital gates belching smoke worse than the kerosene cannon.

Martin went under the large banyan tree in the hospital compound and played on the vines. As the shadows lengthened and the mosquitoes started biting and the nurses began taking the patients in wheelchairs indoors again, he got anxious to know what was going on. He crept indoors and walked the halls, trying to spot his father. He found Victor at the back entrance, sprawled on a wooden bench, his eyes bloodshot. Victor did not even acknowledge Martin's presence.

"I'm sorry about the taxi meter," Martin began, hoping to make a clean breast of it.

"It's going to be a long wait." His father did not even register Martin's words. "Longer than all the other times. There are some complications. I'm going to sleep here. How are you going home?"

"I'll sleep here too."

For once, Martin saw his father look directly at him. Victor's distant features gave way and a smile crossed his face. "No, you won't. This is not your show. I'm the father."

"And I'm the brother."

"You're still a minor."

"Not after you've been to boarding school."

Victor leaned back on the bench and laughed. After a while the laughing became uncontrollable. Then it turned into sobs.

"Having a daughter will complete the family," Victor said. "The one thing I can be proud about."

"What about Mum?"

"Her too," Victor replied a tad too quickly.

"What if it's not a girl?"

"It's going to be—even the fortune teller said so." Victor rose from his seat and re-arranged his crumpled clothes. "Are you hungry?"

"No. I ate *vaddehs* a little while ago."

"I'm starving. Didn't even have lunch today. Had to work right through. Bloody white bosses think we local buggers are slaves."

Just then a nurse came to fetch Victor, saying the doctor wanted to see him. When he returned about twenty minutes later, Victor's face was ashen.

"Nothing will happen tonight—we'd better go home. Doctor says the baby will most probably be born tomorrow."

Victor kept his bicycle tethered at the hospital for retrieval the following day and they took the bus home. In the bus, Victor was reflective. "You know, son, I always wanted the best for you and the rest of the family. But this country does not give us any breaks. Ever since they nationalized everything and made Sinhala the official language, we Burghers have become like tourists—no one wants us here. Can't even bugger off to Canada with all the restrictions. You will have to go one day. I've blown all my chances."

"But we can be all right here. I always come in the top grades in school, even if all the classes are in Sinhala."

"You are different. You have the education in the national language from grade one. We never learned it because it was a native language back then, and of no use when we were under British rule. In the end, we are minorities, and racial lines are very strong here. No, all I can do is to make sure that my sons leave this place and go abroad."

"Not your daughters?"

At which point Victor turned and stared out the window and did not speak for the rest of the journey home.

That night Victor drank more than he should have, and was snoring on the sofa when Martin awoke. Remembering that his mother looked forward to the home-cooked meals she had ordered Kamala to cook for her every day ("Bloody hospital food! Who can eat that? Even my breast milk will dry up"), Martin washed, dressed, went into the kitchen, picked up the neatly plastic-wrapped tin plates that smelled of rice and curry, and headed off on his journey. "*Baby mahattaya* – be careful, the curries will spill and *missie* will be annoyed with me," Kamala pleaded as he slammed out of the front door. Martin had decided to let his father sleep; Victor looked like he needed it.

The hospital was waking up; orderlies were mopping down the tiled floors, and that "smell" had not started to sharpen yet. Martin still did not know where his mother was—surely not in the delivery room? He enquired at the office, and this time the head nurse was more considerate. "Your mother is in the new wing—room 225. Please be very quiet. She has had a very long and painful night. We only finished a couple of hours ago. She is sleeping." The head nurse ordered another nurse to accompany Martin but he wanted to be alone. All he asked was, "Is it a girl?"

The head nurse looked at him sympathetically. Then she nodded knowingly to the other nurse "Go with him."

The feeling of unreality heightened as Martin followed the nurse to room 225. The wing was newer and he was sure his father could not afford the price of a room here. The hospital must be extra nice giving his mother this accommodation.

The nurse held onto him just outside the open door. His mother was asleep. Carmen looked exhausted and her hair was still damp with the perspiration resulting from what she had recently endured. A bundle—the baby—was by her side, held firmly by his mother's encircling arms, protecting the child even in her sleep. Beside the bed, the cradle lay empty.

The nurse said, "Don't go in. Please."

"Is she nursing?"

"Your mother asked to have the baby next to her, before we gave her the sedative."

Martin shrugged her arm off impatiently and entered. He heard the nurse behind him sigh. First he headed for the side table and deposited his food parcel. Then he tip-toed to the bed. His breath was sharp in his throat. He moved the baby's covers gently aside; first an arm, then a leg came into view. His curiosity won him over and he was doing what his grandmother had told him to do in determining the sex of an infant – look *down there.* His breath caught when he saw no testicles, no little rosebud penis, only a smooth mound with a ravine in the middle, just like his mother's, without the hair. "A girl! It's a girl!" he yelled. Just then his hand came into contact with the cold flesh of the baby's pubic area—cold, porcelain, unborn. He squeezed but there was no movement or reaction, just a stiffening flesh like what he had touched when he'd been forced to give his dead grandfather a customary kiss in his coffin a few years ago.

"No!" he was screaming and turning around, the tears too frozen in fear to roll. Suddenly this hospital had become a hostile place, its smell stifling, making breathing difficult. He wanted to grab hold of his mother and the baby and take them away from here. After all, wasn't he Odysseus? But his mother's bed was so far away and receding from him as his feet refused to move. He stumbled into the arms of the nurse, who held him tight and rocked him gently as he passed out.

4. **Daughter on Loan**

Martin remembered the first time the thin man came to their house. He was twelve and they had moved into their new home in Kotte three months earlier. Victor had said that they needed to move because there were too many bad memories in the old one. They had lost Julia nine months earlier and Carmen was still in mourning. In fact, all she did was lay out the baby's clothes on the bed most days, feel them gently and put them away in the suitcase she had taken to the hospital for her unsuccessful delivery. She had started to forget things around the house; Victor got annoyed when items of groceries ran out as Carmen had forgotten to add them to the weekly list.

The thin man was like an ekel broom; a white oversized shirt with ink stains in the pocket draped him. Dark drainpipe slacks that were too short, revealed no socks and his shoes had not seen polish in years, the soles uneven and worn down to their edges. He slouched, and his face was all sunken eyes and jutting cheekbones; straggly black hair falling unkempt over his collar, and the pencil-thin moustache had ceased to adhere to his face long ago, drooping like down-turned fangs beneath his jaw.

The day he appeared, Carmen was in the garden tending her rows of hydrangea and hibiscus. In addition to her rituals with the dead baby's clothes, she spent a lot of time in the new garden, which was supposedly good for her healing. Martin was practicing his cricket strokes, with a ball inside a sock tied with a string to the giant jam tree in the front yard, carefully avoiding the square-cut stroke that would bring the ball within Carmen's range, as well as that of his kid-brothers, Paul and Barney, who were playing marbles. Very soon they would be fighting over who had hit the marble out of base, and Carmen would start screaming at them again. Martin paused when the man came into view; something told him that their lives were going to change—again.

The man hung tentatively by the gate until Carmen straightened up, brushed back the hair from her perspiring face and gasped in surprise at this fellow who was peering at her through the plants by the fence.

"Madam, are you looking for a servant?" he asked, shifting his weight from one foot to the other.

"Who are you?" Carmen asked, taken aback. Even Paul and Barney had stopped playing.

"I heard at the top of the road that you were looking."

It was true that she had "put the word out" about a needing a new servant. Kamala, their domestic, had gone back to her village; her mother was dying and needed care. Carmen was losing her grip on things; she'd never screamed at Paul and Barney before Julia's death, but after her return from hospital and the move to the new house, everything had become overwhelming.

"My name is Jansz, madam. Edward Jansz."

"And where do you live?"

"In Nugegoda, madam. I have a girl for you. Very trustworthy. My own daughter."

Carmen stared at the man from head to foot. "A Burgher like you, giving up his daughter?"

"*Aiyo*, what to do, madam. When hard times hit…"

That's when her generous heart kicked into gear, and she invited him in. He came around to the back of the house and she offered him a cup of tea and asked for details. Martin was ordered to mind his brothers. Martin gave Paul and Barney a chance to hit his ball-in-the-sock (previously forbidden to them) for 10 minutes each, so that he could overhear this important conversation. He knew that he would have to leave in nine minutes to switch brothers at bat because neither was likely to give up this once-in-a-lifetime opportunity.

"Wife died of TB, Mrs. James," Edward Jansz said as Martin came around the edge of the house and paused just out of sight. "I have no job now…only occasional work. Three children to look after. Very hard. God bless you for this tea. I haven't had anything to eat this morning."

Carmen's voice softened. "Yes I know, I have three little ones, and even though my husband is working, it's very hard to raise them."

"Julie-girl is very efficient. She has been raising my little ones for two years now – knows how to cook and sew and wash and iron also."

"How will you manage if you give her up?"

"I want to give the other two up for adoption also. Simply can't manage, Mrs. James."

There was a silence. Martin braved peering around the corner. Edward Jansz was sipping his tea on the back porch. Carmen was in the kitchen but she had her back to Martin. When she turned around, she was sobbing.

"*Aiyo,* please Mrs. James! I did not mean to make you cry. This is my cross. I have to carry it." Jansz put down his tea cup and rose. "Maybe, I'll come again another day when we can talk."

"No, no," Carmen insisted. "Please stay. Is her name Julie, as in Julia?"

"Yes, madam."

Martin heard Barney yelling, "Martin, Paul won't give me the bat!" *Bloody pests, my brothers! No wonder Mum screams at them.*

When he had settled them down, which included giving Paul, the older, a whack on the side of the head for bullying, Martin rushed back to his vantage point. His mother was handing their visitor a parcel.

"Thank you, Mrs. James. God will bless you. More than anything, I was hoping I could get fifty cents for the bus, otherwise I will have to walk back."

"Wait, wait," Carmen was digging inside her purse and Martin saw a rupee note exchange hands.

"I will bring her next week on Sunday, Mrs. James. God will bless you." Edward Jansz slouched off around the corner to the front gate and Martin ran back to attend to his rowdy brothers.

The thin man paused by the gate and glanced back at the three boys. "Hello children. Just like my little fellows," he said, gesticulating towards Paul and Barney. He gripped the parcel firmly in his hand. "At least, tonight, they will have something good to eat."

"This is just what we need, Victor—a daughter." Carmen and Victor were sitting in the verandah after dinner, discussing the day's events. Paul and Barney were in bed and Martin was reading a book in the hall, within earshot.

Victor's voice was hesitant. "She will not exactly be a daughter if she is going to help you with cooking and cleaning and all. More like a glorified servant."

"What's the harm in a little help around the house? After all, we girls were raised to cook and clean and sew and look after children. This will be good training for her."

Victor was silent. Then he said, "And how much does this Jansz want for his daughter?"

"He didn't mention any money. He is just looking for homes for his children."

Victor's laugh was sarcastic. "Don't you go believing that! There's always a catch."

"Well, he didn't mention it." Carmen's tone was edgy. "Why, don't you trust my judgement on this?"

"I trust your judgement, dear. It's just that taking on another person's child has a liability, especially if we are going to give her manual work. What about her schooling?"

"Well, we can send her to school, can't we?"

"Humph. Private school? The boys' school fees are driving me insane. And when Barney starts in two years, it will be harder. I couldn't afford another one."

"How about the government school? Mr. Jansz is not sending the girl to school at all since his wife died. At least, we could provide her with an education."

"The education in the *Vidyalayas* is sub-standard."

"It's better than nothing. We go educating our children in private Christian schools. For what? All the jobs are going to people with connections."

"Now, don't get me going on this." Victor's voice became distinctly irritable. They had covered this ground many times before, always ending with why they could not get passed to go to Canada, where Carmen's sister and family lived. "Bloody fools, all they want are university degrees," Victor complained. "What about honest hardworking people like us who pay taxes, keep jobs and raise families? Doesn't Canada need people like us?"

"But you are not qualified, Victor. That's what they told you the last time, no?"

"Grade Ten was enough for us to get jobs in this country. How many buggers have this university bullshit?"

"We are only two strokes away from Mr. Jansz. What if you lose your job, and I die?" she said, changing her tone.

"Bullshit!" Victor burst out too quickly. "That will not happen. You are getting depressed again."

A long silence followed.

"Well, what do you say, dear?" Carmen said, finally.

"If it helps you, then okay. I am agreeing only if it will bring our lives back to some kind of normality. If this Jansz girl is too much trouble, she goes back."

She got up and kissed Dad on the cheek and he blushed. "Thank you, dear," she said coyly.

Aunty Mala had an opinion on the James family's intended plans. Aunty Mala had an opinion on everything and everyone. She was not really an aunt but the new next-door neighbour and Carmen's closest friend since moving to Araliya Lane in Kotte. Martin couldn't understand why children had to address adults, be they relatives or other, as either "uncle" or "auntie," but that was the custom of the time.

"What the devil are you planning, Carmen? A fully grown girl?"

"She's only thirteen," Carmen corrected, pouring tea for her friend who had dropped in for a chat, a regular activity of neighbourhood housewives.

"Yes. But she will be 'crossing the red sea' soon, if she hasn't already. Then you will have boys chasing her. More problems for you to have."

Aunty Mala took another cream cracker and applied a copious dollop of butter; perhaps she had none at home due to the import ban and was seizing an opportunity because Victor worked as a shipping agent now and received lots of "supplies" on his visits on board the cargo vessels that docked in the Port of Colombo. Her sari could not easily hide the folds of fat that fell around her hips, nor the soft bloated breasts that threatened to fall out of her bodice. Aunty Mala hefted one fat thigh on top of the other, a slipper dangling from the raised foot, the other one lost somewhere on the floor. "Who is this Jansz fellow?" she demanded. "I'm sure I've heard his name before."

"He looked definitely down and out. Like he hadn't eaten in a week."

"That's the pathetic look they all have. Behind that screen they are all bloody crooks. You be careful."

"You are not helping me, Mala."

Carmen was close to tears again. She often got this way of late, and then screamed and shouted at her children. Martin looked anxiously to see where his brothers were. They were playing hide-and-seek with the neighbourhood children—not a good sign—because Barney often got scared hiding alone, and started shrieking, and of course, everyone found him.

Right on cue Barney shrieked and Carmen yelled. "Go and get that child, Martin. He must be in trouble."

Martin grumbled and went off to find his little brother. Sure enough, Barney was in the Perera's garage, behind the cans of oil and the carcass of the old 1948 Austin that Mr. Perera was trying to get roadworthy someday, when spare parts became available.

The other kids were gathered around Barney shouting, "Found you, found you." Barney had his hands pressed over his eyes and he had wet his pants. The kids scrammed when Martin appeared on the scene. He carried Barney indoors via the back door. Little Barney was only eighteen pounds for his three plus years, and trembling with fear. After Martin had changed him into fresh clothes, Barney took a colouring book and slunk off into the bedroom that he shared with Paul. "I don't want to play anymore—with them!" was his final judgment.

"Barney's okay," Martin announced to his mother.

"Well, I must be going, Carmen." Aunty Mala heaved her bulk out of the chair, dusting biscuit crumbs off her bosom. "Can't keep gossiping all the time. Hubbie will be home soon."

"Yes, I have work to do also," Carmen agreed, a bit more readily than usual.

"I will see what I can find out on this Jansz person. He sounds fishy to me."

Everyone has an opinion on Julia—what about me? Martin walked about the garden for the next few days, clinging to his usual daydreaming spots: amidst the branches of the jam tree where he could look out onto the paddy fields, or on top of the wall in the hang of the king-coconut tree. His friends called him "the thinker" because even at that young age, he needed to get away occasionally and put things in perspective.

So what of this Julia? He'd never had a sister. Given the six-year gap between him and his next sibling Paul, Martin had been conferred the title of caretaker of his brothers as his mother was having trouble coping. Having someone else to share this burden would be welcome. Besides, caring for little brothers was a girl's work.

But she was a year older, and Martin felt he would lose the power of being the eldest. *However, I would still be the "official" eldest.* After all, he was the flesh and blood of his parents. That would entitle him to boss her around. She hadn't been to school in a while, and even if she went back, she would be in the government *Vidyalaya* and everyone knew that only the duds went there. Yet he felt that he was going to have to share something with her and that made him uncomfortable.

One night he awoke from a dream in a sweat. Julia had taken over the house. She wore a large sari that resembled one of Aunty Mala's, and sat with a slipper dangling from her toe. With a mighty bat in hand she was ordering Dad to go to work, so he could bring home the money; Mum was banished to the kitchen and Martin was relegated to minding his two brothers; there was no school henceforth for any of them. All Dad's money went towards buying clothes for Julia. Behind her sat Edward Jansz, looking extremely pleased, counting the loot and depositing it into a box.

Martin shrugged off that dream and went back to sleep without any trouble. The following night, he had another, completely different one. He was in the paddy field by the river with Julia. She looked beautiful: silver bangles on her hand and a red hair band held her dark tresses that fell in gentle waves across her shoulders. She wore a blue dress and her eyes were warm and mellow. She read a poem she had composed just for him. When she finished, she held his hand and said, "Martin, I am so happy to be your sister."

"Me too," he replied, and meant it. The whole scene was ethereal and calming. He wanted to stay by the river with her forever.

"When I get older," she said. "I want to marry someone just like you."

His heart leapt, first with joy, then with panic. "Why can't it be me?"

She looked at him and her eyes melted. Then she lay down beside him, hair spilling on the moist grass growing by the riverbank. "What about you? But you're my brother."

"I'm not *really* your brother." And then panic overcame him and Martin awoke. He tried to recapture the dream from where it had been rudely cut off, but it did not return. This time he could not get back to sleep.

"Bloody crooks," Aunty Mala said, scooping devilled chick peas from a tin plate she had brought to the gate to share with her two friends, Carmen and Aunty Soma from the house on the other side. When the ladies only had time for snatches of conversation or gossip between their housework chores, they congregated at the James's gate, between Aunty Mala's and Aunty Soma's. Despite Martin's hearty whacks on the ball-in-the-sock, their conversation kept intruding upon his thoughts.

Aunty Soma was the opposite of Aunty Mala in physical appearance: a shy, retiring skeleton of a woman, whose husband, a lawyer, was hardly ever at home. She spoke softly but deliberately, and had caused Aunty Mala's choleric outburst when the conversation had turned to Edward Jansz. "Carmen, my sister also had a man come to her door with a similar story. His child had another name, my sister's god-child's name. How he finds these things out, no one knows. So my poor sister gave the man lots of money and clothes and food and stuff. To see, he disappeared after a while—never to be seen again."

"And I bet you a hundred rupees, this is the same character," Aunty Mala said triumphantly, choking on her chick peas, so that Carmen had to slap her several times on the back to dislodge the offending scraps trapped in the fat woman's gullet.

Listening to her friends patiently, Carmen said, "Well, we can't go distrusting everyone, no? Let me see when he comes on Sunday. Victor will also be here then."

Martin continued to hit the ball harder and harder, to drown out the neighbours' negativity but ended up breaking the string and sending the socked ball flying into their midst, knocking down Aunty Mala's plate of gram with a bang. She shrieked and jumped, Martin went red and Carmen screamed, "Martin, be careful, child. One of these days you'll kill someone."

On Thursday, just after Martin returned from school, Edward Jansz showed up unexpectedly. Carmen was giving Paul and Barney their showers.

"My mum is busy right now," Martin told the man, playing his role of guardian of the house when his mother attended to other matters.

"That's all right, young sir. I can wait till she is available," he replied, smiling but not dispelling his dejected air.

At close quarters his face looked more haggard than before, and he was wearing the same white shirt with the ink stains. His body odour was sharp, and Martin tried hard not to wrinkle his nose and run inside. "Wait here," he said and withdrew stiffly to let his mother know.

"What? Here already?" Carmen looked flustered and slapped talcum powder on both her younger children, who were struggling with each other for the only dry towel. "Boys, settle down," she pleaded in vain. She was sucking in her breath, trying to retain control. Martin sensed an explosion coming on.

"Shut up!" he yelled at his brothers. "Can't you see Mum's busy?" They responded to him more readily than to his mother. She is too gentle, Martin figured; that's why she loses it, yells and breaks down all at the same time.

In the silence that followed Martin's outburst, Carmen regained her composure. "Here—Martin, see that they get into these dry clothes. I just pulled them off the line. I'll have to get a dhobi soon, the way these boys run through clothes." She straightened her hair nervously, patted down the damp spots on her dress, and went to meet Edward Jansz.

Martin made short work with his brothers, which included wringing Paul's ear when he got too excited, and grabbing the comb from Barney to part his hair exactly in the middle. Red faced and powdered, in their dry clothes, they were deposited on chairs at opposite ends of the dining room with the following options: stay quiet for 15 minutes and get the same amount of time with his now repaired ball-in-a-sock, or break the rule, and get a thick ear. They were wonderfully compliant after that.

When Martin returned to the back porch, Jansz was concluding his explanation, "…so if Baby is all right, I will bring her and come on Sunday, Mrs. James."

Carmen looked tearful and called Martin over, putting her arms around him, more for her own comfort than his. She held a crumpled black and white photograph in her hand.

"Who's that?" Martin asked.

"That's Mr. Jansz's daughter, Julia."

Edward Jansz gave Martin his hangdog smile again. Martin looked down at the photograph and gasped. Staring back at him was the image from his dream of the girl in the paddy field. The long tresses, the limpid eyes—it was all there in the photograph.

"Isn't she beautiful?" Carmen was purring beside him, holding on to her son more tightly than usual.

Martin recalled the recent fragment of conversation. "Is she sick?" he asked.

"No. Mr. Jansz's youngest son is down with a stomach infection, and Julia has to look after him."

Edward Jansz interjected quickly, "All kinds of germs are running around. They're saying that cholera is also coming again."

"So Julia is not coming on Sunday?" Martin asked. At this point he was only interested in her. Baby brothers—well—they were disposable, like his.

"Will have to see, young sir," Edward Jansz replied. "If it's serious, I will need some help at home. Also, can't spread the infection to your house, no?"

Carmen sent him home that day with a larger parcel of food and five rupees. Edward Jansz promised to come on Sunday, no matter what the situation was, to give her an update. He also took back Julia's photograph.

The following morning the school authorities sent everyone home as cholera had broken out in the city. As there was no TV, speculation was rife, and rumour spread very quickly. At one point the "epidemic" was an isolated incident restricted to some shanty dwellers; the next moment, thousands were falling ill, and hospitals were reportedly crammed. On the radio that evening, people were urged to go to the nearest medical facility to get their cholera shots.

Victor took the family on Saturday for their vaccinations. It was a painful injection and Martin's whole arm hurt. For once he felt sorry for his kid brothers; they screamed before and after the needle, and cried all night when they developed fevers, a known side-effect of the vaccine. The following morning, Martin woke up listless. All he wanted to do was lie in bed and sleep but he was excited by Julia's impending arrival. For once his brothers were not driving anyone up the wall: after an exhausting night, they had curled up and slept for most of the day, giving everyone a rest.

During his feverish daydreaming that day, Martin had many visions of Julia. In one, they were running by the water dam. She eventually stopped, breathless, took out a perfectly symmetrical stone from her pocket and gave it to him, saying, "Martin, you are the best. This is for you. I found it many years ago, the first and only time my father took me to the beach." In another vision, he leaned over and kissed her on the lips. He had never kissed a girl before. It felt warm, and his whole body tingled. And he wanted to do it again, and again.

But Edward Jansz never showed up that Sunday.

Aunty Mala had a field day with Carmen on Monday. "I told you; you got sucked in by his tall stories. He really took you for a ride." She had her arm in a sling following her cholera shot; apparently the injection hadn't gone too well.

Carmen countered, "Maybe his child is really sick. Look at us all, even with only the vaccine, we are walking around like zombies. How can you expect that man to do all this at a time like this?"

But Aunty Mala had the last word. "He didn't even give you his address, so you can't check things out. Clever rascal." Martin was mad at her. He wanted her needle prick to turn septic, and for her to die. Instead, *his* arm hurt even more over the next couple of days.

Edward Jansz did not show up for two whole weeks. The cholera outbreak ended. It had sent several hundred people to hospital; a few died, but overall it was a milder catastrophe than rumoured.

When he finally showed up, Edward Jansz looked absolutely horrible. His torso was covered only in a torn undershirt with several stains under his arms; his pants were even dirtier, and he was barefooted. There was a smell of alcohol on his breath. Carmen was careful this time, and did not open the gate, speaking to him over the fence instead.

"What happened?" she asked curtly. Martin saw a flutter of curtains in Aunty Mala's house.

"*Aiyo*, Mrs. James," he began, holding the gatepost and swaying. His eyes were bloodshot with tears, alcohol, or both. "How can I begin? My baby son is in hospital. Bloody cholera."

Carmen gasped under her breath, tears coming to her eyes immediately. "Oh Mr. Jansz, I'm so sorry."

"What to do madam, this is my cross. Sometimes it is too much to bear. That is why I took a drink today. I can't remember when I last slept."

"What are you going to do?"

"I told them not to release Ricky until he is better. Better to die in the hospital than in my house—you know—*cadjan* roof, open to all the insects and things."

"What about the other children? How is Julia?"

"I have found a foster home for the boys. As soon as my Ricky is better, I will be giving them both up there. Then I will bring you Julie-girl. Is that okay?"

"That's perfectly all right. What about your clothes Mr. Jansz?"

"This is all I have Mrs. James. They are falling off me. My shoes have such big holes, it's better to walk bare feet."

That day Carmen made a big clothes hamper: lots of the children's clothes and Victor's worn trousers and old shoes. She also piled in Paul and Barney's discarded toys: dinosaurs without heads, cars without wheels—all still usable, if one had imagination. She did not give him money this time, given his display of intemperance, although Jansz hung around for a few moments after he received the clothes, just in case she had forgotten something.

"Bring me Julia, when things settle down, Mr. Jansz. I really need the help around here, but I will hold on until you are ready. And I'll say a prayer for your children."

"God bless you, Mrs. James."

"Give, give, give!" shouted Aunty Mala. "When are you going to stop giving, Carmen?"

The three friends were at the gate again.

"Be careful, child," cautioned Aunty Soma.

"But what can I do? If this is all true, I'd be a monster to ignore him. Besides you don't even know if it's the same man who conned your sister, Soma." Carmen was close to tears and Martin was considering using his bat on both aunties Mala and Soma.

"That's *what* he did to my sister," Aunty Soma said. "Got her around his thumb with his sob stories. In the end, he got what he wanted."

"You have to put your foot down," Aunty Mala said. "Tell him to bring the girl the next time or don't come at all. If you like, I will tell him for you."

Carmen's eyes flashed. "No Mala, don't interfere. Let me deal with this."

Martin was glad that Mum showed some defiance.

Victor echoed the same sentiments that evening after dinner. "There's no use you giving him all this stuff. He has not given you any proof so far that this daughter exists."

"But I saw her photograph."

"How do you know it is her? She could be anyone's child."

She's the girl I saw in my dream, Martin wanted to say but held off. So far, he was the only one in his mother's camp.

The next time Edward Jansz called—two weeks later—he wore Victor's old clothes and had trimmed his hair and moustache. Once, he may have even been a handsome man. Carmen got straight to the point and gave him the ultimatum in a nice way. "Mr. Jansz, I need to get on with finding some help around the house. There is another party who has approached me. I was waiting for word from you, but now I really need to make arrangements."

He immediately straightened up. "I have some good news this time, Mrs. James. That is why I came. My baby is coming out of hospital next week. He is well. I will bring Julie-girl to you next Wednesday."

"Okay, next Wednesday it is. And please do keep your word." This time no food parcels, clothes hampers, or money exchanged hands.

Martin was in a hurry to get home after school before four o'clock that following Wednesday, the time Edward Jansz usually came around.

As he got off the bus and headed for the entrance to their lane, Martin glanced across the street at the bus shelter intended for passengers heading into the city. Usually it would be deserted at this time, but three children were sitting inside. They looked docile, resembling a row of steps. For a moment Martin wondered why his siblings couldn't be this passive. The smallest, a pale little boy of about three, stared ahead with a glazed look on his face, a pacifier in his mouth; an older boy, a head taller, was playing with what looked like a familiar broken toy, a car without wheels. Then Martin saw the girl.

She was not like the girl in the photograph, although once she may have been. The dark tresses were straggly, even the blue dress was faded and too short, revealing thin knees and sores around the shins; socks hung baggily over her ankles; the shoes, once white perhaps, were the colour of the dust at her feet.

A suitcase, battered and crammed, sat in the dirt. She was reading a book, looking up from time to time at her siblings and then staring towards the entrance of Araliya Lane. Martin followed her glance and saw Edward Jansz walking up the lane, heading towards the bus shelter.

At the sight of Edward Jansz, Martin crossed the road quickly, before he could be spotted. His satchel flew over the fence. Martin followed, slinking through the undergrowth behind the near side of the shelter, making his way to within earshot.

He saw Edward Jansz enter the shelter, pick up the little boy and place him on his lap. He stroked the boy's head gently. Martin could not see the girl from where he was hidden, but her voice came through clearly.

"What is happening, Daddy?"

"I am not giving you up, Julie-girl. I have decided. Finally."

"Are you sure? How will we manage?"

"We *will* manage. When God saved little Ricky here, He was saying to us that we could manage. Together."

The girl was silent. Finally, after what seemed like an eternity of silence, during which Martin could only hear the thumping of his heart, she said. "Then let's go. If we wait longer, you'll change your mind again."

"No, I have done my thinking now, Julie-girl. It has taken many months and I was almost at that lady's door. I am giving none of you away."

A bus came around the bend and approached the shelter. Edward Jansz rose, the little boy Ricky in his arms. "Come on, grab Georgie. Let's take this bus."

As the bus came to a stop and released disembarking passengers, the family held hands together and the girl smiled at her father.

Martin went for a long walk after that, down by the paddy field. He stayed there until dusk, until he knew his mother would start worrying about his whereabouts. Finally, he picked up a stone. It wasn't as symmetrical as the one he had received in his dream. He said goodbye to Julie and threw the stone far until it sank in the soft mud with a plop. Then he picked up his satchel and went home.

His mother was sitting in the bedroom with baby Julia's clothes spread upon the bed. The lights were not on. Her disappointment cut through the gathering darkness. "He did not come. Mala and Soma were right, after all."

There was no need for explanations at that point. Martin put his arms around his mother and held her tight. "Thanks for believing, Mum," he said. "I'm very proud of you."

5. **Paint Butterflies**

Martin loved going to his Grandma's place down Peter's Lane in Wellawatte. She ran a boarding house, the entire second floor of a large two storey building with six bedrooms and a two-floor annex converted into additional apartments. Many people had come and gone through Grandma's boarding house, a place she had occupied when her husband died at the age of 40, leaving her with five kids running around and one "still in the oven." There had been marriages and deaths in that boarding house over the years. Her children took rooms there when they got married, until they were able to afford to get out on their own. Martin had lived there with his parents, when he was a baby, before they moved to Perera Gardens in Kelaniya and later to Kotte. He enjoyed the company of his cousins Jenny, Michael, Shirley and Morgan and the younger ones, all born in the same house. There had been romances between eligible young ladies and single young men—"no hanky-panky, all above-board and clean," as Grandma would say of her boarders. When tenants ran out of rent money, Grandma gave them the benefit of the doubt, and they eventually settled, thanking her from the bottom of their hearts and never forgetting her generosity. "*Aney*, child—I also had unexpected debts when the children's father died suddenly. But people looked after me, so why shouldn't I do the same?" was the way she saw it.

Many boarders, past and present, including the James family, attended the quarterly card party that Grandma hosted. There was Horace, the clarinet player, bachelor for life; Uncle Joe, another long time boarder like Horace, and a widower, going blind but always spick-and-span in his bow tie and two-tone shoes—he wasn't a relative, but tenure had earned him the title of "Uncle;" Pat and Maude, who had met in the boarding house, got married and moved on to start a garment factory that now exported all over the world—they were portly and generous, smoking and cackling away at their luck, or the lack of it; Martin's parents; Victor's three sisters, their husbands and children. The children were not allowed to play, as money was involved; but they spied for their parents by scanning their rivals' hands and sending surreptitious signals. They received tips for their efforts and made side bets with each other as to whose parent would win the next round. During the game, bottles of arrack magically arrived, cigarettes were lit and chips ran counter to the piles of butts and ash in the ashtrays by each player's side. The windows were kept open and the breeze from the nearby ocean, while blowing away the cigarette smell, scattered the ashes all over the dining table and carried the laughter and enthusiasm into the neighbourhood, sometimes to be heard as far away as the top of Peter's Lane.

Martin loved to watch his Grandma play; she usually lost the most yet concentrated the hardest. A cigarette dangled from her lips, dribbling ash on to her ample bosom; excitement reddened her face when she received a couple of trump cards; but she turned crimson when she found out that someone else held higher trumps and beat her just as she was looking forward to replenishing her dwindling chips. Whenever she did win a round, she quickly cashed in some of her chips, gathered the grandchildren around and gave them her winnings so they could run to the nearby *kade* to buy candy. "Go soon," she would say, shooing them away, "before I lose it all again." Grandma also believed in the supernatural, and organized the card parties around the time her fortune teller told her that the stars were aligning propitiously for her.

The grand finale of the card game came around eight o'clock when they ran the consolation rounds. The winner had to win all three tricks of the game of "three cards," and after every round, when there was no clear winner, the kitty was replenished with new bets. By about the tenth futile attempt, everyone but Grandma would be standing around the table, voices at fever pitch, gloating over the swelling pool of chips in the centre.

"Take that—Ace, King, Queen of Trumps," "No look here—three seven's!" On that occasion, Victor was declaring his three sevens with triumph and reaching for the bloated pot when Grandma took a big puff from her cigarette and said, tentatively "Just a minute child, take a look at this, will you?" and placed down three Queens. Wild hand thumping ensued. Victor looked red-faced and sheepish, while Grandma smiled slightly and indicated for Martin to move the kitty towards her. Uncle Joe, who, unbeknownst to everyone, was struggling with the early onset of Alzheimer's, surprised the players by wanting to know if the game was over as chairs were pushed back and the proceedings moved on to post-play analysis.

Not all the boarders were good people. Occasionally, Grandma got taken in. Martin remembered Mahinda as a man in his early thirties. Grandma gave him the top floor of the annex when he came looking for accommodation. He said he managed a cinema in the city, so he worked odd hours. "He is looking to get a part in a Sinhala movie soon," Grandma told the family at breakfast one day. Fancy, she was now going to add a future movie star to her list of boarders! Tall and good looking, yet heading towards premature corpulence, Mahinda had the gift of the gab, when he chose to put it on, always regaling the children with stories of the latest actors he had met at special screenings.

On his days off, Mahinda could be seen on the balcony of his apartment, reading newspapers and magazines. The children kept their distance, and from the bottom of the steps leading to his apartment, enquired about the latest movie showing at his cinema. After calling forth a brief description of the film, he gave them some of the inside stories: how the male lead got injured on the set while doing a fight scene, or how the lead actress was having an affair with so and so. His audience was enthralled to know that all this stuff that they knew nothing about, really happened behind the scenes! He made it a point to throw them a magazine showcasing the latest screenings and the movie stars, and watched their little faces light up with delight. When Jenny asked, "Can we keep it?" he replied, "Sure, and if you come back next week, I'll give you another one." His dark eyes studied them intently.

There were other times when he wasn't so jovial, especially at sunset. He'd be seen pacing in his room, muttering to himself, sometimes displaying outbursts of temper. Jenny and Martin would spy on him through his open window across the backyard from Grandma's kitchen. When they drew attention to this behaviour, Grandma brushed a string of loose hair from her forehead, looked up from the food she was preparing for dinner and said, "Don't worry, children, he must be rehearsing for his part in the movie."

But Martin wasn't convinced. He had spied on him the time when Mahinda had come into the kitchen to grab a snack that Grandma frequently provided for her boarders, even though it wasn't part of their rental package. On that occasion, Mahinda set his plate aside after a couple of nibbles and looked around the kitchen; then he drifted into the living room, studying the family pictures, the giant radio which was Victor's gift to Grandma for her 65th birthday, the piano that Grandma only played at the family carol show on Christmas eve and now covered with her scraps of sewing, the old newspapers, and even the fruit basket with its very ripe bananas that were beginning to smell. He looked as if he was searching for something.

It was around the time that Grandma bought her new steam iron. Martin's family had gone to spend the weekend at her place. The rest of the extended family had also gathered as there was to be the quarterly card game on the Saturday. Grandma had complained that her fortune-teller had forecast bad luck for her that weekend, but relented to pressure from the rest of the family who were just looking to have a good time.

Jenny had arrived with her new paint set. She was keen to show off her oil paints; they came in neat little tubes; one squeezed them like toothpaste and they made bright paintings that didn't run easily—so much better than those messy watercolour palettes.

Martin and Jenny were seated in the back yard between the annex and the main building, a pad of blank papers and the box of paint tubes spread out on an old bed sheet on the sandy soil (very little grass grew in Grandma's backyard due to its proximity to the ocean). "Do you mix these tube paints with water?" Martin was anxious to learn this new technique.

"No you don't," Jenny explained. "You have to use them sparingly."

She was a year younger than Martin, and at 11, was quite the bossy lady when she had access to knowledge that plebes like Martin was not aware of. He beat her at sports— cricket, soccer and badminton—so this was her way of getting back at him. She took a blank sheet of paper and placed three dabs of paint from the tubes—red, blue and yellow— then carefully replaced the covers on the tubes and put them back in the box. "Now we tip the brush in them and paint our pictures."

She launched into painting the face of a man.

"Who's that?" he asked.

"My dream film-star."

"That looks like Mahinda," he said after awhile.

"When he is a film star—my film star," she said proudly.

Just then a gust of wind picked up the paper with the three dabs of paint, sending it whisking across the yard. Martin gave chase and grabbed it just before another blast took it further away. In the process, he crunched the paper and the paints got squished together.

"My paints!" Jenny squealed.

"At least there is no sand on them," he said, opening the two ends of the paper stuck with the paint in the middle. The colours had merged, spreading out on the page into a kaleidoscopic pattern, interweaving colours on both sides, perfectly symmetrical.

Martin was marvelling at the collage when Jenny looked over his shoulder and said, "A butterfly!"

"Yes. And I bet you, we couldn't do it as exactly even if we had painted it ourselves."

What followed was a series of experiments where they squeezed several drops of colour into the centre of a blank sheet of paper, folded it down the middle, and used the handle of a paint brush to spread the colours out in different directions, mixing them into and over each other. They then opened the folded sheet gingerly and looked at the new multi-hued butterfly inside.

Their squeals of delight became louder as each paint butterfly emerged; the prints were gorgeous, each one different. Even Grandma stuck her head out of the pantry window to see if things were all right. They felt privileged for their grandmother's attention, because she had been hard to pull away from her new steam iron and the pile of laundry that she had been engrossed in all morning.

"Are you okay—?" and then she stooped and gasped at the line of papers dangling between the coconut tree and the mango tree: the children had used the empty clothes line to hang up their paint butterflies. "My...how beautiful," she exclaimed. "You painted all that?"

"It's our special magic trick," Jenny quickly chimed in, taking credit for this freak invention.

"I must come down when I have done my laundry," Grandma said, then added, "but this iron is just wonderful. It's so easy to press these clothes. The steam cuts through like butter." Then she popped back indoors, leaving the cousins to experiment further with their discovery.

The card party was in full swing and the adults had lost interest in their offspring. Fevered betting was going on as Pat had requested the stakes be doubled from the customary 50-cent ante. Everyone was keyed up and more than a few drinks of arrack and several packs of cigarettes were consumed to keep tempers and nerves under control.

Michael and the rest of Martin's cousins had gone to the school grounds to play cricket. Jenny stayed behind and suggested that she and Martin paint more butterflies. Martin was getting tired of this newfound hobby, but Jenny was on a mission. So off she went to get her paints. Martin sighed and went through the kitchen to get to the garden through the back stairway. It was around 5:30, and there was still daylight; they could get a few more paintings done before the mosquitoes became bothersome.

As Martin entered the kitchen, Mahinda swivelled around. He had a black bag slung over his shoulder and was standing by the neatly pressed and folded pile of laundry. He looked surprised—understandably—everyone was supposed to be hovering around the card table in the dining room. Mahinda's eyes lit up on seeing the boy; there was a curious hunger in them and it frightened and excited Martin at the same time.

"What are you doing here?" Mahinda asked, zipping up the bag.

"We are going to paint more butterflies," Martin replied, unable to take his eyes off the man's piercing gaze, wilting under the scrutiny.

The spell was broken when Jenny rushed into the kitchen, paint bag in hand. She paused and blushed at the sight of the boarder, then immediately grabbed Martin's hand. "Let's go outside, before it gets dark."

They rushed down the stairs, Jenny in the lead. The string of butterflies was still swaying in the wind, looking vibrant in the twilight creeping over the parapet wall and through the tall trees at the end of the garden. As they spread the blanket and were about to begin their task, there was a heavy step behind them.

"What beautiful butterflies! These are works of art."

This time Jenny could not escape his presence, and she literally swooned. Martin guessed that all kids adore their idols, but are lost when confronted with the real thing.

"You really think so?" she asked, recovering quickly. Martin saw her flat chest with its slightly pointy nipples puff out while her eyes looked for validation.

"Why don't you come over to my place and paint? We don't have to worry about the dark. And I have more magazines for you."

Something told Martin they shouldn't, but Jenny was already mesmerized, because she had been asked by her hero. She began gathering the paints, as Mahinda walked ahead and climbed the staircase to his apartment.

"Maybe that's not such a good idea," Martin whispered in her ear.

"Why not? Besides, he's going to be a film star one day. How can we refuse him?"

"Are you in love with him or something?"

"Shut up!" she hissed. "Well, if you're not going, then I am," she said, and bundling the paints under her arm, trundled off after her leading man.

Martin followed, reluctantly. The stair led directly onto his balcony where Mahinda was already busy re-arranging plastic chairs. He cleared a little table of flowerpots and moved it over for them to set up their painting tools. Martin noticed how secluded it was up here. Mahinda`s balcony overlooked the estate gardens of the neighbouring temple, separated by a parapet wall from Grandma's property: thick overgrowth faced them on three sides and there wasn't a soul in sight; the main building where Grandma lived was behind the annex and out of sight of this balcony.

Jenny was gushing to please. She had the paints out and was dabbing various combinations on the blank white papers. Martin was expected to hold or give her the precise colours she insisted on, like the nurse and the doctor in the operating theatre with all the scalpels and stuff. Only, he was the nurse.

Mahinda pulled up a lounge chair next to the children and murmured encouraging sounds as they worked. His breath was strong in

Martin's face. After awhile, Martin noticed how close Mahinda had come towards him, as Jenny blissfully mixed her paints on the other side of the table.

When a hand slithered up Martin's leg, he froze in surprise, yet he had sensed something like this was about to happen. *How does one know these things?*

Mahinda's hand was cold and he worked it up Martin's leg, out of sight of Jenny. Martin secretly prayed that this was not happening. Mahinda's touch warmed as his confidence mounted, and it did not feel so bad. When the hand started to stroke Martin's testicles, he nearly jumped. Martin felt his penis getting erect, something that was happening lately in the early mornings.

"It's good. Very good." Mahinda murmured; his voice hypnotic. Martin heard Jenny respond. "And the violet looks very sharp here, doesn't it? I wonder what would happen if we mix red in there. Shall we try?"

"Yes, try another one. Take your time. Experiment." Mahinda's voice was entering Martin's head, pulling his skull apart. With his genitals distended, Martin was beginning to feel a guilty pleasure creep up inside, like slurping over the candy at the *kade*. The hairs on his legs stood up, he had goose pimples, and yet felt connected to his assaulter, and believed that he would never be able to break free now. *Frankly, I don't want to!*

Mahinda's stroking became rhythmic, pulling Martin's foreskin roughly, easing back gently; then easing off completely, and just when Martin thought it was finished, starting all over again. Martin's toes had lost sensation and everything seemed to have centralized around his penis: all his blood, feeling, even his breathing. Martin found himself pushing forward when Mahinda eased back, *wanting more!*

Then Martin felt the rush of something gushing out of him and Mahinda's hand caught a thick liquid, that he knew was not pee, and smoothed it back over his genitals, smearing him, rubbing it down over his thighs, minimizing it to a sticky smudge. Martin's energy dissipated, and his panic was countered by a euphoria that crept over his entire body. He groaned involuntarily, and Jenny looked up quickly, as if he had commented on her painting. The angle at which Martin stood next to Mahinda continued to mask the man's groping hands from her.

"Something wrong?" she said, and returned to stare at the butterflies.

"No," Mahinda interrupted in a throaty whisper. "Everything is all right. Keep working."

In that moment, the spell was broken and Martin was able to pull away from his captor and go around the table so that Jenny was now in the middle. He looked down momentarily and saw a stain creeping across his blue shorts. He sat down on one of the plastic chairs so that Jenny would not notice. Revulsion crept over him. He wanted to run away. Painting butterflies appeared irrelevant at that point. He just wanted to curl back in his own bed and die. He felt as if his whole body had changed from the one he was used to. *This is how Buddy must have felt.* He did not even trust his feet to walk back to the house. Mahinda's eyes bored into him across the table, glazed—like those of a dog seeking a bitch in heat.

Then just as she had got him into this mess, Jenny inadvertently got him out. "I'm running out of paint," she said. "The red tube is almost empty. We have to stop."

"I can buy you some new paints. Will you come again tomorrow?" Mahinda asked.

"You will?" again that puppy-dog look of admiration in her face. Martin realized why: if her parents lost money in the card game today, it would be a while before she got new paints.

Martin picked up on the opening. "Let's go," and started moving down the steps, half expecting Mahinda to reach out and swallow him. He had a visual of being imprisoned in this annex apartment forever, being stroked by Mahinda every day, enjoying it and slowly becoming his slave. His legs felt like lead and he had barely made it down two steps when Martin looked back; Jenny was packing her paints and everything seemed so normal. Then Mahinda rose and Martin saw the giant bulge in the man's pants, like his own had been before it had exploded into that sticky stuff.

Mahinda said sweetly, "Before you go, let me give you the magazines I promised." He stepped into his room, and then Martin ran, down the staircase, stumbling over the last few steps and crashing down on his knees at the bottom. Jenny shouted from behind, "Martin, what's got into you? Wait for me."

The pain in his knees burned, but it opened him to the fact that he could now feel his legs and the rest of his body. Martin looked back up to top of the stair at Jenny, a picture of calm, Mahinda handing her the magazines and bidding her farewell. Then the man turned his piercing eyes on Martin "Goodnight, Martin. Please come again, and don't be in such a hurry to leave the next time."

That night Martin clutched a pillow between his legs and squeezed his eyes shut for most of the time, but he couldn't sleep; a horrible dream of being chased by a horde of demon butterflies, intent on attacking his genitals, recurred every time he dropped off. The card game had ended late—around ten o'clock—and many missed the last bus home, so they decided to sleep over on mats and mattresses piled into the living-dining room. Only Pat and Maude went home in their giant Humber, along with most of the day's winnings. Now that all of the rooms in the boarding were occupied by non-family, the family members who had once been boarders themselves had to "rough it out" wherever space was available, as Grandma said. Grandma was in a pretty bad state too, because she had lost about 40 rupees.

Martin slept close to his father on a mat in the living room. He had inspected himself in the toilet after returning from Mahinda's and couldn't understand the sticky goop plastered all over his legs, yet knew it had come from inside him. There was no one he could ask either; he was not going to tell Jenny, or ask any of his older cousins for fear they would tease him, or worse—tell one of the adults. He was scared to take a pee, thinking that that white gunk would come out of him again. By bedtime his bladder was bursting. He finally braved it, as he did not want to pee in his sleep, in particular, as they were sleeping in a public place with all his cousins, uncles, aunts, and parents spread out all around. He held his penis over the toilet and was reluctant to release, until a sharp pain in his bladder made him let go involuntarily. To his immediate relief, it was a stream of glorious yellow urine, and joy flooded in as the pee shot out.

He was troubled by the fact that he had enjoyed this experience so much *while* it was happening. But men and boys? That did not seem to fit. Men and women, or boys and girls being attracted to each other, those were standard—he had seen it in the movies and read about it in books all the time. This was something else; it now frightened and sickened him.

His mind returned to his old friend Buddy and to Brother Joachim? He broke out in a sweat thinking of those days back at the boarding. Buddy died in the end, and Brother Joachim endured a private hell for whatever sin he had committed. Martin took a deep breath—*I am not going to die. I have to find a way out.*

Mahinda had exercised a powerful hold over him on that balcony. Martin thought of Hector and Achilles in the *Iliad.* Wasn't Hector attracted to Achilles as much as he was his opponent? Wasn't that why he decided to fight the strong man, risking death? And to kill this powerful force, was that the only way Hector could free himself from this fatal attraction? But Hector died, horribly. Martin decided to ask Dad—in a roundabout way—as soon as he could.

"The iron, the iron—it's gone!" Those hysterical words woke Martin the following morning from the exhausted sleep he had finally succumbed to around dawn.

Everyone stumbled drowsily from their temporary bedding into the kitchen, where Grandma in her housecoat, top buttons undone, revealing the fair top skin of her huge bosom, was holding her head and wailing over her loss.

"It was always here, child. I had just finished ironing in the morning."

Voices of conscience from the rest of the family:

"Why do you leave these things lying around?"

"Should have put these things away, no? Especially since we were all playing cards."

"Better call the police."

"Bastards—must be one of the boarders."

Grandma quelled the last outburst. "Now, now, don't go blaming the boarders. I screen everyone who comes to live here. After all, you children also lived here once, no? Never had this problem before."

"Call the Police."

Police Constable Perera arrived a couple of hours later. He secured his bicycle to the fence with a giant chain and padlock, then straightened up and looked about him with purpose. He was about forty-five, but looked sixty, with a lean and emaciated appearance, his bald head oily with sweat and a Charlie Chan moustache drooping in the day's rising humidity. Numerous sweat stains of different time periods on his khaki uniform underlined his armpits and one of his hose socks had lost its elastic and hung baggily over his black shoes that had gone brown with dirt and grime.

He opened a well-thumbed notebook and took notes, chewing the pencil periodically and spitting out pieces of wood as he asked questions in broken English:

"So what time this happened?"

"It must have been sometime last night. We were playing cards and then went to bed. I last saw the iron around noon, just before we started the game," Grandma explained.

"How many people in the house at the time?"

Grandma went on to give numbers, names and addresses—all required by PC Perera to be recorded meticulously in his notebook.

"Was back door open?"

"Yes, it must have been. The children were running in and out all day."

PC Perera glared at the "children"—meaning mainly Jenny and Martin who were watching this scene out of a movie; only they were not sure which movie by now: "Sherlock Holmes" or "The Pink Panther".

After about an hour and many pages of notes, PC Perera snapped his book shut. "Okay, I'm going now. Will make the entry in the station."

"But what about finding the culprit?" Grandma looked flabbergasted.

PC Perera stared her in the face and twirled his flaccid moustache affectedly. "Many rogues in this neighbourhood. Hard to say who." Then, as if looking for an adequate response, he hit upon, "…will get back to you."

Grandma fumed even before the man unlocked his bicycle and wobbled down Peter's Lane.

"Those buggers will never find anything," she swore. "When rogues broke into the Fernando's last year and took their gold jewellery, the police did nothing. They say that the cops are in cahoots with the thieves. How can you trust anyone these days?"

An hour later, Grandma, all showered, powdered and dressed in her maroon suit (the one she wore to funerals and weddings), left the house in a taxi. The relatives, who would normally be returning home that Sunday morning, decided to stay on, at least until she returned. Even though Grandma never said it, everyone felt like suspects, and suspects are required to stay at the scene of the crime until "whodunit" is revealed.

She returned just before noon. Carmen and Aunty Phyllis (Jenny's mother) had decided to cook lunch. Aunty Phyllis had won the rest of yesterday's stakes, and was in a generous mood, so sausages and pork curry had been added to the menu. Jenny had managed to scrounge five rupees from Aunty Phyllis to replenish her paints.

Grandma plunked herself on the sofa, wiping the sweat from her brow, her bosom heaving with the labour of climbing the stairs. The relatives crowded around.

"Where did you go?" Aunty Phyllis ventured.

"I went to see a light reader. They are the best for this sort of thing," Grandma replied, taking on an expression of authority. "He told me that it is somebody, known to me, who has stolen the iron."

"That's a fat help," Victor scoffed. "That means you will have to include all of us, and the neighbours, and the charity, and the orphanage, and all your boarders—past and present— wherever in the world they may be, and ...and all the people you have known since I can't remember when! That's a lot of people. Heck, I'd like to be a light reader—bloody swindlers."

"Hush, Victor!" Grandma said. When everyone had quieted down again, she continued, "The light reader said that I will soon receive a sign that will lead me to the thief."

"What kind of a sign?"

"I don't know. That is up to the universe, the light reader said."

The family decided to head home after lunch, which could conclude anywhere between two and four in the afternoon. A bottle of arrack emerged just after Grandma returned, and the men oiled their throats and dived heartily into the topics of rogues, whodunits and movies of the same ilk. Smells of curry and frying sprats emerged from the kitchen.

As the shops were closed, and her paint supply nearly exhausted, Jenny, along with Martin's other cousins and his brothers had embarked on a game of hop-scotch outside. Martin hovered at the far end of the garden, wrapped in his own thoughts and guilt. He felt alone and somehow older than his peers, because he had crossed some invisible threshold, one he could not brag about. He saw his father come out to smoke a cigarette on the rear balcony, the glass of arrack and soda in his hand was losing its fizz in the warm air. Martin inched his way over.

Victor waved his head at the string of paint butterflies below. "What, no more painting today?"

"We ran out of paint."

"Then why are you not playing with the others?"

"I don't feel like it," Martin lied. He sat on the step by his father and looked at the beautiful butterflies. *Come to think of it, if not for them, I would not have had my misadventure yesterday.*

Victor drained his glass, butted out his cigarette and made to go indoors again. Martin decided to brave his question before losing his father to the rest of the relatives and to more arrack.

"Dad, does urine get sticky and white sometimes?"

Victor looked at his son with a curious mixture of amusement and panic. "Have you been having wet dreams? So soon? You are only twelve."

"What are wet dreams?"

Victor threw his head back and laughed. "You'd better ask your Grandma about it. She was the one who educated us when we grew up. No one tells it better than she."

Victor roughed Martin's hair affectionately. Beneath his father's rough exterior Martin always knew there was a kind heart. "Don't worry, son—there's nothing wrong with you—you are just growing up. It's all part of becoming a man."

Just then, Mahinda crossed the backyard, a plastic bag in hand, to ascend the steps up to his apartment. He looked at Martin and waved nonchalantly as he went out of sight up the staircase. *As if yesterday's incident had never even occurred!* At that moment, with his father behind him, Martin had the feeling that he could beat Mahinda. After all, according to his dad, Martin was becoming a man. He wasn't Hector. He was Odysseus, the crafty one. But just as fast as it had come, as Victor scooped up his glass and headed indoors, that brief moment of courage dissipated, leaving Martin very, very alone.

Jenny came running. "Martin, Mahinda has been to the shops and bought me new paints. He stopped by when we were playing hopscotch. He must have a lot of pull to buy them on a Sunday. He wants us to come to his place after lunch to paint more butterflies. We can do that just before we leave for home. Please, say you'll come?"

Martin wondered why she wanted him around, if Mahinda was *her* idol. Despite his attraction, perhaps she too felt the danger of being alone with him. And as much she drove him crazy at times, he felt he could not expose Jenny to any danger.

His panic returned. How could he go back, even with her? But he was Odysseus, *remember?* He was supposed to face his nemesis. Martin must have mumbled something, for Jenny mistook whatever he said and pealed, "Thank you, thank you so much," and ran indoors, then stuck her head out once more to say, "Come along, lunch is served."

Martin sat there for a long, lonely minute. He had to do something before it was too late. The butterflies, flying calmly in the noonday breeze on their line between the two trees in the backyard, looked back at him, telling him what he should do.

He rose, went down the steps and pried one of the butterflies loose. Then he re-arranged the clothes line. Slipping into the house unnoticed, he grabbed the large marker that Grandma used to leave notes on the white board for her boarders, and went to work. Grandma, his mother and Aunty Phyllis were taking the curries into the dining room from the kitchen. As Martin had surmised, Grandma was still in her maroon suit; she always dressed for lunch, part of the colonial custom she had been raised in.

He slipped into Grandma's room; it was a dark, ornate one with a giant teak bed and bureau that was too large for the room: relics from her marriage and the large house she had shared with his grandfather, until his untimely death forced her into more modest lodgings. Martin placed the note on her bureau, where she would leave her earrings and necklace after lunch, when she returned to change into her house-dress.

He played with his food throughout lunch, too nervous to eat. His stomach was a mass of raw nerves, set to run loose at the slightest provocation. He therefore did not eat the pork, or the sausages or the sprats—food he loved. Horace and Uncle Joe, the senior-most of the boarders, were also invited for the repast, and the subject around the table had veered from rogues back to politics and how the new nationalistic government was driving ex-colonialists out of the country. "Even English-educated Sinhalese and Tamils are leaving this country now…And those *Swabasha*-educated university students have high expectations that cannot be met in the employment field…" Martin had heard this discussion many times before, but losing himself in it today was a relief.

He heaved a big sigh when lunch ended, heralded by the men kicking back and lighting cigarettes while the women cleared the tables. Jenny looked earnestly at him, expecting Martin to excuse himself and run away to Mahinda's with her; but he avoided her gaze. His throat constricted when Grandma returned from the kitchen and said, "Well, I am off for my forty winks. I assume you all will be heading home soon? You don't have to wait until I wake up."

"We need our forty winks too," Victor said yawning. He was always like this: a couple of arracks, a rice-and-curry meal, and Dad flaked out for a couple of hours at least.

"Sleep, sleep then," Grandma said. "Pull the bedding out again. But please put it away before you go." Then she disappeared into her bedroom.

Jenny was approaching Martin, a look of secret delight on her face. "Come, we have just enough time to go to Mahinda's."

"Wait," he said, hoping against hope.

"Wait? For what? We barely have an hour." She was annoyed with him. She was about to pout and say her famous dismissive word "Boys!", when Grandma's bedroom door creaked open.

The grand old lady stood framed in the doorway, her housedress barely hanging off her shoulders, top button undone, the note clutched in her hands, eyes wide in a terrible epiphany.

"I have the sign!" Grandma announced to the world at large. No one paid attention to her at first. When she roared, "I HAVE THE SIGN!" a second time, everyone stirred from their drowsy meanderings.

Grandma charged off to the back of the house and the rest of the family stumbled after her. She threw open the back door leading to the balcony and shouted, "Aha—the sign—see it? Didn't the light reader say so?"

And there before everyone's eyes was a line of innocent butterflies, flying uniformly in one direction and pointing in a diagonal line up to Mahinda's balcony, the ends of the clothes line carrying them, tied to the guard railing leading up his stairway.

What followed was an assortment of images in Martin's mind. He recalled the family traipsing down the steps of Grandma's house, across the backyard and up the steps to Mahinda's apartment. Leading the pack was a half-dressed Grandma; Victor had grabbed the empty arrack bottle; Uncle Joe had his old horsewhip; and Horace had even brought his clarinet as a weapon; and the rest of the family followed. Mahinda's door fell under their assault. Inside, he was half-dressed in a sarong; his paunchy belly matted in hair. He was listening to the radio.

Grandma's search was swift. Not only was her iron in the black leather shoulder bag, but a myriad of other "goods", not intended for such a small apartment, were discovered: radios, wristwatches, a brass paperweight awarded by the Legion (Uncle Joe scratched his head and said, "I knew I had put that one away somewhere,") and a pair of gold earrings.

Mahinda crumpled during the search; the bold, brash, budding film star became a snivelling cur as the missing goods came to light. His movement was further impeded by Victor holding him roughly around the neck with the empty arrack bottle poised for a quick strike. Horace stood nearby with the clarinet raised in case additional support was needed. Uncle Joe had misplaced his weapon somewhere but was getting re-acquainted with his missing paperweight.

Mahinda looked at Martin from time to time, terror on his face. Years later, Martin understood that the man's life would have been at risk if he had spilled the beans about the sexual attack. Apparently, child molesters got very poor treatment in prisons in Sri Lanka; few emerged alive. Martin averted his gaze from Mahinda. He never spoke of this incident again. Later that afternoon, PC Perera scratched his head and commented, "All the thieves in the area are living in this man. Everything reported missing at the station, is here."

Mahinda was led away in handcuffs by the triumphant constable, who would ostensibly claim the credit for clearing the neighbourhood of all thieves. Jenny looked crestfallen and was the only one who cried.

The family opened another bottle of arrack, even though it was only tea time, and had a drink to celebrate the solving of the crime. There would be still plenty of time to take the last bus home.

Of course, no one noticed the quick tropical rain shower that came down as the return of the steam iron was being celebrated: a fast, sudden downpour that predictably occurred when the heat and humidity got too high. And it was gone as fast as it came. When Martin went out to the backyard for one last look, before leaving for the bus, he saw the line of butterflies collapsed in the rain, crushed into the sandy soil; the paint, despite its claim to being almost indelible, was smudged all over the place, disfiguring the creatures beyond recovery.

"I'll never make them again," Jenny said from behind him; the resoluteness in her voice was frightening.

As he kissed his Grandma goodbye, Martin held on to her soft goodness for a while. Then he asked her a question; "The next time I come to visit, can you tell me about wet dreams and about becoming a man?"

Her eyes narrowed in surprise, then broke into a smile, "Of course, of course, young man!"

6. **Out on a Limb**

"I'm going to kill that bastard," Bandu said.

"You're nuts," Martin replied, but shivered at the thought. He wanted to kill Maha too, but was scared of the consequences.

"What's the use of you guys living in big houses when you can't face up to things like this?"

"Christo will manage," Martin stammered.

"I am going to kill Maha. Watch me," Bandu said. The old revolver he fingered in his hand made Martin tremble.

"Where did you get it?"

"By the river bank. Where the bodies came floating by."

"You went down there?"

"Yes. You guys chickened out, but I went down there. You should have seen them— heads bopping up and down, shaved. University-level men...and women."

"Does it work?" Martin asked, pointing at the gun and switching from the gruesome topic of the amphibious dead.

"I've oiled it. And I'll oil it 'til I get him."

"Bandu, please. Please think again. Maha's just an asshole."

"And so are you, if you just stand there and do nothing," he said and stalked off.

Christo, Bandu and Martin were friends from different backgrounds. They had met upon entering their early teens, five years after the James family moved to Kotte in '66, long after the seeds of childhood that lay the bonds of friendship for life had matured, and long before a continued association through high school and university could have cemented a life-long relationship. In those short years that they were together, the three friends were fused by far starker events.

Christo arrived in the neighbourhood just before the '71 insurgency. His guardian was his uncle, Bunty, who liked to drink in the evenings. Christo had no parents and he never talked about them either.

"Probably divorced," Aunty Mala from next door said in hushed whispers.

Most evenings, Uncle Bunty was drunk by eight o'clock and played his old Hank Williams LPs on an antiquated record player while sitting on the front steps, crying.

"Broken heart—a lover somewhere," surmised Aunty Mala.

Christo was tall for his age, and had a broken nose. He developed a nervous tic whenever he was among company. He was in Martin's class at St. Bernard's. Martin had transferred to the English medium the previous year, the additional English class having been forced upon the school in order to accommodate the startling number of students who had failed the grade-eight government exam the previous year.

Victor had quipped after having his customary "few shots" one evening. "Martin, you will now be like the one eyed king in the land of the blind."

Christo was very bright but did not care much for his schoolwork. Math came naturally to him, and he helped Martin with his work and sometimes forgot to complete his own. He also had a keen academic interest in guns. He didn't own any, but collected every magazine and book he could on the topic of weapons.

"Why do you like guns so much?" Martin asked him once.

"Weapons protect the weak," was his vague reply.

"Christopher is a good Burgher boy, Martin," Carmen said to Martin during one of her lucid moments. "You *must* be his friend. Bring him home sometime." But then she went off into one of her bouts of absent-mindedness and forgot all about it. Martin was careful to bring Christo home only when she was "normal." On those occasions, Carmen would make them jam sandwiches that Christo dug into with gusto. Even so, one day, he picked up the first sandwich from the fresh plate she had laid out, examined it and said. "Martin, why is the butter spread *over* the jam?"

Christo and Martin usually met at the James's front gate or in the playing field where kids from all walks of life were equal, no matter what class politics existed in the country at the time. It was on the playing field that the two of them met Bandu.

Bandu lived with his mother in a corrugated tin-roofed house on the top of the hill overlooking Araliya Lane, a leftover of the sleepy village that was once Kotte, before they developed new housing for the professional classes (that Victor claimed the James's now belonged to).

In Aunty Mala's classification, Bandu and his mother were, "Poor village trash, come to live in the expanding city. That woman must be a prostitute, to afford sending her son to St. Bernard's."

Martin couldn't refute that observation. Magilin, Bandu's mother, was in her mid thirties and attractive in a sultry way. She wore a *pottu* and had long black hair, usually coiled in a bun, or *konde,* but she left it hanging loose when bathing at the communal well, where she soaped herself voluptuously under her bath cloth and let the men ogle her. She didn't appear to have any fixed work during the day, spending most of that time sleeping, while Bandu always came to school looking like he'd had a disturbed night.

Bandu studied in the Sinhala medium at St. Bernard's. His English was poor but he tried to learn as best he could from anyone. That was another reason why he joined Martin and Christo on the playing field after school. He spoke "Singlish" – a combination of Sinhala and English.

Bandu always got into fights at school. He had been suspended four times already that year. Victor advised Martin not to associate with him. Martin couldn't find anything wrong—Bandu was a good friend, loyal towards anyone who befriended him. He put it down to his father becoming snobbish, now that he had a new job as a hardware salesman and earned more money than he had as a shipping clerk.

"Your father shouldn't think I'm bad," Bandu said to Martin one day. "I would give anything to find out *who* my father was." Unlike Christo, Bandu never stepped inside the James house, although Carmen expected Martin to bring home *all* his friends; the bounds of class and race that separated them were too much for Bandu to cross.

Martin clung to his friends more because this was also the time when most of his Burgher relatives, following the '71 insurrection, had finally woken up and decided to emigrate to Australia, Canada, the United States or whichever anglicized country would accept them. Martin and his friends played cricket, soccer, and in the really hot season, went to the *keera kottuwa*: a marshy field where shanty dwellers grew spinach and other leaves for making *mallum* which accompanied staples of rice and curry. The *keera kottuwa,* with its bushes, shrubs and tall trees, sprawled under a bridge leading into the city and skirted the river. It was their semblance of the wild, living on the outskirts of the fast-encroaching urban jungle that was the city of Colombo.

The *keera kottuwa* was also Maha's hangout. A 25-year-old thug in the neighbourhood, Maha dressed and looked like Elvis Presley, with his jet black cocks-comb, or Yankee bump. Maha was reputed to have helped the Marxist insurgents obtain guns in their recent abortive insurrection. He constantly dodged law enforcement officers, who tried to spoil his various money-making schemes and pin him with evidence. How he escaped the cleansing by the military that followed the insurrection, one could only guess; that his brother-in-law was the local bookie, who also ran a few businesses in the area—not all of them legal—helped. One of those establishments, a bar, was frequented by off-duty policemen, military personnel and local politicians, who got to drink on credit.

The neighbours detested Maha, but also feared him. He was a native of the area and represented the old town before its urbanization. "As long as he does not mess with us and carries on his nefarious activities outside the neighbourhood, what's the harm?" Aunty Mala said, trying to downplay the situation. The one benefit of having Maha, was that other thugs did not move into the area.

"I hate that bastard," Bandu said at every turn that Maha's name came up in conversation. Christo once explained to Martin that it was because Maha paid Magilin visits after dark. "He's her pimp," Christo said bluntly one day. Christo also helped Bandu with his math, even though the medium of instruction was Sinhala; alpha, beta, sigma in math, not forgetting x, y and z in algebra were untranslatable into Sinhala and were used as is. The friends often wondered why the politicians had bothered to proclaim that Sinhala be the national language, as not all the school texts had yet been fully translated from English; students in the Sinhala stream at university were jumping into the English classes to catch up. Maybe that's why the Sinhala university students, tired of being second-class citizens in this country in which they were the majority, had started the Marxist insurrection.

Christo had an enlightened explanation of the revolution. "The standardization system sent village kids to university in droves. They came out with high expectations and could not find jobs, because when you took the spit and polish of university out of them, they were just villagers—no background to work in government or mercantile jobs in the city. At least that's what Uncle Bunty says, before he takes a drink, and when I can talk intelligently to him."

"And see where that left them." Martin said.

"Yeah – dead in the bottom of the river."

Maha ran an illicit still in the *keera kottuwa*, one of his many illegal enterprises. He split his time between this shanty in the bushes under the bridge, his mother's house in the old town area, and Magilin's tin box home. Martin and his friends would often hide in the bushes and spy on Maha's gang as they drank and bragged about their exploits. The men would be sprawled on the open verandah of the little shack in the *keera kottuwa*, with Maha liberally pouring drinks from a big earthenware jug while everyone smoked joints.

"We shouldn't be here," Martin cautioned.

But Christo had an academic interest in watching the degradation of Maha and his gang, while they slumped into comatose mumblings as the evening wore on. "No, hang on. I like to know what they're up to," he said, focusing back on the men in the shanty.

Maha spoke in Sinhala. "Those guys didn't know what hit them," he was saying.

"Yah, we should do it again," said one of his buddies, dressed only in a sarong drawn up over his knees and squatting, spitting streams of red betel juice down the steps.

"No, we have to lie low for awhile. Another drink? Podia, pass the *kala gediya, machang*."

"Nothing to do. Just lying around like this and drinking every day. It's boring."

"You could get some ass at this time," Maha said.

Martin sensed Bandu tense beside him.

"Magilin, now she has a good ass," the betel spitter was saying, and Martin did all he could to restrain Bandu from breaking cover and running, giving their position away.

"Yeah, but Maha's got her all to himself," said Podia, a short man, whose name reflected his size.

"Yeah. And you don't mess with my women," Maha said, leaning back in the single chair on the verandah, an old rattan recliner with extended wing arms. "Try the boys, they are good too. Especially those Burgher boys—cute, fair asses."

The betel chewer grinned. "We are not as good as you Maha. We don't swing both ways."

Maha grinned and scratched his crotch. "You buggers would die if all the women left, you know." Then he leaned forward and got into a conspiratorial whisper. Martin only heard him say, "There's another job coming up soon…"

The three concealed boys couldn't hear any more. Christo said, "Damn!" and pulled on Martin's hand, signalling it was time to go. He already had Bandu by the other hand. It was during moments like this that Martin submitted to Christo's leadership; he was like a big brother, wise beyond his years, although he was a couple of months younger.

When they were a safe distance away, Christo let go of Bandu, who had calmed down. "I know it is tough when people insult your mother."

"You don't even know," Bandu said, kicking the dirt.

"I know," said Christo. Martin wasn't to find out about Christo's mother until many years later.

The fateful incident in the *keera kottuwa* happened the day of the cricket match against the kids from the opposite lane. Martin loved tennis ball cricket—no pads, no gloves—the freedom to hit a soft ball that could not hurt anyone was great, unlike when he played on the school team with the official leather ball. No one gave a damn which stroke was played, and new ones were even invented, especially for the tennis ball.

Martin knew trouble was brewing when Maha swaggered into the playing field, alone. The man walked over to the team at bat (Martin's team) sitting on the benches by the clubhouse and started chatting up the players. He eyed Christo and gave him a playful nudge. Christo needed cheering up as he had opened batting and got out for a duck.

Bandu was at bat when this happened. Martin had to go out just then as the next wicket fell. While batting, he caught glimpses of Maha talking to Christo. Martin enjoyed that inning; Bandu and he hit the ball a lot. They chalked up sixty runs in five overs between the two of them. Finally, Bandu got caught on the boundary and Martin followed soon after. Thanks to their brilliant batting partnership, however, Martin's team won.

As their teammates were thumping each other on the back at the clubhouse and celebrating victory, Christo came over. "We've got to go down to the *keera kottuwa*. Maha's got some new guns he wants to show us."

"Guns? You and your guns!" Martin said.

"Don't you see? He's planning another attack on Bada's grocery store."

"And?"

"We could tip off the police."

"Who do you think we are? The Hardy Boys?" Martin said.

"No, but I'd like to see his ass hauled up by the cops."

"And you think he's going to be so stupid and show you his guns?"

"He's an arrogant imbecile. He thinks he has protection for whatever he does. See how he got off the last time."

"So what makes you think he won't get away this time?"

"Uncle Bunty has a drinking friend who is with the CID. He could do something."

"Is he more sober than your uncle?"

"Yeah, I've met him a couple of times. He is not like my uncle. He's a cop."

Bandu had overheard them. "I don't like this. It sounds fishy," he said.

"Well, then I'm going down to the *keera kottuwa* alone." Christo's determined look said something else: Bandu and Martin had already had their victory in the cricket match; Christo was looking for his.

"I'll come with you, then," Bandu said. "Maha likes boys. You know that, no?"

"We have to take that risk," Christo replied grimly. "This is too big a deal to pass up. Besides, I can defend myself."

Martin had no choice but to go along too. "But we have to be home by six o'clock or my mother will give me hell."

"If she can remember," Christo reminded him.

"Stop screaming you little bastard." Maha had grabbed a struggling Christo by the mouth. Maha had Christo over a branch with his shorts down at his knees and his white butt exposed; Maha was thrusting his pelvis into Christo from behind. From where they were on the ground, all Martin could see and hear were shaking leaves, the two struggling forms, the wild screeching of disturbed birds and Christo's screams interspersed with sobs.

How did we get here?

When they got to the *keera kottuwa*, Maha had met them at his shanty. He was dressed only in a pair of boxer shorts. None of his buddies were around.

"We're going to climb trees," he had said to the three boys. He was looking at Christo, ignoring the other two, annoyed that Bandu and Martin were even around.

"Where are the guns?" Christo's voice barely concealed his excitement.

Maha looked up at the trees.

"Up there?" Bandu exclaimed.

"Where else? You think I keep them around for the *kossas* to find?" He looked at the three of them. "Now if any of you little shits tell anyone about what you see today, one of those guns is going to be pointed at you. Got it?"

"We understand," Christo said quickly and started shucking his sandals.

"Come along." Maha motioned Christo to climb a giant jak tree about fifty yards away from the shanty. "You go up first; I'll be right behind you." Then he looked back at Bandu and Martin, and said, "And you guys stay on the ground. I will only take one up at a time." His eyes betrayed the kick he was getting out of this: three mesmerized kids in awe of the power and influence he wielded.

It was when Christo got to the upper branches that Maha grabbed him from behind, ripped off his pants and started buggering him.

"We…we need to get help," Martin stammered coming back to the present.

Bandu and he looked at each other. Their worst fears were confirmed.

"We can't leave him up there. I am going after him," Bandu was already leaping up the tree and climbing as he spoke. "Maha, take your filthy cock out of my friend."

Martin was rooted to the ground. Off in his peripheral vision, he saw a group of kids, the ones they had just played cricket against, enter the *keera kottuwa*. This was a short cut for many, if one dared to navigate the swampy patches. They stopped and froze, seeing what was happening on the jak tree.

Bandu had almost reached Maha's foot when the man stomped down grinding the boy's hand. Bandu yelped in pain, yet continued to haul himself up. Maha let go of Christo and aimed a kick at Bandu's head. Bandu lost his grip this time and fell two branches, landing on the lowest and thickest one, a couple of feet above Martin's head. Martin finally got life into his legs and swung up on the tree, going to his friends' aid. Bandu had cut his head during the fall and his hand looked twisted. "Get that bastard," was all he uttered, and Martin heard Christo scream again. The other kids began running away shouting, "Maha is coming, Maha is coming."

Martin managed to get Bandu down to the ground; he was too scared to go back up the tree. Then he heard a panting Maha jump off the lower branches. Looking up, Martin's eyes were at the level of the man's stained underpants. Maha caught his breath, his eyes bloodshot and staring, the Elvis hairstyle in disarray.

Maha glared disdainfully at Bandu. "Hey *podian*, tell your mother, that Christo is a better fuck than her." And resuming his swagger, he walked back to his shanty. He emerged a few minutes later dressed in a pair of drainpipe slacks and a nylon shirt, his hair carefully greased and combed once more, and headed off down the pathway leading out of the *keera kottuwa*.

Christo had been forgotten in all this. When the branches shook overhead, Martin and Bandu dragged themselves under the tree again.

"Christo," Martin managed. "Are you all right?"

Silence.

"Christo! Did you at least see the guns?"

Further silence. Then a frail whimpering.

"There are no fucking guns." Bandu muttered, gritting his teeth.

"Do you want us to come and get you?" Martin shouted up into the branches.

"No."

"Can you come down?"

"I don't want to come down."

"You can't stay up there. It's going to be dark soon."

"Go away. Leave me alone."

Bandu stood up painfully. Blood was oozing from the cut above his eye. He stanched it with his tee shirt that he had just stripped out of. Very soon, the tee-shirt was red and brown. "We have to leave him for now. I know that's how my mother feels, after Maha comes and goes."

"But how will he manage?"

"We'll come back for him shortly. Hey Christo, can you hang in there for about half an hour?"

Silence again.

"But what if Maha comes back?" Martin asked.

"He couldn't do it again. Not so quickly. He is a "one-shot" man. I've spent many nights listening to him with my mother. He talks more than he does."

There was so much Bandu knew about sex. Martin envied him.

"Let's go for now." Bandu and Martin limped wearily out of the clearing, holding onto each other for support.

When they returned half an hour later, after going to Bandu's house to clean his wound, Christo was gone.

Martin did not see Christo for an entire week. He was sick, Uncle Bunty advised Martin curtly from the porch whenever he called over to enquire. Uncle Bunty sat with his pint of arrack every evening that week, like he was on guard. He did not play his records either. Just sat there, smouldering, grabbing at his pint from time to time to calm down. Eventually, he would rise, burp and stagger indoors, and the lights would go out in the house.

At school however, the rumour mill exploded:

"Maha cupped Christo."

"In the fucking jak tree!"

"Christo must have wanted it too. What the hell was he doing up there, if he didn't go voluntarily?"

"And I heard Maha also buggered Martin James and that rowdy guy in the Sinhala class—Bandu in grade nine. They say Maha took them one at a time."

Martin tried his best to quell the rumour, wishing that he could identify the kids who had witnessed the incident and then run away, so that he could talk to each one of them. The looks from the other students, even the teachers, were the hardest to get past. After a while, all he could do was ignore everyone when entering the school premises and keep his head high, hoping that this time too would pass.

Bandu did not cope well at all. He got into fights whenever the subject was raised around him; he confronted the rumour-mongers and a punch-up would ensue. By the end of that first week, he got suspended again.

Martin went to Bandu's house on the weekend to check on him. The building was of unfinished brick construction and its rusty tin roof clanged whenever dried fruit or branches fell off the giant *kottan* tree by its side. Inside, the one-room house smelled of soot: bed sheets draped on string separated Bandu's "room", from his mother's. The remaining area comprised of the kitchen, with an open fireplace and a table where they took their meals. They used the communal bathing well and toilets.

That was the day Bandu showed Martin the gun. It was wrapped in a towel and stowed in the little cupboard by the mat he slept on. He stalked out after Martin expressed doubt over his drastic plan of action to shoot Maha. Martin followed Bandu into the little garden. Magilin was nowhere to be seen. Martin tried to change the subject.

"*How* did you get the gun?"

"One of the injured rebels was hiding by the river bank. I brought him food and washed his wounds for him a few times. He was dying. He gave me the gun before he died."

"Did he say anything?"

"He said they had all been shafted. Sent to university and ended up jobless. What job can you get in this country with an arts degree? He cried for his mother before he died."

"Didn't you call for help?"

"He didn't want any help. Didn't trust the authorities. I floated his body downriver with the rest of them after he died."

"Does your mother know about the gun?"

"No. And if she found out, I'd be in deep shit."

"When are you planning…you know…to do it?"

"The next time he fucks my mother and is snoring. He always sleeps for half an hour before he leaves."

The enormity of what they were discussing suddenly hit Martin and he withdrew from this line of conversation. "But Bandu, you will get caught. The police…"

"The police will be happy to see him go. They can't pin anything on him. And they will release me. I'll plead self-defence. He was raping my mother, I'll say. Let her try and deny that. This will be the final test for her to take my side."

"She doesn't side with you? My mum does." Martin was surprised.

"Never. She is ashamed of having me around at times. I get in her way. How is your mother?"

"Not very well. She keeps getting these fits of absent-mindedness. The other day she put salt in the tea, thinking it was sugar. Then she got very upset when Dad gagged and spat the tea out. Dad says, if she does not improve, she will have to go to the hospital."

"If only we had mothers who were normal." Bandu had a far-off look on his face when he said it. "Christo's mother is in jail, you know."

"What!"

"She did something bad according to the police. Something with a weapon. Christo doesn't like to talk about it. He worships her and says she did nothing wrong."

Just then a taxi drove up, and Magilin descended from it. Her bangles glistened in the sunlight. As she bent to pay the driver, her ample breasts squeezed together beneath her bodice and the driver gasped and stared, as did Martin. When he wrenched his gaze away, Bandu was staring at the ground, embarrassed.

"Sorry, I didn't mean to do that."

"She provokes men. She says it's to earn us a living. There are times when I wonder if she's telling the truth."

When Martin walked away from his friend's tin box of a house, with its bed sheets demarcating lives, he wondered if there wasn't something to Magilin's words. Raising a child on one's own without any assistance in a country where the cost of living only went up and drove people to revolution, was not easy. He wanted to believe in Bandu's mother; he wanted to believe in all mothers.

"Pst, Martin. Come here, *machang*."

The elevated but slurred summons coming from the other side of the hedge bordering Christo's yard, surprised Martin. He was heading to the playing field that Sunday evening, a week after the incident. He had by now given up hope that Christo, or even Bandu, would join him at cricket, the one innocent pastime left in life, it seemed.

Martin paused and looked through the hedge. There was Christo, lying flat on the ground staring up at the sky, an arrack bottle by his side.

"Christo! What the hell are you up to?"

"Uncle Bunty is out. Come along. Share my joy."

Martin entered the gate hesitantly. The garden was overgrown. Carmen, despite her mounting illness, always weeded the beds and watered the plants, and Victor cut the grass as he could not trust her with the scythe. In Christo's garden the grass rose like paddy stalks. Irregular patches of wildflowers provided erratic colour. The half empty bottle of arrack drew Martin.

"You're drinking?"

"It's great. Now I know why Uncle Bunty does it."

"But you're fourteen."

"Who gives a fuck?"

"Your uncle would whack you if he found out."

"He couldn't hurt a fly. And he doesn't know how many bottles there are left in the house."

"So you are going to hide here and drink?"

"Yes. I know what they're saying about me in school." Hiccup.

"They are talking about *all three of us* in school. Who the hell gives a damn about rumour?"

Christo took a swig from the bottle. Martin winced at seeing the liquid course through him, burning him, making him forget, temporarily.

"Sorry to ruin your reputations," Christo said. His voice was quiet now.

"Why don't you tell your uncle's cop friend? Get him to arrest Maha."

Christo turned towards Martin; his eyes had lost their life. "He says Maha has protection."

"Did you ask him?"

"Yes. A couple of politicians in high places. That's why they can't pin anything on Maha."

"But he sold guns to the insurgents to fight against the government."

"Uncle Bunty says that these politicians create domestic disturbances and then make money out of them."

"And what did your Uncle Bunty have to say about what happened to you?"

"Not much. He took an extra drink and said the world is all fucked up. That I should grin and bear it. Soon I'll be a man and no-one will bother me then." He slumped into a round of coughing.

"There must be something we can do."

"I wish there were." And he took another swig.

"Stop drinking, Christo. Why don't you come to the field with me and play cricket or even shoot the shit, huh? And I'll go to school with you tomorrow. We'll face the stares together."

"They'll only laugh at me behind my back. No, you go. I'm sorry I pulled you into this. I just saw you go by and wanted to talk."

Martin put his bat and ball aside. "I'll stay with you then. I can always play cricket another time. I'll stay with you until you're ready to go back to school."

"Don't be silly. You'll miss too many classes. I am not planning to go back for a long time—if ever."

Martin argued with his friend for about half an hour, by which time the bottle was empty and Christo was muttering incoherencies. Frustrated, Martin gathered his things and left.

Three days later, in the evening when things came full circle, Martin was particularly sad. An hour ago, his mother had suddenly started emptying the contents of a cooking pan into the garbage. He had run to her aid, sensing something wrong. She was dressed in her nightie, not something she wore this early in the evening.

"Mum, that's the rice you cooked this afternoon. We can eat it for dinner."

She checked herself, ran a hand over her sweaty forehead and continued what she was doing.

"Mum! Stop it!"

She stopped and let the pan fall, spilling the rice on the floor. She bit her lip and tears started streaming down her face.

"It's okay, Mum. I'll clean up." Martin started picking up the spilled contents from the floor. Thankfully, most still remained in the pot and could be salvaged by the time his father came home for dinner. She sat at the kitchen table and buried her head in her hands. After cleaning up, Martin went to her side and put his hand on her shoulder. Part of him trembled inside. His mother had always been strong before his sister was born. After Julia's still-birth, she had never really recovered emotionally. Now it was beginning to show. People said it was the mad streak of the vanishing Burghers who inbred among themselves, but Martin did not believe them.

She started crying. Huge sobs wracked her. "It used to be so easy once, Martin. Now everything is so hard. They turned down our last application. It was because of me."

Martin hid his disappointment. That had been a crushing blow. Normally it was Victor's qualifications that let them down in their attempts at Canadian Immigration; this last time, when his recent promotion had that part covered, Carmen's deteriorating health had disqualified them. It was especially hard as the rest of the extended family were getting through.

"It comes like a cloak—heavy. Pulls me down. I don't remember what I am doing or where I am."

He held back his tears. Here was a woman, 39 years old, fumbling, aging before his very eyes.

"Promise me one thing, Martin. I don't think I will ever make it to Canada, You have to go. Get out of here and take your brothers with you. They killed all those young boys, only a few years older than you—

just because they wanted an equal share of opportunity. How much their mothers must cry for them."

"They were fighting a revolution, Mum. Shit happens." Martin's bravado was not holding. Her attention started to wander again. "So tired…" she started mumbling. He took her hand and led her to the bedroom. She followed like a sick child. In seconds she was asleep. He covered her with a heavy sheet and left the room in case his younger brothers should come in and disturb her.

It happened after dinner. Victor had returned, tired as ever. He now had a company car, a seven-year-old Toyota, reconditioned: brand new cars were only for senior executives, government officials and diplomats. Still, it was better than his old bicycle, he said. Paul and Barney were remarkably quiet at dinner, sensing the gloom that hovered due to the absence of Mum, who was still asleep.

After dinner, while Victor read the newspaper on the back porch, and his brothers played Ludo (quietly, for a change), Martin climbed the old jam tree to be alone with his thoughts. Up the slight hill to the left stood Bandu's tin-box house, and past Aunty Mala's house next door lay the weed strewn garden of Christo's property. It was a peaceful, moonlit night, two days before Poya day and the lane was bathed in a gentle moon-glow.

It was hard to imagine that over the last three months so much killing had taken place in the abortive Marxist revolution. Martin had seen very little of that conflict, for there had been a curfew, and the schools were shut down for two months, forcing ordinary citizens to spend their lives away from the main roads. The radio had played classical music during that time, interspersed with news reports of government victories. And some of the bolder ones like Bandu had seen bodies float down the river nearby.

Martin thought of Christo and what he must have felt up on that jak tree. He'd had similar brushes with child molesters; but now, being on the cusp of manhood, just when one started to feel invincible, to be taken in such an ignominious fashion…just like those young revolutionaries, misled by politicians, and then shot down like dogs…

A scream broke out from the direction of Bandu's house. Martin peered through the dark, as the moon had gone behind a cloud; lights were on inside the little house. Figures stumbled out, through the narrow gate and down the hill, heading his way along the lane that ran between the rows of houses. A man was beating a boy, while a woman hung on to them both. Martin made out Maha, dressed only in a pair of shorts; Bandu rising and falling with every blow; and Magilin, her long hair loose, bodice half open and a sheet wrapped around her lower body.

Maha's hoarse roar was intelligible now. He was shouting in Sinhala. "Son of a bitch – I'll show you how to kill a man. Little bastard." He gave Bandu a kick, sending the boy to the ground for the umpteenth time. Magilin screamed, *"Mage puthe!"* Bandu was strangely quiet despite the onslaught of blows, stifling the pain in his silence, but unable to withstand the force that knocked him down each time.

Lights were going on in the houses on the lane and residents stumbled out into the night. The struggling trio ended up in front of the James's gate. Maha brushed a clinging Magilin aside. "Get away from me you bitch. You and your kid are both treacherous shits."

Bandu's face was bloody; he was having trouble standing up. Martin jumped down from the tree and ran for his cricket bat. He needed a weapon. When he returned wielding the bat, a crowd had gathered outside the gate, the night was flooded in light from the houses and the nearly full moon had broken through its cloud cover. Victor, in his pyjamas, was trying to calm everyone down. Martin caught glimpses of Aunty Mala in her housecoat, Aunty Soma and her lawyer husband looking extremely dishevelled, and Christo hovering on the fringe of the gathering.

"You have to stop hitting this boy," Victor was saying.

Maha puffed his chest and stared Victor down. "He tried to shoot me, the little shit. Look here." Maha pulled something from the back pocket of his shorts and Martin recognized Bandu's revolver. "Came right up when I was sleeping and pulled the trigger several times. Lucky for me, this damn thing did not fire. Useless piece of metal." He flung the gun into the drain running alongside the lane.

"He was only trying to scare you," Magilin wailed.

"Shut up! Bitch. You set him up to this."

"Leave her alone," Bandu managed to cough out, and blood gushed from his mouth. Maha raised his hand to hit Bandu again but Victor intervened.

"That's enough. Let's report this to the police and they can deal with it."

"*Aiyo*, no police please!" Magilin pleaded. "They'll lock us all up."

"Speak for yourself, bitch," Maha shouted.

Magilin fell to her knees and raised her hands together. "*Aiyo*, please, Maha – please have mercy on my boy."

"I don't need his mercy," Bandu retorted, between spitting out clumps of blood.

"Now, quiet! All of you!" Victor yelled. "I'm calling the police." He turned on his heel and went indoors.

Martin heard Aunties Mala and Soma conferring on the side. "She's the trouble maker. Sleeping with all those men. Get rid of her and we will have peace in the neighbourhood."

That's when he saw Christo digging the revolver out of the drain and wrestling with it. A shiver went down Martin's spine in the warm night air. The look on Christo's face, as he swung around, flipping the safety catch back and forth, was deadpan, except for the nervous tic developing on the side of his face.

Maha was saying to Magilin, "You are getting no more protection from me," and pushed through the throng of neighbours, who readily yielded to him—no one wanted to tangle with their resident thug. Martin was surprised and proud that his father had decided to stand up to Maha and call the cops. Perhaps his new job had given Victor more confidence.

"It works!"

Everyone froze at the sound of Christo's voice.

The cops later said it had been an accident. They may have even cooked the records to ease the exit of their nemesis.

"It works!" Christo repeated. Everyone swung around. He was shaking his head at the gun. "See, only the firing pin was stuck." He had the gun pointed up now, as if he was offering it to the adults for confirmation, but it was aimed directly at Maha. The nervous tic on Christo's face was working overtime. For the first time since that day in the *keera kottuwa*, his eyes had suddenly come alight.

Maha's face blanched; he put his hand up for protection as the world shook with the revolver's explosion. Maha's open mouth widened further and spurted red. He staggered back several paces, gurgling, and crumpled in a heap amidst the screams of Aunties Soma, Mala and the rest of the gathering.

And yet the sight that remained etched firmly in Martin's mind took place *after* Christo dropped his arm with the smoking gun. While shrieking and yelling swirled around the James's gate, Carmen stepped out of the house, her white night dress flowing behind her in the light breeze; she was the only one moving deliberately. Christo had a look of resignation on his face, with panic bubbling at the edges. Magilin was spread over the lifeless frame of Maha, screaming, "*Aney*, don't die, don't die!"

Carmen came out of the gate and reached out for Christo. She had a far-off look on her face, as if she was sleepwalking "Come here my poor child," she said to him.

Dropping the gun, Christo fell into her arms with a sob and went inert. She looked over at Martin. "Come here and bring Bandu with you."

Bandu hesitated, casting a momentary glance at his own mother, sprawled hysterically over her dead lover. Then he moved towards Carmen, with slow intentional steps. He went into her arms voluntarily, stepping over all the class and racial barriers that had held him back before. In a daze, the three friends, half-men, half-boys, hugged this demented woman, drawing what maternal comfort they could, muddying and bloodying her nightclothes in the process, trying to hide—even momentarily—from the swirling panic that was the adult world around them.

7. **Screwed**

1974 was a bad year. For starters, Victor James lost his job. Rationalization, they were calling it at the office. "The bastards put a local bugger in the job – the new boss's relative." Victor went home drunk that day.

After the firing, Victor continued to "leave for the office" in the mornings, even when they took the company car away. He wound up home around mid afternoon with arrack fumes emanating from him; people said he was seen wandering in the Fort, playing billiards at the York hotel, or hanging around at the bookie shop.

That was also the year that Martin realized the full impact of standardization, a political ploy introduced to mollify the village youth and prevent future insurrections. Being a city student, his A-level marks were reduced by 15 percent (while his rural counterparts were getting theirs increased by the same proportion). Consequently he failed all his subjects and buried his mother's hope that he would go to university.

"I'm not trying again," he said. "The system is fixed. If I go and live in some one-street village, I could get into the varsity faster than by living in Colombo. I should have listened to Christo years ago." His mother did not register what he said. Carmen had taken to wandering around the house in her housecoat, hair unkempt, unbathed for days. She prayed or sang hymns in her room all the time and Victor had moved into the guest room at the front of the house.

Before long, the household money had dwindled and Martin decided it was time he got a full-time job. After prospecting around the Fort for a few days, occasionally bumping into his father who was ostensibly on a similar mission, Martin landed a job as a clerk in a travel agency.

Victor had an opinion about Martin's relative success and his own lack of it. "One gets jobs in this country through influence, not qualifications. All my influential contacts are leaving and going abroad these days. You got your job because it's at the bottom of the pole. Nobody feels threatened at the bottom of the pole."

1974 was the year when Martin's brothers, Paul and Barney, started getting into fights in school and around the neighbourhood. In fact, Paul now sported a broken nose and scars on both his eyebrows. He was the bigger-built of the two, and by the time he was 12, his voice broke. He began pumping iron by the well each morning, because he wanted to take on "the rowdies" who harassed him and his kid brother. Barney, on the other hand, at 10, was a sickly child, with a drippy nose and running stomach. He avoided his father when Victor was under the influence, especially when the horses had "run the other way." One shout from Victor, would see Paul curse under his breath and disappear into a friend's house for the night, while Barney ran to the toilet.

Barney was the kid that the older boys picked on, especially when Paul was off to rugby practice and couldn't act as a bodyguard. Latha, the new servant, was sent to the bus stop to meet Barney whenever he travelled home alone after school. Usually she got distracted by chatting with the other *ayahs* en-route, and when she was late, Barney met his punishment—swiftly. She would often cradle the trembling boy who had wet his pants while running down the lane from the applied, or implied, threats of the bullies hanging around at the top of the road. And on those nights, Victor would drink and rave some more about the injustice of this "bloody country."

One day, Martin came home from work to find Victor sorting a pile of chits on the dining table. For a moment he thought his father had been betting heavily.

"Are those all yours?" Martin asked, his voice twisting. In recent times he had started to get snappy with his father, especially now that he was financially independent.

Victor looked up. "Are you mad? I wish they were."

"Well then, whose are they?"

"I'm collecting." Victor took a sip from the glass of arrack by his side.

"You're a bookie?"

"Sure, why not? I'm building my customer portfolio."

"But it's illegal."

"Bullshit, it's illegal. Says who? Those bastard politicians can do anything they want—that's not illegal? This is a sport. In England, even the Queen goes to the horses, and even to the dogs."

Martin shook his head. Deep down, he admired his father for trying the underground job market now that the official one had failed him.

"Where do you get your customers from?"

"What do you think I am doing walking the streets in the Fort, calling on all my contacts, while you do the la-de-da in an air-conditioned office?" The hurt and jealousy on his father's face made Martin look away.

"You…you could get a job in an air-conditioned office too," he stammered.

"Nah—I've done that for too long. I'm building my own business now. Those buggers can all go and get fucked." Victor emptied his glass and went back to sorting out his betting chits.

You proud son-of-a-bitch! Martin mumbled, as he went to his room.

1974 was the year that Martin met Rohini when the Senanayake family moved into the old *walauwe* at the top of Araliya Lane. The first sign of the new arrivals was the erection of a huge parapet replacing the rusty barbed wire fence with its myriad of holes that allowed neighbourhood cattle to graze upon the overgrown lawns of the property. Grimy roof tiles were replaced with sheet roofing; new paint went on the exterior, and trucks rolled in with household goods and furniture.

According to Latha, who was deeply plugged into the neighbourhood grapevine, the Senanayakes were rich people; the husband was a skin specialist, and the wife a paediatrician; Rohini, the daughter, was in her A-levels at Young Women's College and the son, Manoj, 12, attended Regal College.

Martin remembered the first day she got out of the family Mercedes Benz. Rohini's lush and shiny black hair fell to her waist. She wore a white blouse and blue dress down over her knees, revealing strong calves, unusual in South Asian women. She paused and looked about her surroundings and at the house that was to be her new home; she was tall, and had an air of superiority, almost of worldliness. She turned in Martin's direction; he was standing on the opposite side of the lane watching the new arrivals move in. Their gazes locked and he saw the glimmer of a smile in those large, dark eyes, the most prominent feature in her heart-shaped face. He drank in her body: wide hips, bosom thrusting against the blouse with no sign of heaviness. *She's perfect.*

The brother was something else; he was fat and slouchy and had close-cropped hair. Manoj slunk out of the car grumbling at something, grabbed a knapsack out of the vehicle and sulked off into the confines of the house. When the parents alighted, Martin saw how the genes had spliced in this family. The mother was like the boy: plump and short, draped in an expensive sari with golden bangles running up her forearms, her grey-streaked hair wrapped in a heavy *konde*. She immediately started giving orders to the movers, hands on hips, surveying the new terrain, appraising the Burgher boy staring at them from across the lane, her thick nose wrinkling in annoyance. The father was tall and aristocratic, with a full head of completely grey hair. He walked into the house with long steady strides, his daughter by his side; even their gaits matched. At the doorway the girl paused, looked back fleetingly at Martin, and went indoors.

Striding home that day, Martin decided to conquer the damsel in the Senanayake fortress, even though the thought made his palms sweat.

Rohini rarely came outdoors, so conquest was not an easy task. Martin occasionally caught glimpses of her leaning on the parapet wall in the evenings, a book under her elbow, dreamily looking off into the distance. Often someone called from inside the house, and she would gather the book and hurry back indoors. On other occasions, she would be in the back seat of the Benz, being driven to and from school or other appointments by the family driver, Banda, an old retainer with a handlebar moustache, who seemed to have been born into servitude within the Senanayake lineage.

Martin tried walking by the parapet wall on those rare occasions when she was outside, but every time he neared, he ran out of resolve and became tongue-tied. What was he going to say to her? She looked imperious, despite her wistfulness; just out of reach, unattainable.

Aunty Mala summed the situation up succinctly when she came over to visit his mother. She was a frequent visitor now, and seemed to be his mother's only remaining friend as Carmen continued to sink deeper into her dementia. "Those people—very proud, *aney*. Don't speak to the neighbours, only keep to themselves. Up-country people—they think the sun shines out of their asses."

One day, as Martin passed by in the lane, he heard a piano playing inside the Senanayake home: classical music, elegant and well-paced. He did not know much about this kind of music, except for what his mother, in her lucid moments, listened to on Channel One of the SLBC. The music from within was similar: no false notes, a practiced artist at work. He almost ducked for cover when the Mercedes came out of the front gate just at that moment. Banda was spruced in a gold-buttoned tunic, and Mr. and Mrs. Senanayake sat in the back: he in Ariyasinghala clothes, all white and flowing, and she in a gold-bordered sari. The car whisked by so fast, all Martin saw was a flash of gold on the woman's side, and a blur of grey-white on her husband's. With the departure of the car, the music inside the house changed dramatically. Out burst an Elton John favourite—*Crocodile Rock*—and he couldn't help tapping his toes in the lane. Martin threw his head back and laughed.

His opportunity to make a dent in Fortress Senanayake came when the old Triumph fell into his hands. A colleague at the travel agency was selling a 15-year-old motorcycle; it was a black blunderbuss that roared and belched smoke, but it did go. In those days, before the liberalization of 1977—when the Capitalists ousted the Socialists and lifted foreign exchange restrictions, ushering in foreign imports and rampant corruption—a 15-year-old motorcycle was still something to be prized. Martin couldn't afford the asking price of four thousand rupees, so he decided to pay a thousand down, and the balance in instalments.

Everyone eyed him with envy, but none more than his father, who after a drink said that Martin had wasted his money on a useless piece of junk. "Wait till the repairs come in. And they can't even get spare parts for those vehicles with all the bloody import controls."

Martin ignored his father; the here and now of owning a bike, of swerving into Araliya Lane, especially when Rohini was at the parapet wall, was worth all the repairs that were to come. She actually paid attention now, returning his wave cautiously as he rode past.

Two weeks after Martin bought the Triumph, he stumbled on Carmen and Victor arguing in the kitchen. Martin knew it must be important; his mother couldn't sustain arguments any more, let alone engage in prolonged human contact. When he walked into the room,

Carmen was sobbing yet holding her own. "If you gamble with all your money, how can you afford it?"

Victor looked up at Martin and growled back. "And if those in the family spend their money on motorcycles…"

"Hey, hey, what's going on here?" Martin intervened, frowning.

Carmen looked up, her red-rimmed eyes defiant, the demented look receding briefly. "Your father has pulled Paul and Barney out of St. Bernard's."

"What?"

"Martin, stay out of this." Victor spouted, getting up from the table.

"You're going to deny my brothers an education? I'll pay for them if I have to."

"They *have* an education." Victor dismissed him, rising from the table. "I've entered them in the government *Vidyalaya*. They'll get education for free now, just like all the other local yokels. After all, this country is where we are going to spend the rest of our days, isn't it?" He looked accusingly at Carmen. "It's time we blended in."

"Blame me. That's what you do now," Carmen said.

"Okay, okay. Calm down everybody," Martin said. "I'll sell the bike tomorrow and give you the money for their school fees."

"No thank you. I will educate the children—my way!" Victor said and stormed out.

Carmen hunched over the table. "I'm so tired. So tired. Everything is dying, Paul." He walked over to her and took her hand. "This is Martin, Mum."

"Martin, Paul, Barney, Julia—lovely names. English names, dying in the dust here."

"Mum, we live here. Yes, the country's a bit screwed up but we will survive."

She looked up at him. Her eyes were puffy from crying; the blank look was returning and it would stay longer this time, Martin sensed.

"Take my hand, Precious Lord…lead me on, let me stand," her voice croaked. "I'm tired, I'm tired…I'm tired." Her voice trailed off. This was when he normally took her by the shoulders and walked her back to her room. But this time she restrained him. "I used to say to you that we had to be resilient. Remember Odysseus? But the energy runs away from me now. Oh, Martin, I only wish I could practice what I preach, sometimes." He led her firmly into her room, laid her on the bed and was about to leave, when her words stopped him cold. "Promise me *—you will do it. Don't let your energy run out.*"

Barney and Paul were non-committal about their new school. "Whatever they want to do," said Paul, shrugging it off. Barney was silent in his usual way; he came home daily after school and stayed in his room reading comic books. Martin decided not to sell the bike after all; the transaction would be a wash at best, a loss most likely, and his proud father would never accept money from him.

He put his domestic worries aside and focused on winning Rohini's affections. One day after work, he plucked the courage to slow down as he turned into the lane and manoeuvred his bike to a stop right underneath the parapet wall where she was at her usual spot.

"Hello, my name is Martin." There was tightness in his throat. He remembered the girls he had gone to dances with, none of whom he'd been serious over; a bit of squeezing, some necking and heavy petting, was as far as girls in his social set would go, because people talked and a girl did not want to ruin her reputation in the Sri Lanka of the '70s. But this girl was something else; she made him feel special even by just looking at him, which she was doing intently now: studying every feature—his body, his clothes, the Triumph, and then back to his body. He felt under a microscope.

"Yes, I've heard about you," she replied in good English. She smiled at him and his heart began to race.

"Who from?"

"Our servants talk."

"Who? Latha and your driver?"

"You have not met our housekeeper Agnes?"

"No. She must be all hidden away—like you."

Rohini blushed, and he thought he'd blown it. Quickly, he added, "Do you go out?"

"Only to school and to music lessons. My parents are strict." A trace of regret crossed her face.

"Then I guess there's no hope for a guy like me, huh?" He knew he was only provoking her by saying all the wrong things in his nervousness, but she seemed to resist and hold on, perhaps appreciating his honesty.

"What do you do?" She leaned over conspiratorially and her blouse parted revealing fair-skinned cleavage, fresh and mysterious. A wild urge made him want to reach out and put his hand on Rohini's breast; put an end to the things that were out of reach for him—like emigrating, or getting into university. Here was another desire, inches from his face, and yet he restrained himself and looked into Rohini's dark luminous eyes instead.

"I asked you what you do?" she repeated.

"Oh, I work in the travel business."

"Then you must go abroad and all?"

"Pretty soon, pretty soon." He didn't want to tell her that this was a pipe dream. All the promotional travel-agent trips doled out by the airlines went to the owner of the agency and his family. All Martin did was take travel vouchers around to the airline offices for ticketing, or go to the Central Bank to get foreign exchange approved on those dreaded P-forms.

A voice called from inside and a look of indecision crossed Rohini's face. "I have to go." She leaned over. "But I want to see you again. Can you come to my school at 3:30 tomorrow?"

"Doesn't your driver pick you up at that time?"

"I'll tell him that I am coming home with some friends. I don't have any more time now. Will you come?"

"Of course." He would have to con his manager, take out some more P-forms to the Central Bank, say he was stuck in the line-up, and head down to her school instead.

Then she was gone. He gunned the bike gently, wishing it would not make such a racket, since whoever had called Rohini must still be in the vicinity. He inched the vehicle forward in low gear, which was a muffled growl at best. As he passed the open gate, he stole a glance and saw an old frail woman, hands across her chest, staring at him, while Rohini, her back to him, entered the house.

He decided to get the lowdown from Latha. The housemaid had been with them for two years and had arrived in the James household when Carmen was no longer able to do the cooking or housework regularly. Martin hung around the kitchen that evening, watching Latha at work. She was younger than their former maid Seetha, in her late twenties, and if not for her protruding teeth, would actually have been attractive. A *vatiya* was wrapped tightly around her ample hips and when she turned, the gold *thali*—the one piece of jewellery she never took off her body—dipped in and out between large breasts bursting up against the skimpy bodice. Latha could be described as buxom, but Martin wondered how long it would be before she turned fat, because she was always eating scraps. Even now, as she put the dishes away after dinner, there was a plate full of assorted left-overs that she would devour rapidly, sitting on the solitary stool in the kitchen. For now, his eyes wandered momentarily over her dark *konde* at the nape of her neck, reflecting on how he'd seen her after a bath on numerous occasions when her hair dropped wildly over her shoulders and down to her hips.

Latha must have sensed her young master hanging around, for she looked up from the sink, "*Mahattaya*, you want something?"

Martin pulled himself away from ogling and tried to get right to the point, replying in her native Sinhala. "The Senanayakes. What kind of people are they?"

Latha smiled knowingly. "Ah *mahattaya*, you cannot mess with them. They are very high-class. Sending the daughter to England next year, for studies."

"Really. How do you know?"

"Oh, Agnes tells me everything."

"The old woman?"

"Yes, she is like my mother. She has been with them for a long time, since the children were babies."

"What about the boy? He doesn't look very high-class."

Latha pursed her lips and bent forward in a whisper. "Shh, don't tell anyone. The son has a problem. Loses his temper and shouts sometimes. They have to give him medicines for it."

Martin felt a movement behind him and turned around to see Victor standing in the doorway. Latha immediately pulled back with a look of panic.

"What's happening here? What's all the *kussu-kussufying?*"

Martin smelt the alcohol on his father's breath. "Nothing," he replied. "How were the horses today?"

"Not bad, not bad." Victor eyed Latha over. "You are still working?"

She kept her head down in deference. "Only putting the washing away, *loku mahattaya.*"

"Good, good." Victor had an air of satisfaction. For a moment, Martin glimpsed his father of old: the man in control of his household. He was surprised that Victor was solicitous about how the kitchen department ran, which had long been the preserve of Carmen, who was now notably absent.

At 3:30 p.m. the following day Martin was outside the tall gates of Young Women's College. The girls streamed through in their white uniforms with square necklines that emphasized the big busted ones and flattened the less endowed. School books cradled in arms, some chatted loudly, others looked glad to be going home, braving the hot mid-year sun and a sweaty bus ride.

Rohini came out alone. She caught sight of the black Triumph and hurried over. She ducked her head behind him and whispered in his ear, "Let's go. Pretend you are my older brother or something." She swung onto the pillion seat behind him. He took off with a burst, her breasts rubbing against his back, sending him into a state of suppressed ecstasy.

"Where are we going?" she shouted in his ear as they hit the Galle Road with its maze of cars, busses, trishaws, and the odd bullock cart, all vying for space and threatening to topple them off their mobile perches at any moment.

"I don't know. Maybe to Galle Face Green."

"To sit on the benches with those illicit lovers?"

Aren't we illicit lovers of sorts? But he held his tongue and said, "Where do you want to go then?"

"We could still get to the Liberty. The movie would have just started."

"Okay." He swerved down into Turret Road and narrowly avoided a trishaw making an illegal turn. He pulled into the back of the cinema parking lot. She dragged him into the building. "I'm going to the toilet. Buy the tickets and meet me inside," she said, leaving him at the ticket window, which was empty as the movie had started 15 minutes earlier.

He bought balcony tickets, even though they were the most expensive. Rohini nodded in approval when he met her by the inner staircase. "Hurry," she said and took the stairs two-at-a-time, letting him follow her breathlessly. He was surprised at her agility, schoolbook satchel and all. They made their way to the rear in the dark amidst the flashing lights on the screen behind them. Couples were already necking in the back rows as could be expected for this time of day—mostly school goers. They found four empty seats in a row and took the two in the middle.

No sooner had they sat down when she was crushing her lips on his with a passion that sucked his breath away. He pulled back instinctively. He was not used to this; the guy was usually the aggressor. Yet her intensity excited him. Rohini's breath was tinged with a trace of cinnamon. Her hot hand fell on his thigh and moved up; before long she unbuttoned his fly, reached inside his pants to release him and began stroking; and he moaned. Just as he stiffened at the point of coming, her mouth descended over his erect penis and he shot uncontrollably into her, shuddering back on the seat, wondering what the hell was happening, dazed, euphoric and frightened.

They remained silent for a while, watching the movie. It was only then that he discovered the film was "Love Story". Their breathing slowly subsided to normal levels.

She leaned into his ear. "Were you pleased?"

"Yes," he said in a throaty, embarrassed whisper.

He could not focus on the movie after that. With her hand tightly clutched in his, all he could think of was that, despite his initial scare, he wanted more of this girl; he had been very lucky to find her. Yet, there was something overpowering in Rohini, in the entire Senanayake family that went beyond the façade of upper-middle class: the *walauwe*, the Mercedes, the starched servants and the well-manicured gardens. He had sought the unattainable; now he had it, and was consumed and troubled by it.

Later, they went to the Green Cabin for tea.

His reticence and withdrawal since climaxing seemed to worry her.

"What's the problem?"

"You are experienced. You have done this before. Many times before," he said, unable to hide the disappointment in his voice.

She bit her lip and took deep breaths. Then she told him about Anil Munasinghe.

"He was my music teacher. We were lovers for a year, before Thaathi found out." Her eyes turned dreamy. "Anil taught me things. He is a married man."

Martin's heart sank. "How long ago was this?"

"Last year. That's why we moved. Amma said she could not face the neighbours any more when the story broke out."

"Why? Why did you go with a married man?"

"I was too impressionable then, I suppose. And I felt trapped by all the restrictions at home."

"You could get into trouble again, if they found out about us."

"Yes." Then her brow creased in anger and she almost spat out. "But I don't care. They keep us caged, like pets."

"Can I see you again?"

"Yes. I want you to. You can pick me up from school. Not every day—I will tell you when."

He dropped her off two bus stops before Araliya Lane and sped away. Even if someone had been at the top of the lane to meet her, the main road curved just before it passed Araliya Lane, and no one would have seen them together.

That night, as he lay in the dark on his bed, he felt deflated. He had wanted Rohini to be a virgin. That would have kept them on the same playing field. Although he was 19, he'd had no previous sexual experiences. He had shied away from them; the humiliations of his grandmother's boarder Mahinda, and in later years, the blatant bisexuality of Maha had sent him into a kind of sexual hibernation, although the urgings of his loins had called frequently; masturbation had been his only outlet to date. And now, to know that Rohini was an experienced sexual being upset him. Yet, he felt compulsively drawn to her. He wondered what it would be like if he made love to her. Would he be competent, or would he shrivel up in the face of her worldliness? He turned around, punched the pillow several times and tried too hard to fall asleep.

An hour later, he was still awake. Only this time his ears had picked up tip-toeing in the corridor outside. He rose and put his ear to the door; it sounded as if a heavy sheet was being dragged across the cement floor with steps gently treading alongside. He was reluctant to open the door, wondering if he would come face to face with his mother in one of her crazy moods, exposing her crumbling mind to him in yet another farcical scenario. Besides, he was too pre-occupied with his own mental turmoil to worry about Mum at the moment. He turned and went back to his bed. After awhile, there was silence. Around dawn, he fell into a troubled sleep.

They met regularly after that to the same drill: 3:30 p.m. outside Young Women's College, a movie, and a cool drink somewhere, before he dropped her off at a random bus stop en-route to home. During those movies, he got more courageous—she wanted him to—sliding his hand into her panties, stroking her thick long pubescence, slipping a finger into her wetness and hearing her sigh in his ears she urged him not to stop his rhythmical rubbing until she came. But he wanted more. He wanted her the way a normal man and woman made love to each other, not in this spurious and illicit way.

One day, over a cokes après-movie at a restaurant, he mentioned this desire to her.

"Be patient. I have to find a time when no one will be at home," she said.

"But you have the servants at home all the time."

"Agnes will help. She understands. She is the only one who understands."

The opportunity came three months into their relationship. "*Amma* and *Thaathi* are going to a medical conference in Kandy for two days next week, and Banda is driving them. *Malli* doesn't come home till 4:30. Come to my place next Thursday afternoon, about two o'clock. I will be home half-day. Agnes will let you in."

Martin concocted another errand at the office: delivering tickets to clients going to the Middle East this time. He parked and locked the

Triumph at the Kotte junction, then walked the half-mile to Rohini's house. The gate was unlocked and he took the side entrance as instructed. The garden was a symbol of man-made order now, with red and white roses populating well-groomed flower beds running by the side wall; even the old coconut tree, once surrounded by layers of cow dung from marauding cattle, looked fresh and was sprouting fruit in its upper reaches again.

The side door opened immediately upon his tap; the old woman stood there. She wore a sari, Kandyan style, with the frill running around her narrow hips; her faded eyes bored holes into Martin. "Come in. Don't stand there." She pulled him inside with a surprisingly wiry strength. "Wipe your feet, please." That was when Martin noticed the shiny red cement floor. He rubbed his shoes vigorously on the thick coir rug embedded in the floor and tip-toed after the old woman into the central hall.

Martin sucked in his breath and paused, taking everything in. The hall was decorated in cane: cane lounge chairs, cane paneled mirrors, a cane ornamental fan hanging from the ceiling. Contrast was provided by large batik cushions on the floor and brass ornaments in every nook and crevice: brass elephants, Kandyan dancers, karma wheels, incense burners, tea-kettles. The dominating fixture was the large two tiered brass oil lamp, used for the opening of traditional Sri Lankan ceremonies, and which was placed in the centre of the room, reposing on a straw mat of many colours. Everything seemed to be in its assigned place and the room sent out a silent command that nothing must be done to upset that order. Martin felt like an intruder.

"Come on up," Rohini was at the balcony at the back of the main hall, summoning him urgently.

"Just a minute, *mahattaya*," Agnes restrained him. She walked over to a side table and from a drawer pulled out a brass knickknack box. She withdrew a plastic pouch and held it out to him. "Use these. I don't want anything bad happening to my little *baby nona*."

Martin felt the condoms squelch in his hand, and the old woman's stare bore into his back as he ascended the staircase to Rohini. At the top, he caught a quick glimpse of Agnes standing at the foot of the stair, hands folded, staring back at him sadly.

Rohini led him down the hallway and closed the heavy wooden door of her bedroom behind him; another large room, big enough to hold half of Martin's house in it. There was a double bed, a stereo player, a small piano, a desk strewn with a jumble of papers, and shelves against one wall filled with rows of hardbound books.

Martin shivered and sat on the edge of the bed.

"What's the matter?" Rohini asked. She was dressed in a tee-shirt and shorts and Martin noticed that she wasn't wearing a bra. This was a new Rohini he had never seen before.

"This is all a bit too much," he stammered.

"Agnes will not tell anyone. She loves me more than life."

"Did she do this with Anil Munasinghe too?" Suddenly he wanted to hurt her. Hurt her for her wealth, inaccessibility, experience— all the things that diminished him.

Her face flushed dark and her voice hardened. "What's all this interrogating? You wanted to come and fuck me. Well, have you got the balls, or haven't you?"

That triggered him. He leaped out of the bed and grabbed her, and she let herself fall into his hands, a wicked lazy grin on her face, daring him. He took hold of her tee-shirt and ripped it, staring momentarily at her ripe breasts with their large dark aureoles; then he was sucking them, moving from one breast to the other while she screamed in delight and pain. Before long they were rolling on the bed, engulfed in passion. Her clothes were shed with every twist and tumble and finally she was naked. He ran out of breath and she used the moment to undo his pants, grab a condom from the pouch and spread it over his throbbing cock. There was a tap on the door and Martin flinched and felt his erection wilt.

"*Baby nona*, are you all right?" Agnes enquired, from the other side of the closed bedroom door.

"Yes, I am all right. Go away." Rohini screamed, focusing on mounting a sprawled Martin.

"I will be outside, *baby nona*—just in case you need me."

The next few minutes passed in a daze. Rohini grabbed his shrinking penis and squeezed it at its base bringing him to life again; then she was astride him and he felt himself slide into her wetness. *So this is it.* She bucked and thrashed on him, her fingers biting into his neck, her long hair brushing his face, smothering him as she moaned and tightened her loins with every thrust, drawing him out. She screamed with each downward movement and he felt his mind standing outside his body surveying this mystical union that men and women had performed over the ages—it seemed so natural and he, contrary to self-imposed doubts, was so able in its execution, despite Agnes hanging outside the door, despite this forbidding house, despite this vixen on top of him dominating him at every turn of the act.

She came first and Martin was surprised again to discover that he was still erect. As her body relaxed, he swung over and mounted her, thrusting with abandon, enjoying his domination, drinking in her body, her scent, her pleasure until he too burst and fell exhausted over her sweaty body.

They made love again but it wasn't as powerful as that first encounter. Satiated at last, they lay side by side, bodies drenched in the afternoon humidity pouring in from the open window, undispelled by the lazy fan turning above their heads.

"You like it rough," he said.

"Anil was rough. That's the only way I know it. Didn't you like it?"

He didn't reply at first. Yes, he had liked it. Yet somehow it was not as he had wanted it. The physical had taken over and made him into something he could not recognize: carnal, an animal.

"Yes, I liked it." He lied, reaching for his pants.

He heard a muffled cough outside and turned to Rohini in irritation. "Why does she go along with this?"

Rohini put her finger to her lips and gestured for him to come over. She whispered in his ear.

"Agnes is scared that I'll take the pills again. I was so depressed when Anil and I broke up, I overdosed on sleeping pills."

A chill settled around his heart. There was a lot he still did not know about her.

"Suicide is not an option in my book," he said.

"You don't live in this prison," she replied, and rolled over on her side, facing the wall.

"We must do this again," he said, trying to appease her, willing her to turn around and say that she was not pissed off with him.

"Yes, we will. You'd better go now. Agnes will show you out. Manoj will be home soon." Her back remained turned to him.

When he stepped out into the corridor, the old woman was sitting on a stool at the top of the staircase. She stood up wearily and led him downstairs. As she let him out of the side door he thought he heard her muttering, "Children, children…"

"You bloody bugger, what the hell are you doing, fighting?" Victor glowed at his middle son Paul, who was standing defiantly at the dining table when Martin arrived home that evening.

"They called me a *Lansi Karapottha.*" Paul said. His voice was high-pitched, as if he had spent several nights without sleep. "I took enough of it at St. Bernard's. I am not taking it anymore."

"And so you go and get suspended by hitting a smaller kid because he called you a cockroach?"

"Big or small—it doesn't matter—I'll hit anyone who insults me."

Martin was surprised at this tit-for-tat conversation, that Victor would even allow it; his father normally dominated every domestic conversation.

Victor pushed back his plate and stood up, glowering at Paul across the table. "If you get into any more fights, I'll whip your bloody neck. Got that?"

Paul flushed red and was about to come back with a retort when Martin intervened. "Paul, you heard Dad. Cut it out."

Paul swung around. A look of betrayal spread across his face. "You…you're all the same. You don't understand."

Barney, who had been silently noodling with his food at the other end of the table, spoke up suddenly. "The boys in the *Viyalaya* are worse than the ones at St. Bernard's." Then having made his contribution and looking surprised at himself for uttering anything, he rose and fled to his room.

"Dad, you have to give them some slack," Martin said. "They're in a new school, after all."

"New school be damned! Fighting only points the finger at you. All we minorities get is the finger pointed at us."

"You're all cowards," Paul yelled back. "If you had the guts you would have got out of this country a long time ago—like Mum wanted you to."

Victor lurched out of his chair and made to catch Paul, but the lad swerved expertly out of reach and darted for the door. Martin stepped in the middle and restrained his father. "Okay, Dad, he is just blowing off steam, let him go." Martin also realized how much smaller Victor was, now that they had all grown up. His father reached only to his chin, despite being broader and heavier. The alcohol on Victor's breath was strong. "We'll settle with him later, Dad."

In his thwarted rage, Victor yelled after Paul, "Ungrateful swine!"

And Paul yelled back, "Servant fucker!" before slamming the door behind him.

Victor's face blanched and he looked shaken. He fell back in the chair. Latha arrived at that point and started clearing the table.

"Fetch me the arrack bottle," Victor grunted at her in Sinhala.

She ignored him and continued her work.

"Maybe, you've had enough for today, Dad?" Martin said.

"I'll tell you when I have had enough."

Martin rose from the table. "I'll bring you the bottle then. We'll have one—together. Then that's it for the night. Okay? Besides, I'm hungry."

Martin went into the kitchen. He filled his plate with rice, vegetable curry and fried dry fish. Beef, chicken and fish had been cut out now due to the impoverished family fortunes; even the 250 rupees he slipped into an envelope under his father's door each month—a contribution to the family budget—did not seem enough. When Martin set eyes on the half-finished bottle of arrack, he grimaced; there was always money for his father's hooch, but none for wholesome food. Martin poured two glasses and topped them up with soda. He hated arrack, except for the temporary buzz it gave him, but it was the only affordable drink today. He did not drink alcohol except at parties, but felt he needed some "Dutch courage" for the conversation he was about to have with his father.

When he returned from the kitchen, Victor was talking to Latha in hushed tones; his father looked like he was trying to re-assert his authority over her. Her prior ignoring of his instructions must have stung

Victor sorely, especially in the presence of his son. They paused on Martin's entry and Latha picked up the pile of half-empty dishes and left abruptly.

Victor downed half his new drink in a gulp, wrinkled his mouth at the aftertaste and swirled the rest of the contents in the glass while Martin dived into his food.

"This family is going to the bloody dogs." Victor said after awhile.

Martin sipped his arrack. *Too much soda.* The soda was flat, despite being from a new bottle. *Who gave a shit for quality control these days?*

"How's the bookie business?" Martin asked between mouthfuls, ignoring his father's comment about dogs and families.

"It's good. My old boss felt sorry for me and introduced me to an MP in his circle. The guy places big bets."

"I'm sorry about Paul, being so insolent. I hope you can earn enough to put them back at St. Bernard's. They'll like that."

"I'll skin that little s.o.b. when he comes home. That's what I'll do."

"He'll probably sleep over at a friend's place tonight. You know he's done it before."

"Whenever he comes home then."

"I thought you said violence points the finger?"

"Now, don't you go getting high-and-mighty. I always thought you had the most sense in this house."

"Dad—let it go. Paul's twelve years old. He's got a lot of anger in him. He doesn't say it, but he hates going to that *Vidyalaya*, among other things."

"You think I did that deliberately? I had no choice."

"You also refuse help when it's offered."

Victor downed the remainder of his drink and stared greedily at his glass. He looked embarrassed about going into the kitchen to get a refill in Martin's presence.

Martin scooped the last dregs of rice and curry with his fingers into his mouth. Then he pushed his nearly full glass over to his father. "Here. You can finish mine. It tastes like piss to me."

When he came out of the kitchen after depositing his plate in the sink for Latha, he saw his father staring at the untouched glass, summoning the will to refrain from drinking, like his son had done.

Martin knew that Paul would be hanging around the jak tree at the end of the garden that night as he usually did when he was banished from the house for his misdemeanours which had been frequent of late. There was no moon and his younger brother looked lost and diminished in the dark, his normally agitated voice sounding weak and tired. He didn't even smack at the mosquitoes that were out in full force.

"You really pulled one today," Martin said.

"He thinks he can push me. They all think they can push me."

"You'll go back to St. Bernard's as soon Dad can afford it. You don't want to piss him off before that happens."

"He's a disgrace as a father."

"Oh, shut up. Don't speak like that."

"Just because you work and are out of the house most of the time, you can talk. You don't know what goes on at home."

"What?"

"Why don't you listen to the noises in the night? The footsteps. The dragging sheets. Barney is terrified."

The hairs on Martin's hands stood upright. Those sounds in the night. Paul and Barney shared the room next to his father's, while Martin's was on the other side of the house, adjoining the room his mother had barricaded herself in. Martin pretended to show no concern. "You'd better apologize to Dad if you want to come home tonight."

"I'm not coming home tonight."

"Where are you going to stay? The church again? Or with one of your pals?"

"I'll find a place. Don't worry, I don't have to go to school tomorrow anyway."

"But you can't do this forever, Paul. You have to come home. And you have to get back to school."

The shadow moved from the behind the jak tree. It vaulted the fence and started to diminish. "Check out the noises in the night. Then maybe you'll understand." Then Paul was gone.

Martin smacked as a mosquito settled on his arm, and felt the blood between his fingers.

That night Martin took action. He waited until all sounds of preparations for sleep subsided in the house. Then he slunk out into the pantry; the clues had to be here. As he had suspected, Latha's mat was empty. She'd made the pantry her bedroom at night, having claimed one of the cupboards for her clothes and other worldly possessions. He hid under the dining table, pulled the chairs around him and waited. He could see the mat a few feet away in clear view. About twenty minutes later, someone slithered into the pantry from the front of the house. The same swish of sheets, the same tiptoe tread.

Latha dropped back onto the mat and turned on the kerosene lamp by her bedding. She buttoned her blouse around her naked bulbous breasts, muttering under her breath. Lying back, she tossed and turned for awhile. Then she pulled back her *vatiya* up around her waist and began rubbing herself between her legs. His own cock hardened, for just earlier in the day he had been doing the same to Rohini. Very soon, Latha was bucking and panting. Finally she gasped and rolled over.

Martin waited a long time, cramped under a chair, until he heard her snoring, then he slunk back to his room. Her last words, before she snuffed out the lamp, still rang in his ears, "Bastard, he can't even finish the job now. All that booze."

Lying on Rohini's bed the following day—this would be the last opportunity for a while as her parents were returning later that evening— Martin gazed out of the window at the palm trees swaying gently in the mid-afternoon heat. The sex had been pre-occupied today, that was how to describe it: slow and hesitant at first, then vigorous, urgent and fast as they got aroused; the quick rush, then a pulling away into their separate sides of the bed. They lay absorbed in their own thoughts now.

He couldn't blame his father, could he? The draw of the loins, the physical need for a woman; he had experienced this over the last couple of days. Wasn't he, Martin James at the age of nineteen, also doing something he shouldn't, beckoned by the weakness of his flesh?

He had not wanted to visit Rohini today, but some force within him had compelled him to find an excuse at work and arrive at the appointed time; motor bike parked at the junction, through the side entrance of the Senanayake *walauwa*, up the stairs followed by the aged retainer, to engage in his carnal desires. How could a kid like Paul understand all this? Not yet. All Paul understood was betrayal.

Rohini stirred at his side. She cradled her face in her hands, elbows on the bed. "You don't approve of this do you? I'm a slut in your eyes."

"No, that's not what I was thinking about."

"But that's what you *feel*—right?"

He was getting tired of her constant seeking for validation. "What's with you? You want to know my problem? I'll tell you: I'm sleeping with a girl who is way more experienced and high-class than me, who may get suicidal if we break up, whose parents would go crazy if they found out. On top of that, I have a mother who is out of her mind, a brother out of school, I've got debts to pay and my father has become a bookie and is sleeping with our servant. Do you want more?"

She looked alarmed at his outburst. Then she burst out laughing. "Oh Martin, you are such a dramatist."

"All you can do is laugh." His feelings about her were crystallizing. *I am only a plaything to her, that's it—an amusement.*

Then she became serious. "I didn't mean to hurt your feelings. Yes, *Thaathi* and *Ammi* would create a big stink, but I don't care."

"That's because you're their spoilt and cherished child whom they would go to the ends of the earth to protect. I wish I had parents like yours."

"That's not fair!"

Now he wanted to hurt her. All his problems in the world seemed to have their apex in her, just like Victor saw his in Paul. "Go on," he threw back. "It's true, isn't it? After they break us up, they'll move house to another place and start up again, to preserve Dear Daughter's reputation. And old Agnes will have more secrets to hide."

"Martin, stop! You're hurting me!"

Their voices were so raised that they did not hear the commotion outside the bedroom door, which was suddenly thrust open. Framed in it, were a gulping Manoj and a harried Agnes shouting, "Aney *baby nona,* I tried to keep him from coming in."

Things moved in slow-motion for Martin after that.

Rohini grabbed the bed sheet to cover her naked body and screamed, "*Malli,* no!"

The boy opened his mouth; no words came out at first; then he started to form them and his face twisted in a mixture of hate and disgust. "Bitch—you are destroying us. Again!"

Manoj flung his school bag at Rohini, who ducked on her way towards him; the bag bounced against the wall behind Martin. This nudged him into action. He was on his feet struggling into his pants, grabbing his shirt from the floor. Agnes wailed, "*Aney nona,* be careful. They sent him home from school. He did not take his medications today."

Rohini encircled Manoj who thumped her with his fists and they went down in a heap on the floor, the boy spitting and kicking at his sister viciously.

Martin had his clothes on by then and he went over and pulled Manoj away. The boy was weaker than Paul, and Martin, having broken up plenty of fights between his younger siblings, had no problem with Manoj. Martin held the boy at arm's length as Manoj punched the empty air around him. "Settle down, Manoj. We can explain this," he pleaded, hoping this hysterical piece of flesh would start to calm down. Suddenly Manoj went limp in his arms, and collapsed.

"*Aney mage baba!*" Agnes screamed and rushed towards Manoj, who was sinking to the floor as Martin gently let him go. Rohini crawled across to her brother; she had blood on her face from scrape marks.

"What the hell's wrong with this kid?" Martin said.

"He is manic depressive. Random things set him off."

Manoj may have been down but he wasn't out; in fact, he must have been faking it, seeing how he took everyone by surprise with his next move. Just as Agnes bent down, he snarled awake and spat in her face. His features resembled those of a caged animal. "Fuck you all! Wait till everyone hears about this!"

Then he was up and backing out towards the door. He kicked at Rohini, but she was out of reach. Martin dived at him but Manoj ducked deftly and escaped downstairs. Martin gave chase with Rohini behind him, still wrapped in the bed sheets. From the corner of his eyes Martin saw Agnes running towards the telephone.

Manoj moved with a nervous agility that Martin could not keep up with. At the foot of the stairs when he thought he almost had him, the boy pulled a large brass pot into Martin's path. Martin just managed to dodge the obstacle to see the giant ceremonial oil lamp wrenched off its perch and heading his way, sending it crashing into him; Rohini, bringing up the rear, fell on top of Martin as Manoj made it to the front door.

"The son of a bitch!" Martin hissed.

"We have to stop him, Martin," Rohini's voice was panic-stricken. "He's dangerous when he's like this."

Martin held back Rohini just before they exited the house. "You can't go out like this. Look at you, you have no clothes on."

Rohini's eyes widened in realization. "You go after him then."

When Martin stumbled out of the front door, an astonishing sight met his eyes. There, in the centre of the lane, Manoj and Paul (where the hell had *he* come from?) were circling each other.

"Your brother is a fucker," Manoj yelled at Paul. "He's fucking my sister. Do you know that? He's a third-class fucker."

"Shut your mouth, you bastard. Don't you talk about any of my family like that," Paul threw back.

Martin's first inclination was to break them up. Then he paused, a thought crossing his mind. Why was Paul here? Had he come back home to make up with Victor? If so, it would be better if Paul got out whatever residual anger was still in him. Making mincemeat of this crazed Manoj was just the answer. Besides, Manoj needed a good hiding, his parents obviously having spared the rod all these years.

Manoj rushed; Paul feinted and stuck his leg out sending his attacker stumbling in the dust. Then Paul jumped on Manoj's back and grabbed him in a half Nelson. "Say you're sorry you bastard, before I break your bloody neck."

Manoj screamed. Rohini stumbled out behind Martin and rushed to her brother's rescue, her hair loose, a shirt hastily tucked into a pair of jeans that had its fly undone. Martin held her back again. "Let them settle it."

Two things happened then: a dusty Mercedes chugged into Araliya Lane on one side; and a solitary figure got off the bus from the main road and walked up its other side: Victor.

The car screeched to a halt and Mrs. Senanayake came stumbling out, mouth open, swallowing her dismay, trying to look authoritative. Her husband got out from the other door, surveying the scene objectively. Victor, looking like he'd had more than his usual quota for the day, staggered up too, unbuckling his belt with one hand and holding up his trousers with the other.

Mrs. Senanayake and Victor reached the two grappling boys simultaneously and almost collided with each other.

"You son-of-a-bitch. I told you 'no fighting,'" Victor yelled and down slashed the belt, missing a ducking Paul and whacking Mrs. Senanayake squarely on her ample backside. The woman yelped, more in shame than pain, and went pale, as Victor tried to correct his shot.

Martin sailed into the melee, separating the various players before more damage could be done. Mrs. Senanayake grabbed her son, who started sobbing like an overgrown baby, "*Ammi, ammi.*"

She held Manoj at arm's length and yelled in his face. "Did you take your medications?" Before the boy could reply, she turned around and glared at Victor, to remind him that she had not forgotten, nor would forgive his accidental swipe at her behind.

"No *ammi*, I forgot." Manoj was like a snivelling cur in front of his mother.

"Get in the house—now! And take your medication immediately!" She assumed her signature pose: hands on hips, watching her son grovel away across the lane and through the gates of the Walauwe.

"I told you no fighting," Victor was yelling at his younger son in the meantime, blissfully oblivious of his stray belt swipe on his neighbour's rump and of her dagger-like looks.

"Dad, calm down," Martin intervened. "Paul wasn't fighting. Manoj had some kind of a fit."

But Victor was beyond listening. He snarled at Paul, who had risen and was dusting himself. "Call me a servant fucker, huh?"

Paul looked up, defiantly. "I came back to apologize."

"I don't want your damned apologies. You're not fit to be my son. Disgracing me in front of these people."

"Dad—" Martin grabbed Victor roughly by the shoulder and pulled him away. "Dad, stop it now!"

Victor brushed him off, staggering to get his bearings, still focusing on Paul. "Wait till I finish with you, you little bastard. You'll be sorry you came back."

Paul's face was a study of disappointment, tears lurking on the edges, lips quivering. He turned towards Martin. "If not for you, I would never have come home. I'm leaving. This time I'm never coming back."

"Paul... settle down." Martin tried to lower his voice. Behind him, Mr. Senanayake had entered the fray, ordering his daughter in a calm voice to "go indoors and stay there. And zip up that fly so you don't exhibit yourself to the whole world."

And Paul was running away now: down Araliya Lane towards the main road, faster and faster, his sobs the only impediment to flight. Martin gave chase. "Paul, come back. I saw what you did. You defended me. I'll explain to Dad. Please stop."

Witnesses later said that the child had jumped in the path of the fully-loaded bus that careened round the bend; the driver, already fifteen minutes behind schedule, was trying to avoid stopping at Araliya Lane.

No one will know what went through Paul's mind at the time. All Martin heard was the screech, the thump of body hitting metal and the crash of bone. A splash of blood squished out as the bus ran over Paul's body, like when the fattened mosquitoes were squashed during the monsoon season.

1974 was indeed a bad year, and it wasn't finished yet.

Carmen was strangely reserved while Paul's body lay in a closed coffin in the house before the funeral. She placed candles on the mantelpiece and a full glass of water by the casket. "The poor child is going to be thirsty." She filled the glass, whenever the water evaporated beyond a certain level. "See, he drinks!"

Victor tore his hair out in drunken grief all through those two days, constantly threatening to open the coffin to catch a final glimpse of his mutilated son. "My son, my bloody son! God help him!" His shrieks resembled the hoarse gratings of a tortured soul. Barney spent a lot of time going to the toilet, and all the while, Martin sat smouldering. Many people came for the funeral: all the neighbours, the few relations who had not already emigrated to Canada or Australia, even some of the neighbourhood bullies who had plagued Paul, but respected his resistance when he was alive. Prepared food arrived magically from various neighbours. Aunty Mala did yeoman's service, filling in for Carmen in the role of chief mourner and hostess, flitting everywhere, talking to everyone, as if it were her son's wake they were attending. For once, Martin was grateful for her intervention.

Mr. Senanayake also came and paid a short, respectful visit, not saying much, just nodding and smiling reverently among the gathered mourners. None of his family was present. Before he left, Mr. Senanayake came up to Victor and offered him his card. "Mr. James, I know this is a hard time for you and your family. If there is anything I can do for you, please let me know."

Victor paused from his chest-beating and scratched his head after the skin specialist left. "That's the first time a Sinhalese was genuinely nice to me."

There was a moment during the wake when Carmen sat with Victor, stroking his head, while he allowed it, like a drowning animal would a lifeline. They did not speak. Speech seemed superfluous.

After the funeral, Carmen withdrew to her room once more. Her silences grew longer and she no longer sang. Victor would disappear for a couple of days at a time, but whenever he came home at night, drunk, Martin heard the animal-like howling of grief emanate from his father's room. Victor began to visit Carmen's room whenever he was home and sober. Once Martin walked in on them; Victor was sitting talking to his wife about the old days, while she had lapsed into one of her blank moments and was staring into space. Her temporary "absence" did not seem to deter Victor; he was animated, as if addressing a very interested and engaged audience. Whenever Victor went into Carmen's room, he left a pile of ten-rupee notes behind. As for Latha, she stayed in the pantry and paid no more night visits to the master.

Martin moved into Paul and Barney's room and slept in Paul's bed. He did this to keep young Barney's company during this period of adjustment, and also to connect with his dead brother if that were at all possible. He tried to imagine what Paul must have been thinking on that last day, in those final moments. Was it Paul's courage that had held the mirror to Victor and enraged his father so much? After a while, it dawned on Martin that he had not really known his brother at all. Brothers were to be tolerated when alive, but they left deep holes when they were dead.

He read Barney stories at night until the boy fell asleep, the same stories of Odysseus that his mother had read him in times of crisis. Having lost two siblings, Martin suddenly felt very protective of Barney, knowing he would never have any more.

One night, Barney gushed out. "Do you think Paul's watching us?"

"He probably is. And he wants you to grow bigger and stronger than him. You've got the chance now, I guess."

"No, I don't think he'd like that. I'll always be his little brother. That way he'll protect me from the bullies. Like you do."

Just before he fell asleep, Barney mumbled, "Martin, thanks for taking me to school in the mornings."

"No problem, buddy."

Barney started chuckling uncontrollably. "You know the bullies in school lay off me now, when they see you get off your bike and look around the school yard and then help me off the pillion. They're scared of you and your bike." Barney's chuckling was turning hysterical.

Martin went over and ruffled his brother's hair. "Settle down, little guy. Go to sleep. No one will bully you in future." Soon the boy calmed down. After a few minutes, Barney was sleeping soundly.

Martin looked back at Paul's bed. He wanted to cry too, to get hysterical, to miss Paul overtly. This was a time when he wanted to believe in God, not just in the way they had parroted those hymns and prayers at St. Bernard's, but in a kind and loving God. But God was strangely missing in his life, and His gatekeepers, like Brother Joachim, had only been perverse creations. There was only hollowness, as if he had accepted losing as his lot in life, as if the countervailing reward—if it was out there—would never be visible to him in this incarnation.

The nights that Victor did not come home, Martin visited his mother in her room. There were moments when she was lucid, and others when she just was on another planet. The transitions came faster now than ever before.

One day, she surprised him with her insight and the duration it lasted.

"Do you love that girl?"

"I'm not sure. I'm not sure I know what love is. Besides, it's not meant to be. There are too many barriers."

"Don't you think your father and I have barriers?"

"I suppose so."

"But he will never leave me. Despite all I have done to blast his chances of going to Canada, deny him a baby girl and all."

"Mum, it's not your fault. Any of us could have problems."

"He sleeps with the servant. But he will never leave me."

Martin exhaled deeply. He did not know what to say to that.

Carmen continued, undeterred, "Your father loves me. When you feel that way for that girl, then you'll know what love is."

Then she seemed to lose it again. "*Why has my child left me? Why did he go? Must he, too, be forgotten?*" Martin realized that she was repeating a line from the Odyssey. Her voice turned conspiratorial "I see him walking with me at night."

"Who?"

"Paul."

"Paul! You see his ghost?"

"He was not long for this world. That's why God placed him in the middle, so we would not pay too much attention. He served a purpose."

"He sure did. Taught Dad a lesson."

"Taught us all. Taught you, mainly."

"Me?"

"Yes, he reminded you of your promise to me. To leave this place. Continue your journey. Or you will leave like him."

Rohini wrote him a letter about a month after Paul's death. It arrived in regular, post office mail:

Dear Martin,

I am so sorry for what happened. More importantly, for what happened to us as a result of that awful day. My parents have decided to arrange a marriage for me. They say that I am safer married. I suppose they are right. My husband-to-be is a doctor in London. A good Buddhist Sinhalese from a high caste, and our horoscopes match. He is however, quite old—39, but Ammi says that I will not have to worry about anything financially. Martin, I am sorry to have to break this to you at this time, but I think we both knew that there was no future for us together. Please wish me luck. I do have a lot of fear about where I am heading to but I have no choice. Love! Ro.

P.S. I will write you and give my address when I am in England.

It was the end of the third month of mourning, and the cool winds that followed the monsoon were signalling that Christmas would soon arrive. Victor came home one Saturday evening, cold sober and greatly agitated. He retired to his room and Martin heard static as the shortwave radio in his father's room switched on. Victor had tuned into the BBC's Saturday Special program that ran commentaries on the horse races in England. Martin shook his head—his father was gambling again—not only was he a bookie, he was placing his own bets now; a complete wash of earnings, no doubt, and the home finances would deteriorate once again.

As the evening progressed, Martin hovered outside his father's closed door. Instead of the cries of agony he had been hearing these last three months, today there came muffled shouts of joy every time a race result was announced. Martin was perplexed, his father normally had the shittiest luck, losing more than he won; today seemed an anomaly. Finally, around eleven o'clock, when the final results were in, Martin couldn't hold back any longer; he knocked on his father's door and entered, without waiting for permission.

Victor was in an agitated state, calculating something on a piece of paper. Martin noticed how bedraggled his father had become in recent months: the shirt crumpled and stained under the arms, the trousers long having lost their sharp creases, the dull shoes and lack of socks. For a moment he resembled Edward Jansz, the man Carmen had said "was only two strokes away from us," those many years ago.

Suddenly, with a loud "Fuck!" his father jumped up jubilantly. "We've done it boy—we're clear!"

"So you're betting again now." Martin said, unenthused by his father's ebullience.

"On the contrary, no!"

"Then why are you so happy?"

"MP Somaratne won a hundred thousand rupees on yesterday's horses and placed a twenty five thousand rupee bet today."

"So? You made a commission of ten percent. That'll help for a couple of months' expenses if you don't blow it on gambling or drinking."

"That's not it boy. You don't get it, do you?" His father was grinning and Martin saw glimpses of Victor's youthful freshness peep through, last seen when Martin was a little boy and his father had read him those cowboys-and-Indians stories.

"Okay, I'm listening."

"*I held back the bet.* There was no way he could get it right two nights in a row. All his horses ran out today."

"What!"

"Yes, I am holding onto twenty five thousand rupees that I can use to put some things right around here."

"My God!"

"Yes, my God indeed! I can pay for the rest of the funeral expenses. Put Barney back in St. Bernard's. And—"

But Martin was already grabbing his father in delight. "Oh, Dad, that's the best thing I've ever heard from you. Barney will think he's died and gone to heaven." He held onto his father tightly and Victor returned the embrace. For a moment they hung there together, two men, unembarrassed.

"Yes. And now that I have only one to educate, I think I can afford to pay St. Bernard's fees." Then Victor started shaking and sobbing. "Oh, Pauli boy ..." And Martin held onto him, for a longer time, until his father calmed down again.

Finally, Victor broke loose and walked over to the cupboard. "There is one other thing." He took deep breaths and blew his nose into a dirty handkerchief.

"Yes?"

"I will have just enough to pay for a proper attendant for your mother. An older woman: someone to wash her and look after her basic needs. I can't do this all by myself anymore."

Martin nodded. This was the inevitability he had been dreading. They had to talk about what they were going to do for Mum, sooner rather than later.

Victor continued. "Your mother and I have talked about it. It is her wish that one day she enter the mental home in Angoda. She does not want to be a burden on us anymore. And I want her to stay with us as long as we can have her."

"Thanks, Dad."

Victor hesitated for a moment then seemed to will himself to make the next statement. "And I am giving Latha notice. The bottle, I will keep. It's my one solace."

Martin paused in the doorway, one thing still bothering him. "What would have happened if the MP had won his bet?"

Victor looked up slowly then looked away quickly. "When you hit the bottom, you don't think of consequences. I didn't think. I acted. And God heard me. Perhaps my little Pauli heard me too."

"But now you wouldn't do it again, would you? When the next big bet comes around?" *It will be like living on the edge of the volcano from now on. Perhaps God had indeed answered him, or Victor, but in a most ironic way.*

Victor looked directly at his son and this time he did not look away. The doubt was all over his face; but there was pride and a semblance of wisdom too. "Martin, I don't know. Just be grateful for today. We have not had a lot of good days in this family. Tomorrow—tomorrow can go fuck itself!"

Then Victor opened the cupboard, pulled out a bottle of arrack and poured himself his first tot of the day.

8. **Welcome to Canada – the Express Way**

The three men had staked out prominent corners of the former YMCA building in the Fort in Colombo, now used for many mercantile pursuits, not all of them legal. The man nearest to Martin, one-eyed, was the UK consultant; the grey-haired skinny guy, with his namesake *pottu* and powder daubed on his forehead, specialized in Canada, while the bald fat one in the nylon shirt covered Australia. If one did not know the inside story on them they could have been mistaken for bookies talking to their punters, or for fortune-tellers reading horoscopes.

The UK agent had two Tamil students at his table. The Australia connection had a few families gathered around, and in their midst, Martin was surprised to see a sprinkling of Burghers still around, fair skins amidst the brown. The Canadian section had chairs lined up in two rows, occupied mainly by Tamils. The customers' faces were weary, but hope hovered on their edges. This was 1984. Last year, many had lost their homes in the ethnic conflagration that had swept the city. Now that there was a full-scale war in the north, he couldn't blame any of them for seeking another home.

Martin too was seeking another country; that's why he had come today. His job was a dead end. He had managed to claw his way up from clerk to booking agent at the travel agency, but all the senior positions were reserved for the proprietor's family. The proprietor had thrown Martin a few crumbs over the years, such as a shopping trip to Singapore and another to Dubai. Last year, Martin's cousin, Jenny, had gone to the Middle East to work as a receptionist. Hers was the only fairy tale: she had met an Australian engineer, was getting married next month, and was heading off to Australia to settle down.

Carmen was finally in a mental home, oblivious to everyone, shut away in her dark world, forever. Victor continued to drink—to "drown his sorrows" as he put it—and played the horses, both as a bookie and a punter. Barney had entered the seminary. The rest were dead.

The James family's official attempts at emigrating had all failed, for one reason or another. Martin had even tried getting a student visa once, but that had required a lot of money for tuition abroad; money he could not come up with on his modest salary. However, the travel industry had opened his eyes to the various scams in operation: transporting women, who came up with the money for the initiation fee, as "housemaids" to the Middle East (initiation fees were even deducted from future earnings if the women had no money but looked attractive and could live on their wits in the male-dominated petrodollar societies); merchant seamen traveling to various ports in the world from which they would simply vanish; students who went abroad and got resident status. All this needed money.

His scruples had prevented him from succumbing to the temptations that colleagues and friends in the travel industry had long acquiesced to. Like taking *santhosams* for clearing waitlisted airline seats for groups of illegals to travel abroad; bribing the immigration and security personnel at the airport to look the other way; greasing the palms of hospital and morgue workers to provide chest X rays of otherwise healthy people who had died in accidents so that they could be used in the medical reports of would-be immigrants who were perhaps not as healthy. These same colleagues now drove the BMW's and Mercedes' that were flooding the market after Sri Lanka had gone capitalist in the late '70s, while Martin drove to work on a modest reconditioned motorcycle, purchased after his old Triumph had just refused to start anymore.

It was Christo who awakened Martin to his scruples trap. Martin met his old friend at the airport one day, after a lapse of nearly 12 years, as he was sending off a group of clients who had booked through the agency.

Christo was sitting in the waiting area with a solitary duffel bag by his side. The hooked nose and the twitch were still prominent, more so, as he had lost weight since his teenage days. His eyes were bloodshot and he looked tired and old for a man of 28.

Martin was thrilled to see him after all this time. Christo and his Uncle Bunty had moved out of the neighbourhood shortly after the Maha incident. All Martin had heard were second-hand reports from unreliable sources such as his gossipy neighbour Aunty Mala about an elopement and a marriage that had gone nowhere, of heavy drinking, a stillborn child, divorce—fragments of the life of his old friend trickling in through dubious channels.

"Christo, don't you recognize me?" Martin said walking up to him and pumping his limp hand vigorously.

Christo looked up, straining to recollect; then a faint glow at the back of those dead eyes; an old man in what was still a young body. Finally: "Martin—my God!"

"Going somewhere?"

He smiled. "Joining a ship in Halifax."

"You are in the merchant navy?"

"I've been on a few voyages." Christo studied Martin closely, as if trying to gauge his friend's trustworthiness after all these years. Then he leaned forward conspiratorially. "This time I'm not coming back."

Martin saw hope stirring somewhere deep within those lifeless eyes. "Legal?"

"Shit, no."

Martin didn't want to push for further information. It was none of his business. Yet it seemed like Christo wanted to talk.

"There is a place down at the Fort," Christo said. "The old YMCA building. All sorts of deals are hatched there, even arms deals."

"And they got you this gig? How much did you have to pay?"

"I did some 'transporting' for them on my past sailings. So I got this as a freebie."

Looking at those deadpan eyes, the rumpled Gucci shirt, and the Reebok sneakers of a model not in the local market, Martin momentarily longed for those days down at the *keera kottuwa*, before all those bad things had happened.

"Have you heard from Bandu?" Christo asked.

"Not a word."

"He is already in Canada. He also went through the YMCA channel."

"And he had the money?"

"He made a lot before he left, conning tourists."

Martin felt ashamed at his immobility while friends and family were leaving the island through any means at their disposal.

"Why don't you leave, Martin? This place is fucked up. Wait till the Marxists start up again, like in '71, and the whole country will go up in smoke. The government can't fight on two fronts."

That's when Martin finally said, "Give me the details of this place…"

Now, standing in front of his three options Martin recalled Christo's parting advice.

"The UK is the cheapest, everyone goes there as a student, but the fees on the other side are high. You can arrange payback to a local sponsor but that could take you several years. Canada is the easiest to get into, but the waiting list is long. Australia has its fits and burps, but could be easier if you have a Burgher relative living there. Don't pay any money until you see the papers and have received your instructions."

Martin decided to try the UK option first.

The one-eyed man slurped and studied him. The two earlier students had not bitten, it appeared; they were walking away muttering between themselves. Martin quickly told the man that he did not have the money for overseas tuition.

"How much money do you have?" the man asked.

"About ten thousand rupees."

"Shah! Not much you can do with that. For fifteen thousand I can get you in as a refugee."

"How? I am not a Tamil."

"Lome," One-eye said.

"Lome? As in Nigeria?"

"Yes, lots of oil workers needed there."

"I don't have the experience."

"We get you the papers and the medical clearance. That's what you pay for."

"And what would I do in Nigeria? Migrant workers have to return, eventually."

"Who said about returning?"

"I don't want to be a resident of Nigeria."

"Your plane goes via London. That's all I will tell you for now. Give me a deposit and we can go over the details. Five thousand now and the rest in two instalments."

Shocking images fuelled by recent newspaper reports of would-be refugees destroying their papers en route, and putting their hands up for refugee status at European airports, flashed before Martin. Lome was the decoy, London was the target.

"No thanks," he said, moving away towards the other two counters. The one-eyed man called after him. "You're making a mistake. Last offer—twelve thousand." Martin moved on, leaving one-eye looking hungrily for other customers.

The *pottu*'d guy ("Pottu" was the man's pseudonym, Martin later found out) at the Canada counter did not seem to have any difficulty attracting clients. Martin had heard of prices around 30,000 rupees to get into Canada, yet this guy was busy. Many of the Tamils had money, jewellery, even land to trade for the passage across. The dowry system endowed them for ventures of this kind, even though a lot of property had gone up in smoke in the ethnic rioting last year. Unfortunately, the James family did not subscribe to the dowry system, or any other that managed, multiplied and bequeathed family fortunes to subsequent generations through marriages that were also lucrative business arrangements. The Burghers, in their European tradition, were supposed to enter into "love marriages"—none of this arranged-marriage stuff. As Victor would say, "I wish we had a dowry system. How to live on love and fresh air alone?"

The Canada counter also drew Martin because this was the country his family had always wanted to emigrate to. He remembered the fourth and last time they were at the Canadian High Commission for their interview, attempting to immigrate the official way...

Victor had prepared with great effort, rehearsing answers in front of the mirror the previous day:

"I was recently promoted to sales executive...no, no scratch that. I have territorial responsibility for the whole southwest region of Sri Lanka...how am I doing, dear?" And Carmen nodded, beaming with encouragement. "Now, you make sure to be in your best mood tomorrow, dear. Take a tranquilizer if you have to, and get a good night's sleep," he reminded her when he wrapped up his practice performance.

The males in the family were all dressed in ties and pressed white shirts for their interview and Carmen wore her best taffeta skirt and pink blouse. Paul and Barney were threatened under pain of death by Victor to keep their mouths shut, their hands on their laps, and to speak only if spoken to; they were forbidden to look at each other lest they start another ruckus. They were all pretty nervous.

Victor had answered all the questions asked by the second secretary. "Yes, sir—you see, since our last attempt at immigrating, I have upgraded my skills. I am now responsible for hardware sales in the entire island and I have twenty sales reps under me." Martin couldn't understand how his father had been promoted from managing just the southwest region to being responsible for the entire island literally overnight, but decided this was not the time to ask for clarification.

The second secretary lowered his head impassively and pored over their thick file. The silence made the children fidget, and Victor started to lose the fake smile he had worn since entering the High Commission building. Carmen began to take deep breaths, as if she were trying to stop a hiccup.

Suddenly the second secretary looked up at her. "And Mrs. James, how do you think you will contribute to Canada?"

His sudden onslaught set her off. Carmen blanched, her face went blank and Martin groaned.

It was as if a veil had enveloped her over and transformed her into another person. She rose staring at a picture on the wall of a Canadian pastoral scene. "What a pretty picture," she said.

"Mrs. James…"

Then she started singing, softly at first, then louder, swaying on her heels, even doing a pirouette in the centre of the floor. Victor's face was ashen; Paul and Barney started giggling. Carmen waltzed over to the second secretary and gently stroked his face, saying in a soft voice, "You Canadians live in such a beautiful country." The second secretary went red in the face.

"Carmen!" Victor's voice was so menacing that something must have clicked in her, for she snapped out of her trancelike state, looked embarrassed, and slunk back to her chair with bowed head. She started sobbing uncontrollably.

"I'm sorry, sir," was all Victor could mumble.

"Well, Mr. James," the second secretary gently flipped the file shut." I think you all need to be in the best of health to immigrate. Canada will make a lot of demands on you, as well as provide you many rewards. I suggest you focus on your family's health first." He winked at them, trying to look jolly, but failing. "Come and see us when you are…are… feeling better – eh?"

That was twelve years ago. The family had not applied again.

The line took forever. The customers rose and advanced along the row of chairs every time the ones in front of Pottu left smiling or grumbling. Hushed conversations, most of them in Sinhala or Tamil worked their way down the line. He understood the Sinhala, and people close to him in the line translated the Tamil for him.

"The price has gone to forty thousand now."

"They're tightening the loopholes for refugees."

"If you get a lawyer, it is easier, but more expensive."

Martin was five chairs away from Pottu when two dark-skinned men in jeans and tee shirts rushed in, heading straight for the counter. They spoke to Pottu in whispers. Pottu listened to them, a look of annoyance crossing his face. Then he nodded abruptly and started shoving his papers into a briefcase. The two men helped him clear his table and chair. The UK and Australia guys also began closing shop.

"Tomorrow, tomorrow," Pottu said to his waiting customers who were looking on in mounting apprehension. "All of you go home now." He scurried off through the rear exit, followed by his cronies. The customers began rising and complaining to each other when someone yelled "Police!" The crowd immediately scattered. Martin made for the back door, but it was locked. Turning around he saw a police inspector enter the front door, followed by a pair of constables. The other customers were filing out quickly, some with heads bowed in respect or fear, others talking nonchalantly as if not to attract attention to themselves. The inspector made his way over. He had picked Martin out.

"You!" he shouted loudly in Sinhala, his thick moustache working itself around his upper lip. He was a short man with an air of disinterested authority. "What are you doing here?"

"I came to see a friend," Martin lied. Christo had prepared him well for contingencies.

"And where is he?"

"He has not shown up yet."

"Tell me another one." The sudden glint in the inspector's eye sent shivers through Martin. He had heard about and seen the results of police brutality: bodies of young students floating down rivers, the infamous fourth floor of the CID building where people just "fell out" of windows while undergoing interrogation.

Martin stammered but held to his story. "He has not shown up yet. That's all I can say."

The inspector looked him over from head to foot. "Burgher, huh?" That must have saved him; Burghers were non-political relics of the country's colonial past and a fast-disappearing ethnic group. All that Burghers did was to "Burgher-off" to western countries like Australia and Canada. Burghers did not make good terrorists or revolutionaries. The inspector's eyes resumed their disinterest and he yawned. "You can't stay here. This place is off limits. Clear out."

Martin bowed respectfully. "Okay, officer." He picked up his shoulder bag and made for the front entrance.

Outside, Pottu was in the police car with two constables on either side of him. The driver was smoking a cigarette. The other two "immigration reps" were nowhere to be seen. Pottu was in animated conversation with the policemen. Martin walked across the street to a tea stall, ordered a tea, sat down at the only available dirt-streaked, marble-topped table and watched the action. After about five minutes, the inspector came out, followed by the two constables who had accompanied him into the building. He looked about him then nodded to his men, who got on their bicycles and rode away. The inspector walked over and got into the front passenger seat of the police car, without even a glance at Pottu in the rear. The car drove away.

"Pottu will be back tomorrow," a voice from behind said.

Martin turned around, and there at the next table was one of Pottu's customers who had been sitting a few chairs ahead of him in the earlier line-up. A middle-aged man with his slicked greying hair parted in the middle, wearing a white cotton shirt and striped sarong. "I've had to come back three times already because of these raids," he explained.

"Are the cops in the game?" Martin asked.

"Who knows? But this is one way for them to check into Pottu's records and fix the right bribe."

"No wonder the price has gone up to forty thousand," Martin said, sipping his tea. He figured that was also why the inspector had let him off so easily.

"You have any relations in Canada?" Pottu was peering at Martin; the hair in his ears standing out. It was five days later, and Martin was finally first in line.

"I have an Aunt but I don't want to involve her. She sponsored us many times in the past but we failed every time." He went on to tell him about Victor's earlier lack of qualifications and of his mother's deteriorating health that had got in the way.

Pottu puckered his brow. "You people with European blood should have no problem normally. How much money do you have?"

"Not much," Martin replied hesitantly. "Ten thousand rupees." This was the crunch. Pottu had so many prospective prosperous customers, why would he take Martin on? Then the man's frown collapsed into a kindly smile. "You know, my first boss was a Burgher. A good man. Gave me a promotion in the Immigration Department."

"You were an Immigration Officer?"

Pottu leaned back in his chair and looked at the ceiling. "Those were good days. None of this shit."

"Then why are you doing this?"

"Must survive, no?"

"What happened?" Martin was curious, yet wary of probing too far.

"Government changed. All got fired. Mr. Van Langenberg, my boss, he went to Australia with his family. But us locals, we had no relatives abroad in those days. Now I am too old to go." Then Pottu shrugged and resumed his businesslike manner. "Now, let us see what we can do for you. Getting lawyers and pleading cases will not work for you. You have no money, no overseas relatives. You are like me, in those days. But I will help you."

"Thank you." Perhaps the man was not altogether a shark. Martin waited for his next suggestion.

Pottu scratched his nose, dug in his ear and cleared his throat, spitting into a corner of the room.

"You need to speak to Vedha. He works for me on special cases only. Give me your phone number. Vedha will call you in a few days."

Martin provided his office number, as there was no phone at home. "What's the plan? I need to know whether I can carry it out."

"You are going on a shopping trip to Bangkok. That is all you need to know. I need ten thousand rupees—payment from you *before* Vedha calls."

"How can I trust you?"

"You can't." Then he waved at the long line-up of people sitting behind. "You think these people will come to me if they don't trust me?"

"I'll think about it."

Pottu glared at Martin, his voice rising. "I don't waste time with people like you. Bring me the money tomorrow at this time or I don't want to see you again. Next!"

Martin walked over to the tea stall, fished out some loose change, bought a cup of tea, sat on the only bench outside and contemplated his future.

Ten grand was all he had: his hard-earned savings from working the last 10 years. To blow it all on a gamble with a shady operation was asinine. Yet, all the legal attempts his parents had made to emigrate had failed. Why not one of these? The whole country was corrupt. Ever since the Capitalists had come to power, corruption was reaching newer heights: ministers had huge real estate holdings in other countries, making them among the wealthiest even in those lands; aid was being siphoned off; development contracts had huge commissions attached to them. This was the word on the street, not in the newspapers which were government controlled; yet this was supposed to be a democracy. Now, the Marxists, badly defeated in 1971, were making a comeback in the south. Rumour had it that they were going to start another revolution while the government was pre-occupied with its battle in the north with the Tigers. So, why not this little deal? Despite Christo's warning, all he could do was blow his savings or start fresh and give himself the break his parents could never provide him. He knew that he wanted to do this.

The following day, he cashed in the fixed deposit, losing the interest of 20 percent in the process. In later years he discovered that the finance company too had made a killing on his savings: the inflation rate in the country was in excess of 50 percent at the time, although official statistics hovered around 15 percent. He took the money to Pottu.

Pottu smiled as he counted the cash, secured an elastic band around it and deposited it in his briefcase. Then he said, with an air of satisfaction, "This is only a fraction of the price—you know that, no? Your air ticket alone will cost this much."

Martin kicked himself. He should have seen this coming. Christo had been right.

"I can't pay you anymore."

"Not now. But when you are in Canada, we will expect payment in instalments over two years from your earnings there."

"What is the total?"

Pottu whispered the sum. When Martin blanched, thought of grabbing the briefcase with his money and making a wild dash for it, Pottu smiled. "Don't worry, it's not a lot in Canadian dollars. The exchange rate is about eighteen to one and the rupee is going down every day. You will be able to pay this without any problem. Many others have done so; otherwise we would not have so much business. Besides, everyone in Canada is paying off one loan or other, you'll fit right in."

As he was now committed, Martin tried to convince himself that this indeed would be the case; that the debt would be manageable. He asked Pottu what the next step was.

"Vedha will call you. When he does, read him this code." Pottu scribbled something on a sheet of paper: seven digits, a jumble of letters and figures that made no sense.

"Memorize it," he said.

"Right now?"

"Yes."

It took Martin a couple of attempts to get it right.

"Now go home and wait," Pottu said, tearing up the piece of paper.

The next day Vedha called at 4:30 p.m.

"Mr. James?" The voice was husky.

"Yes."

"How do I know you are Mr. James?"

"Who are you?"

"Read me the code."

Martin did, realizing who he was talking to.

The voice asked him to read it again.

Silence.

Just when Martin thought that the caller had hung up, the voice said, "Meet me at Vihara Maha Devi Park at six o'clock tonight, opposite the Town Hall building. Hold an *Observer* newspaper in your hand."

The line went dead.

Two weeks later, after three meetings with Vedha in the park, Martin had his verbal instructions. He was to leave for Bangkok the following Sunday. Travel documents would be delivered at the airport. The schedule was subject to change at any time. And it did change.

Martin received a call from Vedha on the Friday evening, two days before his departure, just as he was about to leave the office for the last time. Vedha informed him that there was a slight "delay." Now he would be flying out next Wednesday. The plan changed a couple more times after that and Martin began to wonder if this was all a hoax and should he go to the police. But what good would that do? He might end up in jail. He was in too deep to turn back now.

He went to work as usual, not telling anyone of his travel plans; those were Vedha's instructions. In the evenings he took long walks in the neighbourhood, trying to say goodbye in mind to the country and the events that had shaped his life in the suburb of Kotte. He climbed the old jam tree; it was easy now that he was a full-grown adult. He could look out across the rooftops to the paddy fields in decline, encroached on all sides by new housing. He was going to miss some of the old sights: the clotheslines with dripping wet clothing, especially the women's brassieres and panties, whose stain marks never came off, despite how hard they were hammered on the washing stone at the communal well; schoolgirls walking down the lane in their uniforms and long dark plaits; the bullock cart carrying sand for the construction workers in the shrinking paddy fields; the smell of drying fish in Bada's old market; the dampness and humidity after a sudden rainfall; his jungle that was the *keera kottuwa* coming alive in the evenings with the hum of insects. The

Senanayake *walauwe*, empty once again and up for sale—if those walls could only talk! From the books he'd read and the pictures he'd seen, Toronto seemed a sterile city by comparison; Toronto, from what he could make out, did not pull out the intimate details of nature and life and put them on public display like it was done in Sri Lanka.

He recalled the day Maha was killed, back in the '70s; an accident, the police hastened to say and closed the case. Christo, who had pulled the trigger, returned to school after that, and no one bothered him again. For awhile he walked about with an aura around him; after all, he was the guy who had taken down the neighbourhood crime kingpin. But Christo never recovered. He sank more and more into alcohol, like his guardian, Uncle Bunty. They later left the neighbourhood, like Martin's other friend Bandu and his whoring mother. In the end, none of Maha's gang came after Christo. How could they take revenge on a 14-year-old and save face? And what of Rohini Senanayake, now married with three children, living in her cozy house in Kent? She had written once but Martin had never replied. Let old ghosts be.

He decided not to visit his mother. He couldn't bear to hold a final image of her in those shabby regulation clothes, being escorted by stern and uncaring attendants, her hair uncombed, eyes staring without recognition. He took her wedding picture with him instead; Victor wouldn't miss it. Martin wanted to hold his mother to him as beautiful as the day she had married, and he dreamed about the happy life she had wanted but had never been granted.

The next time Vedha called, Martin instinctively knew the game was finally on.

"Be at the airport tomorrow at 7:00 a.m. Meet me in the parking lot by the public toilet. Bring only one small suitcase with clothes."

Click.

It broke his heart that night that he could not even say goodbye to the rest of his family: to his father, however drunk he was, or Barney up at the seminary in the hill country. Instead, Martin decided to leave them a note that he would mail on his way to the airport. He wanted them to understand why he was taking this step.

Dear Dad and Barney:

I have decided to go abroad. I can't give you any details as that would mess up my plans. Suffice to say that I am going to a better place. If things work out well, I will sponsor and bring you over in a few years. I promised this to Mum the day Maha was shot. It has been our family dream to go to a better place, a place where we would not live in fear or be forgotten. Let me at least take a chance of realizing this dream. I love you both, even though I haven't always shown it. Keep well, keep the faith, and pray for me. I will pray for you too. Say goodbye to Mum for me.

> *Yours,*
> *Martin*

The stench of the public toilet repelled him from a hundred yards away. Perhaps that's why Vedha chose the spot; people did not hang around here, and only visited if their bladders or stomachs were badly in need of release, and if they could prevent themselves from retching at the smell. Vedha was standing by a parked Hi-Ace minivan. Despite his husky voice, one wouldn't pay him much attention while passing him in the street: he was of slight build, wearing a white shirt with sweat stains under the arms, faded dark shiny slacks, and sneakers. He wore dark glasses at all times, even when Martin had met him in twilight at the park on previous occasions.

There were five other travellers with their identifiable "small suitcases." Martin was surprised to see that the man who had talked to him about Pottu in the tea shop, whose name he soon found out was Pillai, was also in the group. Pillai looked like he had lost weight and sleep. He was dressed in a white shirt and black slacks and sported a multi-coloured tie for the occasion. Two other travellers had even brought pillows, which Vedha quickly confiscated and threw into the van. Pillai's tie also got tossed into the vehicle. "Nondescript" was the dress code demanded of them that day.

Vedha addressed the travellers, sometimes stopping to translate from English to Sinhala to Tamil. "You are going to Bangkok. For shopping. That is what you will tell the customs and immigration people, or anyone else, if they ask you. Got it?"

Everyone nodded. The six strangers exchanged nervous looks, bonding in their tenseness.

"I am giving each of you a passport and a return ticket to Bangkok. When you get to Bangkok airport, you will not go to the

Arrivals, but walk to the duty-free section in the transit hall. Look for the signs. Go to the electronics store."

Vedha watched their faces for acknowledgement. When convinced that they had got it, he continued, "You will be met at the electronics store by a man called Navaratana. He will have a sign saying Lanka Tours—my company. Got it?"

The travellers were trying to remember all these details amidst their anxiety. They looked at each other for assistance; if one of them forgot, would the others help? Or would they forget everything and piece together the whole set of instructions incorrectly?

"Can we write this down?" One of the travellers asked.

"No! You will memorize everything I say. I will repeat it only one more time. No writing anything down. Got it?"

They nodded timidly.

"Navaratana will take your passports and the return portions of your air tickets and give you new instructions."

Pillai spoke up. He looked the most nervous of everyone. "Vedha sir, we are still going to Canada, no?"

"Yes, my friend, you are all going to Canada." Vedha smiled crookedly and started to hand out the travel documents.

Arriving in Bangkok, many in Martin's group, who were in an airplane for the first time in their lives, showed signs of several ailments: stomach pains, gas, diarrhoea or plain-and-simple nerves. In addition, Martin's sinuses were blocked and his ears hurt upon landing. They bunched together at the exit gate, trying to get their bearings.

"Those Thai air-hostesses were good, no, *machang?*"

Nervous laughter.

"But the food was terrible—no rice and curry. I have gone to the toilet three times already."

"You're bloody nervous, that's what."

"There's the Lanka Tours sign. Let's go," Martin said, getting everyone in motion again.

He managed to steer them through the throng of air travellers, mainly western tourists in shorts, tee-shirts and sandals, flesh burned raw in the sun. Interspersed between the tourists were Thai families and local business people in suits, looking harried in the close confines of the airport lounge. They passed rows of cosmetics, gifts and clothing shops on their way to the electronics store where the Lanka Tours sign waved vigorously in the hands of a short man. En-route to him the group got side-tracked by the latest in consumer durables, unseen before in Sri Lanka. Not all of them had the money to spare, being already indebted to their immigration consultants, but they were still captivated by the novelty. If this was only Bangkok, one could just imagine what Canada would be like!

Navaratana had a scar across his pock-marked face. A bristly beard grew in between the pocks, and a bandana draped his head as if he was in the sun. When they had gathered around him with sheepish grins, he barked above the din of the airport. "Okay, give me your papers." They meekly handed him their travel documents.

"Good." He then produced new air tickets and a red booklet for each.

He pointed at the booklets. "These are seaman's books. You are registered as Panamanian seamen joining a ship in Halifax. Your tickets are Bangkok-Amsterdam-Montreal-Halifax. When you get to Montreal, you land at Mirabel airport. You will be met and cleared as seamen and escorted to Dorval airport. In between those two points we will give you further instructions on how to get to your final destinations. Okay?"

Navaratana seemed to have memorized these lines well; his English was well articulated. When one of the group asked him, "What do we do in Amsterdam?" he looked frazzled and struggled with the explanation. "Changing planes there. You go on this airline, okay (pointing to the logo on the airline ticket). That plane over there. Then to change in Amsterdam for another plane—same company. Flight number…plane number—it is all written inside."

"He must do this all the time," whispered Pillai before running for the toilet.

Martin noticed his name and picture in the seaman's book; he had managed to become a sailor without ever having gone to sea. He bet all six of them would drown if their life boat capsized.

Pillai was Martin's traveling companion on the way to Amsterdam and from there onto Montreal. They had seats next to each other, while the others were scattered elsewhere in the economy cabin.

Pillai recounted his story, not unlike many Martin had heard and witnessed before: his brother's family, who were in Colombo at the time, witnessed their grocery store and apartment go up in smoke during the riots of '83. One of Pillai's nieces died in the fire. The brother's family holed up in a temple which had been hastily converted into a refugee centre. Then they joined the first arrivals who were granted easy asylum in Canada. Pillai and his family lived in Trincomalee and were spared the racial conflagration in Colombo. However, economic conditions for his printing business went downhill after that. His brother opened a Sri Lankan grocery store in Toronto upon arrival, and although mortgaged to the hilt, had told Pillai that there were many opportunities in Canada. Pillai's first and second immigration applications were rejected as he couldn't provide sufficient proof of being under threat where he lived. Pottu became the only alternative. Pillai had sold his printing business to afford this trip. Like Martin, he was also indentured for two years to pay $250.00 a month to a "collector" in Toronto.

As the plane flew over lights at night, Pillai wanted to know which country they were flying over. "My last and only chance to see these places, no?" he explained. "I can write back to my family and tell them." He interrupted their conversation to look at the next clump of lights that appeared. "This must be Pakistan, no, if we passed India half an hour ago?" The passenger next to him suppressed a smile.

In Amsterdam, a couple of the guys in the group disembarked, drunk and belligerent. They did not stick with the rest as Navaratana had urged the group to do. Martin last saw them straying into the airport duty-free shops, wide eyed and excited, like kids in an amusement park. He guessed Amsterdam had done what Bangkok had failed to do, and tipped them over the edge, helped by the booze they'd had on board.

"That Siva and Banu—young bucks—think they can disobey orders." Pillai shook his head in disgust. The remaining four in the group huddled near the boarding gate for the next flight, longing for this odyssey to end.

At boarding time, Siva and Banu had still not showed up and announcements for them echoed throughout the airport.

"What to do?" Pillai asked nervously.

"We have to keep going. That was Vedha's instruction." Martin reminded him.

Boarding commenced. This time everyone's papers were scrutinized extensively. The gate agent shook Martin's seaman's book, twisted the photograph, held it under a light on his desk, looked at the bearer several times and then at the book, and asked Martin which ship he was joining. After going blank for several seconds, Martin gave him the memorized answer. Finally, after repeatedly scratching his head and scowling, the agent let Martin through.

Just before entering the boarding tunnel leading to the aircraft, Martin heard a commotion behind him. A terminal car, one of those silent electric mobiles that were constantly zipping late and elderly passengers around, had whizzed up to the gate and disgorged Siva and Banu, loaded with duty-free shopping bags. Both guys were garrulous and began arguing with the ground staff.

Pillai, who had also cleared behind Martin, turned around. Martin pulled him back into the tunnel, "Come on. Let's not hang around those guys. If they get caught, we're all in the soup."

Inside the aircraft and buckled up, they felt like prisoners, not knowing when the authorities would come in and take them away to join those two assholes and be deported. Instead, just before departure time, the curtain of the front cabin parted and in staggered the two assholes themselves, escorted by a stern looking flight attendant, who set them down in their respective seats a few rows in front, took their many shopping bags and deposited them wherever free space was still available in the overhead bins.

As she passed Martin, the flight attendant rolled her eyes at her colleague who had also come to the rescue, "Seamen, jah!"

It was another long flight and their nerves were now on their sharpest edge. Siva and Banu ahead were ordering scotch after scotch every time the drinks cart went by, until the purser came along and had a word with them. Martin wished for a couple of stiff ones himself, but his sinuses were really clogged now, and the pain in his ears had spread to his head; he did not want to add hangover to his ever-increasing list of discomforts. Next to him, Pillai kept going to the toilet regularly.

After a while, Martin fell into an exhausted sleep, only to be nudged awake by Pillai.

"They are eating their seaman's books."

"Who?"

"Siva and Banu."

"Where are they?"

"In the toilet."

"Together?"

"Yes"

"Shit!"

While Martin had slept, Siva and Banu had awoken from their alcoholic stupor and panicked that they would be discovered upon arrival. They had therefore decided to eat their seaman's books and pretend that they were stateless. They had muttered this to Pillai as they made their way to the toilets in the rear of the cabin. There were recent reports of people who had got through on that ruse. In the past, Martin had heard of people flushing their passports in the aircraft toilet but now ground crews were sharp, and could dig through the refuse to produce the destroyed papers even before the would-be refugees arrived at the immigration counter. It had been reported back on the street in Sri Lanka that eating was best these days.

"Should we do the same?" Pillai was panicking.

"Your stomach won't stand it. You're having loose motions already," Martin reminded him and decided to hold his ground. "Where are we?"

Fortunately, they did not have to go by Pillai's guesswork anymore, the big screen on the bulkhead that had shown blurry movies with poor sound, had now turned into a digital map and indicated that they were over Canada, somewhere between Nova Scotia and Montreal.

"We should be landing soon," Martin said, answering his own question.

As if to confirm his conclusion, the captain announced that they were going into their descent and could everyone take their seats and buckle up; the plane lurched downward and Martin felt his ears start to pop again. This time they popped so badly that he lost most of his hearing for the rest of the flight and for most of the next day. He could barely hear anyone close to him speak anymore.

Pillai was saying something.

"What?" Martin yelled in pain and annoyance. Pillai pointed to the rear. Martin turned to see Siva and Banu returning to their seats; as they passed, their faces looked green despite their dark complexion. Martin decided to ignore them and focus on his ears. He swore he would never embark on a silly voyage like this again. Next to him, Pillai's lips were moving; he seemed to be praying.

"Welcome to Montreal's Mirabel airport, ladies and gentlemen," the cabin attendant's announcement came faintly to Martin's ears as the plane touched down flawlessly. It was sunny and bright outside.

"Thank God, there is no snow." Pillai exhaled, grinning hysterically.

"It's August." Martin reminded him, glad for the gentle easing of pressure in his ears, although his hearing was still shot.

They rose from their seats. Considerate passengers passed the many duty-free bags from various overhead compartments, fore and aft, to Siva and Banu. The two still-drunken travellers nevertheless grinned helplessly and staggered out with only their carry-on bags, leaving the merchandise behind on their seats. The cabin attendants shrugged, and the helpful passengers looked at each other chagrined. Pillai wanted to help, in his typical Sri Lankan neighbourly fashion, but Martin restrained him. "Don't. Those buggers are so cocked, they don't know if they're coming or going. They will surely kick up a stink at the immigration counter. You don't want to be seen carrying their bags."

A bus that locked into the aircraft ferried the passengers to the terminal. They walked through several narrow corridors to the immigration counters strung between them and freedom.

For their bad luck, Pillai and Martin got stuck behind Siva and Banu while the other two in the group—the guys who'd had their pillows confiscated in Colombo—were right behind them. Passengers were quickly forming other lines in front of the many counters. Martin wished he had not followed the drunken duo, but it was too late to change now without attracting undue attention.

"*Adey, ya*—we forgot our duty free shopping." Siva had suddenly awoken from his stupor and was croaking at Banu.

"I can't go back now." Banu replied, rubbing his stomach. "I am feeling…very…sick. How long this queue is going to last?"

Martin whispered to them from behind, "You can't go back now. The ship's courier will be outside waiting for us. We have to stick together."

Siva turned back and his eyes lit up. "*Adey,* then you can go and get it for us, no?"

"These fuckers are drunk," Pillai groaned. "Ignore them. Please God, ignore them and let this nightmare end!"

Martin squeezed Pillai's hand but his own was clammy with sweat, which probably panicked his companion even more. Martin glared at Siva, as if to say that there would be no more favours from this point on. Siva hiccupped and turned back helplessly to Banu who was tugging him forward. The immigration counter in front of them was now open.

The two drunkards lurched to the counter together. The immigration officer frowned and said something which Martin's blocked hearing could not pick up. The officer waved one of them back. Siva began to step back to the red line, when with a mighty heave and an "Arrrrrr!" Banu spewed a flood of vomit all over the immigration counter, through the slit in the glass and at its occupant on the other side, and on the floor all around him. The immediate stench was overpowering; the yellow goop was embellished with scraps of paper, red cardboard and photo paper. Kudos to whoever had to put that seaman's book together again for evidence against this illegal immigrant.

But the most ridiculous sight came when Siva wobbled over to his friend's aid. Overcome with the stink and puke that he walked into, Siva immediately added his contribution to the party, giving the immigration officer a fresh daubing of red-coated, whiskey-flavoured gunk.

Pandemonium reigned. Angry growls from several passengers, shrieks all over, yells from the hapless immigration officer, and all lines stopped. The other immigration officers left their stations and came over to help their beleaguered colleague who was dragged away gagging and in shock.

"Quickly, let's move over to another line—at the far end. " Martin grabbed Pillai in the scramble and pulled him away, their pillow-less companions following like puppies. This had been the perfect diversion they needed. It couldn't have come at a better time. When the lines re-arranged again, the remaining four illegals were far away from Siva and Banu, who were being led away by two uniformed personnel to a room in the back.

"How long are you going to be in Canada?" the female immigration officer, very young, French accented, and friendly, asked Martin, inspecting his seaman's book. Martin was surprised. He expected threatening macho types to be manning the borders of this country that so many desperate people were trying to get into.

"I am joining a ship in Halifax tomorrow night. My agent is waiting outside to take me to Dorval airport."

"Any alcohol? Cigarettes?"

"No"

She stamped his book and customs form disinterestedly and handed them back with a smile. "Okay,'ave a nice day." It took him a few moments after passing the barrier to realize he had entered Canada. *I have entered Canada! Do you hear that Dad, Mum and Barney—I have entered Canada!*

The same euphoria, bordering on tears, enveloped his traveling companions who followed. The immigration lady must have got bored with the pattern of arriving seamen and had ushered them through before taking on her next challenging passenger seeking entry into the country.

The familiar Lanka Tours sign drew them, wheeling suitcases, over to the smiling shipping agent Hanif (according to Navaratana's briefing).

"There are supposed to be six of you." He said scratching his head, the smile slowly vanishing. His Sri Lankan accent had an added veneer of North American twang. Hanif pronounced "supposed" as "sapposed."

Martin quickly related what had just happened.

"Fuck!" The venom in his voice took them all aback. "Those bastards have ruined our scheme." Then he was all business again; the smile returned, but a sense of urgency overlaid it. "Come, we must get out of here. Follow me."

They made it out of the parking garage inside a nondescript mini-van in less than 10 minutes. The broad and never ending highway they flew down blew Martin's breath away. Cars whipped by really fast here. He was beginning to like where he had arrived already. There was an air of order and peace, that he had never seen back home. No bullock carts, tooting horns, bicycles, tri-shaws or pedestrians walking in the middle of the road.

Half an hour out of the airport, Hanif pulled off the highway and burst out laughing. "I guess the boss will have to come up with a new arrangement now. He always does." Then Hanif got serious again and fished out a piece of paper, "Pillai?"

"Yes, sir," Martin's faithful companion answered eagerly.

"You are being dropped off in Kingston at a motel. Our people will contact you there."

The other two—Martin never found out their names—were being dropped off in motels in places called Belleville and Oshawa respectively.

Martin was the last. "And you—James? You are going to downtown Toronto." They would all be met by Hanif's "people." And a ship would sail out of Halifax tomorrow with six fewer crew members.

The four newly-arrived refugees embraced each other fondly as they parted company, one at a time, at the appointed drop- off points. This experience, short though it had been, had bonded them like soldiers in the battlefield. They would never see each other again.

Pillai bid goodbye to Martin tearfully, "Martin sir, thank you very much. I couldn't have made it here without you. God Bless you!" Then he was gone, swallowed in the darkness surrounding the dimly lit motel, his interim destination, a hundred yards away.

And that is how Martin James arrived in Canada. The mini-van dropped him off last, at the corner of two main streets full of neon signs and crowds of people, mostly women, walking in skimpy clothing and revealing cleavage, legs and bare arms. Beautiful, well-groomed people who did not seem to have a care in the world. He looked up at the tall CN Tower that rose majestically over the rooftops and felt that he was walking through the Promised Land. He could smell the freedom in this place, even though he was yet to be free. What beat him was that, despite the anxiety of the airplane ride, it had been so easy in the end. It hurt him that his parents who had tried so hard and honestly to get into this country, had got nowhere. Money had talked. *Money that I am now to earn over the next few years to pay off my huge debt.* Like Pottu had said, people in Canada were all in debt. Martin had just joined the club.

Part 2 – Adventures Abroad

"It is not possible to fight beyond your strength, even if you strive" – Homer

9. **Underclass**

"You're a free man now, huh?" Hanif said, the gold fillings in his teeth glinting as he stuffed the final payment into his jacket pocket and made for the door.

Martin followed him. Hanif had filled out in the last two years and the grey at his temples had spread. He paused on the threshold, his belly pressing against the door jamb, "You have done well, Martin. Not like those other fellows."

"Thank you." Martin was anxious to see the back of this guy, to never see him again if possible, even if the man had shown occasional streaks of benign self-interest.

"But you cannot say anything, like those other fellows, okay?" Hanif surveyed his client.

"I understand."

"See what happened to that Pillai guy. Got too cocky. Tried to leave and go to Vancouver without paying the bill."

"Yes, I read the newspapers. You guys didn't have to throw him off the tenth floor, though. He didn't make a pretty corpse."

"We don't do the throwing. That is all outsourced." Hanif extended his hand. "Good luck. Your new student visa is good. Very soon you can get a good job here. You can even become a citizen. But you must keep secrets."

"I hope you will do the same."

"Of course. Otherwise it's not good for business. We are like the 'other' Canadian Government. As long as you pay your taxes, the Canadian Government leaves you alone. As long as you pay our bills and shut up—you live. Good day."

Martin sat in his armchair and let Hanif and his bad vibes recede before venturing out into the afternoon. There were a couple of real estate sales calls to make; hopefully, at least one would turn into a closed deal. And then on to his evening date with Ivana.

Hanif had kept his word despite the dubious world he inhabited. Immediately upon his arrival in Canada, he had found Martin a job in a light-engineering factory, and an apartment with two other illegals in the heart of the city. Martin rarely saw his fellow tenants for they worked opposite shifts; all they left behind were traces of curry and gingerly oil. The only drag was that one of the guys slept in Martin's bed when he was not around and left oil stains on the pillow. There wasn't a lot of room for three men in a one-bedroom apartment.

Those first months had been an unending round of shift work: operating various sizes and types of lathes, assembling moulded parts for industrial equipment, and packing finished goods in the dispatch area. Distracted by the repetitious mind-numbing work in a hot, cavernous environment full of lubricant fumes, Martin did not always follow safety instructions and cut his hands several times on the machines. They were little nicks at first, but with the constant of lubricant, metal dust and other workplace junk, they started to get infected. Seeing a doctor was not an option, as he had no official landed-immigrant papers yet. He wrapped his hands in tissue from the men's room, slipped them back into his thick industrial gloves and kept going. He needed the money and he did not want to attract attention.

Gradually the wounds began to hurt and soon he couldn't even pick anything up without wincing. One day as he struggled home, Martin felt the glands swollen under his arms and he was running a high fever. He dosed up on Tylenol and buried himself under the sheets, determined to be fit to go to work the next day. He tossed and turned, sweated and ached right through the night. This whole new world had turned hostile: the closed apartment building with its curtains drawn, the echoing workplace with workers of every nationality speaking in tongues he could not understand. *I thought this was Canada?* He lulled himself to sleep with the image of his mother applying balm to his bruises from his first day at school, those many years ago. Somehow those days that had once been hostile and foreign at the time, seemed less threatening, even comforting. He missed Mum, especially out here.

The next morning he could barely walk to the washroom. He collapsed on the bed and it must have been noon when he awoke. A couple of Tamil men were talking just outside his room, gesticulating at him. They smelled of gingerly oil and stale sweat, and Martin wondered which one of them had been sleeping in his bed.

"Hi" Martin said weakly. "Speak English, or Sinhala?"

"Sar," one of the guys responded in accented English. "What problem?"

"Sick. Infected cuts." Martin raised his hands from under the blankets. They had started to ooze pus and his makeshift bandage was stained. "Know a doctor who won't ask too many questions?"

The two men sized up the issue immediately. They nodded without alarm. Perhaps they had been there before. "Yes, sar. Wait. Will bring."

An hour passed and Martin dozed again and woke up to Hanif staring down at him.

"Ay, ay yar, Mr. Martin. We can't have this happening to you. Come let's go right away."

Martin got another taste of the underground network for illegals that day. After all, he could not die on the smugglers; there would be too many questions. There had to be lots of doctors, lawyers and other professionals working "on the side". It grieved him that he was an underclass in this country. Nothing seemed to have improved from Sri Lanka. At least in the old country shit happened in the open; here it was all covered up, but there was still shit.

Hanif took him down some side streets in Agincourt to a South-East Asian man wearing a white lab gown and a stethoscope. In a room behind a grocery shop, they dressed his wounds and gave him an injection. "Take these." The doctor tossed some tablets in an unlabelled plastic vial at him. "Antibiotics. Take all."

On Hanif's advice, Martin called in sick for work and rested a week. His roommates obliged by sleeping in the living room. The TV blared all day and he had to listen to South Indian music. But they bought him a steady supply of *chapatis, thosas* and *sambol.* When he was better, Hanif came to see him again.

"I have a new job for you. Factory is too dangerous. Here, go to this address," Hanif gave him a slip of paper.

"Thanks," Martin said.

"We look after our people." Hanif grinned. "Oh, by the way, there is this little bill to settle." He handed Martin another piece of paper. It was an invoice, handwritten for $500.00.

"Sorry medicines very expensive here," Hanif said. "Especially, as you have no OHIP coverage."

"You could have told me this before you took me to your doctor."

"You were in no state to argue, my friend. We don't like problems. You can put this on our instalment plan if you like—add it to your monthly payments."

Martin bit his tongue and refrained from a smart-ass reply. "I'll look this place up," he said.

The "place" was a bungalow in the suburbs, with an overgrown lawn. The man who answered the door had a craggy face with a droopy moustache.

"Hanif sent me," Martin said, extending a still-unhealed hand. The man took it gruffly squeezing it and sending Martin into a spasm of pain.

"You immigrants not used to shaking hands?" the man asked, leading Martin into an unfurnished living roomfull of pamphlets and boxes of books.

"I'm just getting over an injury."

The man squared his hands on his hips, surveying Martin. "Okay, I'll get to the point. We sell encyclopaedias here. See all these books? All the knowledge in the world if you care to read. Frankly I don't care if anyone reads. Just sell the books. We pay a fifteen percent commission. And there are no benefits. You get injured you don't get paid, capiche?"

I thought this was the land of milk and honey? "Sure," Martin said, picking up a volume and thumbing through its pages. Ironically, he was at the section on Greek Mythology. He couldn't resist holding up the chapter on *The Odyssey*.

"Hey, hey—no reading,"

"Aren't I supposed to familiarize myself with the product?"

"You're a sharp one, eh? Listen, son—you can take a set home and get familiar on your own time, okay? Not on mine."

Martin put the book back.

The man took a pile of pamphlets and shoved it at Martin. "This is your bait. You go out in the neighbourhoods and drop them in mailboxes, or hand them out to pedestrians, especially to kids. People like these books. The pictures are good. If you see an immigrant, stick one in his hands. Immigrants like to adorn their houses with these books.

Makes them look kind of special—working up the social ladder, you know."

"What happens then?"

"If they write back—and a two percent response is good—then you go out at night and sell them a set of encyclopaedias. I pay you the commission in cash, capiche?"

"Got it. Can I start now?"

"Keener, eh? Sure. Grab some pamphlets and start walking. I'll give you some maps of areas we haven't covered yet."

Martin rose from the armchair and got into the shower. No more grimy walls from that first hole-in-the-wall he had shared with the other two illegals, he noted smugly as he soaped himself. This apartment block was mainly inhabited by white-collar workers. And the scars on his hands were just faded lines now. Encyclopaedias and real estate had been his way out of the ghetto of the underclass.

After that meeting with his new "boss," Martin dropped hundreds of pamphlets each morning according to the maps he was given. The offer was for free extracts from the encyclopaedia, and gifts to those who wanted to sample the wonders of knowledge. Surprisingly, people responded. With a five percent return rate, he had sufficient contacts to call upon who would not slam the door in his face. After all, he was bringing them a gift, and he had observed how Canadians, especially the new arrivals, loved free things.

Immigrant homes lapped up his offering. Martin focused on the children, with their newly-forming Canadian accents. Their tired yet hopeful parents looked on and spoke in broken or accented English, hanging onto his words. Martin pushed the premise that the encyclopaedia, with its embedded knowledge, would lift them out of the ghetto and into prosperity in their new homeland. In some homes, a premium set of encyclopaedias was purchased even before a VCR. He got good at this game in no time.

Before long, sales commissions were pouring in. He even contracted two students to drop the flyers so that he could focus on qualified door-to-door sales.

When he moved into this apartment, the two Tamil boys were sad to see him go, but wished him well. The payment of $250.00 a month to Hanif was now easily affordable, though he did not want to accelerate payments in case his minder smelled money. Illegal immigrants were supposed to live hungry and appreciate every day of freedom they enjoyed in this country.

And what of freedom? On Hanif's "premium plan," Martin could buy a student visa and, if he got a community college diploma in sales management or marketing and a job in the field, he could apply for resident status. With added sales pouring in, his confidence was at an all-time high, and he went for it; it cost him an additional $3000.00, but commissions held him afloat. Before long, he received a Sri Lankan passport, oddly similar to the one he was given for the trip to Bangkok. It even had the date stamp of when he landed in that country. The passport now had a Canadian overseas student visa on it as well.

He enrolled in marketing management at a community college and took additional courses in real estate. For months the habit of studying, absorbing, going for long walks, studying again, became his daily routine. Recreation was selling encyclopaedias at night. He would look enviously at what he called "normal" Canadians shopping casually and extravagantly in malls, strolling and playing in parks, idling over coffee or wine in food courts and restaurants. Life was taken for granted by these people. Had he really escaped the underclass?

He did not have to do much in the way of earning a living—door-to-door sales of encyclopaedias on evenings and weekends would be sufficient—or so he thought. Good things don't last long, he soon discovered. Just as immigrants were flooding in, so were a lot of inexperienced encyclopaedia salespeople, who soon began wrecking it for people like him. He started to get doors slammed in his face.

But another door opened. After months of slogging, he had just obtained his real estate license. Commissions were now in thousands of dollars for a sale, not hundreds. Despite the load of overhead to start off: realtor license fees, driver's license, a second-hand car, Martin was bullish on his new career. By the time he had set up his real estate infrastructure and received his business cards from the printer, he was back in debt again before even selling his first house.

He slaved hard for that first sale. But he also promised himself that he would not cut commissions for he had seen the encyclopaedia market erode that way. His two students added real estate flyers to their daily drop. During the day he ferried home-buyers between listed properties, and at night he knocked on doors selling encyclopaedias. Sometimes he called on the same customer for both products and hoped like hell no one would report him to the real estate board for conflict of interest.

Then he found a hook: a premium set of encyclopaedias to go with the new home if they bought from him, compliments of yours truly. Canadians loved gifts—he made his first home sale!

Martin went into his bedroom and looked at his naked body in the mirror. Gone was the angular frame, the lines on his rib-cage, hallmarks of life in the tropics on a diet of rice and curry. He was filling in nicely now, thanks to hamburgers, fried chicken, and pizza, grabbed at odd hours between studies, sales and women.

He sprayed himself with aftershave, cologne and applied deodorant, something he had never used in the old country; didn't even know it existed. Ivana liked her men smelling good and if things went smoothly tonight he would get lucky. There was not a lot of inducing necessary to make it with Ivana. He slipped on a tie and put on his blazer for business had to be attended to first.

He stepped out of his apartment, overcoat in hand. He did not slam the door any more, since cooling it with Jamila from across the hall. Jamila with her moon face, buxom body, big breasts and romantic heart. He had made the mistake of asking her out on a date when he had first moved in, more out of loneliness than attraction. As he hauled his few belongings across the hall that day of his move, she had come over with cookies and eaten most of them herself as she had helped him arrange his empty apartment; then she sat and talked to him about the neighbourhood, romance writers and about her work as a bank teller. The date, two days later, had been a disaster: all Jamila had talked about was of finding a suitable husband from among the immigrant class—

someone like him, for instance—of buying a five-bedroom house in the suburbs and staying home to have lots of babies. He had been avoiding her since.

The elevator door opened to disgorge a puffing Jamila with shopping bags in both hands. He tried to smile and ease himself into the elevator but she blocked him.

"Why, it's Mr. Handsome. Avoiding me these days, huh?"

"No. I've been kind of busy—studies, clients. You know."

"When are we going out for dinner again? My father was also enquiring about you."

"Your father knows about me?"

"My whole family knows about you. What do you think? You take a girl out and her family should not know?"

The elevator door closed, leaving them both standing in the corridor. Jamila's ample bosom heaved spastically. "Here, help me take these to my apartment. My father and mother want to meet you."

"Jamila, I am running late for my class." He pressed the call button for the elevator again.

"What? Is it true that you have found another girl?"

"And what if I have?"

Her eyes widened in horror. "What? And I thought you were interested in me."

"We went out on a date. That was it."

She blanched. "You...you don't know how much I have waited for you to call after that day. Always avoiding me whenever we meet. People say you are running around with a Russian woman. Is that true?"

"That's none of anyone's business."

"So it's already over between you and her? So soon? Then why are you so...stand-offish?"

"Jamila...listen, I have to go, okay. As for the two of us...we are not an item...we never were. I'm sorry you thought otherwise."

The elevator had arrived. He quickly jumped in. She was still recovering from his words as the doors slid shut. Her insults and curses followed him as he descended and vainly trying to shut out the clamour.

Getting into his eight-year-old Mazda, he focused on his client, Vigo Matinsen. Vigo had homes in Florida and Europe. He was trying to negotiate the seller down on a four-hundred-grand property and was pushing Martin to get the job done for him. Martin had worked it down from a list price of $450K to $425K, which he thought was pretty good in this escalating market; but Vigo wanted more. This was also the highest-valued property that Martin had worked on, and he kept wondering if he was biting off more than he could handle. This meeting was going to be the walk-away for both of them if they could not reach an agreement.

As he drove into the downtown area, he tried to focus his mind on more pleasant thoughts. The evening ahead with Ivana was one of them. He had met Ivana at a strip club on Queen Street two months earlier. She worked as a hostess and had looked at him more than cursorily as she ushered him to a table at the rear. The main strip show had been dull, the women too flat breasted, and Martin had preferred the jazz musicians who started up afterwards. As Ivana had walked by he had invited her over for a drink. She told him that she was going off duty shortly and then she could meet him outside.

That night had begun a whirlwind of vodka, marijuana and sex. They met twice a week at her place after that, and Ivana wanted all those stimulants to wrap up an evening of working at the club, which suited him well. He liked the sex and the vodka, but drew the line at the weed; somehow the lack of control it induced did not sit well with him. Years of watching his back had conditioned him.

Did he *know* her? Other than the fact that she was a recent émigré from Russia, had a son somewhere in the old country and was studying computer programming when she was not working, he really did not know anything about her. But he knew and delighted in her body: every contour of her well-sculpted breasts, her curvy hips, the vertical streak of pubic hair, strong legs, blue-dyed hair cut in punk style; the tattoos on her shoulder, around her navel and on her bum. He wondered whether she had become his addiction. But her apparent lack of values, other than for earning money, had bothered him from the time they had met. When he had asked her about her son, whether she maintained contact with him, she replied, "Nyet, he is with his father."

Now as he parked and entered the old commercial building with its creaking elevator, he wondered how long this relationship would last. Was he holding on to her just for the sex?

Vigo Matinsen occupied the entire breadth of his desk, or so it seemed. Martin was ushered into his fourth-floor office by a nervous elderly secretary. Vigo was the only broad thing in this narrow building with lean corridors and frayed carpets. The man was a curious blend of the steely-eyed northern European living in a world of saunas, and the emotional, sensuous southerner living on a diet of wine and pasta; Vigo's mother was Italian, he had explained to Martin when they had first met.

Vigo lumbered up, a wide grin on his oily face, and extended a hand to Martin. "Ah, Martin, you have brought me good news?"

Martin fiddled with his briefcase, gathering his thoughts, angry now that Ivana had invaded them when he should have been preparing for this crucial meeting. *Stick to the key points.* He felt his throat go dry. Vigo's grey Armani suit, so out of place in these drab surroundings, was intimidating. *Stick to your points.* "The offer is ready to go if you accept four twenty-five."

Vigo sat down with a sigh. "Ah, Martin, you disappoint me. I told you, this building is not worth anything over four hundred thousand. Three hundred and ninety nine grand would make me feel very good."

"Mr. Matinsen, consider the features: the house is on the lake, with a brand new furnace and air conditioning, a new roof and solid hardwood floors."

"I know, I know, Martin, so are dozens of other houses. Why did I come to you, Martin?"

"I'd like to think your colleague, Mr. Sorensen was happy with the deal I worked for him."

"Right. Sorensen said 'Martin's your man'. So I come to you. To buy the house so I can bring my family here from Finland and give them what they are used to: lakes, sauna, wood, snow etc., etc. And you are offering what I can negotiate for myself?"

Martin flushed and tried to calm himself. "You would have got the list price, sir. This is a seller's market. Prices are going up daily."

"And you people are making fat commissions, for little work, no?"

"Mr. Matinsen, I'll leave it to you to shop around and see if you can do any better on this deal. I have had three rounds of intense discussions with the owner and his representative. They are not prepared to budge any more. And they might receive another offer any time now."

Matinsen rose and walked over to the window. He moved the curtains gingerly and looked out. "How much commission are you making on this deal, Martin?"

"That, sir, is confidential. You can check out the real estate board's guidelines on agent commissions. I play by those rules."

"Very good, very good." Matinsen turned away from the window. "That is a good speech. I tell you what; I give you three hundred and ninety nine g's right now. No mortgages, no bank loans and all that crap. You get them to sign."

Martin did quick mental math. Accepting this offer would mean parting with almost his entire commission to close this deal. He would be left with $500 to cover his expenses. And he had been counting on this deal to wipe out his debt and get him on to a new path.

Martin started to put the papers back in his briefcase. "Mr. Matinsen, I'm sorry I've taken so much of your time. You obviously need another kind of an agent."

"Wait!" Matinsen shouted as Martin reached the door. "Four hundred and ten—last price."

"Four hundred and twenty five, sir."

Martin held his breath, wanting to hear "deal" being shouted back. But nothing happened as the door clicked behind him. Dejected and angry he walked to the elevator. He wanted to throw the file in the garbage. *Cheap bastard!* The drab surroundings of this office building should have alerted him to dealing with Matinsen.

When he got to his car, his beeper went off. It was his second client: a South Asian immigrant family looking to buy a starter bungalow in Scarborough. He dialed on his car phone.

"Ah, Mr. James, ah, how are you?" the accented voice came faintly over the line.

"I am well, Mr. Patel. Are we still on for this evening? I was just heading your way."

"Ah, Mr. James, this is why I called. We already purchased the house."

"You what?"

"You see, the owner fellow, he wanted to deal directly with me."

"But that is not how it's done here, Mr. Patel. What about the owner's agent?"

"The owner fellow did not want to deal with him either. So I simply paid him today and he signed the papers. I was calling to tell you not to come."

"Mr. Patel, I have taken you and your wife to see over a dozen houses in the last month."

"I know, I know, Mr. James. You are a good man. But what can I do, when the owner fellow..."

Martin dropped the phone back on the receiver. "Fuck! Fuck them all!" he thundered as he wrenched the wheel and jerked the car onto the main road.

He drove in a haze of rage, west on Queen Street, swerving narrowly to pass a streetcar, not stopping for passengers disembarking, and getting tooted at from other motorists. He pulled up in front of the Pink Flamingo club. He was early, and Ivana would still be on her afternoon shift of hostess duty. Time to grab a drink or two at the bar and watch the table dancers entertain middle-aged businessmen who had to leave early to their wives. And boy, did he need a drink.

He slipped in through the side entrance and headed directly to the bar; no sign of Ivana. He ordered a double scotch on the rocks. *What the hell, let me just pile on my debts.* The scotch burned, and the sense of shame burned even more. Here he was drowning his sorrows in a seedy strip joint, having worked all day with shady immigrant smugglers, slimy businessman and unprincipled immigrants. All he could look forward to was more booze and sex with an immoral Russian whore. Mum would be proud of him. He had sunk even lower than his father.

He turned around, the anger and shame mixed with the alcohol, and saw a crowd of men gathered around one of the tables. There seemed to be only one girl on duty today, but she was attracting quite a crowd; the oasis in the desert. And he was drawn to the oasis, his loins crowing for release, if only that would help ease the pain in his heart.

He was unprepared to see Ivana writhing gently on the table, revolving her naked breasts in the faces of the onlookers, only a hat and a G-string covering the rest of her body. He gagged on his drink as she started to peel the string off too, grabbing the notes tucked into the waistband by her ogling fans and placing them under her hat.

He pushed the men standing at the rear and parted a way to the front of the circle of onlookers amidst jostling and shouts of "hey!" and "fuck-off!" Now he was standing directly in front of her as her eyes widened upon seeing him, a half smile tempered with a touch of panic. "Martin, you are early," she said, shifting her eyes back to her patrons, trying to recapture the seductive look she had been in control of thus far.

"Is this hostess duty? Or a way to earn pocket money?" he yelled.

"One of the girls called in sick." She tried winking at him and smiling at her customers at the same time, failing at both.

"And we are fucking done, you whore!" He flung his drink at her. It splashed across her breasts and a man in the front took an angry swipe at him. Martin punched back and the man went down. Martin grabbed a chair and swung it in front of him. "Come on you bastards. Who's next?"

He wanted someone to come at him, to feel the chair crash down on bone. But in the end these were middle-aged men having a little afternoon fun; no heroes here.

The bouncer grabbed him firmly by the neck from behind. "Drop the chair, Martin."

He dropped the chair as his windpipe contracted and let the bouncer frog march him to the exit. It felt good being manhandled. He could add pain as another outlet for the release of shame and hurt. Out of the side of his eye, he saw Ivana resuming her dance after giving him a final, ugly look this time. That was all this breakup seemed to have cost her, an ugly look. The onlookers had regrouped around her table by the time the bouncer slammed him against the wall by the entrance.

"Okay, Martin, you've been a good customer here," the bouncer said. "Leave now before, I get really mean."

Martin resisted the temptation to take a swipe at the man. Self-preservation kicked in; after all, he was still an illegal immigrant on a purchased student visa. This was not the time for getting involved with the cops. He straightened his crumpled tie, tugged his jacket, torn at the sleeve in the scuffle, and walked out into the evening.

The drive home passed with conflicting thoughts, even self-hate. *I'm as fucked up as my stupid parents.*

He found a half-empty bottle of Vodka in his apartment. He took several gulps and sat in front of the TV, trying to be mindless, letting the images of free-trade talks between the US and Canada flash past him: a vast moment of opportunity for both nations, the politicians were hailing, while the critics talked about the loss of Canadian privileges and subsidies. What privileges, what subsidies—he had seen none to date.

The phone rang. He let it ring. If it was that bitch calling to apologize, he was going to let her stew. She could pick up one of those ogling old men to screw tonight.

Ten minutes later, the phone rang again. He grabbed it. "Fuck off!" he shouted into it.

"Martin?" Vigo Matinsen's raspy voice came over the phone. Martin instantly sobered.

"Mr. Matinsen?"

"You are having a fight Martin?"

"No...no." His alcohol sodden brain grabbed for an excuse. "Some...some crank callers have been bothering me. Sorry."

"Nothing to be sorry for Martin. Let's close the deal. Four hundred and twenty five is a good price. You have done well."

Martin could not believe what he was hearing. He reached for the Vodka bottle. "You... you are buying the house from me? Really?"

"Yes, really Martin. Be in my office tomorrow at noon with the buyer's acceptance. Now go and have yourself a drink."

10. **Super Salesman, Super Lover**

Martin closed his notebook and looked at the young woman seated in the row across from him in the lecture room. She was new to the class, yet seemed to grasp the substance of the last four weeks of lectures that she had missed. Her blonde hair fell in a lush wave across her shoulders and framed a well-defined face: prominent chin, aquiline nose, wide lips and large blue eyes. She was dressed in a white shirt that accentuated well proportioned breasts, and when she leaned back, her long legs, set in black spike-heeled shoes with pointed toes, stretched out elegantly.

She had asked the lecturer—an old duffer who had left the corporate world long ago and seemed stuck in a fog of ancient theories—some pointed questions on his recommended timing for abandoning obsolete products, and had sent the class into a titter as he had pontificated vainly in a bid to answer her.

Martin had signed up for this extra course because he wanted to complete his marketing diploma early. Yet he wasn't learning anything new. As a real estate salesperson he had already put into practise all the theories being presented. Even divesting of old products—well, he'd done that: he had ditched the encyclopaedia business at the right time and narrowed his focus to selling houses and commercial buildings. Still, he realized how much this country valued credentials and connections.

Connections he seemed to be gaining. Impressed by how Martin had handled the purchase of his lakefront property, Vigo Matinsen had recently approached him with an offer: head of sales for Telstra Properties. Martin didn't even know that Vigo had any connection with Telstra, a property development company that had burst onto the scene a couple of years earlier and was giving the established names a run for their money. Word on the street was that Telstra was over-leveraged, but even so, they continued to outpace the competition. The downside of this offer was that Martin would have to give up or curtail his own real estate sales activity. Vigo ran the marketing for his firm and brought customers in; Martin's job would be to convert prospects into sales. He had asked for time to consider the offer and put renewed vigour into completing his diploma so he would at least have academia off his hands.

Yes, the future looked bright after all this time spent among the underclasses: a diploma after years of study, a lucrative job offer, and his real estate sales career taking off despite its feast-or-famine nature. And now, after having dabbled with losers such as Jamila and Ivana, this pretty woman across the aisle was intriguing him.

The lecture was ending, and Martin sidled up to the row where the young woman was sitting. She did not seem in a hurry to join the crush of students heading for the exit, and was casually putting her papers away into a soft leather briefcase. A couple of the male students sitting next to her tried opening conversations, but she only nodded politely and focussed on packing up. Martin waited until she was alone. He had moved right beside her, and picked up a faint whiff of her perfume. Musk.

"Good questions you asked," he opened, wondering if she would just get up and walk away.

She looked up, brows furrowed inquisitively, even suggesting annoyance at his intrusion.

"This class is a waste of time, isn't it?" he persisted, palms getting clammy. "You already know everything."

Her blue eyes widened in a smile. "Glad I'm not the only one who thinks that way." She was appraising him. Good thing he had put on a jacket, as he had a client to visit later in the evening; otherwise he would have been in sweats and jeans, and she somehow did not look like a sweats-and-jeans type of girl.

"Martin James." He extended his hand.

"Your accent's not Canadian, but your name could be."

"I'm an old colonial. Dutch Burgher from Ceylon."

Her eyes widened even more and she rose, a trifle quickly. "I'm privileged. A rare specimen, I believe."

"Don't you think it's time you tell me your name?"

"And a pushy one too." Her lips had parted and there was a distant look on her face as she studied him. "Why don't you walk with me to my car while I consider whether I should tell you my name?"

The parking lot was huge and poorly lit. She was parked on the fringe and she edged closer to him as they walked.

"Are you a refugee?" she asked with a directness that caught him off-guard.

"No. I came for other reasons." He hoped the vague response would satisfy her.

"Economic?"

"Isn't everything about economics in the end?"

"I suppose so."

"What do you do for a living?" he asked.

"I don't have to do anything for a living, if I don't want to. But I work for a consumer goods marketing company. Hopefully, this diploma will earn me the jump into the management ranks."

A rich girl, he thought. *Just my luck.* The prospect excited and disappointed him. When they neared her BMW, her social status was confirmed.

"Nice car," he said, glad that his old Mazda was parked a long way off in the opposite direction.

"Daddy's gift for my last birthday." She got into the driver's seat.

"So, do I qualify to get your name?"

She studied him, elbow on the open window as the car's engine rumbled to life, purring like a giant tiger. "I still don't know anything about you. Where you work, what you earn, your hobbies. My family is pretty picky about who I associate with."

He felt smacked. The blood rushed to his face and he was glad for the darkness. "Okay, then Ms. Rich Girl, I'll throw these cards on the table and you can decide if you want to play. My name is Martin James. I am an immigrant. I am a real estate salesman by day. I intend to build my career in the business world and I have only just started. And I aim to be successful. That's the sum total of my credentials."

She put her hands up to silence him. "Passed with distinction! Well said, bravo and all that. My name is Virginia Summers. I'll see you in class next week. Goodnight!" She gunned the engine and took off in a hail of stones and dust.

He had spent the afternoon, as he did most of his free time, in the mall, after two showings at opposite ends of the city. Christmas decorations were already out—it was only mid-November and already the Season was in full swing. He had no friends, he realized. It was too late to make life-friends, like Bandu and Christo, again. He wondered where they were; somewhere in this vast country, struggling with their own challenges of gaining landed status and marketable skills, amidst paying off debts; all that just to get to the base that most Canadians were born into.

The few guys he'd befriended at the community college, and occasionally went out for beers with, were temporary; their conversations would meander from politics to movies, sitcoms (none of which he watched), and finally to hockey or basketball. He had tried to study the big names in the NBA and the NHL so that he could name-drop and belong, but he could not hold his ground when the conversations got more technical. He wished that he had gone to school here; then he would have been a product of this place and would be able to converse and interact unselfconsciously. His only other contacts were customers, and these he kept at arm's length for professional reasons. He deliberately stayed away from the Sri Lankan community, because people were nosy and he did not want to talk about his origins in that country. Hanif's warning still rang in his memory.

A troupe of carollers in top hats went past, melodiously singing their repertoire in four-part harmony. Tired parents lined up with restless kids by Santa's chalet to get their pictures taken. He remembered when Christmas carols ebbed and waned back in the old country, depending on which political party was in power; and the year there were no fireworks when his sister was born, and died. Joy had been rationed back there; frowned on as something never to be pursued. Whereas here it was everyone's right to be happy, to consume, and to ignore the unpleasant. How he wanted to show Barney, Dad and Mum what Canada was really like: the snow, the Christmas lights, the packed malls overflowing with gifts and food that were often remaindered or thrown away. Christmas cards from his father and brother arrived by sea-mail, sometimes long past the event. But the remnants of his family were now in their own isolated worlds, too hard-coded in their imperfections to pry loose and re-unite.

He shrugged off the family memories and tried to focus on the options at hand: to accept Vigo's offer, or not. If he did, he would have a title and a permanent job, and that would impress women like Virginia Summers. Virginia seemed to understand the economics behind relationships. But he would also be throwing away his chances of building something for himself. Choices, choices, why was it such a pain?

He tossed his coffee cup into a nearby garbage can. He loved the order here: no throwing things all over the place and spitting freely in the street—something that had always alienated him from the old country.

He drove back to his apartment; it was time to get ready for his evening class. He passed the unemployment office on the way. People were still in the line-up, as it was not yet closing time; they were laughing and talking among themselves, coffee cups in hand, parkas out against the blustery cold. If only Dad could see this: *you did not lose your dignity just because you lost a job in this country; the government propped you up.* People even played the government for a sucker and cashed in unemployment cheques in every province where they had registered under fake names. That was another of Hanif's package options that Martin had politely declined.

As he dressed for school, the bottle of Vodka on the kitchen table caught his eye. It would be so easy to take the evening off, get drunk and wallow in old memories. That was what Dad had done, and finally Victor had caved into the bottle completely. Martin shook himself. No, that was the road to skid row. He quickly closed the door behind him and left his apartment.

There was no movement from Jamila's side of the hall. Now, whenever they both happened to come out at the same time, she would immediately step back inside her apartment and slam the door. The only other collateral damage from their breakup was the occasional phone call he would receive at night, accompanied by her heavy breathing over the line. The silly woman continued to play the same Madonna music in the background—"Material Girl"— she would obviously make a very poor stalker. After letting her breathe for a few minutes he'd hang up. Once she had called at 3:00 a.m. and he had said, "Aw Jamila, for heaven's sake, call at a decent hour," and slammed the phone down. Now the calls came with declining frequency, before 11:00 p.m. He was hoping she would eventually get over him.

Virginia took his breath away that day. Gone were the smart business clothes he was accustomed to seeing her wearing. She had dyed her hair red and wore a rainbow-coloured sweater, faded denims and cowboy boots. To top it off, a small baseball hat perched on the crown of her head. The transformation was shocking. *So she is a sweats-and-jeans kind of gal after all.* He could not take his eyes off her during the class. She nodded in his direction when she first saw him, but was soon absorbed in her usual pastime of interrogating the lecturer, who now tried avoiding her questions whenever possible.

Today Martin was determined to take their association to a new level. The last few classes since their first meeting had followed a polite routine: casual walks to her car, once for coffee at the cafeteria, and another time over to the library to collect a book she needed. On those occasions she'd asked him more questions than he was able to ask her. He felt as if he was interviewing for a job. Today, he was going to change that.

"A new look for the Season?" he enquired casually as they met after the class.

"I'm expressing myself," she said, straightening the cap on her head.

"I'm sure that cap keeps you warm."

"It's a fashion statement, idiot."

"I bet you didn't go to work like that."

"I took some time off to do my Christmas shopping."

"And what did you buy?"

Her face clouded over and she seemed to be wrestling with a thought. "I haven't started yet. Do you want to help me?"

"What do I have to do?"

"Hold my bags and tell me what a nice purchase I've made each time."

"When do we start?" he asked eagerly.

Her face brightened at his eagerness. "Tomorrow. I'll pick you up at ten o'clock. Where do you live?"

Martin gave her his address. Not wanting to risk another Jamila encounter, he quickly added, "I'll meet you downstairs."

He walked over to his car with lightness in his step. The noose was closing and he hadn't even had to try hard. The attraction was definitely mutual. But there was something else in Virginia that went beyond sexual attraction: her background, her attitude to life, her expectations —they were all so foreign to him, and yet so appealing. Somewhere deep in his DNA, these same longings—which his European ancestry's two hundred year sojourn in Asia had not erased —must have existed.

Virginia, Ginny, as she liked to be called, tossed her head back as they raced along the Don Valley Parkway.

"Your credit cards took a beating today," Martin said.

She laughed and her voice was off key, hysterical in its euphoria.

Martin continued, "Now I know why Canadians have the blahs in February." He was giddy with enthusiasm himself. The morning had been a blast of shopping, only at the best shops —Holt's, Ashley's and in the tiny boutiques of Yorkville. The back seat of the car was strewn with dresses, sweaters, scarves, bone china and leather. His first reaction at the entrance to every high-end shop was not to go in, and Ginny would do the opposite, just push the door open as if she were entering her favourite aunt's house.

"I could get used to this, you know," he said.

"Why don't you? You sell enough houses don't you?"

Martin nodded, even though her comment bothered him. He hadn't sold a house in a month despite taking dozens of clients on showings. The bottom always fell out of the market during the winter; people only window-shopped and vendors held out for higher offers that were sure to come in the spring. That's why Vigo's offer (Martin hoped it was still on the table, as he hadn't called the man back) was so tempting.

"I will get down to paying those bills, you know." Ginny took her eyes off the road to look at him pointedly for a moment. "Daddy only pays me a fixed allowance. I don't ask him to bail me out on my binge-shopping."

Daddy pays her a fixed allowance? Must be nice.

"Why does one need so many clothes?"

"Oh, come on Martin. You only have one life. We work hard. Why not play hard too? That's what my parents have done. They both come from good hardworking stock. You'll meet them one day."

"Oh, I will, will I. Glad I qualify."

She smirked and smacked his arm playfully.

She pulled up at a new apartment building just north of Yonge and Sheppard. A security password typed into a keypad let them into the residents' underground parking lot.

"Will you help me with my bags?"

Why do all Canadian girls interested in a guy, ask the poor sucker to help them indoors with their shopping bags? This time however, he wasn't turning down the offer.

"And bring the gift I bought you. I want you to try it on for me."

He grabbed the only masculine articles in the back seat. They had spent a long time in the men's department at Holt's, looking through various shirt styles until Ginny picked exactly the right shirt: indigo blue with a hint of purple when it caught the light at an angle, and a wingtip collar. The undershirt was a ribbed red. This was going to be a new look for him as he was used only to button-down collars and ties. He followed her into the cosy foyer. A security guard sat at the reception desk, dwarfed by a giant mural of Canadian forest life on the wall behind him. The elevator took them to the fourteenth floor.

"You live in the penthouse," Martin mused, his excitement mounting.

"The top floor," she corrected, unlocking and pushing open the ornate wooden door.

The apartment was tastefully decorated: matching pale pink broadloom and curtains, a heavy dining table and chairs visible to the right, white leather sofa and loveseat in the large living-dining room that ran the length of the apartment, and a ceiling-to-floor bookcase next to an AV cabinet that seemed to have all the accoutrements: stereo, TV, VCR, and speakers. By comparison his apartment was almost bare. He made a mental note to buy those remaining items that make up a typical Canadian home, articles he insisted his clients equip their houses with before listing them.

"It's early for a real drink," she said, going over to a portable bar by the kitchenette. "But I could do with a beer."

"Make that one for me too." He peered through the curtains. Over the bare trees covering the Don Valley, Lake Ontario shimmered under an icy blue sky.

She microwaved two sachets of pre-prepared Chinese chicken stir-fried noodles and they ate it with their beers. She flipped a remote close to hand and a Mozart symphony played in the background.

"You have it good here," he said.

"It will do. For now."

He noticed two closed doors running off the living room, one on either side.

"Is this a two-bedroom apartment?" he asked casually.

She smiled mischievously at him. "I haven't gotten around to showing those off yet."

"I'll wait with bated breath," he said scraping the remnants of his food.

She poured them two small glasses of sherry after their late lunch and curled up on the sofa in the living room. When she faced him, her eyes took on a dreamy look. "Try on your new clothes. Let's see how you look," she said.

"Where do I change?" *Was he sounding too eager?*

She pointed to one of the closed doors. "You can use my bedroom."

He picked up the shopping bag and stepped inside. This room smelled different: soft, feminine; it smelled of when he came near Ginny, only stronger. This was her nest, and he had finally earned the right to enter it. The giant queen-sized bed with its pastel-coloured comforter and pillows, the dresser neatly arranged with perfumes and lotions of varied size and colour, the clothes on hangers visible in different parts of the room, draped over the bed frame or on the dresser stool—ordered disorder—welcomed and soothed him; it made him want to plunge into the bed, pull the covers over him and breath in her essence.

He unbuttoned and tossed his shirt on the bed; the shirt smelled of sweat, and he changed his mind and moved it to the floor. He wished he had bought deodorant and cologne while shopping. The new undershirt was soft, and when he buttoned the indigo shirt over it, it almost completely hid the red underneath. He tucked both garments into his pants. He heard a click behind him. Ginny had followed him in.

She surveyed him. "Oh no, that is not how you wear it. You keep the outer shirt unbuttoned."

"No way! In my country you would be called a rowdy, a hooligan for that."

"Oh, you colonials are such conservatives." She came right up to him, looked deep into his eyes—that dreamy look again—and pulled the shirt and undershirt out of his pants. Then she undid the shirt's buttons, until the outer garment hung like a jacket framing the red underneath. She stepped back and surveyed him. "Much better."

He turned and looked at himself in her wardrobe mirror. He had to admit he looked contemporary. And the cut of the clothes conveyed rugged elegance, not even a hint of hooliganism.

"Those pants don't match," she said, sitting on the edge of the bed.

Their eyes met. He could see the hunger in hers. His heart was beating rapidly and he felt the sweat start from under his arms, staining his new clothes.

"I could take them off," he said gently, deliberately.

She lay back on the bed, throwing her arms over her head. "Please do," she whispered, eyes closed.

When he got home later that evening, he didn't shower. He wanted her warmth, her scent to linger with him. Their lovemaking had possessed an ephemeral quality. Not the carnal, animal grunting and thrusting that occurred with all the women he had slept with before. It was as if carnality had no place in this bedroom with its feminine essence that was now permanently embedded in him and invoked whenever he saw Ginny. She led and he followed, rapidly losing himself in her, pleasing her, and feeling the joy that erupted in his heart as a result.

Surely, this must be love.

He would like to have asked his mother, but she was beyond him now.

Later that night, he went through his bank book and checked his savings. There was enough to put down a deposit on a new car, and on some living room furniture. He would be in debt after that if house sales did not come through. But he was not going to bring Ginny to his apartment in its current state. And tomorrow he would call Vigo.

Martin's heart sank when a breezy Vigo announced on the phone, "Ah, Martin? Why have you taken so long? I hired another guy."

"Sorry, Vigo, it's been a tough decision to make. My own sales are at risk if I accept your offer."

"Ah but you could make much more with me. I have the marketing, Martin, the marketing."

"I know. I'm sorry it's taken so long to come to this conclusion."

"Tell you what, Martin, tell you what. Let's have lunch, okay? The King Eddy. Tomorrow at noon? We can talk about...possibilities."

Martin arrived fifteen minutes early, pacing the cavernous lobby, staring at the photograph of the Queen on the staircase, hoping she would confer some mysterious favours on him through her imperious stare.

Vigo breezed in thirty minutes late, the revolving doors squeezing and thrusting him out into the lobby.

"Ah Martin, you look well. Sorry for the delay, pressing business. Come let's eat. I'm starving."

Over steaks that dripped blood, washed down by a heavy Merlot, Vigo got down to business. "It's like this Martin: I...Telstra...builds these housing estates. Various models: two-bedroom, three-bedroom, with in-law apartments and without. I give them names: the Viscount, the Presidency, the Serendib—all fancy names, marketing, you know. We are on TV, in the newspapers, on flyers, you name it."

"Yes, I've done my research on Telstra Properties. You have many far-reaching tentacles."

"Indeed. You see, I hired this guy to recruit and manage our salespeople. He came highly recommended. Selling our properties in this market—that should be a slam dunk, no? But sales are slow, or at least, he says they are. And he does no selling himself, just sits in the office and waves his hands about at the other staff." He chewed a chunk of steak and blood oozed from the edges of his fat lips. He swallowed, took a swig of wine and said, "Perhaps, I need another sales manager, eh?" Vigo's eyes narrowed and Martin thought he heared clicks going off in the fat Finn's brain.

"It takes time to build a team," Martin said, trying to sound impartial.

"But the leader must be in front of the charge, no?"

"I guess so. At least, that's how I would play it."

"Precisely." Vigo wiped his hands on his napkin and looked at his watch. "I have to leave for an appointment in two minutes. Tell you what Martin, here is the address for our showroom. Get down there this afternoon. I have asked them to give you an associate's badge. Look around. Tell me what's going on, eh?"

"You want me to spy for you?"

"I wanna know if these guys are goofing off. Please Martin, do me this favour, eh? If I go myself they all look so serious and act like they are working hard." Vigo had the ability to go from bullying to pleading in a flash. The pleading look on his face won Martin over.

"Okay. I'll take a look. But only for this afternoon. I'm sure they are not going to take too kindly to a guy like me showing up out of the blue."

"I already phoned Jones—he's the new sales manager—and told him that I had taken on an associate for mutual evaluation. You will be okay."

Vigo tossed some cash on the table, spilling a pile of crumbs from his dark pinstripe suit as he rose from the table. He belched and said, "Before I forget, if you make any sales there this afternoon, you keep the commission, okay?"

Martin called Ginny before he set out for the showroom. He desperately wanted to speak to her, to hear her voice, to tell her that he was making a pitch on a permanent job; he wanted to win her. He couldn't wait until next week when they would meet at class. But her answering machine simply said that she was out and would return calls later. Disappointed, he left her a message. Suddenly he panicked that she might not call back. He tried to recall their moments in bed, their passionate kisses. Surely he amounted to more than a one-afternoon stand? He was not merely the guy who had carried her shopping bags and got a free fuck as his reward? Winning was paramount in his mind when he pulled up at the model home showroom.

The showroom was completely different from Vigo's moth-eaten office off Adelaide Street. Here, the atmosphere was one of quiet elegance. Smartly dressed sales associates stood around smiling and handing out information to the few prospective clients who browsed the miniature models located in the centre of the room. Other rooms led from the main area to a model bathroom, kitchen and bedroom. Martin immediately knew what was wrong here; this was a showpiece, not a hardscrabble sales arena.

A glass-fronted office overlooked the sales floor. Martin went over and knocked. A bearded heavy-set man in his fifties rose, arching an eyebrow.

"I'm Martin James. Vigo sent me."

"Ah yes." The bearded man studied him closely. "The new hire. Bob Jones. I normally hire my people."

"I'm not a new hire. I am an associate with Bradley Realty. I thought I would spend an afternoon here before deciding whether to come on board."

"Or we decide to take you on." The man's voice had edge. He fished inside his drawer and tossed a badge on the table. "Vigo tells me you know the ropes. Just some words of caution: we don't discount, and we treat customers with respect."

No training, no orientation—this guy wants me to fail.

"What's your sales quota for today?" Martin asked, feigning innocence.

"Eh?"

"Aren't you supposed to sell a certain number of units per day?"

Bob Jones look flustered. "Well, uh, we have monthly quotas. We don't break it down to daily numbers. That would lead to competition among our associates, price cutting at the end of the day, and all other unsavoury things. Mr. James, this is a quality establishment. I will be watching you on the floor."

Martin persisted. "Have you sold any units today?"

"We are close on a few." A nervous tic had started to appear over Jones' right eye.

Martin nodded and went back to the sales floor. He could feel Jones' eyes burning holes in his back.

He studied the models and mingled among the customers and sales people. He did not clip on his associate badge yet. The Presidency was the most elegant and the priciest house on sale. People hovered there and quickly moved down to lower-priced models. Martin noticed that sales associates had staked out their turf by model type, they were experts on a model or two at the most; when a customer moved between models and out of the range of knowledge of a sales person, the new associate would start all over with no history on the prospect's inclination to buy.

Martin went back to the Presidency. A middle-aged professional-looking couple were shaking their heads with the sales associate and starting to walk away. Martin followed them and drew within earshot. The woman was the picture of elegance, while the man was dressed conservatively.

"It's a shame that interest rates are going up again. It's going to be out of our range," the woman was saying, casting a longing look back at the miniature model.

"Well, we have to sell our home first, anyway. I doubt we could do that before they jack up interest rates again and the prices go up," the man said, putting his arm around her as they neared the door.

"I don't understand why we can't sell our home in this hot market. Maybe, we're asking too much, Bill."

"Let's sit this out until spring, Elaine. As much as the price goes up on these houses, it will go up on our home too."

"But these models will be all sold out by then."

Not at the rate these jokers are selling them, thought Martin, slapping on his badge and intercepting the couple at the door. "I couldn't help but overhear you, madam. But perhaps I might be of assistance?"

The man looked annoyed. "And how could you, young man? Your very helpful colleague has given us all the information we need. We have too much of a price and time gap to bridge."

"But if you wait till spring, the gap can also widen, no?" Martin said politely.

"He has a point, Bill."

Martin closed in. "Look, I am also a real estate agent with my own listings and clients. Where is your present home located?"

The man fished in his pocket and took out a newspaper clipping. Martin looked at it and immediately recognized the property. He felt his pulse quicken. It was a four-bedroom bungalow in the high-end Willowdale area. Perusing the listings daily, cruising the length and breadth of the city, checking out houses with clients, he knew the background on this property very well. In fact, he had tendered an unsuccessful bid on it very recently; the papers were still in his car. There was certainly a play here, he realized. *If I go about this the right way.*

"Sir, this listing is familiar. I took my clients there three days ago but we were fifteen thousand below your asking price."

"Well, we don't want to undersell in an expanding market."

"Or your agent may have got ahead of himself in his valuation."

"What the hell—?" The man's face was turning a dark crimson.

The woman looked uncomfortable. "Bill, please –"

Martin was used to these outbursts in his daily line of business. "Sir, if you are prepared to go down ten, I'll get my client to go up five. Your home will sell today with a closing in two months. That's a fair market price. I will square things with your listing agent; he'll still earn his commission on the sale. I will also speak to the sales manager here and get you two months deferred payments on your purchase of the Presidency, if you sign today. That will coincide with the closing of your property and you will avoid double payments."

The man gulped and the woman looked adoringly at Martin.

"Do we have a deal, sir?" Martin looked directly at the man, holding his stare.

"How...how are you going to make all this happen?" the man stammered.

"Please have a seat here, I'll be back in a moment."

Martin made sure that the couple were safely ensconced in the foyer and went into Bob Jones' office. "How would you like to sell one of the Presidency models, today?"

"What?" Jones nearly choked. "And we've been having trouble selling the lower-end units because of these damned interest rate hikes they keep talking about in the papers."

"Are you prepared to extend two months of deferred payments?"

Bill Jones started to smile. "Ah, price cutting again are we? Is that how you became the star that Vigo is anxious to hire?"

"Two months extended? Yes or no?"

"Look Mr. Smart Aleck, let's see you work for your commission. I'll extend one month. That's our limit, and only in exceptional cases. Let's see you close this deal."

"Done. I may need to take a short ride across town, after which I'll need your office for an hour with the clients, while I make a few phone calls. Perhaps it's time you spend some time on the floor. There are a lot of deals just walking out the door out there."

As Jones blundered out onto the floor, Martin slipped out through the back door to his car. He rummaged among his papers until he found the old offer-form, crossed and re-crossed and still $15,000 short of the asking price for the property in Willowdale owned by William and Elaine Purvis. He called his client, the prospective buyer on his car phone. Mercifully, he answered after the first few rings.

"Mr. Davidson, its Martin James. Remember the property in Willowdale, the one you and your wife liked? I've got the vendor to come down ten grand…it's an exclusive to you only for the next fifteen minutes. Even his agent doesn't know it yet. Shall I go ahead? I'll just increase our sign-back by five thousand and get his concurrence. Then I'll come over to your office in the next half-hour and get your countersignature. You can call your wife and tell her the good news while I am on my way. The vendor is with me now on another transaction but I can't hold him for long. It's a good deal, Mr Davidson. If we wait any longer, and the rates go up, we'll be paying more than the incremental five thousand for any comparable property. …Thank you, Mr. Davidson, I knew you would go for this. I'll see you shortly."

Martin revised the sale price down by ten thousand and ran back into the showroom. He gave the form to Bill Purvis. "Please sign here, sir. And then we'll get the buyer's counter-signature. Sorry, it's a little ass-backwards, but it will be all sorted out, you'll see."

After he had the signatures, Martin said, "Let's go for a short drive to see your buyer, and we can be back here before closing time to buy your dream home." He bundled them into his car and drove like a maniac across the city to his client's office. Never leave clients to wander when you are hot on the close of a deal; keep them where you can see them—a mantra he had learned from many a botched deal. Leaving them in the car, he darted up four flights of stairs to Mr. Davidson's office. His open-mouthed client couldn't believe that he was buying the house by paying only a five thousand dollar premium over three days ago. Martin shook his hand vigorously. "I'll be back with champagne later this evening, Mr. Davidson. Thank you for the business."

Leaving his nonplussed but happy client, Martin dashed back to his car and waved the signed agreement at his two passengers. "You have just sold your house. Now let's go buy you a new one."

"Bravo!" said the woman in the back seat, smiling from ear to ear.

Back at the Telstra showroom, Martin ushered them into Bob Jones' office and they went over the sales agreement for the Presidency. At the section where the payment commencement date was, Martin scrawled "two months deferred" with a start date of Feb 1ˢᵗ 1987.

"I'll get my sales manager's signature on this one and be right back," Martin said. "Mr. Jones is still on the floor."

Elaine Purvis grabbed him by the sleeve before he stepped out. "Martin, we want to tell you how grateful we are for what you have done today. How can we reward you?"

"Oh, no need. Mrs. Purvis. But if you get a chance, you may want to phone this gentleman. He's the owner. Tell him how satisfied you were with Telstra." He slipped her one of Vigo's business cards.

Outside, Martin pulled out his cheque book and wrote a cheque for eighteen hundred dollars, equal to one month's payment on the Presidency after down payments were accounted for. He figured his share of the commission on the sale in Willowdale and the sale of the Presidency would more than compensate for this little kick-back—and it wasn't going back to the client directly.

He found Bob Jones idling around a sales associate who was explaining the merits of another model home.

"Mr. Jones," Martin interrupted him. "I need your signature on this contract of sale."

Bob Jones' eyes widened. He did not seem sure whether to praise or criticize at that moment. Instead he took the document and scanned it, dumbstruck. Suddenly, he pounced on the amended section. "I said one month deferred, not two."

Martin handed Bob Jones his personal cheque. "And here is your second month's deferred payment. You are not out of pocket."

"But this is unethical."

"It sells houses, Mr. Jones. You got your price, the clients got their house sold at market price and bought their dream house. No one loses. Are you going to sign? Or do I tell Mr. Matinsen that his outfit is not worth joining as you never sold a single house while I was here this afternoon."

Martin heard the man's teeth grind as he signed the papers.

Martin smiled. "Now, Mr. Jones, as sales manager, I'm sure you will want to finalize the paperwork and talk to your new clients and tell them what a fine purchase they have made."

When he got home after the champagne toast with the Davidsons, Martin felt exhilarated by the dual sale, but disappointed as he still had no message from Ginny. He stared at the silent phone with its unlit message light. Where the hell was she? Was she avoiding him after what had happened?

The phone rang and he grabbed it.

"Martin!" It was Vigo. "Martin, fantastic job, my boy. I thought those models were never going to sell."

"Word travels fast," Martin replied, deflated that it was not Ginny. "Did Bob call you about it? Hope I wasn't too much of a distraction for him today."

"No, Martin—our customers, the Purvis's, called. Mrs Purvis couldn't stop singing your praises."

"Oh, well thank you. I was kind of lucky because I was familiar with their existing home."

"No, no, my boy, you have the instinct. And you understand the customer—what is good and what is bad for them. And they appreciate it."

Martin continued to stammer his thanks.

"Listen Martin, you have the job. You can start tomorrow."

"But Bob Jones—"

"There is no more Bob Jones. I gave him notice after Mrs. Purvis called."

"But—" Martin couldn't believe his gamble had paid off.

"There are no 'buts,' Martin. We can't leave the showroom unmanaged. I need you in there ASAP. Do you accept?" It was more a command than a request, and Martin couldn't help suppress a laugh. The exhilaration slowly began to seep in. Vigo was a bastard and would fire him too if productivity dropped, but that was something Martin could handle.

"Sure boss. I'll see what I can do to help."

When he put down the receiver he felt like screaming to the walls, to his absent Ginny, to tell her that he had just won a battle for her.

11. **Moving up the Food Chain**

Martin did not see Virginia again until after the Christmas holidays. Following their romantic tryst, she did not show up for the next class, the final one before the holiday break, and that left him chewing his finger nails until the New Year.

He poured his focus into the new job and into upgrading his apartment. His coup on the sale of the Presidency model had earned him brownie points even before he arrived at Telstra. The staff looked up to him for leadership and he put some immediate changes in place, converting the sales team into "customer agents." They were to trail their prospects from the time of arrival to the time of departure, and had to become familiar with every model of home on the floor. The staff had to compile data sheets on each customer and follow-up, since sales often concluded months after the initial visit. The mere "brochure bunnies," he fired. Sales started to pick up, as Martin added himself to the list of active agents and introduced an incentive for the highest-selling agent of the month.

He put down a deposit and drove off with a brand new Cadillac Seville, and ordered a suite of living-room furniture from Simpsons, a splurge made possible by the commissions he received on the sales of the two properties for the Purvises. As the delivery men started to fill out his bare living room, he mused on how little he had left Sri Lanka with: a suitcase with a few clothes and personal belongings. Despite his early misgivings, this *was* the land of opportunity.

The day before he returned to class he saw an article in the newspaper that got his heart racing: an immigration bust. The grainy picture showed Hanif being escorted in handcuffs between two plain-clothes cops. Hanif did not even have the customary hood over his face. Would the immigration authorities limit their efforts to merely cutting off Hanif's pipeline of clients waiting to enter the country, or would they go poking around in his backlist as well—uncovering people like Martin, now on visas and gainfully employed? Martin had that uneasy feeling of being watched creep into him again. He figured that the only avenue open to him, now that he had a permanent job, was to apply for landed immigrant status and put as many official barriers between him and the unofficial ones that had first brought him to this country. He would probably need an immigration lawyer as he was going about this ass-backwards, being in the country already, and applying for landed status from within. To his advantage were the rumoured paperwork snarls in Immigration and lack of proper record keeping, but there was also talk of improved automation coming in to provide more efficient processing. He had to move now, before his murky trail could be more easily unearthed.

Ginny showed up in class the next day, back in her formal business attire, hair returned to blonde, which he now knew was her natural colour. She nodded briefly, averting her eyes as soon as they traded silent greetings, and focused on the instructor for the rest of the lecture. Martin caught up with her at the door as she hurriedly made an exit along with the rest of the students.

"Ginny, what's going on? You didn't return my calls."

She brushed past without answering, but he kept on her heels. When they were out in the courtyard, she eased up and turned to face him. "This was probably a bad idea."

"What? Us?"

"We live in two different worlds, Martin."

"We live in Canada, Ginny."

"I spent the holidays with my family in Rosedale. That's when it came home to me. My world is full of people with big suburban houses, cottages on the lake, boats, golf, drinks at the club. The men my parents constantly introduce me to are solid corporate jocks: Upper Canada College, McGill or U of T stars, looking for the trophy wife who will bestow them two spoilt children they can indulge for the rest of their lives. Don't you get it?"

Martin's eyes flashed. "And do you like that world?"

She walked in silence, head bowed. "No. But I can't seem to do anything about escaping from it."

"Oh yes, you can. We all can. If I tell you my life story one day, you will *know* that we can."

She paused and looked back at him. "Walk with me to my car. Let's just talk okay? I'm fragile at the moment."

He had parked the new Seville strategically next to the space she normally parked in. They walked in silence until they neared her car. She allowed him to hold her hand tentatively.

When they arrived at her parking spot, she remarked cynically, "Nice car, that Seville. Glad I'm not the only rich kid in school."

"Must be one of your big jock types, come to learn some practical skills," he said, and clicked the door locks of the Seville open with his key fob.

She gasped. "That's *your* car?"

"There were a lot of things I wanted to share with you over Christmas, but you weren't around."

Her look of dejection seemed to have temporarily vanished. "Tell me more."

"Get in first. I'll take you for a spin. I promise to bring you back before they close the gates on us."

Inside the Seville, the new smell of the upholstery had special appeal to him today with Ginny by his side. He told her about the new job.

"And all this in a couple of weeks?" She was wide-eyed.

"Where I come from you have to move fast, Ginny. Or there are lots more people to take your place."

"I envy you, Martin. I seem to have everything made for me. There is nothing to try for. I insist on working and making my way in life because that little bit is mine. You see what I mean? My parents push the hard-work ethic at us but it's difficult to feel serious about it when my brother and I have large inheritances coming our way."

"And I envy you too. Does that make us a couple?" He was smiling now. They were pulling back into the parking space beside her car. On impulse he reached out and pulled her to him, and she let him. He closed his lips on hers, and they kissed hungrily for a long time.

"Goodnight, Ginny. I'll talk to you in the morning," he said confidently. "You will pick up the phone, right?"

She smiled as she lingered with her hand in his. "Yes. This time I will."

"Promise?"

"Promise."

As he backed his car out, she called after him, her voice small and feeble. "Martin—"

"Yes?"

"There are a lot of things you don't know about me. But thanks!"

For the next six months, theirs was a picture-book romance. Evenings spent mostly at her place, studying together, taking breaks to make love, sipping wine by the fireplace, and having meals delivered in. She loved Italian and Japanese food. The first time she came to his apartment, she nodded approval at the way in which he had furnished it. He had gone to the extra trouble of setting up candles in every room, buying some classical CDs and stocking up on expensive red wine and liqueurs. The cheap Vodka he poured down the sink, and he trashed the empty bottles. The visitor washroom was elegantly decorated with soaps, towels and hand creams—all matching.

"A functional bachelor apartment, suitable for a woman. Do you have many lady visitors?" She looked at him teasingly, stretching out on the new leather sofa that was still exuding its factory-fresh aroma. For once he wished it wouldn't smell as if he'd bought it only to impress her.

"You could drive them all away," he said going into the kitchen to open the wine.

The phone rang in the living room and she boldly picked it up before he could take it. He continued to pour the wine. When he returned she was amusedly hanging up. "You certainly have lady stalkers," she said.

Oh, damn! Jamila.

"This is a crazy country, what can I say. I get all sorts of cranks calling me," he replied keeping a straight face, trying to be nonchalant.

"I'd say. Whoever she was, that woman sounded pretty pissed to hear me on the phone. Sounded like a jaded lover."

"Well, you're starting to drive them out already. Cheers!"

She raised her glass slowly. "Cheers!"

He put on a Beethoven symphony; the sixth, gentle, bucolic.

"You would tell me if there are others, wouldn't you?" she said.

He went over to her, kissed her on the eyes, and said, "Look at me, there *is* no other. You are the biggest gift I have received since coming to this country."

She studied his face carefully, inspecting, verifying, until the doubts started to fade. She smiled and kissed him back. "Tell me about your life. About your other girlfriends."

"I'll tell you about my life," he said. "Girlfriends have come and gone. Not one left a mark."

"Tell me about life in Sri Lanka. My Dad still calls it Ceylon."

He got up and paced. He had never told anyone in Canada about his life in Sri Lanka. There were parts that he couldn't disclose. But that life had been sitting like a millstone around him for many years. The only way he could bear it was to bury it and embrace the new life and its own set of challenges. To sit and pause and talk about the old—he did not know how he would handle it.

"There are a lot of bad parts..." he began.

"Start slowly. Tell me the easy parts first. The happy parts."

He poured more wine.

He began to talk...slowly.

He enjoyed those months. Gradually he was able to unburden everything that had been hidden inside. There were times when he cried. And she cried too, though not at the same parts. She cried when he told her about his sister's birth. He cried when he talked about his mother's descent into dementia, while Ginny remained strangely quiet. There were parts when they both had to stop, go for a walk, and continue later. His tale unfolded only in his apartment; her place was for the present, he told her—it was his escape; he did not want to tarnish it with ghosts.

There was only one blemish during that time, and it occurred on the day he came to her apartment unexpectedly and found her asleep at noon. After many rings of the doorbell, he was about to leave when he heard a sound on the other side of her door.

"Ginny, it's me. I dropped in to take you out for lunch."

"Go away." Her voice sounded heavy, muffled.

"Hey, don't spoil the surprise for me."

"Go away. I'm not feeling well. I can't go out."

"Then I'll bring food in. Italian or Japanese? Or do we want to try something from a completely different part of the world?"

"I'm not hungry. I just want to sleep."

"Then I'll come in and sleep with you."

"You'll live to regret it."

The lock scraped, and she stood in the doorway, dressed in her pyjamas, her hair a tangled mess, eyes puffy and red. It was the way in which she looked at him that was creepy: a cold, piercing stare that sent a chill down his spine.

"These exams are screwing me up. Too much pressure," she said.

"Perhaps, I'll come back at dinner time, then."

"Whatever," she said staring at him. "Call before you come. Never come unannounced."

He stayed away that evening, disturbed by this new image of her. When he saw her at class two days later, she was back to normal, ebullient, professional, her charming self. It was as if he had seen a stranger on the previous occasion.

In the spring, they both passed their marketing course with distinction and had a joint celebration at her place, making love several times throughout the evening and into the following morning.

Summer was starting to arrive when she asked him how he had come to Canada. Who had sponsored him? This was the part he had omitted in all his unburdening.

"I can't tell you about that yet," he said.

She looked quizzically at him.

"There was an irregularity with my landing papers. I am seeing a lawyer to get it fixed. When it's in place I will tell you. It's confidential."

"You told me you weren't a refugee. So what's the problem?"

"I'll tell you when I am ready to talk about it."

Summer also brought a thaw across the corridor. He heard sounds of a huge commotion in Jamila's apartment as he waited for the elevator one morning. Suddenly she poked her head out, saw him, and stepped out into the corridor. He was taken aback by her transformation.

She had lost at least fifty pounds, had cut her hair short and done a face makeover. She looked quite pretty. And she hadn't been phoning him in the last month.

"Jamila. You look great!"

"I'm getting married!" she announced triumphantly, a hint of haughtiness in her posture.

"Why, that's wonderful news." He was happy for her, and relieved. Perhaps now the calls would cease altogether. "Who's the lucky guy?"

"My second cousin in Guyana. My parents arranged the marriage. He is coming over to Canada next week. We're getting married next month."

"Wow! Congratulations!"

"Of course, I don't love him." Her voice had dropped down to a whisper, as if worried her parents might overhear. "Not yet, anyway."

"Oh, well, you'll grow to love him over time. It happens in all arranged marriages. At least, you won't have to waste a lot of time in the searching stage."

"And you? I've seen that white girl you bring over all the time. Is she the Russian?"

"No. She was born here."

She looked at him enviously. "So have you also finished your searching stage then?"

He sighed. He wished it could be as easy as Jamila suggested. "I'm not sure yet, Jamila. I'd like to think that I have. The gods may conspire to send me on another adventure before my search ends."

"Best of luck, Martin. I'm sorry we didn't work out. Will you come to my wedding?"

"Of course. All the best to you too." He stepped into the elevator.

As he descended he wondered what had prompted him to make that prophetic statement. He still had to meet Virginia's family. And why had it taken so long? Why was she keeping him like a well-hidden secret away from the rest of her life? At the same time, he had been content to enjoy those evenings with her in her apartment, and the confessional-like therapy in his.

He drove to his lawyer's office. He had met this lawyer twice already, and paid dearly for each visit. His case was dicey. There were two years of his life that he had to erase: the ones preceding his receiving the student visa. And yet he had been in Canada during that period, selling encyclopaedias, working in factories, leaving a record of his presence on people, none of which could come out when he tried to upgrade his student visa to a landed immigrant's.

His lawyer, Jim Duffield, was in his late fifties; bald, thickset, but with a kind smile, as if he saw things in the future that his clients could not foresee.

"I've prepared your case as best as I can, Martin. Let's submit it, and see how it progresses."

"What are my chances?"

"Fifty-fifty. If they accept it on the surface, you should be okay. If we stumble on an ambitious young officer who decides to go digging, we could have problems."

"But you have contacts..."

"I may bend the law Martin, but I don't break it. There are parts of your case that are... let's say...murky. I accepted your case, because I think you are a fine young man who will pay this country a lot of taxes over his working life, and who deserves a break. And you have been honest with me. I have seen far less worthy people get through."

"So I have paid you a lot of money to only get a fifty-fifty chance?"

"Yes."

Before Martin could reply, the door to Duffield's office burst open and a younger man in a dark suit hung on the door.

Ignoring the client-lawyer discussion in progress, the intruder announced, "Our clients on the Waterford project are here."

Duffield looked annoyed at this disturbance and put down his pen, leaning back in his large chair. "I am still in this meeting, Tim. I'll be over shortly."

Tim grinned nervously, but stood his ground. Martin gave him a stare, as if to say, *Asshole, does my money not count?* Tim stared through Martin as if he did not exist.

"You know how sensitive they are at this stage, Jim. I wouldn't like to keep them waiting too long."

Duffield, picked up his pen again. "I'll be right over. Give them a cup of tea, and have a nice little chat. Close the door, will you, Tim, so I can get this meeting concluded." Duffield turned back to Martin's file. The door clicked shut slowly. Martin suppressed a smile.

"As I was saying, Martin, unless we get an ambitious young immigration officer," he gestured with his head towards the door, "like my junior partner out there, we should be good. Leave this with me for now." He rose and extended his hand, that faraway into-the-future look returning to his face.

As Martin passed the boardroom on his way out, he saw the junior partner serving tea to three dark-suited men with grey hair, who were poring over various files and folders. Yet Martin had not even warranted a glass of water all the while he had been there.

"Would you like to come to my parents' cottage for the weekend?" Virginia popped the question out of the blue one evening. Then she added quickly, "No one will be there. My family is down in New York at a wedding of one of my mother's friends."

"Is this my introduction to the inner sanctum?"

She smiled. "I thought I'd show you the cave first, one of the caves, anyway, before I introduce you to the animals."

It was the weekend of Jamila's wedding. But this cottage visit was more important.

"Sure," he said without batting an eyelid.

That evening on the way home from work, he stopped in at Holt's and bought a silver dinner platter, and had it gift-wrapped. He appended a huge wedding card and delivered it to Jamila's apartment. Her mother, a dowdy woman with unkempt hair, dressed in an ankle-length housecoat, came to the door.

"Jamila's not home," she said, keeping the door ajar.

"I have this gift for her." He held it out. Immediately the door swung open and the woman beamed.

"Acha, you have spent a lot of money on this, no? Come in and have a cool drink."

"No, I can't stay. Please give this to her. Also please tell her that I cannot come to the wedding. I have to go away on a business trip."

The woman showed disappointment, but quickly took the gift from him. "Ah, I will tell her."

He left her turning the gift over in her hands and looking as if she would like to tear open the wrapping to check the contents.

That night, he got the famous stalker call again. Only this time, the stalker decided to talk.

"Martin, are you there? Why are you not coming to the wedding?"

"Didn't your mother give you the message?"

"She gave me some cock and bull excuse. Why are you avoiding me again?"

"Listen Jamila, we are both moving into different worlds now. I am not sure we were ever in the same orbit, even though we live across the same floor."

"But I don't love him, Martin. And he is twenty years older. Married and divorced with two teenage children also."

He genuinely felt sorry for Jamila, a sheltered girl from the colonies. He'd seen plenty of them in his time; and this progressive society had only helped to further shrink Jamila into her nook of limited experience. She wouldn't get quality from a divorce´ straight off the boat. By the same token, with her narrow view of the world, she'd drive a man in this country crazy, or into the arms of another woman.

"Jamila, you are going to have to stop calling me like this after you marry. Your husband will not take kindly to it."

"Do you think he will beat me up? Someone related to him, who is living in Toronto, told me that he beat up his first wife."

"Well, if he lays a hand on you, you let me know. But otherwise, I think I need to tread my own path for a while."

"Okay, okay Martin. I will leave you alone for now. But I'll call you if he turns nasty, okay? Thank you for the help. My parents don't understand. They only want me settled, by hook or by crook."

"Goodnight, Jamila. And good luck."

They drove out into Muskoka, where the road meandered through woods, and lakes appeared around every bend. Boat yards, fish & tackle shops flashed by, and powerful motorcycles and jeeps suddenly burst into view and disappeared down the road. Turning off highway 169 just past the town of Gravenhurst, Ginny's car ambled down a gravel path until it ended at a fence with a wrought iron gate. She parked the car, opened the gate and hauled her bag out. "Come along."

He followed her into a glade of pine trees that went uphill and then veered sharply down towards the water. The lake ran at a hundred and eighty degree arc in front of them. The cottage—it looked more like a large bungalow—lay on the down-slope to their left; its front, propped up with wooden pillars, facing the water. Two boats sporting outboard motors lolled in the gentle waters, slopping against the long white-boarded dock.

"Good. Smithy has taken the boats out of the boathouse."

"Who is Smithy?"

"Oh, he's our caretaker. Lives in town but looks after the property. I phoned him to stock up the fridge and the cellar."

"Hmm, this sounds more like a first-class hotel than a rustic cottage with outdoor toilets and no running water."

"Outdoor toilets?" she said, feigning a look of mortification. "That went out of fashion when my mother was a child. She often reminds us of her good farming stock and their heritage, whenever she wants Tim and me to put extra effort into life."

"I'd like to meet your mother."

"Don't be too sure about that. She is not called the 'dragon lady' for nothing."

The house had six bedrooms, each with its own shower and toilet.

"My parents entertain a lot," Ginny explained. "But we can use my bedroom."

Hers was on the ground floor towards the back of the house, and was a replica of the one in her apartment: same colours, same soft comforter, even the same dresser. "My home away from home," she clarified as he raised an eyebrow.

After settling in, they sipped beers on the deck. Smithy had done his job: the fridge was full of beer and white wine; the reds were in a ceiling-high rack in the kitchen. The pantry was stocked with tinned goods and the freezer loaded with steaks, sausages, racks of lamb and fish fillets.

"Does Smithy also cook?" Martin asked after the second beer had mellowed him.

Before she could answer, a man, wearing a white canvas hat, stepped out from behind the trees on the extreme right end of the property and waved.

"Smithy, what are you doing here at this time of day?"

"Hi Miss Virginia. I come down to trim some bushes over on this side. Nice to see you." He surveyed Martin with a mixture of curiosity and amusement. He doffed his hat at Martin. The man was bald, trim and red faced in the heat; he must have been about seventy.

"Can we get the barbecue going, Smithy?" Virginia asked casually.

"Oh sure, miss. What'll you be wanting—hamburgers? I got some fresh ones in the store this morning. They are sitting in your fridge waiting to go."

"Let's do the fish instead, Smithy." She looked at Martin for acquiescence and he nodded. "I'd leave the meat for Father and Tim."

They lunched on a sumptuous repast of garden salad, jacket potatoes and halibut filets sautéed in Smithy's concoction of spices, washed down with a mild Sauvignon Blanc. Afterwards, Ginny made them cappuccinos from the machine in the kitchen.

Smithy cleaned up and departed after lunch, taking extra containers of the left-over fillets and salad with him "for the Missus."

"Let's ride the lake." Ginny pulled him down to the water, when Martin would have preferred to snooze in the hammock under the trees.

She took them out in one of the boats, skillfully navigating through water skiers and a couple of daring, or drunk, jet-skiers trying to outrun each other across the water.

"I grew up on this lake," she said as they cruised into gentler waters, in the shadow of tall spruce that skirted the water's edge. "Summer was an unending series of swimming, boating and bonfires at night. Later, we had parties and there were boys, but none who interested me. They all seemed cut from the same mould. I guess I'm like my father. He's an old colonial; served in India and the Middle East in the sixties; loved to travel in the east."

"Did he ever take you to Asia?"

"He got too busy building the family empire after he married Mother. We only managed to go as far south as Italy for holidays, and once he took me to Japan on one of his business trips."

"Ah, that's why you like Italian and Japanese cooking. Would you like to eat Sri Lankan one day?"

"Isn't it the same as Indian? Dad likes curry."

"It's different. It's hotter. I'd like to think that our rotis, hoppers, string hoppers and sambols are unique. But like Canadians living in the shadow of all things American, Sri Lankans seem to live under the shadow of their northern neighbour."

"Okay, I'll try Sri Lankan. Will you cook it for me?"

"Sure. It's been awhile, but I'll try the next time at my place."

Later that evening, they dined in town, at an elegant restaurant with a strict dress code and where reservations were required. Many of the diners looked like regulars and nodded at Ginny, while looking curiously but politely at Martin.

They sat in the open-air patio deck that ran out above the lake; the water slapped gently against the pilings underneath as they sipped Merlot and counted the stars. The carrot soup was lightly tinged with ginger and the game fowl was deliciously herbed with a mixture of parsley, cilantro and oregano, and bathed in a red wine sauce.

They kissed before bed, out on the dock back at the cottage, as the moon rose overhead and covered the lake with a healing glow. "Do you think the two of us will work out, Martin?" Ginny asked, a worried frown on her face.

"Of course. Why not?"

"I don't know. This is just too perfect, I suppose. It looks like a scene out of a movie, and I don't dig sappy movie scenes."

"I've not had too many movie scenes in my life. Horror scenes, yes. So I'll buy this one." He buried his face in her soft hair, gleaming in the night as the moonlight caught it.

The next day she took him out to play golf. He had never swung a club in his life; Colombo had only one golf course, and it was reserved for the elite, most of whom could not swing golf clubs either, but used membership to highlight their status. Martin had never been able to afford the membership fee, a set of clubs, or the tips to the caddies.

He soon realized that his ability to play cricket was an immense help here. Golf was also a mental game, and the calmer he was, the better he hit the ball.

"Calm your mind and play the same stroke repeatedly," Ginny advised him as she swung her driver off the fourth tee for 180 yards. "It was a recommended therapy for me."

"What were you suffering from?"

She sounded dismissive as she lined up her next shot. "Oh the usual stuff of growing up in a rich family."

Despite her advice and his attempts to "calm the mind," his competitive nature interfered and he lost quite a number of balls by the time they had completed the last hole.

"I'll be back," he concluded. "This looks like another challenge worth attempting. I need to take lessons."

As they drove back to the club house, he looked at the manicured fairways and picture-book greens nestled in groves, water and sand, and wanted to belong in this environment. He had been shut out from the good things in life for too long.

On their last evening, she took him for a long hike into the woods. They skipped along dry ski trails, down narrow animal pathways, deeper into the underbrush, and as the sun went down, the temperature dropped rapidly; mosquitoes hummed and loons cried off in the distant water.

"Don't worry I've walked these paths several times and cross-country skied them in the winter," she said.

He let her lead the way, comfortable in her ability to get them back to the cottage. The woods were benign compared to the dry, snake-ridden jungles he had walked through in the old country. And the mosquitoes here did not carry malaria, nor did the woods harbour terrorists or insurgents.

"Sometimes, when the cottage was full of guests, I'd come camping out here for the night. Tim was supposed to accompany me, but he'd get bored and head back. Dad would come out before I went to bed to check on me. I loved reading a book under my flashlight and listening to the frogs croak."

"Well, there's one thing we have in common—frogs. There were lots where I was growing up. Some even came inside the house during the rainy season."

He put his arms around her and she leaned into him. He kissed her again. "You don't have to be worried about us, Ginny. I'll take up any test you want me to stand."

"You never give up do you?"

"No. Giving up was never an option for me."

"Let's head back. Those pesky mosquitoes are really starting to bite now."

The invitation to the Summers' city home in Rosedale followed soon after that visit to the cottage. This time the rest of the family would be gathered to meet him, Ginny told him.

Martin spent a sleepless night before the visit. He had his best suit dry cleaned, bought a new shirt and tie from the Georgio Armani store, but opted not to buy a new pair of shoes for fear of getting a blister and giving the game away. He scrubbed and polished his pair of black tasselled dress shoes instead. He left work early and visited the hairdresser. He showered, and perfumed himself well. He was going to be as ready as ever. But as he left his apartment, he felt the dampness under his arms and his palms were clammy.

Ginny picked him up outside his apartment and while she drove, he refreshed his memory of the family history, driblets of which he had received from her over the months. Ginny's mother, a fifth generation Canadian had inherited several farms in the country. Ginny's father, an English immigrant, and a management accountant by profession, had helped convert the farms into a holding company that funded several successful start-up ventures. Martin did not know much about her brother, but decided to wait until he met him.

The house was a huge three-storey stone monstrosity with a turret on one side. The gardens were immaculately manicured and coloured with white and red roses, orange poppies, hyacinths, daisies and more exotic flora that Martin couldn't identify. A sprinkler worked idly on the close-cropped drenched lawn.

The entrance hall was cavernous with large Renaissance paintings on the east and west walls. A giant fish tank ran across the south wall and assorted fish titillated the eye with their vibrant multi-hues. For a fleeting moment, Martin felt like he was in a giant fish tank himself, but shook off the feeling and let Ginny lead him into the living room. He remembered the old Senanayake Walauwe; even though the furnishings were different, that sense of not belonging was as strong as ever.

The family was gathered in the living room, standing about the bar. The father, a short, portly man, threatening to burst out of his dinner jacket, had red hair, a florid complexion and handlebar moustache dapperly accented by a crimson bowtie; the mother, dressed in a black evening gown, was angular and silver-haired with a neatly contrived black streak running down the centre. He later recalled that the mother had studied him far more than the others all evening, even though she generally exuded a detached air. Martin stared when he saw the brother, close-cut hair already thinning at the top, with stooped shoulders and wearing a sweater that accentuated his soft pot belly. This was the young lawyer who had interrupted him and Jim Duffield the other day. The brother dropped a quick hint of recognition, nodded absently, and turned away.

The father had already walked up and was extending a hand. "George Summers. How do you do, young man?"

"Martin James, sir. Very well. Glad to meet you."

Ginny slipped her arm around her father and kissed him affectionately on the ear. "Oh, do call him George, Martin. I do."

"They all do," the father laughed throatily. "Can I get you a drink, Martin?"

"Beer, sir...er...George."

The mother wrinkled her nose from her perch by the bar and the brother turned to refill his glass of red wine.

Ginny sensed the remoteness of her mother and brother and said loudly to Martin, gesturing with exaggerated flourish, "And this is my mother, Clarissa, Clarice as she is known around here. And my wastrel older brother, Tim, who will never find a woman worthy enough to marry."

"Touché," her father said raising his glass of scotch and ice.

Tim grimaced at the bar.

"It will be Mrs. Summers to you Martin, if you don't mind," Clarice said, detaching herself from the bar, white-wine glass in hand. "I'll see if dinner is ready." She sailed out of the room without a backward glance.

"Mother takes some time to warm up to people," Ginny explained, blushing. "I'll go and lend her a hand."

Martin figured that they were going to have a little "talk."

"Oh, don't worry about Clarissa," George said, handing Martin a beer in an ornate metal tankard. The elder Summers immediately launched into reminiscences of working in the Middle East and India. "In Oman, they rarely had air conditioning. We slept with the refrigerator door open on hot nights. Come to think of it, every night was hot."

He wanted to know if Sri Lankan curries were like those he had tasted in Madras where he had also been stationed. Martin explained the subtle differences in the flavouring. "We eat meat and poultry in Sri Lanka, whereas the Madrasis are mainly vegetarian."

"Do you guys eat dogs, too? Like they do in the Philippines?" Tim suddenly piped up from the bar. He had a silly grin on his face, taunting, almost.

"No we don't. I had a dog once as a pet."

"How come you speak English so well?" Tim continued unabashed. "The Sri Lankans who come to our office to get my senior partner's help can barely string two words together."

Martin smiled back. "Perhaps you have the wrong types of clients. My mother tongue is English." He left it at that. If Tim wanted more he could go figure it out.

"Dinner is served," Ginny announced, coming out of the dining room.

Dinner was a disaster, Martin recollected later. To his left Tim kept up his periodic barbs, while directly in front of him, Clarissa continued to study him as if he were a lab rat: how he handled his cutlery, how many times he picked up his napkin to wipe his mouth, how much wine he drank, how he talked between mouthfuls. Ginny for the most part was silent, observing too, letting Martin deal with the situation without trying to be overly helpful. The only time she jumped in was when Tim asked Martin what his major in university was; Ginny interrupted with a, "Well Tim, Sri Lanka does not have an Upper Canada College and a University of Toronto, so you will not understand the equivalents of what Martin has studied. But he is a Marketing graduate from Seneca College, same as me." Martin used this interruption to duck the question and resume a conversation with George Summers.

Clarissa asked questions about Martin's family. He had prepared for this one.

"They are all dead," he said. Explanations would have been too complicated at this stage. Ginny raised her eyebrows but said nothing.

George was by far the most affable and accommodating, elaborating on his business ventures: the family owned a printing company, a photography studio and the most recently opened semi-conductor factory. Martin gathered that the first two were stable cash cows while the new venture was on a rapid growth path.

"We took some risks and they paid off," George said, with a self-satisfied burp, downing his glass and reaching for the red wine yet another time.

George had poured wine liberally during the meal and Martin had been helping himself to a few glasses whenever offered; it took some of the edge off the evening.

"What risks have you taken in your life, Martin?" Clarissa asked coolly, as the maid took away the remnants of the main course of roast duck.

The wine was starting to hit him at this stage, and Martin decided it was time to loosen up.

"Living in Sri Lanka was one."

"How so?"

Martin downed his red wine and launched into an account of the '71 insurrection. "Everyone knows about the present Sinhala-Tamil conflict in the north of the country, but we had one in our own backyard in Colombo, when I was growing up." He described with growing vividness the bodies floating down the river, the curfews, tension in the streets when one did not know who was an insurgent and who wasn't; the futile end to the conflict with so many young students dead, and the country still teetering on bankruptcy and slumping into the throes of an even deeper conflict between the Tamils and the Sinhalese.

"Barbaric," concluded Clarissa.

"Balls. This looks like something out of a B movie," said Tim, who had been listening despite his feigned air of disinterest.

"You have to live there to really experience what I have told you. My recounting makes it sound like a scary fairy tale."

"I can imagine that." George surfaced from the dazed stupor he had slumped into during Martin's recounting. "Vietnam was a similar story."

"And how did you get across to Canada, Martin?" Tim asked sweetly.

"I took a plane," Martin said and focussed on the excellent dessert of crème brulée.

"Isn't he a survivor?" Ginny exclaimed. "He also likes Homer. I call him my "Ulysses Man.""

Driving back with Ginny later that evening, Martin was quiet. Had he passed the test?

"I'll call you in the morning," she said. "It's been a long day for both of us."

"How did I do?"

"You were yourself, Martin. Except for the bit about your family. Why did you say they were all dead?"

"Do you think your family will ever meet mine? Sri Lanka is a world your folks will never set foot in. And mine are never going to come out here. Why complicate things at this early stage by saying that my father is an alcoholic, my mother a lunatic and my brother is lost somewhere in the country?"

She nodded quietly. "You did well. And for that, I am proud of you."

"Tim took an instant dislike to me. And your mother—"

She placed her finger on his mouth. "Shh. Forget about them. I reached a conclusion at dinner while watching them at their horseplay. I am not one of them, Martin. If at all, I resemble my father, that's why I love him so much. And I am going to do what I damn well please, just like he did. Goodnight. I need to sleep on all this—alone."

"Goodnight, Ginny." When he walked up the steps to his apartment he had a sudden misgiving that she would drive away and her mother and brother would chain her in that cavernous dungeon of a house and never allow her to see the light of day—or him—again.

12. **The Price at the Top**

Martin sold three houses that day. Vigo was ecstatic; he visited the showroom before closing time and popped a champagne cork. "To the best damned salesman I've ever met," Vigo said toasting loudly with the other staff, who begrudgingly had to admit that the big boss was right: Martin had chalked up the most sales among the team since coming on board, and this was in addition to his supervisory responsibilities.

Martin later took his sales team out for drinks at the pub, and they got very drunk indeed. By the end of the night they were patting each other on the back and promising, "all for one and one for all."

As he was over the limit, he left his car in the office parking lot and decided to walk home. The cooler breezes of early October had started to blow. Fall was here. Yet what a summer it had been: long, hot nights with Ginny, the cathartic recounting of life in the old country, frenetic selling in the office as the real estate market had gone onto higher peaks, the weekend at the Summers' cottage, even the testy dinner with her family. He had not been re-invited to the Summers' residence since, but Ginny was even more attached to him now. And she did not bring up her family again in their conversations.

He stopped at another bar and downed a couple more. What was eating him? He should be on top of the world; but he'd been edgy all day. That's why he pounced on those sales—almost for release. If he really put his finger on it, he was feeling like he was trying to climb a mountain that held a safe refuge for him at the summit. But the mountain was too tall, and he kept slipping back. And everyone on the ground watching him fall was laughing.

Staggering out of the bar, on impulse, he hailed a cab and went to Ginny's apartment. Outside the entrance to her building he gave the cab driver his home address as their next stop, and told him to wait for him no matter how long it took; he gave the man a twenty dollar bill as incentive. The crisply attired security guard frowned at Martin's inebriated condition, yet decided to let him in as he pocketed the cash extended in the young gentleman's hand.

Martin had difficulty standing erect in front of Ginny's apartment, but managed a large grin when she opened the door and looked upon him with a bemused smile.

"Where have you been partying?" she asked raising an eyebrow.

"Marry me," he said trying to focus on her and not slur his words.

"What?"

He went on his knees and looked at her. "Ginny, I may be drunk as a friggin' skunk right now. But this is a moment of clarity. I need you. We will be tops—you an' me. Marry me."

"Well, Martin James..." She drew her dressing gown tighter about her and tried to look stern. "For starters, you could try asking me that question when you are stone cold sober."

"It ain't going to be any diff'r'n't, sveet-tart. Why waste time? I feel like...like I have been on a bloody ship for sooo long, stopping in port after bloody port and never finding any happiness. You are the lasht port. Why sail anymo'? Marry me, please."

This time she put her hands on her hips and smiled widely. "Martin James. You take the prize for the most original and honest proposal. People whom I know normally propose in the most bizarre places: on top of the Eiffel Tower or on the Empire State building, at the Grand Canyon, under Niagara Falls, you name it. You do it on my doorstep and without flowers or a ring."

"Oh shit." He staggered up. He felt ashamed, he'd forgotten to prepare. *So much for impromptu performances.* "I forgot the ring. Hang on, hang on honey. I'll be back." He staggered over to the elevator.

Behind him, he heard her gentle laughter. "Go home safely. Did you take a cab?"

"Yes I did...no problem. I'll be back."

He must have passed out in the cab, for when he next surfaced, the driver was shaking him. "Your address, sir."

"We have to buy a ring," he managed, remembering his task.

The driver puckered his brow. "Sir, the shops are closed now. Tomorrow."

"Oh shit. I must be pretty pissed. Am I pissed?"

The driver suppressed a smile. "I think you can do with a good sleep, sir."

"Right. Right." Martin straightened himself and took a deep breath. "I think I better do that."

Martin gave him more cash, without counting and staggered into his building. He remembered getting into his apartment on auto-pilot and sprawling on his bed, fully clothed. He was out before he could take another breath.

The next morning the ringing doorbell woke him. The bedside clock said 9:00 a.m. *Shit, I'll be late for work.* He smelled of booze, his throat was parched and his clothes were crumpled. He immediately recalled what an ass he'd made of himself the previous night. *My God, I was like my father in one of his drunken moments.* He wished the caller would go away; his head was throbbing incessantly and the ringing doorbell added to his discomfort. He panicked. *Ginny's never going to call me again. Maybe that's her at the door, come to tell me personally!*

He staggered to the front door, swung it open and nearly fell backwards. Standing in his face, elegantly dressed in a green pantsuit and scarf in her hair was Clarissa Summers.

"Oh," she said surveying him coolly. "Is this an appropriate moment?"

"Clarice...I mean Mrs. Summers. How did you get here?"

"I drove. You are not hard to find. Virginia told me that you had proposed to her last night."

He held onto the door jamb, trying to gather his thoughts. This was a tight-knit family indeed; word got around fast. Or was Ginny so pissed with him that she had complained about his behaviour to her mother? But why was Clarissa here alone? Was she here to congratulate or to castigate him? And where was George? Did he not agree with this caper? Martin needed more time figure all this out. He stepped back from the door. "Would you like to come in?"

"Thank you," she said, stepping inside. "What I have to say is best not said in hallways."

He backed into the living room trying to keep his distance from her so she could not smell his breath. A vice gripped his heart as she followed him, looking about her like a municipal inspector checking out a blackballed restaurant's suspect kitchen. She came to a halt in the middle of the living room. He had arranged the place before going to work yesterday, yet her lip was curled in distaste.

"Would you like to take a seat?" he offered.

She ignored his invitation and held to the middle of the room. "You seem to have had quite a celebration over your proposal," she finally said. "You look like you still need time to recover."

He grinned sheepishly. "Well, we had a celebration at the office. We had some record sales to celebrate."

"And then you drop in on my daughter and say, 'Oh, by the way, can we get married?'"

"No, Mrs. Summers it wasn't like that. I've been meaning to ask Ginny for a long time. I guess I couldn't hold it back any more last night."

"It was the drink talking, young man."

He felt the bile rising but decided to bite his tongue.

"I'll get to the point, Mr. James. Ginny stands to inherit a lot of money. This is money that my family has built up over several generations. My husband, with his financial acumen, was able to multiply that many times over. I do not want to see these assets getting into the wrong hands."

"I don't want her money Mrs. Summers. I want Ginny, if she will have me."

"That's what they all say in the beginning."

"Does your husband share your opinion? Why isn't he here?"

Clarissa flushed, but quickly regained her composure and laughed sarcastically. "George is busy managing the various Summers' businesses, Mr. James. I secure them."

Martin suddenly felt like grabbing this haughty bitch and pitching her out on her ear. "Well, thanks for letting me know your feelings Mrs. Summers. I hate to push you out of here, but I am late for work and I need to take a shower."

"I will not bother you anymore. I suggest you leave my daughter alone. She is twenty-six and can make up her own mind, no doubt. But hers cannot be a marriage of love to just anybody. We have too much at stake, Mr. James. Good day."

He slammed the door behind her, angry, impotent, wanting to throw something at someone. When his head cleared after a long shower, he found that something did not quite add up: if he had really pissed Ginny off last night, why would Clarissa have bothered to call on him about protecting her assets? Was he that much of a threat?

He had just stepped out of the shower when the phone rang. His call display indicated it was Ginny calling from her office. He grabbed the instrument.

"Martin, are you all right?" Her voice was all concern. "I phoned your office and you had not come in."

"Ginny, oh Ginny, I am so glad you called. Look, I am sorry for making such an asshole of myself last night. Please forgive me."

"Forgive you?" she was laughing, her voice a trifle out of pitch again. "That was the most romantic proposal a girl could ever expect to get."

"You mean...I passed?"

"Now...I haven't accepted your proposal yet. But I told my parents about it. Just to get their reaction."

"Yes. I know. Your mother came to see me a little while ago."

"What?"

"She asked me to lay off."

"Darn! She had no right."

"Look I'm sorry for all this mess. Can I do this properly again? Today?

"You can do it as many times as you want. It makes a girl's heart sing." Then her voice got serious. "But tell me about Mum, what did she tell you?"

"Oh, it's too much to go over. Perhaps I can tell you after my repeat performance tonight. Can I come over at seven?"

"Sure. I can hardly wait!"

He called the office and said he would not be coming in. After all, he had already fulfilled his sales quota for the month with his performance yesterday. And the team could do with less supervision; they might even take some risks and sell more properties. He dressed and went down to the Eaton Centre and trolled the jewellery shops. He did not have Ginny's measurements but tried to visualize things as best as he could. The diamond had to be visible but not overly pretentious.

The chosen ring in his pocket, he walked around Nathan Phillips Square for a couple of hours, watching other strollers. Seeing the falling leaves race across concrete that would turn into a skating rink when the weather got colder, he asked himself whether he really wanted to marry Virginia Summers. She came with a lot of family baggage and complications, and there were times when he wondered if she had a split personality. Love was one thing, and he knew he was madly in love with her. But living together? They were from two different worlds. Finding an eligible woman from his own cultural background in this city was like looking for the proverbial needle; every woman he had met here was from another culture, the only things he ever found in common were sex and English. He had to integrate; the Burghers had run their course with his generation. And if integration was inevitable, why not with someone who would pull him out of his past circumstances and place him on another level? Managing the likes of Clarissa and Tim was the price he had to pay for upward mobility. Another challenge worth undertaking?

His mind rationalized for the moment, he went home to shower again and dress for the evening.

He showed up at her doorstep at 7:00 p.m., a large bouquet of flowers in one hand, a bottle of Dom Perignon in the other.

She opened the door; she had changed from her work clothes into a revealing low-cut evening dress; her hair was brushed back and a gold chain he had never seen her wear before, tapered down to a cross that nestled in her cleavage. He could not take his eyes off her.

"You look stunning," he stammered, the cross riveting his eyes towards her breasts.

She looked at him impishly. "Come in, lover boy."

He knelt on the threshold again and offered her the flowers first. As she took them gently in her hand, her eyes melting, he laid down the bottle of champagne, fished in his trouser pocket for the ring in its box and held it out to her with both hands outstretched. He did not say a word, content to mime the actions that she silently followed. Her mouth opened in delight and astonishment as the diamond sparkled back at her. Then he popped the bottle, and the champagne smoked but did not spill on the floor. He fished in his inner jacket pocket for the two flutes that he had carefully stowed before taking the elevator, and filled them, all the while watching her eyes as they opened even wider in amusement.

"Now, will you marry me?" he said at last, extending a glass to her.

She kissed him tenderly, "Of course you romantic lost soul. Of course."

"Come in, Martin," George Summers said, rising from his pool-table sized desk, extending his chubby hand in greeting, a fatherly smile on his face already. Martin was responding to a call from Ginny the day after his formal proposal that "Daddy" wanted to see him.

Martin stepped into the large office and took in its contents: Indian paintings of Mughal periods, an Arabian scimitar on the wall, a bookcase with faded hard copies, the titles of which he could not decipher, a bar with a wide collection of spirits in the glass cabinet behind it, and heavy brocade curtains hanging from tall windows on either side of the desk.

"Have a seat." George ushered Martin to a round conference table at the far corner of the room. "Drink?"

"Water, please."

George poured himself a small tot of scotch and got a bottle of water for Martin from the mini-refrigerator. "I always have a snifter before lunch."

When they were settled, George studied Martin for a moment, sipping his scotch, the handlebar moustache twitching ever so slightly. Then he set down his glass.

"I'm glad you came today. These matters unfortunately have to be gotten out of the way in a family as complicated as ours."

"Ginny told me that you would have the coolest head."

George leaned back. "I was once in your position, the outsider entering the family fortune. It was only after twenty years of marriage, and after I had demonstrated that I had what it took to, not only manage the fortune, but to grow it, that I was cut in for a share. Clarissa considers her custodianship a sacred trust from her pioneer ancestors."

"I understand. She has already made that clear to me."

George smiled. "She also acts impulsively at times. I am sorry Clarissa behaved the way she did, without consulting me."

"She sounded very deliberate, George."

George downed his drink and coughed, wrinkling his mouth as the alcohol coursed down his gullet. "I'm not as good at drinking this stuff as I used to be. Doctor has asked me to lay off due to my blood pressure. But years of habit are difficult to give up that easily. Okay, down to business." He opened the file folder that was sitting on the table. "This is a prenuptial agreement. Take it away with you and read it. We would expect you to sign this before you get married."

"Does Ginny agree?"

"She has no choice in the matter, if she wants to maintain her share of the inheritance."

Martin looked down at the reams of wording; it looked like a real estate contract, a purchase. He used to frown on those loveless arranged marriages back home, with dowries and property thrown in. Somehow he did not seem to have escaped that fate even in this part of the world.

George softened his tone. "Martin, this is not a big deal. I see you as a self-made man, like me. I don't think you'll be happy living off a woman. All this does is reassure the family that you are not a money-grabber."

"I'll read it and get back to you," Martin said picking up the folder and rising.

"There is something else I need to tell you. Sit down." George waved his hand deliberately. Martin sat again.

"Ginny suffers from a form of depression that has run through her mother's family for several generations. It came on in her teen years when she was experimenting with drugs, the bane of teenage life in this country I'm afraid."

"I see. That explains some of her erratic behaviour at times."

"She has been well treated and will be well treated in future. You have nothing to worry about. But I thought I should at least tell you that."

Martin set his jaw. The more obstacles this family was throwing in his way, the more determined he was to break through them. "My mother suffered from dementia. I am well used to mental illness."

George digested this information and nodded. "I see," he said, and continued to nod. Then he got up, came around and put his hand on Martin's shoulder. "Martin, I am not getting any younger. If the family needs to continue to run its various businesses, Ginny is the only one, despite these medical weaknesses, who would suit the role as the next chairperson. Tim unfortunately, is weak and has no business skills, even though he is his mother's pet. You see our dilemma?"

"Thanks for sharing this with me, George. You are right; I will not live off Ginny, under any circumstances."

"Attaboy! And congratulations! Ginny is very happy with you, and that is enough for me. Clarissa will give me hell for going this far, but I'll manage her; after all, she is my wife...and my problem."

"Thank you for your support."

"Good luck. You and Ginny make a great couple."

In his car, the file folder still in his hands, Martin called Ginny. She answered too quickly, he thought.

"What did he say?" she sounded breathless.

"He wants us to sign a prenup."

An exhalation on the other side. "That's all?"

"That's all? What the hell do you think this is? A sale?"

"Martin, slow down. A prenup is the least of our problems. This means that Daddy likes you."

"I'll wait to see how Clarice reacts before I cast any votes."

"Oh, there'll be fireworks over at Rosedale tonight, for sure. But Daddy has always worked to make me happy. He deserves a big hug and kiss from me."

"Not at Rosedale tonight, I suggest." He was starting to calm down. Perhaps a prenuptial agreement was not such a bad idea after all. Maybe it was just part of his ongoing Canadian experience.

"I'll plan on an April wedding," Ginny said.

"April? Do we have to wait that long?"

"That's only six months away, honey. That's cutting it. There are so many people to invite, hall arrangements, my gown, the honeymoon. We'll be swamped with preparations in no time."

"Ginny, this is about us. Why can't we keep it simple?"

"Martin darling, this is one that you or I, will not be able to duck. The Summers believe in grand weddings. At least, let's go through this to keep my parents happy."

When he put down the phone, he was wondering whether he had underestimated all the obstacles to upward mobility.

Two days later, on Monday October 17th, a day in infamy among financial markets, Martin's world took a sharp detour he had not anticipated.

It started with a call from Vigo's assistant, asking Martin to report to Vigo's downtown office immediately. He drove down, still bathed in the euphoria of his upcoming marriage. Given his recent appreciation of classical music—thanks to Ginny's influence—and wanting to polish his knowledge in this area, Martin played a classical music tape all the way to Vigo's office without listening to the radio.

When he arrived, just after nine, he sensed an air of tension as the two assistants were fielding an unusual barrage of phone calls. One of them waved him over to Vigo's office where the door was ajar. Martin caught a glimpse of Vigo pacing the room, cordless phone to his ear, issuing commands. He heard the words, "sell, sell, sell" repeated with an edge bordering on panic. Then the door slammed in his face and the sounds inside became muffled. He took a seat in the waiting room, and that's when he saw the bold headlines in the already ruffled morning's newspaper: "BLACK MONDAY".

He went over to one of the office phones and called Ginny. It took several attempts before he got through to her. Her voice sounded frantic.

"It's crazy over here, Martin. Everyone's in a panic. Daddy's locked up in his office too. I can't get through to him either."

Martin promised to keep in contact, gave her the number he was calling from, and hung up. He called the showroom. The senior salesperson answered. "Boss, it's dead in here today. Have you heard the news?"

"Yes, I am with Vigo. It's just panic. I think the buyers will be back as soon as this blows over. Hang in there. Let's have a meeting to regroup as soon as I get into the office."

But it was a couple of hours later before Vigo popped his head out. He looked like he had lost twenty pounds and sprouted multiple grey hairs since they had last met.

In the meantime, Martin had managed to glean from the papers, the radio, and from talking in snatches to the two office assistants, that financial markets everywhere in the world were tumbling like dominoes. Asia and Europe had collapsed in the wee hours of the morning and Matinsen Holdings' many offshore investments were useless pieces of paper now. He tried Ginny again and was told by one of her colleagues that she had taken the rest of the day off. Realizing that she must have gone to check up on her father, Martin tried calling Summers Enterprises to locate her. He got through to an assistant who had last seen her go up to the executive floor, to her father's office an hour ago.

Vigo was gesturing at him from the crack in his office doorway. Martin dropped the phone and grabbed this propitious window in his boss' busy schedule.

"Martin, this fucking place is exploding," Vigo thundered, pacing, grabbing a bottle of water, and mopping his sweaty face with a handkerchief.

"How serious is this?"

"I don't know yet, I have my accountants figuring out the damage."

"What do you want me to do, boss?"

"Go back to your office. See me later this evening. I'll be here till midnight at this rate. Keep the troops calm, eh? And sell more houses."

Martin went to the showroom. The floor was empty of customers, the staff full of enquiries. Martin ordered pizza. "Might as well take advantage of a slack day," he said, even though there was a nagging feeling at the bottom of his stomach. After lunch, he sent some of the sales people home and covered the floor himself, but the only callers he received were a couple who had signed a sale yesterday and wanted to know if they could cancel. No word from Ginny all afternoon.

At 5:00 p.m. he shut the showroom and returned to Vigo's office. The two assistants were not around and the boss himself was sitting at the reception desk. Vigo's bald pate was shiny with sweat as he sat fanning himself with an empty file folder; his tie was hanging down his chest. Even his shirt buttons were undone and Martin noticed for the first time that Vigo had a chest of matted black hair—a gift from his Italian maternal ancestry, perhaps.

"Ah, Martin. It is finished."

"You probably need a drink, right now."

"More than that, Martin, more than that. I am shutting down the operation here."

A chill settled over Martin's heart. The misgivings he had been having all day came full circle.

"Why? We have been running a profitable business so far."

"The bottom's going to fall out of real estate for awhile. If not now, then soon. My lenders have called in their loans. I'm broke, Martin."

He rose and lurched into his office, returning with his briefcase, his overcoat loosely thrown over his shoulders.

"I've given my assistants their notice already. Tomorrow, I will do the same for you and your staff. I'm sorry Martin. Business is like sword fighting—thrust and parry. Now is the time to parry. I am going back to Finland for some time. To take lots of saunas, and to parry. Maybe, I'll even go and visit my Mama in Sicily."

Martin felt the bitterness well out of him. "You're quitting, Vigo. Just as times get tough."

"I am not a warrior like you Martin. I am a coward, just like money is a coward and runs away at the first sign of trouble. I am like money. Goodnight. Turn the lights off before you leave."

Vigo put his hat on head and slouched out of the office.

Martin sat for a long while. For the first time in his life he realized he had been fired. Everything seemed so transitory to him. He hadn't built anything permanent despite all his career climbing. Or was the pace of economic development such that in these developed countries' fortunes could be made and broken in a day? So what the hell was the Summers family trying to protect? Perhaps they too must be losing all their money while he sat here.

As if on cue, the office phone rang. He wanted to let it ring, but realised it was the phone for which he had given Ginny his contact number earlier in the day. "Martin, thank God I found you. I was calling all over." Her voice sounded off key, hysterical.

"What's up?"

"It's Daddy... Oh Martin. He collapsed in the office an hour ago. I'm calling you from Toronto General Hospital."

"I'm coming right over," he said, dropping the phone and springing for the door. He forgot to turn the lights off.

13. **Closing the Deal**

The onset of winter was depressing. Martin sat in the mall watching the carollers stroll past. Unlike the previous year, when there had been promise, there were now only losses.

George Summers had suffered a massive stroke and was paralysed. Summers Enterprises' investments took a beating in the meltdown. The printing company and photography studio—the only solid tradable assets—had gone on the block to pay off the losses. Ginny had given up her marketing job and taken over the helm at Summers Enterprises as temporary CEO, but everyone knew that George was not coming back.

Vigo let the whole team at Telstra go with two months' notice, and for Martin, that money was nearing its end. Martin had taken the team for a final drink the day they received their notice and they had kissed and hugged and promised to stay in touch realizing that they would rarely, if ever, see each other again in this big city.

He saw Ginny infrequently. They made hurried calls during breaks; very rarely spent weekends together, and when they did, she was distracted most of the time. He kicked around in malls while she worked at the Rosedale home or at her father's office, trying to understand the family business and looking for come-back opportunities. Each time he saw her, she had lost more weight while dark rims expanded around her eyes. It was as if Summers Enterprises had swallowed her up whole and was sucking the lifeblood out of her. There were anxious moments when he wondered whether Ginny had not only taken over her father's job temporarily but had also inherited her mother's sacred duty of preserving the family fortune handed down over the generations. Her dedication to the firm was total.

The only person making money unconcernedly, was Tim Summers, who suddenly had a slew of clients wanting bankruptcy protection, one of his specializations.

The one bright spot Martin remembered in all this angst occurred on the evening when he rushed to the hospital to console Ginny over her father. Clarissa Summers was pacing the corridor outside the ICU, dressed for once in a shapeless sweat shirt and slacks. Without make-up, her facial features were plain and creased with wrinkles and she looked twenty years older. They were alone together in the corridor. Clarissa brusquely explained that Ginny had gone for coffee. He decided to stay and not go in search of her. He wanted to see the old lady in the heat of her suffering; it was good to know that rich bitches also suffered.

"You have been a bad omen to us," Clarissa said, fishing a tissue from her pocket. "Two days ago I heard that Ginny planned on going ahead with this silly marriage, and today...this."

"We all lost today, Mrs. Summers."

"Can you even begin to compare your losses to ours?" She had a mortified look on her face.

"At least, you have your family. I lost mine a long time ago. Today I also lost my job. I only have Ginny now."

"And you'd be better off giving her up and leaving us alone."

"Listen, Mrs. Summers, I don't quit and I am not quitting on Ginny, especially in her time of need. Come to think of it, there is very little that separates your family and me now. We are all kind of broke, aren't we?" He saw that the detachment with which he uttered the words had the intended knife-stabbing effect, as Clarissa arched her back and glared at him with an expression of loathing and disdain.

"We will never be broke, young man, remember that. Hurt, maybe; broke, never."

Ginny arrived at that moment, a tray of coffee mugs in-hand. She sensed the tension in the air. "Martin, thank God, you've come." Turning to her mother she asked, "Is he out of ICU yet?"

Clarissa shook her head. She picked up a cup of coffee, poured two sachets of artificial sweetener into it, and kept pacing.

"Can we talk?" Martin asked Ginny. He motioned with his head to imply "outside."

"There is a little garden around the corner. Mum, you'll send word if they bring Daddy out, won't you?"

Clarissa sipped her coffee and continued pacing without even a nod.

"He had passed out across his desk," Ginny recounted, holding Martin's hand, sitting on a bench in the outdoor green-space where patients wheeled their chairs and nurses took their smoke breaks.

"The company was important to him," Martin said. "I recall the pride with which he told me how he had multiplied its revenues. It must have been tough watching it slip away in a day."

"Everything is different now. We'll have to sell some of our holdings. I have decided to step into Daddy's job until he recovers. The management agrees. My internship at the firm two years ago will help."

"What about your own job?"

"I am going to have to quit. I can't let Daddy down."

"It will burn you up. There is so much to learn."

"This is the chance I was waiting for. To break away from the pre-ordained path and tread my own." There was a fiery determination in her eyes.

"What about your...your moods?" He did not want to say the d-word.

"This will be a good test for that, won't it?" she said, sniffing stubbornly.

"Well, I'm there for you if you need me."

"Thank you, Martin. We'd better get back. I don't want to miss Daddy when he comes out of the ICU."

That promise now burned as he sat in the mall watching the carollers. He couldn't complain; even though he rarely saw Ginny anymore, he just had to be available whenever she called and needed a sounding board. The few times they had talked, she appeared to be holding her own. She always tried to involve her senior managers in decision making, so there were endless rounds of meetings and conferences to decide on courses of action. Martin found this hard to understand, for he liked to operate as a lone wolf most of the time. But this seemed to be the Canadian way of corporate governance.

He also realized that as she grew through this cruel baptism, Ginny was changing. Gone was the naivety and idealism that had so charmed him: the girl who opened her mouth in wonder as he recounted his adventures in far-off climes. She now had her own real-life adventures to draw from. He had been right in saying to Clarissa that there was little separating them anymore; the same was true of the differences that had led to the attraction between him and Ginny; they seemed to be shrinking.

For his part, he had decided to resurrect the only asset left to him: his real estate sales licence. He re-registered as a sales-representative with Bradley Realty who was glad to have him back on board. The Toronto housing market was still strong, property values were still high and holding—for how much longer, no one could tell.

George Summers survived his stroke and was now at home, confined to a wheel chair, his speech slurred, the right side of his body paralysed. Clarissa hired a full-time nurse to look after him. Whenever Martin visited, George seemed to want to tell him something, only to give up in frustration each time.

Martin rose from his seat in the mall. It was time to be getting home; to his apartment, to eat a solitary meal and watch TV or read a book. There was no chance he'd hear from Ginny today; year-end was looming and Summers Enterprises was still wrestling to shore up its damaged finances.

Martin looked out over the sluggish rolling waters of Lake Ontario with patches of ice. It was a bitter February day: a minus 20-degree temperature redoubled by a numbing wind chill. The coffee shop was inviting, and people were blowing in from the street to huddle in corners over steaming mugs. He was on his second cup, waiting for Ginny—who had asked to see him today—to emerge from Summers Enterprises across the street. He thumbed idly through the pages of the "How to" manual he had been following these last couple weeks. His new homeland had taught him that self-sufficiency in everything was the key to survival.

Everything in the news was gloomy: the free-trade deal recently passed was forecast as good for Canada but bad for Ontario's manufacturing belt. His Canadian customers had all but stopped buying houses. The only bright spot was the surge of immigrants pouring in; last year's newcomers were already getting bullish about buying houses. He had managed to sell two properties in January, just enough to keep out of poverty's clutches.

There she was, crouched and darting across the road, hair billowing, mouth set in a tight grimace against the cold. She looked about the coffee shop anxiously and made her way over as soon as she saw him. He slipped the book into his briefcase.

"Coffee?" he asked after he hugged her tightly and she had released the tension in her body.

"Oh, yes please." She started shedding her coat and gloves as he went to get her favourite blend of Colombian.

After she had taken her first hurried sips, he asked, "Still tough going?"

She looked out at the lake, a sadness wafting over her like the steam from her cup. "There are days when I wonder whether this is all worth it. I take two steps forward and end up three steps back."

"You're on a steep learning curve, honey. It's a pity that George has everything in his head and is unable to tell you about the short cuts."

"In the evenings, on my way back from work, I stop by to see him in Rosedale. I sit across from him, willing him to speak. We write things across the table to each other, but even his writing is undecipherable. He leaves me notes when he is rested and able to write a few lines, but by then it's too late, I needed the information yesterday." She was twirling the engagement ring as she spoke. "Sometimes I wonder whether it would be better to sell everything and invest in fixed paper investments. We could still have enough to keep the two houses going and provide mother an income to live on. I have cut my allowance and gone without a salary for the last two months."

"You said you wanted to chart your own course, Ginny. Most successful business people have gone bankrupt a few times in their formative years."

She gave him a look of horror at the mention of the b-word. "We do not have that option, Martin. This is not my money I am playing with. It's the family's."

"You could always hire a professional CEO."

"We can't afford one. Besides, I am not sure what a professional CEO can do. They are making semi-conductors in Asia now, and our customers are pressing us for price concessions."

"I'm sure this will give Tim and your mother one more reason to hate Asians."

The loose ring on her finger was starting to make him nervous.

"Why did you want to see me today," he asked gently.

She held up the ring in full view. "I wonder why couples use a ring to symbolize their union. Is it another fence? I feel surrounded by fences."

He took a deep breath. He knew what was coming. "You want to put the wedding off," he said slowly.

"I haven't done a stitch of work on it, Martin. No invitation lists, no location booked, no nothing done. And I don't have any money to spend on it."

"And your mother is not dashing to help on this one either, like other mothers usually do."

"Oh, leave her alone. She's got enough to deal with, with my father."

"She's got a nurse to help. I don't see your mother even pushing his wheelchair."

"Are we going to sit here and fight?"

"No. But you are not the only one suffering over the ills of Summers Enterprises these days."

"Oh Martin, I know. I'm sorry. I haven't been there for you. You've had your share of difficulties as well. It seems like the whole world is conspiring to keep us apart."

"That's one way of looking at it. Or we could simplify this whole wedding ceremony and everything would be fine again."

She shook her head. "No, that wouldn't do. We have to put the wedding off to the fall."

"No!" He was standing up, the blood hot in his face. "*I* will organize this event. I have some money, not a lot, but I can pull it off. Give me your lists and I will schedule everything and carry it out."

She looked beaten, the last thing she needed in this fragile state was a fight with him, and he knew it.

"We are only two months away from April."

"Plenty of time. I am already holding a booking at Casa Loma."

She looked at him in amazement. For a moment that naive wonder was in her face again—the expression he loved so much. "You're kidding!"

"I've booked a band, the priest and the venue, and I have a printer working on invitation designs which I'll have in a few days. You need only go and pick out your dress, and we'll be ready to rock and roll."

She put her arms around him and hugged him. "Oh Martin, you are such a life-saver."

He didn't tell her that he had taken a $25,000 line of credit, and that the payments were hurting; if he did not sell another house this week, the next cheque was going to bounce.

"Well, you go back to work and don't worry yourself over the wedding. I'll send you my schedule tomorrow. Just make sure that you can cover your tasks on it, and we'll be fine."

Martin put aside his well-thumbed "Weddings for Idiots" primer and rubbed his eyes. It was past 11:30 at night, and he was tired. He had gone over the invitee lists repeatedly to ensure no one had been left out. And it was an extensive list. Clarissa had slipped in an "addendum" at the last minute when she realised that they had passed the point of no return on the wedding going ahead. The addendum was longer that the original invitee list. Tim had made a fuss about not being able to attend as he had client appointments that he could not back out of. After two changes to the time of the service, Tim finally relented, but said that he would be leaving early.

Martin was expecting a financial contribution from the Summers family, but was reluctant to ask. None was forthcoming. Ginny cashed in a savings bond of $10,000 and gave it to him as her contribution. He concluded that he was marrying into a family that had been used to amassing a lot of money and indulging themselves with it, but quite unaccustomed to doling it out, especially now, when supply was tight. Fortunately, he had three house closings in March, and that helped keep the rubber off the cheques.

Two weeks earlier, his landed-immigrant application had finally been accepted and he felt a hollow victory. Fifty-fifty had worked in his favour. He'd had to leave the country and come back to get his passport endorsed on re-entry. The border immigration officer at the Niagara crossing looked bored, stamped his papers and waved him through. Martin felt none of the apprehension of that first arrival three years ago.

Tonight, as he put his handbook away, two weeks before the wedding, he felt tired and the doubts of climbing this mountain had returned. He checked his schedule; there were a few tasks still left, including renting a tuxedo for himself. He had no best man and had opted to go without one. The only best men he could have counted on were his brother Barney (lost somewhere in a seminary in Sri Lanka), Christo (lost somewhere in Canada) and Bandu (ditto).

The night before the wedding, he took Ginny out to dinner at an Italian restaurant in Cabbagetown. She looked pale and tired. She let him do the ordering. He ordered her favourite pasta and herbed chicken and a bottle of Valpolicella. She picked at her food, pre-occupied. He ordered her gelato for dessert and a cappuccino to round things off. At one point during dessert, she smiled, the coquettishness returning for a fleeting moment, "Are you trying to fatten me for the feast tomorrow?"

"I want you to relax and be happy. 'Tomorrow is the first day of the rest of our lives,' my guide book says."

"Are there any tips in there for running a company and being a good wife at the same time?"

"That's a dilemma of the times. We have no role models in our families, unfortunately. This yuppie generation of ours is writing about it a lot in the newspapers these days. That, and juggling kids and aging parents, and all. No one has the answers yet."

"Kids? I don't think I can even think about kids at this stage."

He hid his disappointment; he did not like her talking like this. "Summers Enterprises won't be down for long. Besides, you forget you'll have a husband who can also pull in the dough."

She sipped her cappuccino. "This coffee reminds me of old times...was it just last year? There was so much optimism then. Now I feel like a runner falling over the finish line, dead last."

"But you completed the race," he said, smiling.

She reached out and took his hand. "Yes. And I owe it to you, Martin. Thanks for sticking with me."

And what a wedding it was! It rained, poured, as elegant couples dashed up the steps of the castle with umbrellas and raincoats, the women lifting long black dresses above ankles and trying, more than anything, to preserve their elegant coiffures. Martin wondered whether God Himself was finally telling them not to go through with this event.

Inside the austere castle foyer, guests were served champagne by stiff white-gloved waiters who looked spiffier than the wet guests stumbling in. Clarissa Summers was at her radiant best with a smile that never left her the entire evening, greeting everyone, shaking wet hands and apologizing for the bad weather, without any show of empathy.

George Summers looked pathetic in his wheelchair, forgotten and moved off to the side of the entranceway. He had lost about fifty pounds and looked anxiously about him, constantly mumbling to the nurse who never left his side. He had lost his grip on his surroundings, on life itself, and looked like he was on the verge of tears all the time. Martin went up to him and placed a champagne flute in his hand, winking at the nurse.

"George, for this once, you can join us in a toast, the doctors won't mind, I'm sure."

Tim arrived in a flap, cursing the elements and frowning at his sister, as if blaming her for insisting that he attend this wedding, since it compromised his schedule so much. He ignored Martin, grabbed a glass of champagne from a passing waiter and got immediately absorbed in a conversation with a clutch of Summers Semi-Conductors senior managers and their wives.

The United Church minister read a simple service, terribly watered down from the ones Martin had witnessed in his childhood. He had knocked Ginny down to the abbreviated version: middle of the road, don't rock the boat, be politically correct—the operating mantra of this upper crust gathering.

But Ginny simply took his breath away. Dressed in a traditional white lacy wedding gown with a short train, natural blonde hair shiny and down over her shoulders, wearing a subtle blend of make-up that ignited her blue eyes with life and promise, the gold chain and cross that rested just above her half bared and thrusting bosom—Martin wanted to have her right then and there. Her strain and fatigue of the last few months seemed to have been hidden away by either make-up or medication. His thoughts during the service were not on "do I take this woman to be my wife?" but on "what have I done to earn this prize?" Despite all the obstacles thrown in his way, and his determination to fight them, was he worthy of this payback? God had plucked him out of a third-world country and put him up here on this perch, like Poseidon had sent Odysseus into the arms of the goddess Calypso. But that mythical union had been a loveless one, sustained only by Calypso's charm and divine allure. Was this marriage going to end that way too? *Am I worthy of maintaining my position in this arena, or have I reached the pinnacle of my own incompetence?* He shook his head and focussed on the minister. When he heard, "You may kiss the bride," he kissed her not with passion but in desperation.

During the dinner, Ginny took Martin around and introduced him to the guests, who were all names to him so far on the well-thumbed and cross-checked invitation list: old ladies who smiled politely all the time, grey-haired men with taciturn faces, younger men and women who seemed interested only in where they were taking their next vacation, or how they were going to decorate the new cottage or the upcoming baby's room in their new house in the suburbs. After a while, Martin adopted a fixed smile, showing interest, and looking like the new tropical animal in the petting zoo. He had resolved to drink only mineral water during the whole event, being wary about making the slightest mistake.

Clarissa did her own introductions; introducing Virginia Summers (Ginny was retaining her family name after the marriage) as the new CEO of Summers Enterprises. Martin noted that the people Clarissa was courting seemed to be those on her addendum list. So the old dame had used this wedding as a marketing event, the coming-out party for the new head of the family business.

George had to be taken home early for his rest, just before dinner commenced. He had his nurse summon Martin and Ginny before he was wheeled away. He pulled an envelope from the folds of his jacket and handed it to Ginny with quivering hands. His eyes were alight as he pointed repeatedly, asking Ginny to open it. She did, and gasped, embracing her father with a sob, "Oh Daddy...thank you...thank you sooo much!"

When he was able to pry the envelope from Ginny, Martin read the letter, scrawled and undecipherable in some places and, judging by the different colours of ink, obviously written over many days. The enclosed bank draft for $250,000 made his eyes open in amazement:

Dear Ginny and Martin,
As I near the sunset of life, I have realized that money is best put to use by younger people—people such as you who have never wanted for effort and enterprise when that was called for. This is my share of Summers Enterprises, a share that sits outside prenuptial arrangements and other encumbrances. I want it to be for both of you in equal measure. I hope it gives you the start in life you need.
I wish you many happy years together and hope you will give me many healthy grandchildren.
Love and kisses!
Daddy

Clarissa and Tim came over at the sight of the emotional hug-fest. Martin restrained them and merely held up the letter triumphantly; he kept the bank draft in his hand for safekeeping. They read the letter with paling faces. When Ginny straightened up from her father to announce the good news, Clarissa and Tim had already resumed looks of beaming generosity. Clarissa followed George and his nurse out, and for the first time at this event, Martin saw her in animated conversation with her husband.

Everything was taking its natural course; the dinner was at the entrée stage, waiters were clacking dishes and men were returning from the washroom to sit down once more and gorge their stuffed stomachs, while women dabbed their noses and savoured the red wine that had now followed the white and the champagne. Tim excused himself from the right-hand side of the head table and walked up to Ginny and Martin saying it was time for him to leave for his client meeting. He then made a production of kissing the guests around the head table and waved gloriously to everyone else in the great hall. No one was paying the slightest attention anyway. He even went up to the microphone and said goodnight, which caused Virginia to rise quickly and announce to the puzzled guests that it was only Tim leaving and that everyone else still had the main course and the rest of the evening to look forward to. On his way past, he whispered in Martin's ear that he would like to "have a word" outside. Martin excused himself and followed Tim out, ignoring the look of apprehension on Ginny's face.

The rain had stopped. Tim paused just outside the huge double doors. He didn't waste time getting to the point. "Good luck, you son of a bitch. You even conned my father. If not for my sister's feelings, I would have turned you in to the authorities right away."

Martin was taken aback by this sudden outburst. "What the hell are you talking about?"

"You should know. You fuckers come into this country through the back door and parade about like you're loyal Canadians."

"I am a landed immigrant, just like your forefathers were."

"Landed immigrant, my ass!"

Martin felt the blood gush to his face. "Do you want to see my papers, asshole?"

Tim smiled at his opponent's discomfiture. "My forefathers did not gain entry into this country *the way you did.*"

A shiver went down Martin's spine. How much did Tim know? Martin had read about lawyers hiring private detectives. Had Tim gone that far to protect his family's interests? Or had he merely snooped inside Martin's file when Jim Duffield was not in the office? Tim was frightening and revolting at the same time.

Martin grabbed Tim by his collar. Tim's bow-tie came loose in his hand." Listen you son of a bitch, I am as legally entitled to be here, just as you are. People have come to this country over the centuries in many ways. I have worked my ass off to get here and have worked even harder to stay here."

"Tim! Martin!" The high-pitched voice from behind made both men swing around. It was Clarissa Summers. The wide smile on her face was missing for the first time that evening. She looked upon them in stern admonishment. She turned on Tim. "Stop that immediately. You will not behave like this at your sister's wedding."

Tim quickly straightened up as Martin let him go. Tim made to say something, changed his mind, mumbled an apology, and swaggered off to the parking lot.

Martin straightened his jacket. "I'm sorry Mrs. Summers. I shouldn't have fallen for his needling. But I guess this was coming for some time."

Clarissa looked him up and down, the curl in her lip a pure animal expression. "Martin, your class—or the lack of it—shows. You'd better do some growing up if you want to stay married in this family." Then she turned on her heel, hoisted her dress slightly and swept indoors.

Martin broke his resolve for the evening and grabbed a Scotch from the bar before returning to his seat at the head table. He was determined to enjoy the rest of his already spoiled wedding.

14. **Birth Pangs**

Martin sat in the back rows of the school auditorium and watched the children practise for the school concert. He took time off work to bring Jamie to the rehearsals these days because it re-affirmed his belief in the world. It also beat his old habit of hanging around malls and watching life go by.

The choir had just finished their number and the music teacher, an angular woman in her forties, ushered them down to the front row seats. She looked at her program sheet and announced: "James Summers." The surname still rankled, but it had been a concession worth making, given the disruption James's birth had caused the Summers dynasty. Martin insisted on making his family name the child's first name, so that he would maintain a stake in the kinship. The Summers clan reluctantly accepted. Thanks to Clarissa, "James" quickly morphed into the pet name "Jamie."

The slim boy in curly blonde locks walked shyly over to the piano. Jamie placed his black music binder on the piano stand and adjusted the seat so that his feet reached the pedals. He tentatively tried a few keys. Then he looked up at his father and took a deep breath as if remembering something. Martin raised his hands, both thumbs up, beaming. This was the moment he had been waiting for.

The opening adagio of Mozart's sonata number 14 wafted subtly through the hall. Beneath its glittering surface Martin could feel the lyricism and and passion exquisitely drawn from the keys by the nimble fingers of this child prodigy who seemed suddenly possessed by the music's power. Martin had tears in his eyes. This was his gift: after all the years of struggle, to be handed this boy, despite Ginny's desire not to have children, despite the obstacles that had loomed in the path leading to Jamie's birth.

The music took him back to when it started to go wrong...or right...

Martin and Ginny had bought their dream home in Willowdale soon after the wedding. It was a four-bedroom house in the heart of an area where prices were going up 30 percent a year. George went on a hand-me-down rampage, not stopping at the money he had already given them, but also dividing his art collection between Tim and Ginny. Ginny ended up with the giant Ming vase, a Monet, a handmade Persian rug and a set of Egyptian daggers.

Clarissa berated her husband for his generosity. It was too early to give the children their inheritance, she complained. George didn't seem to care, and appeared to be in a hurry. Barely six months into Martin and Ginny's marriage, just as they were about to move into the new house, he passed away quietly one morning with a satisfied look on his face, according to the nurse who had gone in to wake him.

Ginny seemed to lose the struggle to fight for Summers Enterprises with her father's passing and went into a deep depression. She would stare into space at the breakfast table, pick fights over the slightest disarray or change in plans that affected her equilibrium or burst into tears without encouragement or provocation. She took time off from work and hired a retired CEO, Joe Peterson, to help with the day-to-day operation of the company. Martin suggested a trip to the Caribbean or to Europe or somewhere they could cool off, but she would not hear of leaving the scene of her grief. His own business was picking up too, and now being officially the sole bread winner (Ginny was still not drawing a salary from the firm) he decided to stay put, and the idea was shelved. Instead, Ginny went up to the family cottage and stayed until Christmas. Martin visited on weekends, but the time always seemed to go by too fast and they never got a chance to get to the heart of the issues that were pulling them apart. However, she felt relaxed amidst the familiar surroundings of her childhood and he decided it was best for her. They spent those times together taking long walks in the woods choked with fallen leaves, usually in silence; donning parkas and raincoats to take the boats out on the icy cold lake, and firing up the barbecue to huddle around during the evenings. Ginny gave up alcohol and drank only herbal tea from that time on.

Clarissa aged after her husband's death. Gone was the erect bearing and haughty manner. She developed a permanent hunch. Her acerbic remarks however did not abate, and she cut Martin up whether they were in private or in company. Martin, for his part, tried to stay away from her as best as he could; in fact, after George passed away he gave the Summers residence in Rosedale a wide berth. Clarissa decided to spend more time at the cottage, often with Ginny for company. Due to these forced separations, Martin decided to make use of the time by studying for his broker's licence.

When Ginny came home at Christmas, after a month at the cottage, Martin decided to have a heart-to-heart with her. He had been missing her and had started to find solace in the extra drinks that were quickly becoming his regular companions in the quiet evenings. He was feeling rejected, like a toy that had outlived its short life. Ginny and he were like strangers, barely a year into their marriage. On her return this time, he noticed that she had cut her hair short and her face had become angular and hard. He could see the veins in her hands now. In anticipation of her homecoming, he had put up a Christmas tree and decorated it with lights. He had also strung a "Welcome Home" sign over it. Although he felt as if he was going through the motions just to make her happy, *he* was far from content himself. She didn't seem to notice his forced cheerfulness, for she hauled her bags wearily into the house and immediately hit the shower.

"How does it feel to be back?" he asked after dinner on that first day of her return.

She thumbed through some mail that had been collecting for weeks and didn't reply.

"It's been hard here," he said. "I missed you."

"I've decided to go back to the office," she said, her eyes taking on a strange fire. "Joe Peterson has not made an ounce of difference."

"Be careful, the manufacturing sector is taking a hit with free trade. Semi-conductors aren't hot anymore."

"I have to make it up. My family is depending on me."

"Honey, your family's businesses were successful under yesterday's paradigms. You inherited these companies, you did not create them. So don't beat yourself up too hard because of the tough times they are in. Remember our old lecturer and the theories we argued about: when to stay, and when to jettison old products? Perhaps it's time to sunset semi-conductors."

She flung the mail at him. "How dare you say that, Martin? No bloody way. You may cut and run. I won't."

Biting his tongue, he picked up the fallen letters, leaving them in a pile on his side of the table. He got up and walked around the neighbourhood for the next half hour, talking to himself. *So much for romantic homecomings.* When he returned to the house, she was asleep.

After Ginny returned to work, it was as if she was still at the cottage. He rarely saw her. She would often work late and then go to her mother's for the night. Martin swallowed his irritation even though he could not understand what drove her to seek to solace with the cold fish he knew Clarissa to be. Ginny needed attention, love, assurance; all the things his watered-down wedding vows had said *he* should provide. Yet she seemed to prefer her mother's company. As resentment burbled inside him, he had to remind himself that two depressed people were not going to solve the problem; he had to keep his head up, however tough the situation was.

When he broached the subject one day, she cut him off. "Mother is very lonely and could be gone very soon too, and then I will have lost both my parents. I need to spend as much time with her as possible before that happens."

"And you take me for granted while all that is happening?" The complaint came out of him involuntarily. *So much for self-control!*

"Martin, our marriage was one of bad timing with everything that was happening. I should have listened to my intuition. You wanted to go ahead with it. Now, you have to put up with the fallout."

Matters came to a head on the day he received his broker's certificate. It was a Friday and he was banking on Ginny being home at a regular hour for the weekend. He was overjoyed when he saw her car in the driveway. He drove around the block to the LCBO and picked up a bottle of champagne, ready to celebrate. Later, he would take her out to a dinner-theatre show downtown.

"Honey, I'm home. I passed!" He threw his jacket on the stairwell, kicked his shoes off and waltzed into the living room only to find her surrounded by a sea of papers spread all over the floor, tears streaming down her face.

"We can't meet the overdraft, Martin," was all she said. His words had gone over her head or she had not heard him.

"Honey, I said, I passed."

She snapped out of her pre-occupation and seemed to comprehend momentarily. Then she looked back helplessly at the papers spread before her. "Oh. Congratulations."

"We are going out tonight, honey. Put all this stuff away. I've got it all laid out for when I set up my own brokerage. We'll be out of the woods soon."

Her lip curled and he saw the outburst coming too late. "It's fine for you to go celebrating. How the fuck am I going to get us out of this mess?"

"Ginny, all you've done since I married you is to beat this dead horse called Summers Enterprises. Don't you know when to call it quits? The business is done. You've given it your best shot—let it go. Sell it. And sell it now before it has to go on fire-sale."

Her blue eyes were like ice. "Go on—laugh! Gloat at my misfortune. Mother is right. It's been nothing but misfortune since you entered my life. You go from strength to strength and my family goes down the tubes."

Her words stung him. "I am also your family. My success is yours. If you continue to treat me as an outsider, there is no point in my sharing anything with you." He put the champagne in the fridge—it would have to be for another day. "I guess I'll be going downtown by myself to celebrate on my own."

"And while you're down there, get one of your immigrant girls to keep you company since I am of no use to you anymore."

He came up to her grabbed her by the shoulders, raised her from the pile of papers and shook her. "Ginny, Ginny, listen to me. What has become of you? Of us? All we do is fight."

"I should never have married you. Mother was right."

Her eyes were pools of venom and envy. This was another person he was gazing at. Where was his sweet Ginny? Had her father's death been enough to swing her over to the other end of her gene pool? Was she really another Clarissa-in-waiting? *My God, what kind of a life have I consigned myself to?* He let go of her as if singed, and she fell back limply, scattering the papers further across the floor.

"I'm moving into the spare room in the basement," he said. "When you come to your senses, we'll talk. And don't keep me waiting too long." She lay where she had fallen, succumbing to tears again, this time sobbing uncontrollably.

He went out on the town that night on a solitary binge. In a fit of loneliness, he thought of calling his old girl friends Jamila or Ivana but they had spun off into other orbits and he had lost contact with them. In fact, women were the last people he wanted to see at that moment; right now they were the most changeable, unpredictable chameleon-like creatures he had ever encountered. He wracked his brains for a description. Circe from the Odyssey came to mind; even the sweet Helen, who had launched a thousand ships, unleashed the destruction of Troy, and then gone back to her husband Menelaus as if nothing had happened.

Their silence continued for several weeks. Martin crossed Ginny sometimes on his way out the door, or whenever they pulled in or out of the shared twin-car garage. She appeared as embarrassed to see him he was to see her. He wasn't used to this cold war. He would wake up in the night and reach over for her warm body and feel the absence, the emptiness. There were many times he thought of breaking the impasse and walking upstairs to her room and begging forgiveness for his thoughtlessness. But was he the only heedless one in this whole deal? Convinced that he was not, he would steel himself, stick a pillow between his legs and try to fall asleep.

He tried to drown his worries by focussing on new plans for the brokerage. He had picked an office location near the house so that he could walk to work if necessary during the warm weather. He went down his list of agents and picked the ones he wanted to solicit to hang up their shingle with him. Foremost among his picks were team members he had mentored and developed at Telstra Properties.

Within a month he was ready to open for business with two sales representatives committed to come on board. The rest of the team would be built up as results warranted. Just for the heck of it, he slipped a flyer, announcing his grand opening, under Ginny's windshield wiper on his way to his new job that day.

The brokerage office smelled of the fresh coat of paint he had given it on the weekend, and the new furniture had just been delivered, still encased in plastic. The phones were being tested by the installers as he walked in.

"Are we ready to roll?" he asked, puffed with pride that he was finally master of his own destiny.

"You bet, sir," said the technician, winking, as he put his tools away.

Martin looked in the display window to see that the listings were as he had arranged them the previous night—colour photographs of high-end properties in the neighbourhood—he was going upscale, targeting those who always seemed to have money. Talk of that dreaded R-word was heavy in the air during this spring of '89 with reverberations of the stock market crash of '87 and the recent Toronto MLS crash still in the air.

Martin walked into his own cubicle that he had made private by extending the glass walls up to the ceiling and sticking in a door. He had adorned the credenza with two pictures at either end: one of his parents (the old picture he had filched from the family album before leaving Sri Lanka) and the other a wedding picture of him and Ginny. Not only was there a generational difference in the texture of the photographs, but also a cultural difference that he found difficult to fathom. He had set his chair and desk so that the pictures were on either side of him, to remind him of the vast chasm that he was still bridging. Some day, he hoped, he would feel comfortable enough to place them side by side.

"Ready for the opening, boss?" Marnie Rogers, one of his sales representatives stuck her head in. Young, energetic and street-smart, she had been on the other end of a couple of deals with him in the past and he was impressed with her tenaciousness. She was also attractive: brunette, curvy and using her body to emphasise her whole person in closing the sale.

"Sure," he grinned. "Vinod in yet?" Vinod Sharma was his other salesperson, formerly of Telstra Properties.

"He's gone for coffee. Do you take yours with one sugar?"

"Good guess."

She slanted her eyes at him coquettishly. "I remember. The Cunningham deal—we drank lots of coffee while the buyers made up their minds."

He laughed. Those times looked so innocent. *Why does the past always look so nostalgic even though it often wasn't really that pleasant?*

"I'll need a hand with the refreshments and the hobnobbing this afternoon."

"No problem, boss. I've got lots of business cards too." She smiled, bouncing off to her cube.

The opening was a hit. Most of Martin's loyal customers were in attendance, including the Purvises who were currently in the market again, downscaling from the Presidency which had been ostensibly too big for them (although Martin considered their new move an intelligent property flip). Marnie and Vinod's clients and prospects were also out in full force. Vinod, in his early fifties, had been in real estate for many years and was well entrenched in the South Asian community. So the wine-and-cheese was actually, wine, cheese and samosas, and Martin was heady with a sense of multi-cultural harmony and general goodwill. If only he could find such bonhomie at home.

As he got up to make his speech of welcome and raise his glass in a toast, someone tapped him on the arm. It was Ginny. Dressed in a smart blue business suit and a red scarf around her neck, she looked stunning. She must have spent the morning at the aesthetician's, for she looked rejuvenated and confident: the old Ginny. He was open-mouthed and wanted to put his arms around her, scared that this beautiful elusive image would suddenly disappear again.

She raised a glass of orange juice to him. "Congratulations, Mr. Hotshot Broker. I wish you much success."

It flashed across his mind that she might have come to embarrass him in front of his customers, to escalate the home-front cold war into a public dog-eat-dog battle, and he instinctively looked around for cover. Then he shook himself. He looked deep into her eyes: gone were the envy and hurt evident the last time they had fought, replaced now by a sparkle of genuine pride in his accomplishment. He raised his glass to her in return. "Thanks for coming, honey."

"I thought the best place I could be today was beside you."

In a sudden swoop of headiness, he grabbed her and swept her to the front of the office.

"Ladies and gentlemen, I want to thank you for coming here today to help us launch James Realty. My wife Virginia and I (he saw questioning looks, especially from the South Asians, among whom mixed marriage was still a novelty; even Marnie Rogers had an eyebrow arched) would like to thank you for your custom in the past and we look forward to giving you the best service in future." He held Ginny's hand high as he toasted everyone.

After the party, he left his car at the office parking lot and drove back with Ginny. Even for the short distance, he could not hide his exhuberance. "I am so glad you came, honey. I've missed you like crazy this last month."

"I've missed you too, Martin. For longer than a month; since Daddy died, in fact."

He was burning to ask her what had caused this tsunami of a change. It could not just have been the flyer he stuck on her car? Was it the nature of her depression: descending and lifting with the winds of change? She gave him the answer.

"Today, I presented to the family my plan for proceeding with the business. I have recommended a sale of Summers Semi-Conductors to an Indian company looking for a beachhead in North America."

"Wow, that's terrific that you've got a buyer."

"They approached me. They are willing to pay top dollar. I don't think we'll get another offer like this."

"And...did they agree? The family, I mean."

"Frankly, I don't care. I've paid my dues. If Mother and Tim accept the offer, we could still salvage the house and the cottage and keep Mother with an allowance into her old age."

"Honey, I'm proud of you. It must have taken some balls to go up against the old lady."

"It was like a weight lifted when I delivered the news to them this morning. We have until tomorrow to give the Indians an answer. I spent the rest of the day at the spa, cleansing myself of all the emotional baggage I have been carrying."

They had reached the house. Martin pecked her gently on the cheek, still uncertain, still wary of raking up something negative at such a delicate state of their relationship. She reached out and pulled him to her and they kissed awkwardly across the front seats of the car.

"Can I move back upstairs?" he asked when they broke for breath.

"I was hoping you would," she replied, smiling.

The next few weeks passed in bliss: life couldn't have been better. The brokerage was a hive of activity despite the recent market crisis; Marnie was on fire, selling five properties in the first two weeks, and Vinod was almost equally productive with four sales. Martin knew that he had the right team.

The rest of the Summers family decided to take Ginny's advice, and the business changed hands. Ginny had a fit of nerves on the night of the closing. Martin found her pacing the house when he returned from work.

"Honey, what's wrong?"

"Did I do the right thing, Martin?" She looked panic-stricken and had that crazy fire back in her eyes as she paced, clenching and unclenching her hands. "This is my doing. The others only caved in. Would Daddy have approved?"

He put his arms around her and rocked her gently. "Honey, I see this with most of my clients; 'seller's remorse' they call it. It will settle. Look at it this way, based on today's set of circumstances—and it could be different tomorrow—you made the right decision."

She relaxed in his arms and her tension washed over him.

He carried her upstairs. "You need loving, my dear, long, tender loving..."

She clung to him, swabbing her tears in his collar as he took her to bed.

With the business in full swing, Martin took two weeks off in July and spent the time with Ginny at the family cottage. Mercifully, Clarissa was vacationing in Europe that summer. The bright weather, the water, and the trees had an aura of promise about them that Martin found exhilarating. They made passionate and carefree love at night, making up for the lost first year of their marriage. They built a fire on the edge of the lake at night, doused themselves with insect repellent and watched the stars come over the woods framing the lake.

One night when the moon was full, Ginny leaned back on her deck chair and caught Martin by surprise. "You know about my clinical depression, don't you?" she said.

He sat up in his chair, looking down at her. But her face was staring at the full moon, objective and serious. "Your father mentioned it to me once," he confessed.

"Daddy's death triggered it again."

"Honey, you were under a lot of stress. You went from employee to CEO in a flash. Besides, you had just gotten married. Isn't that enough to send anyone around the bend?"

"But the hurtful things I said. That was not me."

He remained silent. He did not want to get into another argument and spoil a perfect evening that had been laced with barbecued shrimp and a vintage Chardonnay.

She sat up and looked at him. "I've done a lot of research into the illness, recently. My grandmother on Mother's side suffered from it and it's known to pass down the family line."

"Can it be treated?"

"Yes, they experiment with various types of drugs until you latch onto the right one. Until you do, the side effects can be worse than the actual symptoms. They found me one quite a while ago, but it doesn't last indefinitely. I think I'm now wearing it out after all these years."

"Why do we need to bother experimenting with new drugs now? You're fine, stress-free, and everything *is* okay, isn't it?"

"I think I am pregnant, Martin. And I don't know how I will react to being a mother."

His eyes opened wide and he let out a whoop of joy. "Pregnant! Whoa! That's the greatest news I've heard in ages!"

He sprang out of his seat, lifted her clean out of the deck chair, and twirled her around in the sand. "I love you, honey. We are going to have the best baby, ever."

He carried her gently into the chilling but refreshing water and held her and her growing foetus safely to him as the moon went over the trees.

"You were good today, Jamie," Martin said as he turned onto their street. "I've obviously missed a lot of your growing up—on the musical side."

"Grandma's tutor wants to increase my class to two hours a day, three times a week." Jamie was pre-occupied in assembling and dissembling his Transformer toy.

"Practise makes perfect, they say."

"I'd like to play the guitar. Like Manuel Gonzales of Spain."

Martin shook his head. At six years of age, he had been spent his time running around in Perera Gardens with a bicycle rim, trying to save a sick dog. His son was in a different league.

Martin pulled into the garage and Jamie took off into the house.

"Remember to shower. And you're reading for an hour before dinner," Martin called after him.

Martin took his briefcase and limped in through the side door. Ginny was not home; she was at a support group meeting, which one, he could not tell. She belonged to several now that she had decided not to return to work: divorced mothers, breast cancer, MADD, orphans in the developing world. None of these causes directly touched her personal circumstances. Martin would have understood if she had been part of a depressed woman's group or a poor self-image group. But that would have been too close to home, and he was not sure that she could manage radical therapy of that kind.

He went into the kitchen and pulled out the chicken breasts he had put into a marinade before setting out to work. The vegetables: cauliflower and broccoli, in a light crème sauce would have to do, along with rice that he put in the the rice steamer.

He poured himself a glass of wine and set to cooking. He had stirred up memories during Jamie's rehearsal—the relatively good parts. The rest was buried inside him, threatening to surface if he let his guard down.

He put the timer on for the chicken in the grill. The vegetables simmered in their sauce, and the rice steamer would knock off automatically. He topped his glass and headed into the living room. Right now it was a fully inhabited room again, signs of life everywhere: Jamie's grand piano (a gift from his grandmother), music sheets spilling out of their folder, Ginny's pile of self-help books on the writing table, her computer that she toiled at most mornings writing minutes for the various associations she belonged to, her knitting (a new hobby) with its balls of wool and needles lying on top of her latest creation, the present shape of which did not convey what it would end up as. His own collection of real estate and business books sat in the bookcase against the wall, accompanied by a set of the old encyclopaedia he used to sell. Two older volumes, their dust jackets long missing, looked out of place, the lettering on the spines faded, *The Iliad* and *The Odyssey*, gifts from his mother on his twelfth birthday, two items that had made their way over in his solitary suitcase on that nightmare journey out of Sri Lanka.

It was good to be in a room with signs of vitality, of family, however eccentric or diverse its members were. Just a few years ago there had been only the bookcase and its contents, and he had spent many lonely evenings accompanied by a friendly bottle of Vodka to pacify himself.

He felt his phantom toes shriek out in pain, and winced. He took a gulp of his wine; the alcohol helped, sometimes. He gently massaged his left foot and stretched it out. The foot reminded him of too many bad things, and, except in the shower, he never took his socks off, not even in bed.

The pregnancy was a difficult one. After the morning sickness had passed, Ginny decided to join a fitness class for new mothers. Martin would find the time in between the office and clients to drive her to classes and checkups as he did not want anything untoward to happen to her in this delicate state. A change to the anti-depression drugs was postponed until after the baby arrived.

In the sixth month, Ginny abruptly gave up her classes, saying that she was too exhausted to continue. The gynecologist prescribed vitamin supplements and home exercises. Things returned to normal for about a month over the Christmas holidays. Then one evening Martin found Ginny sitting on the living room floor, hair dishevelled, as if she had just gotten out of bed. She was staring at a point in the floor.

"What's the problem honey?" he asked gently, wary of her mood changes.

She did not appear to hear him and kept staring at the imaginary point.

He put on a CD, hoping that would distract her.

"Shut it off!" she shouted.

"Talk to me."

"I'm a bad mother." The look on her face was near maniacal as she turned toward him, eyebrows arched and nostrils flared, eyes as cold as blue ice.

"No, you're not," he said forcefully. She was slumping back and he had to head her off. "Have you taken your supplements?"

"No."

"And your exercises?"

"They don't work."

"Let's go for a walk."

"I don't want to go for a fucking walk."

He walked over and took her by the shoulders. "Look honey, you're on the home stretch. We can't quit now."

A tear lurked at the corner of her eye. She started breathing hard as if trying to hide a sob. "I'm going to fail, Martin. Again."

He was beginning to get exasperated; a hard day at the office and now this at home. For a moment he had a flashback of his mother in her last stages of sanity. *Does one have to pay the piper twice?*

"Why do you think that way, even before you fail?"

"I failed the company."

"Oh, that again."

"I didn't marry into my class."

He felt smacked. The real Ginny would never talk to him like that. This was another person, in a trance, as if he were not even in the room.

She kept talking, unaware of his grimace. "I would like to go the cottage. I hate this house at this time of the year."

"It's January. It'll be pretty miserable up at the cottage."

"But I could take walks in the snow." She rose and walked over to the window. Snow had started to come down gently outside.

"Okay...I'll see if can take a few days off."

She kept gazing out of the window. "The cottage would be nice."

Then she went upstairs, dragging her feet on the stairs. He followed her ten minutes later, but she was fast asleep by then, a bottle of sleeping tablets on the bedside table. He heaved a sigh of relief. She took a sedative when in these dark moods, and when she woke, she often felt and acted better. He stretched out beside her, fully dressed. He wondered how his father must have felt when his mother descended into her lower depths, never to return: abandoned, surely, a stranger to the woman he loved, useless, a candidate for another woman's charms, or the bottle. Victor had chosen both and then settled on one. What was he, Martin, supposed to choose? Or were those choices not open to him?

Martin awoke from a troubled dream of being chased through the forest by a fat baby who looked like Vigo Matinsen, with Ginny sitting on a tree, laughing. He was sweating, despite the cool of the cottage. He blinked in the dark; the creak of leafless maple branches rubbing against each other in the front yard came to his ears.

He shook the dream off and replaced it with recollections of driving to Gravenhurst earlier that evening through a freak snow storm. It had engulfed them suddenly, and the road had disappeared in a whiteout. He had been able to hook onto the taillights of the truck in front and follow it at 20 km/hr all the way from Parry Sound. Ginny had been sighing all the way, saying it had been a bad idea to come out, after all. It was too late to turn back when the snow hit, so he kept going. He had ignored her negative prattling and concentrated on his driving, particularly as the road signs were obliterated with snow. He had to go by the familiarity of certain bends in the road to figure out where he was, or speed up in places to keep pace with the truck ahead.

He parked the car at the side of the main road and they walked uphill to the cottage as the turn-off pathway was snowbound. Martin cursed under his breath: this was no weather in which to come out to the cottage, but he had been grasping at straws, trying to please, trying to cater to her whims. They took only essentials with them up to the house, the rest could follow in the morning when the storm cleared. He was hoping that this snowfall would leave them with a calm winter wonderland that they could frolic in and forget the blahs. After all, these were the winters of her childhood, when life had been carefree. Ginny had stopped complaining as they neared Gravenhurst; she now clammed up and slumped deeper into her parka. When he stopped the car, she followed him wraith-like into the house, hauling what bags he would let her carry. Smithy had turned on the generator and packed food in the refrigerator. After eating a bowl of soup, she retired to bed.

Now he reached for her in the dark. The bed was icy cold and empty, the blankets pulled away. He jumped up with a start and groped for clothing. Shivering, he switched on the light. Her side of the bed was empty, but her dressing gown hung over a stool nearby.

He ran into the living room. Empty. Her parka was gone from the coat rack, so were her boots, cap and mitts. He donned his parka, couldn't find dry socks, slid his bare feet into boots, pulled on gloves and grabbed a blanket as well, just in case he needed it. He fished out a flashlight from the kitchen. A blast of cold air shocked him completely awake when he opened the front door. The snowfall had subsided and the moon was out on the lake. It was indeed a beautiful winterscape, the sinister and dangerous magically transformed into benign tranquility.

He flashed the dim beam around the front yard calling her name. Only a dog barking in the distance answered. He ran down to the dock; both boats were moored and their coverings caked with a thick layer of snow. He turned back towards the woods, looking for footprints. His panic increased and he kept dragging himself about the yard through knee-high drifts with no plan of attack. Then he caught himself and decided to pan the area in widening arcs. Finally, he saw them, behind the house, heading for one of the animal paths that Ginny had taken him down during the summer. The path was undistinguishable in the snow, but he followed the break in the trees and the deep footprints that went down the middle, as if the walker ahead was burdened, or drunk.

Snow had crept into his boots and his feet began to freeze. He gritted his teeth and continued on.

He almost stumbled over her. She had collapsed like deadfall across the path, wrapped only in her brown parka. He scooped her up and flashed the light on her face. She wore a silly grin that made him wince.

"It's like camping," she said.

"It's freezing fucking cold, Ginny. Let's get you inside." He hauled her up and she lay limp in his grasp. His toes were beginning to lose their feeling altogether. He slung her right arm over his shoulder and turned back toward the cottage. The flashlight fell out of his hands into the snow. He swore. He lowered her down gently and crawled back for the light. As he picked it up, the beam flashed over their footsteps. He froze: a red stain was scribbled across the snow, from the point where he had picked her up to where she now lay.

He hauled her up, and at her feet were those incriminating red spots.

"We have to get you to a doctor."

"I told you, I wasn't going to make it, Martin. But it was good to go camping one last time." Her voice was off-key but triumphant.

He could see the cottage through the trees and the moon was fully over. He dropped the flashlight to get a better grip on her and half dragged, half carried her to the house.

He laid her on the sofa, propping her legs up on cushions. He called 911 and was advised that there would be a delay in getting to him as the roads were snowed-in and there had been a lot of accidents during the storm. He asked what he could do in the meantime and was given some stop-gap tips: keep the patient warm, turn her head to the side, no fluids, keep her feet up – all intended to prevent haemorrhagic shock.

"Can I drive her over?" Martin said, unsatisfied with the response he was getting.

"Better not," said the calm operator. "Your chances of getting through to the nearest hospital are as good, or as worse, as ours. She shouldn't be moved."

He gave the man directions to the house. "A kilometre out of the town, you'll see a grey Cadillac Seville pulled off to the side of the road. The way up to the cottage is on the path uphill from there."

Hanging up reluctantly—somehow the operator seemed to link him to the world of sanity—Martin settled Ginny as best as he could in the way he had been instructed, and limped around the house, praying to a god he had never believed in, to help her and the baby. He checked the clock—2:30 a.m.—too late to call Smithy or the locals for help. What could they do anyway? No, this was his cross, and he had to bear it.

Suddenly he felt a burning in his toes—shit—he had forgotten about his own situation. He stepped out of his boots. His toes were red and swollen and the last two on his left foot were a sickly purple-white. He touched them and felt no sensation. He limped into the washroom and turned on the hot water tap—shit again!—the water heater had been turned off. He switched the heater back on and bound his feet in towels to keep them warm. He limped back to Ginny who was groaning; the sofa under her was staining red.

She gripped his arm tightly, her eyes urgent. "Save the baby, Martin. I'm not going to make it."

"You will make it," he roared, screaming at the rafters. "You will make it. We will all make it. My fucking toes will make it, the baby will make it. We are going to make it…" He stumbled back into the bathroom and lukewarm water dripped on his toes, warming them up as the flow increased in heat. There was still no sensation in his feet. He wet towels and limped out again, placing them on Ginny's swollen belly. *Keep the patient warm, the man had said.*

"We've been through worse, honey. Don't give up now. Please don't," he begged her, squeezing her frozen hands, trying with all his might to infuse energy from his cold body into hers.

He didn't know how long he stayed, embracing her close to him, warming her with his body, pulling out reserves of strength and forcing them down to her, swearing at the top of his voice when it looked as if they were both going under. He crawled over to the phone and pulled it over to the sofa. He dialled 911 again, and this time he got a woman.

"We can't hold on much longer," he pleaded. "I called earlier. We may lose the baby. And my wife is going into shock."

The woman coolly put him on hold and said she would check where things were. He was about to slam the phone down and turn back to Ginny when the woman came back on the line. "Sir, the paramedics are at the bottom of your driveway making their way over. Sit tight."

"God Bless you!" he yelled and crawled to the door to make sure the porch lights were still on.

The front door opened and Ginny walked in just as the timer went off in the kitchen. Martin rose from the sofa, shaking the memories of the past away from him. "You couldn't have timed it better. Dinner is ready. How was your day?" he asked.

Ginny threw her keys down on the side table and stretched. "Tiring. They want me to run for president." She was thinner now, hair cut short, beginning to look a little like her mother: angular, flatter breasts and wiry arms from all that exercise in the gym.

"Congratulations!" he said. "And which association is this, refresh my mind?"

She looked annoyed. "Oh Martin, you never pay attention. This is the Divorced Women & Single Parent's Association."

"Sorry," he said sheepishly, going in search of another glass of wine. "How do they account for the fact that you are not divorced? Or a single parent?"

"I could have been. We were close to the edge. Remember?"

He ignored her comment and repeated, "Dinner is ready."

"How was Jamie's class today?"

"The child is gifted and a gift to us. He ran through the Mozart sonata like he was the maestro himself. Blames it on his grandmother's influence."

"Well, that's all well and good, as long as it doesn't take over his life. There are plenty of starving musicians around."

"Honey, this kid is not going to be a starving musician. He is a prodigy."

"We'll see. I'm famished. All I had was a salad today."

"That's part of your routine, isn't it?"

"It's fine for you men to be smug about our diets. I'm not sure where you stow your food."

Martin grinned. "I must have picked up worms, growing up in the colonies. And they still reside in me...Jamie!" Martin knew he would have to issue the summons a few more times before the boy actually responded.

Jamie lumbered downstairs, the spring in his step gone in his mother's presence.

"How was your day, young man?" she asked, as they passed the food around serving each other. "You'd better eat more vegetables there."

"I hate vegetables," Jamie said, and looked at Martin for acquiescence.

Martin shrugged. "No help there buddy. Veggies are good. And you'd better eat up if you want that guitar."

"What guitar?" Ginny's eyebrow was raised.

"Oh, something I promised him if he brings the house down at the school concert."

"And do I not get consulted in these matters?"

"Oh, Mum, I've always been asking for a guitar," Jamie said, his hands on his head, pouting.

"You're in grade two now, honey. It's time for some serious studying."

"He's ahead of his class and the youngest member too. Cut him some slack, Ginny. It's a junior acoustic guitar anyway, nothing serious. And I'm not buying the amplification unit yet, just the guitar for now."

Ginny put her fork down, her tone getting serious and her voice slowing down. Martin did not like this stage of their conversations. "You know how much time this child spends on musical instruments, especially when they are new. Mother's paid for music lessons are time-consuming enough. When is he going to have time for swimming and hockey?"

"I hate swimming and hockey." Now it was Jamie's turn to throw his fork down. It clanged on the plate and sent scraps of food splattering on the table.

"Jamie!" Ginny flushed.

"Okay, okay, cool down," Martin interrupted. "Let's have a peaceful dinner, shall we? Then let's get through the concert. Then, only then, will we take the next steps, in a civilized fashion."

Martin could not avoid the look on Jamie's face again as the child picked up his fork and went through the motions of eating, very slowly. The rest of the dinner went by in silence.

He looked across at Ginny and Jamie, and his foot throbbed. Despite the frostiness, it was good to see them both at this table. His mind went back to when the paramedics arrived that night...

"We are going to rush her to the hospital and try to save the baby," the lead paramedic, a chunky man with a beard said, as the stretcher, bearing a tightly strapped Ginny, hooked up to an IV drip, was hauled out the door by his assistant and the driver. "I'm sorry we couldn't get here earlier."

Martin stood inside the open doorway, blankets draped over him, feet covered in towels. "I'm coming too."

"Better get your boots on, Mr. James," the man said.

"I don't think I can get them on. I've had my feet exposed in the snow."

The man came back indoors, a terse look on his face. He forced Martin down on the sofa. "Let's have a look at that." He began peeling away the towels.

Martin was getting impatient and angry, using the anger to keep the numbness in his feet from spreading. "I think this can wait. Why don't we get my wife to the hospital first?"

The man took one look and was already onto his radio phone. "I need one of you guys back here. We need to get this gentleman into surgery. A bad case of frostbite."

They amputated two of his toes at about the same time that Jamie was delivered prematurely in another section of that regional hospital.

At seven and a half months, the baby was seriously underweight and was required to be in incubation for two weeks. As much as he was grieved to hear this news, Martin was relieved, because it gave Ginny time to heal from her ordeal, and for him to strategize on how the baby would be cared for. He couldn't trust Ginny any more. He tried to get news about her: that she was in the ICU in a critical condition was all the nurses could give him. Out of a sense of duty, he called Clarissa and left a message on her phone, providing as much detail as he could. Clarissa never called back.

Two days later, they moved him into a wheelchair; he immediately asked to be taken to see his wife and child.

A helpful nurse wheeled him into the neo-natal area. There were more nurses and parents walking around than babies. She led him towards a heavily panelled door and requested that he wait there until she got the necessary paperwork completed. Both his feet were in bandages and his left was throbbing. He laid his head back in the chair and gazed at the bright overhead lights. He could not believe that his entire family was in this hospital at the same time, suffering from three dissimilar conditions.

The nurse returned, swung open the giant doors and wheeled him inside. Three incubators lay in the centre of the room, their tiny contents inert, with tubes entwining them.

She stopped at the middle one. The label said "Summers".

"His family name should read 'James,'" Martin said.

The nurse looked at her papers. "I'm sorry that's what it says in the hospital record. The mother is Virginia, correct? Your wife?"

"Yes."

"The last name of the baby is given as Summers." She said reading the papers again and nodding her head emphatically.

"Can you leave me in private for a minute?"

"Of course. I'll be outside." The nurse withdrew quietly.

The baby was small, tiny, not more than four pounds. An oxygen tube covered his face and electrodes were attached to his bony chest as he lay in a comatose state. Martin wanted to reach out and touch. He placed his hand on the outer wall of the incubator; the baby's tiny toes were directly on the other side. He imagined stroking those toes—at least—this little infant had all ten of them. Tears poured out of him and huge sobs of relief wracked him. *My son, I'm not sure we are starting off on the right foot, but I swear that I will raise you to realize the freedom we all desire but so few of us have.*

A hand tapping him gently on the shoulder brought him back to the present. "We should leave now, Mr. James," the nurse said. "I will take you to your wife." She wheeled him out, backwards, so that he could continue to gaze upon the receding incubator and its occupant.

"I want to correct that hospital record," he said. "The child's first name is James. I'll sign any papers you need to make it happen."

"You wife will need to co-sign too."

"I never signed the original."

"I can't answer for that, sir," the nurse said, looking nonplussed.

"Take me to her then." The determination on his face cut out further conversation.

Virginia had come out of the ICU the previous night, the nurse informed him, as they ascended the elevator.

She wheeled him down a corridor, a female section for women with brightly decorated rooms in floral and feminine art forms.

They turned into a private room. Virginia was asleep, her hair sweaty and plastered to her forehead, wearing a similar orange uniform like the one he was in. An IV stuck out of her left arm and her feet were propped up on pillows and draped with a thick blanket. A figure stirred in the chair beside the bed and straightened abruptly—Clarissa. Catching sight of the nurse, she immediately seemed to bite back the words threatening to spew out of her mouth.

"Leave me here," Martin told the nurse. When the woman withdrew, discreetly shutting the door behind her, Clarissa burst out, "How dare you put us through all this?" She had drawn herself to her full imperious height, looking down at him in his chair. Despite the recent stoop she had developed, she looked to be in full flight. Her arrogance only served to bring out the bitterness in him.

"What the hell do you mean?" he shot back. "Perhaps you should ask your daughter that question?"

"She almost died through her experience."

"And nearly took us all with her."

Their voices had elevated to the point that Ginny began to stir.

Clarissa immediately went over to her daughter. "Perhaps we should defer this discussion for another time."

Martin gripped the edges of his wheelchair, his knuckles white. "Perhaps, not. Perhaps it's time that Ginny faces the reality of her situation and chooses between me and her damned heritage."

Clarissa turned, hissing, "Don't you dare talk like that...you...you..."

"You, what? Go on spit it out, woman. You never liked me from the day I came into your house. Do you think the sun shines out of your ass? Do you?"

"Martin, stop it." It was Ginny.

Martin turned on her. "The boy's first name is James. I want you to sign that change to the birth certificate."

"And if she doesn't?" Clarissa interjected. The old lady was looking as if she had been slapped and was desperately trying to regain her composure.

"Then I'll fucking go to court to have it done."

Ginny held her head and fell back in the sheets. "Oh Mother, please do not shout. I can't stand it. I'll sign, Martin. Whatever you want. Now please leave me alone."

Their raised voices brought in two nurses, including the one who had wheeled him in. "I'm done with my visit," Martin said to them. "Take me back to my room."

Jamie excused himself after dinner and went up to his room; he knew that his parents wanted to have a serious talk, about him. Martin was sure the child would be listening from upstairs.

He looked at his wife across the table and wondered where love had gone. They went through their roles as man and wife, as parents and keepers of a respectable household, but intimacy seemed to be in another place, too far out of reach. Even sex occurred with clinical regularity: twice a week and with a marked lack of spontaneity; it was part of her infamous "schedule," a rostered wifely duty like doing her share of the cooking and laundry. He often wondered why Ginny would not simply divorce him. He had considered it too. But the thought of Jamie being swallowed up in the Summers' camp, only to be released on select outings with his father, was too difficult a bridge to cross. Maybe it was difficult for her too, for the same reason. Besides, however hostile she would become with him during her "moods," he suspected that she still viewed him as her pillar of stability—the whipping boy who would not leave his post. But for how long would these psychological restraints be in place before they came unshackled?

"Mother has opened an account for Jamie's university education twelve years from now," Ginny opened cautiously.

"He is a lucky boy," Martin replied, grimacing. "My father could barely afford to pay my high school fees."

She ignored his comment. "The caveat is that he follows a medical, engineering, business or law degree."

"Clarissa develops Jamie's right brain with all this musical stuff and then expects him to be a logical left-brained nerd?"

"You really have to stop picking on Mother."

"I will, when she stops picking on me."

"Music and the arts are only part of one's rounding. We were all sent to music lessons, art classes and given Charles Dickens to read when growing up. The Arts is not a place for a decent career."

"But it can be a calling. It's Jamie's calling."

"If you keep encouraging him with this guitar business, he will easily get confused into *believing* that it is his calling."

"I think I have heard your point on this. I am still buying him the guitar if he does well at the concert, and that's it. I'll make sure he does not neglect his study time."

She flung her napkin down, like she always did when he was intransigent. "When will you listen, Martin?"

"We are in two different worlds, aren't we?" he said, rising from the table and picking up the plates.

"Now I realize what that means."

"There are thousands of people in this country—millions—doing what they were not supposed to do in life. You were there too, when you took on your family's business. Do you want that for our son?"

"Let's not go over this again. Jamie needs to earn a living and a lifestyle. Being a musician will not get him there."

"Ginny, we can still meet in the middle, you know." He was standing there, empty plates in hand, waiting for her to reach out and break the ice, not only of this conversation, but of the many they had had over the years of their marriage.

She ignored his suggestion, rose and went into the living room, to her computer.

Martin was released the following day from hospital and given crutches to move about. Jamie came out of his incubator but was in the care of nurses until his mother recovered. He was taken to her twice a day for breastfeeding and returned to the nursing staff afterward. Ginny spent a month recuperating in hospital. Her condition was still weak at the end of that period, and when she and the infant were finally released, Clarissa suggested that Ginny and the baby move in with her at the Rosedale house.

"No way," Martin insisted, brooking no further argument. "I am not letting James close to Ginny until she is emotionally capable of caring for the child on her own."

Not wanting the mental and emotional stability of her daughter to become the subject of another heated public debate, Clarissa caved in. Martin hired a day-nurse who would live with him in Willowdale to care for the baby until Ginny was willing and able to return home. He was hobbling around with the aid of a walking stick by that time, and felt reasonably mobile to look after his infant son.

The next three months of Jamie's life went by with no mother's milk to wean him, a fact that broke Martin's heart when he remembered how much of his own mother his siblings had suckled on in their formative months. He couldn't wait to get home every day, for when he would dismiss the nurse from her day-time duties, prepare the formula and feed the little guy, place him on his chest and sing to him, let their heartbeats coincide, and watch Jamie fall sleep murmuring peacefully.

Marnie Rogers visited and bought Jamie a cloth puppy and a set of plastic blocks of many colours and shapes. She noted Ginny's absence.

"Ginny's staying with her mother for a few days," Martin explained curtly, carrying Jamie and trying to position one of the blocks in the baby's hand.

"Overwhelmed mother?" Marnie asked, surveying the baby's room. "You seem to be coping very well."

"I'm getting lots of practice," he said, finally latching Jamie's tiny fingers around the block of plastic.

"Yes, there is so much...order...here," she noted. Martin was scrupulous about tidying the baby's bedroom and did an additional round of cleaning after the nurse left each day.

He tried to make light of it. "First-time parents tend to overdo it."

"Well, if there is any way I can help, let me know. You are a lucky man, Martin. I'd love to have my own baby one day."

"I guess I am lucky," he said. *Despite all the shit that has happened.*

The evening after Marnie's visit, the phone rang. Martin heard breathing on the other end, a little out of rhythm. A crazy thought occurred to him: *Oh no, Jamila? Not after all this time?*

"Martin," Ginny's voice was tentative. His heart leaped.

"I'm getting better, Martin."

He gulped. "It's nice to hear from you, honey. How are you?"

"Better. I'm on the new pills. They found the right type for me."

"What pills?"

"Anti-depressants."

"Oh. That's good to hear."

"How's Jamie?"

"He's well, catching up for lost time. He's growing up big and strong. Coos all the time—very musical. He's trying to turn on his belly now."

"I miss him. The little time he spent at my breast was wonderful."

"Would you like me to bring him over?"

She quickly said, "Not yet. I'm not fully there yet. I can't screw this up again. I want to be perfect for him."

"We don't want perfection, Ginny. Just normal would do."

Her voice receded for a bit, as if she were thinking out aloud. "I'm on a schedule. It helps me keep organized. Mother got me this very good psychiatrist."

"We'd both like you home soon, honey. We miss you."

"I miss you too."

But it was another three weeks before she called again. She sounded agitated. "Can you come today? With Jamie?"

"Today? It's 6:30 already. Jamie's asleep."

"Oh. It's just that I steel myself every day and then lose my courage. Today, I felt sure I could manage it."

"How about tomorrow?"

She seemed to think for a long time. He thought the line had dropped. "Hello, Ginny—you still there?"

"Tomorrow?"

"Yes, I can bring him over tomorrow at around five in the evening."

"Okay. I'll prepare for it."

Her transformation was spectacular. She had trimmed her hair and wore a dark blue dress. She had lost weight and her face seemed to have matured in the intervening weeks, like someone coming back from a near-fatal car crash and developing reserve and a deeper perspective they'd never had before.

She held out her hands for Jamie who was dressed in a jumpsuit. Martin tenderly handed the baby over, warily watching her every move, relieved at the care she was demonstrating. He rested his cane and sat down heavily on the chair. He was glad that Clarissa had not yet put in an appearance. Perhaps the old dame was watching from some secret peephole, ready to pounce the moment he said something untoward.

After Ginny had exhausted herself kissing and petting Jamie, she turned to Martin. "How is your foot?"

"It'll hold. I lost a couple of toes. They hurt now and again."

"I'm sorry." The remorse in her face was palpable.

He shrugged and remained silent. Just then his phantom toes made their presence felt and he winced.

"Martin, there's been too much conflict these last two years. I'd like to come home. Things will not be the same, but I want to make them the best they can be under the circumstances."

Looking at her then, he realized that even though she and the baby were now safe, something between Ginny and him had died. The bond, which was their spontaneity, had been battered to pieces by the prevailing forces that had engulfed them ever since their marriage. They were now different persons.

Looking at her now as she worked on her computer, typing endless lists of action items and scheduling activities, he realized that they still had not re-established that magical bond. Their marriage ran like a well-oiled business partnership, with activities—including sex— scheduled in an organized fashion. This schedule kept her balanced, with some help from her lifelong companion: anti-depressants. It was like one of those arranged marriages back home: a pillar of stability, a springboard for the family-run business, a crucible for birthing unemotional but enterprising children who would in turn make loveless marriages and propagate the family dynasty.

He shrugged his shoulders and went upstairs to see how Jamie had made out with his reading.

15. **Cheating**

On the morning of the day of Jamie's concert, Martin received a call at the office. "Martin, how are you?" the old wheezy voice said.

Martin sighed. "Hello, Vigo. Are you back in Canada?"

"Yes, yes, the time of parrying is over. Time to thrust again, Martin. I hear you're going from strength to strength: a married man, a broker... Aha, my boy, I knew you would go places."

"And I don't have you to thank for that, Vigo." Martin was feeling less and less enthusiastic as the call progressed.

"Ah, but come, that was business, no? Listen, I got a deal for you. It will be good for your business."

"I am not working for you again, Vigo."

"No, no, you don't have to work for me. We can be partners, yah?"

"Well, I'm rather busy. Can we talk some other time?"

"Look Martin, let me see you for a few minutes today, okay? This is a really hot deal. It cannot wait or we will lose the whole thing. Can I see you at four o'clock today?"

As much as he did not want to have anything to do with Vigo, business was business. "My son's taking part in a concert. Can we make that earlier, say three o'clock? At your old haunt, the King Eddy?"

"Ah yes, please. I will see you there. Thank you, dear Martin."

Vigo was waiting for Martin, pacing up and down the lobby, an unlit cigar—in deference to the anti-smoking sentiment sweeping the city—between his fingers. The man had put on even more weight but looked paler.

"Martin!" Vigo was all over him hugging, kissing him on both cheeks, beaming magnanimously. "Come, we need to talk. Tell me about your family." *Vigo the family man—perhaps he has spent too much time with his Italian mama.*

Over tea and cake served in the lobby restaurant, Martin gave Vigo the headlines on his marriage, on his son, and on the brokerage, keeping out the unnecessary details.

"That's great, Martin. I knew you were a survivor. I am very happy for you."

"What's this deal about, Vigo? Sorry I don't have a lot of time to spend chatting today."

"Ah yes," Vigo leaned forward in his chair, looking to either side of him before speaking. "Let me explain..."

The Garibaldi deal was simple. A giant shopping mall had opened in north Toronto in the early eighties and taken off as it had fulfilled a need of the growing number of residents in the area. Enrico Garibaldi, the owner-developer, had taken the project a step further and begun building an office tower next to the mall but had run into the crash of '87. He had let the project sit the last few years and was now interested in re-activating it. He was looking for partners. Garibaldi was promising a 25 percent return. It was 1995; the recession was over, the glut of real estate in the downtown core was easing, and office towers were once again growth opportunities.

"What do you want me to do?" Martin asked.

"I want you to get me the investors. And I will also appoint your firm as sole leasing agent for all the offices in the tower."

"How much are we talking?"

"We need a million dollars to get our overdraft extended and complete the construction." Vigo's beady eyes were studying Martin intently.

"I'll come up with half of that, you can fetch the other half."

Vigo chuckled. "You are a good boy, sharp as usual. You want my...skin in the game...is that how you say it in this country, Martin?"

And your balls too, for security. "Yes, that is the expression," Martin said wryly. "What is your connection in all this?"

"Ah. Enrico is my business partner. Matinsen Properties—that's my new company, by the way—will be the lessor of the office space."

Martin placed his tea cup back in its saucer and rose. "I'll think about it, Vigo. Now I have to go, or I'll be late. I'll call you tomorrow."

"Think well on it, Martin. Dream on it. And give my kind regards to your beautiful wife and talented son."

The final coda of the sonata rippled along the walls of the auditorium. Everyone's eyes were on the diminutive pianist running his fingers frantically over the keys, an agitated little creature, who had started off as a waif-like little boy too short for the pedals. Now he was on his feet, head swooping down towards the keys and then up in a graceful arc as if pulling notes from a heavenly source, hitting perfect time, adding trills where least expected, taking the lows and highs of the piece with quiet or deliberate intensity, creating contrasts that sent goose pimples along one's forearms—all this from a boy not quite seven?

Martin heard Ginny gasp beside him in that dramatic pause between the piece's end and the audience's spontaneous rise to its feet. On her other side, sat Clarissa, politely clapping, a look of satisfaction cracking her austere face. Martin had winced when he heard that Clarissa was coming to the concert as well. But it did make sense; she was, after all, checking up on her investment in her grandson's musical lessons. They hadn't spoken a word to each other, just politely nodded and maintained their distance, keeping Ginny in the middle wherever possible.

As the angular music teacher, dressed for the occasion in a dark evening gown, came up on stage to make her closing speech, Ginny wiped her nose with a tissue, shaking her head, "To think that we almost lost him," she whispered, stifling a burst of crying.

Martin saw his opening. "Do you think he's earned his guitar?"

She didn't reply, but he could see her nodding to herself several times.

Jamie came out of the green room carrying his gold medal. He waved it proudly. Clarissa ran forward and embraced him. She made sure that she stood beside him when the photographer came around to take the souvenir pictures as the children and their families mingled for coffee and refreshments.

Jamie managed to break away at one point and grabbed Martin's hand. "Dad, did I do well?"

Martin embraced him and lifted him up. "Fantastic, buddy!"

Jamie was looking directly into his eyes, "And the guitar..."

"Sold!"

"Gee, thanks Dad!"

"I want you to work with me on this deal," Martin said. He had summoned Marnie into his office and briefed her on the Garibaldi project. He would bring in the investors; she would sell the office space. Both were co-dependent activities: the more she sold, the more those investors would be tempted to chip in.

"Good. I need a new challenge to focus on," she said, hands circling her third cup of coffee for the morning.

Martin paused and looked at Marnie. The last seven years of their business association had seen her emerge from a high-energy sales person projecting little emotional depth, into a mature, attractive woman still possessing that instinct for the kill but with more restraint and consideration for her clients' needs. There were moments when he caught her off-guard and saw a trace of sadness in her face. Her sales had flattened out in recent months and he was concerned about her.

"How are things since the divorce?" he asked in a measured tone. "Sorry I don't get much time to talk to you. It gets so busy in this place."

She sipped her coffee. "Jim settled on giving me the condo and he took the cottage."

"I mean on the emotional side."

She sighed. She took a gulp from her cup and there seemed to be more than coffee in her throat.

"That's a wasteland, but thanks for asking, Martin."

"I've found that marriage is not the romantic ideal we make it out to be."

"Yes. Jim and I should have just stayed lovers."

Martin remembered partnering with Jim once at the firm's annual golf outing. Jim had been pre-occupied with his handicap (five) and with the new set of clubs he was researching for potential purchase.

Martin sighed gently. "I've heard of golf widows."

"Childless golf widows are even more pathetic." She drained her cup, tossed it into the waste-bin and stood up, straightening her suit. Martin gave in to a moment of weakness, when he gave into daydreaming about imagining her warm body underneath: full lips, breasts and hips; and a generous and compassionate disposition, despite being an aggressive salesperson. *God, those golf addicts must be nuts.*

"I'll drop the Garibaldi file off on your desk shortly," he said shrugging off the image of a naked Marnie.

"Looking forward to working with you on this, boss."

She gave him her customary wink as she left the office. This time he felt himself flushing and hoped that she hadn't noticed.

Martin heard the guitar notes in Jamie's room. He paused; something was not right. Jamie had been practising with the guitar for only two weeks; it was too soon for near-perfect strains to emanate from the instrument, even for someone with Jamie's potential.

He peeped inside the room. Jamie was seated cross-legged in the middle of his untidy room, cradling the guitar that was too big for him. He was playing the notes from a music book spread out in front of him. There was a frown of concentration on his face.

"How's it going, buddy?"

Jamie did not appear to hear him and kept playing, protesting under his breath from time to time. Martin loved watching his son in this state—the concentration, the desire to find those elusive notes and execute them to tempo—a beautiful study in the evolution of the species.

Martin tapped on the door this time, and Jamie shook his head, "I heard you the first time, Dad. It's just that I can't get my fingers to these chords quick enough."

"Don't you need to practise some more before you get there?"

"But this should be easier than the piano. It's cool watching Manuel Gonzales."

"Yeah, and he has practised for how many years?"

"Aaah! My fingers don't reach these stupid notches."

Martin rubbed his son's shoulders. "Come on buddy. The way you are growing up, very soon, your fingers will no longer have that problem. Let's give this one a rest, shall we? Fancy an ice-cream?"

"Double chocolate with whipped cream?"

"Well, if you hurry up before your mum gets home from her meeting, we might manage that. And..."

Jamie leaned the guitar against the bed. "And...what?"

"If you eat your dinner, including the vegetables."

Jamie grinned. "I think I can handle that."

The selling was well oiled. Vigo gave Martin an open account at the King Eddy and Enrico Garibaldi extended his private skybox at the baseball games for entertaining prospects. "Bring your targets there and make sure they eat and drink well," were Vigo's instructions.

Martin quickly lost track of the number of cocktail events that he and Marnie attended at these venues, where they both worked the crowd, he on likely investors, she on prospective tenants. Garibaldi's own contacts would occasionally show up at the baseball games, but they were the dark-suited types who huddled in corners, nibbling caviar, sipping champagne, talking in monotones, oblivious to the baseball action. Martin's alcohol consumption ballooned with all the liquid lunches and dinners, and he found himself increasingly in Marnie's company for most of the working day and night.

Martin had also run into a snag in finding investors. After collecting investment funds from the clients who had shown interest, he was still $100K short. Without consulting Ginny, he took out a loan secured against the equity in the house on Willowdale. He reasoned that there was no sense in bringing her into the equation at this late stage; it would only add to her sense of instability. The office tower was a few short months away from completion, and Marnie had already sold six tenants and had a dozen warming in the pipeline. When asked to have both signatures on the loan application form, Martin reproduced Ginny's familiar signature on the form next to his. The loan would be retired inside three months; what harm could there be?

Yet, the fact that he had so easily forged Ginny's signature bothered him, even as they completed a good round of entertaining at the Dome. However, a couple of vodka and sodas soon drove that worry away. Garibaldi's dark-suited types were in the majority at the skybox that evening. Not having any of his own clients to schmooze, Martin had little to do but drink and enjoy the game; in fact he had come out to the Dome to keep his conflicted thoughts about the loan at bay and to cut loose a bit. Marnie, on the other hand, had taken the opportunity to hype her sex appeal; and this time the dark-suits were smiling, ogling, and falling for her charms.

They each had a drink to chill out after their guests had departed and Martin offered to drop Marnie off at her apartment. She was equally high, both from one too many glasses of wine and the fact that one of her own prospects had finally agreed to come on board at that evening's event. And many of the dark-suits had promised to get back to her.

"This has been the best damned job I've worked on, Martin," she said, rolling down the window as they sped up the ramp onto the Gardiner Expressway.

"Yeah, that Ruscoe fellow was staring down your front all evening."

She threw her head back and laughed out loud. He had not seen her do that in a long time.

"He signed in the end. For that I'd have been prepared for him to see me naked." Then she caught herself and held her hand modestly to her breast. "Oops, sorry."

He felt bold. "I'm sure a lot of Garibaldi's guys would want to see that."

"I take it you're not one of them."

"I might be. I'm only human."

"And you're married to a bitch, if you don't mind my saying so...boss."

"You can stop calling me 'boss.'" He did not want to reprimand her further. It was a known fact in the office that Ginny treated him shabbily at times. His staff had witnessed the number of times that Martin had left early on days when he had to suddenly cook and do the domestic chores because Ginny had called to say that she was "sick" again, and they had heard the ingratitude in her voice whenever she had called for Martin during one of her moods and had wanted him to come home no matter what, even when he was occupied with a client on an important deal. While Martin put this down to how one should treat a depressed person—after all, his mother had become infinitely worse as she went downhill—his staff took Ginny's behaviour as a sign of disrespect.

"Why is it that all the good guys get taken?" Marnie muttered. The last glass of wine she had downed just after their guests had left was taking effect now.

"Opposites attract, I guess."

"Are you attracted to me Martin? I know I am being bold today. But I've known you for seven bloody years and if I can't ask you that question now, I'm just full of shit."

He remained silent. He was afraid to answer. He found her terribly honest, attractive and dangerously tipsy.

"We'll be pulling over at your place in a few minutes. Then you can sleep it off and we can forget we ever had this conversation."

"Are you going to fire me Martin? For stepping over the line?"

"No." He sighed. He felt his resolve weakening. "We go back too far, Marnie."

He turned the car into her driveway and instead of stopping under the porch of the apartment building, drove into one of the visitor's parking spots.

"You coming in," Marnie said. It was more a statement than a question. "I'll make you a coffee, or a nightcap. Or anything you like."

He suddenly reached across the seat and drew her to him. He smelt the alcohol in her breath, saw the hunger in her eyes, fuelling his own appetite that had been submerged by routine sex over the last six years. "You asked me whether I was attracted to you. And I didn't answer," he said.

"And..." her eyes were goading him on; her full lips curling into a smile.

He crushed his mouth on hers and drank thirstily of what she had to offer.

He woke with a start. Marnie was lying on her back, snoring gently beside him, her bulbous breasts with their large areoles heaving gently like buoys in a harbour. The room was warmer than his at home and the sheets were still wet with their sweat. Neon glittered in the window. He wanted to ignore the nagging thoughts and immerse himself in her welcoming warmth again. It had been like taking a steam bath after breaking rocks in a quarry all day; he had moaned as he had thrust himself inside her. She in turn had been so accommodating, taking him into her with joy and delight, enveloping him with her strong arms and caressing him; an act that he could remember only from a long time ago.

This is wrong. He rose silently and started pull on his clothes. *Yet, is it?* There was nothing wrong in two people consensually giving each other what they could not get in their private lives. *Are we breaking a law?*

"Martin?" Marnie's voice drifted over languorously from the bed.

"I have to go home."

"Please stay a bit longer."

"No. It's past everyone's bedtime."

He heard her sigh in understanding.

"You won't fire me now, will you?" She switched on the bedside lamp and held the sheets up to her naked bosom. She looked delicious with her eyes wide in question, no longer as confident as she had been during their dance of intimacy, worried as he was, as the cold dose of reality washed over her. He had to pull himself away from dropping his pants and diving right back into her bed.

"No, I can't afford to do that now, can I? Goodnight, Marnie. I'll see you in the office tomorrow."

He let himself out the front door and tiptoed to the elevator. He drove carefully, mindful of the police and their RIDE patrols at this time of the evening. He knew his blood alcohol was still on the high side, and he could smell Marnie all over him. He couldn't suppress the thought that he had followed in the footsteps of his father after all: booze, broads and bets with other people's money—well, he had succumbed to all those temptations in a single day, hadn't he?

The following morning they avoided each other, partly because the office was busy and partly because of the aura of embarrassment now hovering between them. At three o'clock Marnie hung outside his door. Steeling himself for emotional fallout, Martin waved her in. But she was all business.

"Martin, I've had those three guys in from last evening— Garibaldi's contacts—who want to sign up immediately. I know I'm a good salesperson, but I didn't think I was that good."

He was relieved to be able to focus on business. "Check out their credit, before you take them on."

"Well, that's the problem. They're paying cash!"

She was studying him, he felt, as he busied himself looking over the paperwork; not just for his verdict on these customers, but for any sign of leftovers from the previous night. Finally, he put the papers down.

"Let's get to this in a minute," he said rubbing his eyes. "I am sorry for yesterday. I took advantage..."

She reached out and placed her hand on his. "Why do you have to be sorry, Martin? Wasn't it good? For both of us?"

"Yes. But..."

"There are no 'yes-buts'. I felt wonderful last night."

"We were both drunk, Marnie."

She withdrew her hand. She rose slowly. "Well, I'll be in my office when you've finished with those papers, boss."

"Oh come on Marnie, don't start that cold shoulder crap. I get enough of that at home."

"You don't know when you have a good thing going, Martin James." She made to walk out of the office.

"Wait." He picked up the papers and stood up. Through the thin glass walls of his office, he could see the other agents hurriedly returning to their work. Once there had been only him, Marnie, and Vinod; now there were seven agents and an office administrator, and invariably, a handful were in the office at any given time.

He handed the papers back to Marnie. "I'd take these guys on board. Just check out these companies that are leasing the space, what kind of business they run, etc. And let's have a drink after work. There is no privacy in here."

"Thanks, Martin." The gratitude in her eyes warmed his heart.

Martin walked out of the clubhouse to his designated golf cart. He was surprised to see another player already at the wheel. The man, in dark glasses and Panama hat, extended his tattooed hand. "Hi. My name Boris. Come, get in."

"Is this the Garibaldi party?" Martin asked, noting that his own golf clubs were already strapped to the back of the cart.

"Yes. Get in. Mr. Garibaldi is already on the first tee."

Martin got in and let himself be driven through plush lawns, down a gully and onto the first tee, which overlooked a man-made lake and an assortment of sand traps on the outer bank. Emerald Lakes was a private course, exclusive to members and their guests.

A chunky but athletic man in his late forties dressed in a red shirt, white canvas hat with a leather headband to match crisp white slacks and classic two-tone golf shoes, was warming up his swing in the tee box. A Boris-like clone sat in the driver's seat of the second cart parked to the side.

The chunky man stopped in mid swing and turned around as Martin and Boris drove up.

"Hello. Enrico Garibaldi. How do you do?"

"Glad to finally meet you, Enrico." Martin said, disembarking and taking his host's hand. "Sorry I was late getting here."

Garibaldi was anxious to get started. "You first," he said. "Please."

Martin felt the prick of anxiety as he flexed his driver over the ball. Despite having taken some rudimentary lessons and playing more frequently the last few years, he was not comfortable with the consistency of his swing. This was a game he wished he had learned as a child. That was also why he did not want Jamie to give up his piano playing in his formative years.

He swung and sliced the ball to the left. Luckily it cleared the lake but landed on the tip of a sand trap.

Garibaldi stepped up and with just a quick swipe cleared 250 yards, over the lake and dead centre down the fairway.

"Great shot!" Martin had practised the art of complimenting his opponent, especially as they were invariably clients whom he courted.

Garibaldi shook his head. "Not good enough. But let's go. It must get better from here."

Martin looked towards the cart drivers. "Aren't they playing?"

Garibaldi got into the passenger seat of his cart. "No, they just drive, and and keep their eyes and ears peeled. Come, let's go."

Martin's anxiety eased a little on the next few holes. Garibaldi swore whenever he scored bogey or higher. Martin was jubilant if he could make double bogey.

"What's your handicap?" Garibaldi asked him on the third hole.

"I've never had it assessed. I'll be happy the day I break a hundred."

Garibaldi grimaced. "Ah, that is not the way to play. You have to set targets all the time and start to lower them."

On the ninth hole, as they paused for a drink, Martin decided to ask Garibaldi what he wanted to talk about.

"Plenty of time for that. Now focus on the game. I never lose my focus."

Martin started to go downhill on holes 14, 15 and 16, losing a ball in the forest that had suddenly sprung up on the left, and another in the river that skirted the right boundary. He decided to play it safe on the par-3 17th and managed to land his tee shot on the green.

"Good comeback, good comeback." Garibaldi nodded and then dropped his tee shot closer to the pin than Martin's. "Ah, but not good enough."

Garibaldi drained his putt for a birdie, while Martin had to be content with two putts to make par.

As Martin teed up for the last par-5 hole trailing behind a giant 275 yard tee shot from Garibaldi, his host suddenly asked him. "Your sales lady, Ms. Rogers, she's good, no?"

Martin straightened, not taking his shot. "Yes. She is the best I have."

"She asks too many questions."

"What do you mean?"

"Please make your shot. I did not mean to interrupt you."

Martin teed off, but clubbed down on the ball and sent it no more than fifty yards.

"Ah, ah...poor shot," Garibaldi said shaking his head. "Concentration, si?"

Martin pulled his number-3 wood, walked up to the ball, tried to freeze out the sudden panic and managed to clear a 180-yard second shot.

"Better, better," Garibaldi said, getting into his cart and motioning to his driver to take off.

They did not meet up again until the green. Garibaldi was waiting patiently for Martin, sporting a grin, pleased at getting to the green in two shots.

"What about Marnie?" Martin asked as Garibaldi prepared for his 10 yard putt for eagle.

"Later...later," Garibaldi murmured as he measured the distance again and took one more practice putt.

"Don't keep me in suspense, Enrico," Martin snapped, just as Garibaldi stroked his putt. The ball veered an inch away from the hole. Garibaldi threw his putter down on the ground. "Damn, that would have been my best score this year. I told you, no talking!" His eyes blazed with anger.

"Sorry." Martin bent down over his ball, turning his back on Garibaldi, feeling somewhat jubilant. His was a long putt: 20 yards or more, downhill with at least two turns in the cut of the turf. He had already consumed his five strokes just to get to the green. *Double bogey, if I'm lucky.* He took aim and sent the ball off in the direction of the hole, reminding himself to follow through. The ball rolled evenly at first, then turned left, caught the downhill lie and rolled faster, correcting course to hit the lip of the hole and fall in.

"Phew! I'll take that bogey." Martin grinned. Garibaldi picked up his ball without finishing his putt.

"You have a lot to learn about golf...and business, Martin," he said, looking at his watch. "Sorry I can't stay for a drink, I have another meeting to get to. But please help yourself to the bar; there is an open tab in my name."

"Thank you. I won't if you will not join me."

Garibaldi waved his two goons off to the club house with the carts. "Come, let us walk back together."

Garibaldi put his arm around Martin's shoulder, squeezing tightly. He seemed to be letting out the tension of the last hole. "Tell your Ms. Marnie not to ask too many questions about her clients, si? These people are my associates. If they want to rent or buy space from me—that is okay, no?"

"Marnie's just thorough. She is acting on behalf of her client and your partner Vigo Matinsen and Matinsen Properties. We do due diligence on all our deals."

Garibaldi paused on the steps of the clubhouse. "But these deals, they are good ones. No need to check further. Do you get it?" The look in his eyes was one of pure steel.

"Fine. If you and Vigo are comfortable, and are willing to sign for it, I'll ask Marnie to back off."

"Good. Ask her to spend her time with you instead. Goodbye, Martin, and happy selling." Garibaldi stepped into the Lincoln that had slid in under the porch of the clubhouse with Boris at the wheel. The car purred away, leaving Martin still grabbing for a suitable come-back.

He reached for her in his sleep. Instinctively, he groped for the large breast that he would cradle in his hand, taking comfort in its velvety softness; the fleshy rump of buttock in which he would snuggle his manhood; the tangle of hair over her shoulders that he would inhale from as if injesting a sleeping draft, sending him back for more needed sleep. Instead his fingers cradled another familiar, smaller breast with tiny hard nipples, his penis nudged into bone and his nose bristled with the short-trimmed hairs of a boyish hairstyle. He woke with a start, frozen, gathering his bearings, heart pounding as if he had been caught stealing candy.

A hand reached out and took his away from the breast, as if to say, "Not now, darling." He eased back into his corner of the bed ashamed of this transgression, this unscheduled and unannounced overture towards intimacy. On her side, Ginny—by now he was fully aware that he was in the matrimonial bed at home in Willowdale—pulled the covers tighter around her, having lost no more than a trifling moment's sleep.

He lay on his back staring at the ceiling in the semi-dark; birds were beginning to chirp outside and a glimmer of light was poking in through the blinds. He was getting too used to Marnie, to their frequent after-work trysts in her warm nest. Over the last two months these meetings had added a new dimension to their lives, re-awakened an old appetite. And they both indulged in it, silently drinking off each other in blind abandon, shutting out the world. Words only brought guilt, so hands and lips did the talking and the fires in their loins administered much needed healing during those moments of congress. When they did talk, it was over Greek or Chinese take-out food that followed the satiating of that other hunger, a gentle postlude to the passionate coda. They talked of loss in love, and loss along life paths that might have taken them in other directions had they made different choices. They even talked, with resigned frankness, about the futility of their present reality that found sustenance only within the cover of her apartment walls.

He recalled similar conversations with Ginny in the days leading up to their marriage; they had been full of optimism about the things they were going to do with their lives and careers back then, some of which had come to pass in ways they could never have imagined. But now those talks never happened. Instead his hand was taken coldly away and put back in its place.

He had agonized over whether to call it off between him and Marnie. Nothing good would come out of it; all the advice books on relationships pointed to the ultimate collapse of the classic office affair built up of adultery, cheating, and mortal sin. Were there no positive words to describe this pass? But every time he was on the verge of calling it off, he paused. Why deny himself a fleeting fragment of abandon at the end of a hard working day when there was no comfort awaiting him at home? Is that how his father Victor must have felt every time he summoned Latha to his room? Martin wished he could have a heart-to-heart with his father right then. And just like his mother knew about Victor's infidelities, did Ginny know about Marnie and him? Was that why their mechanical sex act had dropped off from once a week to only twice for all of last month, and none at all this month, with no explanation beyond the frozen iciness offered? *She must know. The whole world seems to know; how the hell does Garibaldi know?*

Martin rose and dressed in the dark. He tiptoed out of the room only to freeze by the door. Ginny's voice was surprisingly crisp and alert for that early in the morning. "Will you be late coming home today, too?"

"I might be. We're working on the Garibaldi closings. I'll call you."

"I'm going to my MADD meeting. You'll have to eat out."

"I'll do that." He left before they could get into a further exchange. That's what he did these days: stay out of her way. It was safer.

16. **Bandu's Canadian Experience**

Bandu sped along Highway 401. He had to be on duty by 10 o'clock and was pulling a 12 hour shift today. There was serious and dangerous work ahead.

His eyes often flicked to the pictures on the dashboard: Sumana and Ravi. He thought about them a lot. They held much more pleasant memories than any of the others he had of Canada during the decade he had lived here.

He had married Sumana six years ago, after finally agreeing to his mother's oft-repeated plea to marry a girl from back home. In Canada, his only female contacts had been the table dancers and hookers he'd indulged in periodically. Sumana and he were strangers to each other on their first night in bed, just like the hookers had been. She was a compliant new wife, supportive of everything he did. Magilin, his mother, had aged in the years he'd been away and had lost a lot of weight, yet she bounced around the little apartment on Kirula Road, lavishing meals upon her prodigal son and his new bride during their stay with her; after all, she was the one who had made all the arrangements, from matching horoscopes, to making the proposal, to setting up the first meeting between the young couple.

In the three months he had spent in Sri Lanka, Bandu fell in love with Sumana, and then it was time to leave. Her dark hair falling down to her waist, her gentle eyes that lit up in his presence and her earthy smell ignited a yearning in him he had never felt before. He etched that feeling into his soul for the long separation he knew was to come.

On the day he left, his mother embraced him. "*Puthe,* I know I haven't been the best mother to you. But I am happy how things have worked out for you." He returned her embrace, feeling the sharpness of her spine for the first time. "You did your best, *Amma,*" he replied, no longer feeling the anger and shame towards her as in years past. "I will be happy with Sumana."

His fabricated excuse to exit and return to Canada while still a refugee was that he was visiting a "dying mother" back home. The excuse turned to reality a month after he returned to Toronto; he received a letter from Sumana saying that his mother was in the hospital, diagnosed with cancer. Magilin had masked her illness well during his visit. The letter also said that Sumana was pregnant.

Before getting out of the car in the mall parking lot, he glanced at the pictures on the dashboard again. It had taken him five years to bring them across to Canada. He never made it to his mother's funeral; her death had come too fast. His wife and son arrived last year. He was a stranger again to his wife, and certainly to his son. Sumana had stayed strong during their five years of forced separation, always encouraging her husband when most avenues to get his refugee status regularized had run aground. Finally, a favour from a lawyer, who had flagged a ride in his taxi to one of those "discreet" places, led to his case being re-opened and a sympathetic judge ruling in his favour.

Bandu worked long hours. Ravi was still distant from him and knew him only as *"thatha"*, the title Bandu preferred, instead of the word "dad" that the other kids used in school. One day he hoped to have the time to take his wife and son to Disneyworld. He had set aside a savings account just for this trip but expenses always made him dip into it, especially when the car broke down.

The security office was deserted; the guys were on their patrols. *Probably having a smoke outside and pretending to be busy.* Even getting a security job needed "pull" these days and if not for Uncle Sunna's influence, he wouldn't have succeeded. The taxi trade had become competitive and Bandu needed a steadier job when Sumana and Ravi had come over. Now, with Sumana in school upgrading her skills and taking ESL classes, he supplemented his present security guard's salary with lucrative "side jobs."

Bandu busied himself with the log sheets, making sure they were updated. Good, Guna and Toby would be on duty tonight; the two dumbest guys he had ever known. *How the hell did they ever get security jobs? Shows you needed pull.* He went over to the alarm system. Tonight, just before the mall closed, he would disable the router that transmitted information to head office and to the local police station. He would only keep the mall's internal system running; he'd figured this out long ago. Uncle Sunna had shown him. "Make sure both connections, internal and external, are working during your checks, otherwise the system is useless." Uncle Sunna in his zeal to make his protégé a great security guard had revealed all the flaws in the equipment at Mall Security.

The day was busy; it was September, and despite the schools re-opening, kids were still hanging around the mall. These days, the girls were so aggressive, *they* were ogling the boys. They never could utter two words without saying "fuck." He wondered how Ravi would make out with girls like that. When the time came, would his son be better off marrying a girl from back home too?

Nothing out of the ordinary happened on this shift; a couple of kids scrapping opposite the department store and a senior passing out at the subway entrance—pretty routine stuff. On his rounds he checked out Zenith Jewellers; shop attendants were busy serving customers and overhead lights accentuated the gold in the wall-to-wall glass cases.

On his three o'clock round he came across three men in business suits standing in the centre walkway, not far from Zenith Jewellers; one, dressed in a navy blazer was waving his arms expansively about him and talking loudly, while the other two in grey suits were nodding impassively and scrutinizing the shops on either side. Wondering if these guys were last-minute monkey wrenches to his plans, Bandu drew near and tried to overhear their conversation above the hum of shoppers and strollers. He had his back to them and watched their actions in the reflection of a shop window.

"This is a convenient location for your employees," the man in the navy blazer, who looked familiar, was saying. "They can do all their shopping on their breaks here. There are great restaurants, and even a gym."

The other two merely nodded. When Bandu turned around, they were exchanging business cards. *Salespeople! Nothing to worry about.* Bandu resumed his rounds. But he was pre-occupied by the face of the man in the navy blazer. Then it hit him. He reversed his steps and rushed back, but the three men had disappeared. He circled the mall again, trying to spot them. He located the two men in grey suits having coffee in the food court; the man in the navy suit was missing. Bandu grabbed a coffee and edged up to the table next to them to overhear the grey suits in conversation.

"He's a good salesman," one man was saying.

"I wish the property was as good as him," the other replied.

"It's a good location, for someone doing business in the city."

"I think it's overpriced. I'd like to try further downtown. For those prices, we could get closer to the action."

"So do we strike this one off our list?"

The men crushed their coffee cups and stood to leave.

"I'd keep it only if we hit nothing further south."

"In that case, I don't think we need all these brochures. Hang on to yours. I'll toss this one." The man dumped his brochure kit in the garbage and walked out with his companion.

Bandu waited until they were gone and dove into the garbage bin. The brochure was soiled with coffee and food stains, but as he suspected, inside was a business card of the realtor, the man in the navy suit. Martin James. The card said that Martin was the sole agent for rentals of the new offices in the adjoining office tower that was under construction. *Now here is a guy who has made it in Canada.* Bandu was taken back to the "old days." They hadn't been happy ones, but looking back, they seemed safer and more predictable than the unknown waters he now treaded. He had lost all contact with Martin since coming to this country. He slipped the business card into his pocket.

Around nine he grabbed a Coke and went down to the public washroom. Patrons were leaving and he did his bit to announce, "The mall is closing in fifteen minutes." He saw Lennox, the 'Ox', washing his hands by the sink. Bandu took a pee as the last of the visitors exited. There was only Lennox and him in the washroom.

"Got your cell on 'vibrate'?" Bandu liked teasing the lanky Lennox who had his hair braided and wore pants that threatened to fall off at any time, while a heavy silver chain around his neck gave him a permanent stoop.

"Shut up, motherfucker. Just call me at the right time and I'll get the job done."

"You better not screw up this one."

"Listen punk, I'm a professional—okay?"

"Okay."

Lennox went into a stall and locked the door. He was to stay there until Bandu gave him the signal. It would be a long wait.

Bandu couldn't resist a parting shot. "Remember—vibrate!"

"Fuck off!"

Bandu laughed, took some putty out of his pocket and stuffed it into the urinal. Then he pulled on the flush several times. The water spilled over and ran on the floor.

Outside, he placed a red plastic cone on the floor and stuck a "Closed for Repairs" sign on the door. He told the cleaner, who was pushing his cart over, to cool it for the night. The washroom needed a plumber first, and that wouldn't happen until morning.

When he returned to the office, Guna had already arrived for the night shift.

"Where's Toby?" Bandu asked.

"Probably drinking somewhere," Guna replied.

"Bloody alcoholic. You never know when he is on or off the wagon. I don't know why Uncle Sunna keeps him."

Guna shrugged. He worked three jobs, including the night shift; half the time he was too comatose to have long conversations.

Now that the mall was empty, Bandu went by the video recorders and scanned the monitors, particularly the ones at the north-east exit that had Zenith Jewellers' frontage centred in their sights. All was quiet, not a soul around. He switched the three north-east cameras to "freeze frame" while the recorders kept running. Tomorrow, he would come in early and switch them back. All Guna and Toby would see tonight on those monitors would be a peaceful and deserted Zenith Jewellers. This stuff was so easy; they were even making movies about it!

"I'll do the lock up," Bandu said and went out again. When he shut the northern door, he left it unlocked. Tomorrow, he would lock it before the mall officially opened. Walking the halls back to the office, he checked every nook and cranny; the building was deserted except for a few workers inside their shops, cleaning up. These stragglers would leave by the back doors of their respective premises that opened onto the parking lot. By 10:00 p.m. the only living creatures inside would be the security guards, the mice crawling about the food court, and the Ox, of course.

At 11:00 p.m. Toby and Guna would do their rounds and then alternate on the hour—cursory surveillance for movement or visual anomalies. There would be no checks on locks or other detailed inspections. As the night progressed, their degree of rigor would deteriorate and by 3:00 a.m., it was questionable if anyone went out at all. They'd be snoring back in the office.

"Toby's late, the bugger!" Guna said looking at his watch. It was almost 10 o'clock and the night shift had commenced at nine. Time for Bandu to head out, off-duty. He was reaching for his car keys when the door opened and a short, grey, round figure puffed in.

"Uncle Sunna!"

"Had to come in. Toby called in sick."

"But it's your week off, no? What about the wedding?" Bandu began to have misgivings.

"The wedding is on Saturday. In between, duty calls."

"You'd better sack that bastard Toby."

"Now, now, Bandu, we all have problems. You've had yours."

Uncle Sunna threw his jacket on the chair and got to work going through the day's logs. "Quiet day, ha? Good! Hope it will be a quiet night. I can do my daughter's wedding bills in peace. Who did the lock-up and cross-check?"

"I did," Bandu said.

"Good. You can go then. Give my regards to Sumana and the boy. You are coming for the wedding?"

"Of course!"

As he headed for the Crown Victoria, Bandu felt bad. This was the first time he had pulled a side job so close to home. He did not want Uncle Sunna involved in this. Sunna was the only soul who had been kind to him, selling him the car for a measly five hundred dollars when it was probably worth 10 times that, and introducing him to the taxi ring that got him his start in Canada. Sunna was a saint in Bandu's eyes. The old man had built three careers in his own life: one as an executive in a large mercantile firm in Colombo, and another as a bank executive in the Middle East, before seeking refuge with his family in Canada 15 years ago due to the ethnic conflict back home. Being too old to get in at the levels he had worked at prior to arriving in Canada, Uncle Sunna never lost hope and joined this security firm. His compassion and leadership skills had seen him promoted to supervisor at the mall. Sunna always saw the good in people and was a role model. Bandu did not want Uncle Sunna to lose his job over what was going to happen tonight.

When he had first met the old man, Bandu was angry and frustrated with bouncing from one employment agency to another in search of work. Lacking formal education and having just a grasp of the colloquial English spoken here, he could not land a desk job.

"You've got to pay your dues," Uncle Sunna had said.

"But they don't give you a chance. How to get the Canadian experience when they don't give you a job to get it?"

"You have to keep trying. Eventually, when they know you are really keen, they will take a chance on you—a small chance, maybe. That's when you prove yourself and show them that you are smarter than someone home-grown."

"You've been here over ten years. You haven't even got close to where you were."

The old man looked pained and Bandu felt badly for shooting his mouth off. "Well, you are right. I arrived a bit late and had fewer options. You are in your thirties. You have more time on your side."

Bandu got into the Crown Victoria and lit a cigarette, his fourth for the day. He looked at his watch. From his vantage point in the darkened parking lot, he could see the windows of the security office on the second floor. At 11:20 p.m. or thereabouts, the lights would go on in the office, signalling that the guards had returned from their rounds. He would call Lennox on his cell phone, hoping the jackass hadn't fallen asleep. Lennox had half an hour to do his work and get back into the washroom with the loot. At 11:55, just before the guards headed out for their next walk-around, a diversion would occur outside the mall to distract them. Bandu would call Lennox again and the Ox would cross the remaining frozen camera lines and make his exit by the unlocked northern door. A traceless crime, the most difficult type to solve; undiscovered until employees arrived at Zenith Jewellers the next morning.

He had an hour to kill, so he drove around the city. The guilt inside him was deepening. He stopped at an all-night pizzeria and ordered a slice and a Coke. He didn't much care for this food, although it was prepared fast and readily available and reminded him of the *rotis* back home. The few stragglers in the pizzeria were hunched over their food:

tired night workers like him, mostly new arrivals into this city, at the bottom of the pecking order. It inflamed him that he was still at the bottom, part of the underclass. Hopefully, Ravi would do better. Ravi wouldn't have to play in the pit with these underworld snakes. Bandu too was going to get out as soon as he had enough money to establish himself. But he did not want to get Uncle Sunna in trouble tonight.

He fished inside his pocket for the business card he had picked up earlier. On impulse he went over to the telephone booth, and given the late hour, dialled the home number listed on the card. He was surprised when a woman with a Canadian accent answered. "Hello, this is Ginny."

He felt tongue-tied and couldn't respond. This must be a wrong number. Martin James couldn't be living with a Canadian woman. That was almost like a betrayal. How could he have become so…so Canadian…so soon?

"Hello?" the voice persisted.

Only his deep breathing on the line came through.

"Oh, go to hell, sicko!" the woman yelled and slammed the phone at the other end.

Bandu placed the receiver back on the cradle, sighing, relieved at the preserved anonymity. He returned to his table.

Go to hell, sicko—the words reverberated through him. That's what he amounted to: another crank caller, a sicko.

Forcing himself to get up, Bandu emptied his pizza tray into the trash bin, collected a few napkins for later, and headed back to the car. It was time for the final act, although sitting in the pizzeria he had resolved to rewrite the script.

He drove back to his customary parking spot at the mall; the lot was empty except for a few cars. It was 11:00 p.m. The lights in the office dimmed; the guards were going out on their walk. Twenty five minutes later they returned. They had taken longer today; the old man was more painstaking. Bandu dialled Lennox. He got him on the third try; the idiot still had his phone on "ring" and was probably listening to his music. *Where do these dumb bastards come from? And why did the criminal masterminds who ran these operations hire such losers?* Maybe they thought Bandu was a loser too when his phone had rung the day he got that fateful recruitment call: "Heard you are looking to make some extra cash?"

"You've got twenty minutes." Bandu said into his cell phone when a voice finally came on the other end.

"Thank you, motherfucker."

Bandu swung his car out of the parking lot and drove to the next intersection. He parked on a side-street and ran back to the public phone at the corner. He dialled the security office and placed a paper napkin over the mouthpiece. Guna answered sleepily.

"Get me your boss. It's urgent!"

"Hello? What is this?" Guna was just stirring.

"Get me your boss, motherfucker!" Bandu liked his imitation of the Ox.

"Who's there?" Uncle Sunna was now on line.

"Listen carefully. This is a tip off. There will be a couple of drunks coming by shortly to distract you. Do not go out. Go down to the public washroom on the ground floor instead, the one that is under repair. There is a burglary in progress. Do it now." He hung up.

He ran back to the car and headed for the mall. From a safe distance he watched the two drunks, deposited from a black car that sped off. A few bottles of booze would be their reward for this gig. They shouted, exposed themselves, and urinated on the mall doors in full view of the security office. The guards did not come out—good, they were acting on his tip-off! Bandu looked at his watch. 11:55. He gave it another five minutes and dialled Lennox. Ring, ring. No answer. Great! The Ox was spacing out on his music again and still had his phone on ring. *Good, this time I'll ring until you sink, you bastard.* Bandu kept calling and disconnecting, calling and disconnecting. Finally, he heard a throttled "Hello, Motherfucker? Is that you? What's up, man? Some shit has locked the washroom door!"

Bandu clicked off the phone. "Fry in hell then," he said into the dead instrument. He swung the car out of the lot and headed home. It had been a very long day.

He hoped that with Lennox being caught, the cops would not go snooping elsewhere, like in the back of the security office among the video recorders. He spent a restless night hoping that the Ox would not spill the beans, hoping that Lennox too had received the same tag line when he was recruited. "If you get caught, you're on your own, brother. Don't ever rat on your buddies or we will come after you, even in prison. Welcome aboard."

The following morning, Bandu was in at eight o'clock. He didn't want to arrive too early and draw attention. He went in through the staff entrance and made his way quickly over to the north door of the mall. There was yellow tape all over it and the lock looked shattered. *How did that happen?* He'd left it unlocked. Besides, Lennox could not have gotten that far if Sunna had locked him in the washroom. The entrance to Zenith Jewellers was also taped and a cop stood outside. The glass cases inside the store were smashed, shards scattered over the plush carpet. This was *very* strange! Despite his attitude, Lennox was a professional locksmith and safe-cracker; he was not supposed to have a left a trace of his activity last night. Bandu went into the security office. It was deserted except for a tired-looking Uncle Sunna slumped over his desk. His uniform was torn and his hair tousled. An ugly bump graced his forehead.

"What's happened?" Bandu said. "Here, I bought you a coffee."

"Thanks. Sit down. We had some action last night. The cops were buzzing in here until a little while ago."

As Uncle Sunna gave him details of the break-in, Bandu started to feel uneasy.

"The thief got away?"

"With two hundred and fifty thousand in jewellery. And he gave me a souvenir too," Uncle Sunna said, feeling his head gingerly.

There were so many questions buzzing in Bandu's mind but he tried to remain calm. He'd lost control of this script. He hung up his jacket and pretended to look busy. "Well, you'd better get some rest. You've got a wedding this weekend. I'll take over now."

The old man stretched and yawned. "Yes, as soon as I'm done with this incident report."

With a pile of log sheets in his hand, Bandu casually made his way over to the three frozen video camera consoles. *Shit!* The cameras were back on "record." Sweat broke out on his brow. He looked over his shoulder; the old man was still poring over his papers. Bandu inched around the alcove and headed quickly over to the router. The external connection was firmly plugged in place! *Damn!* A wheezy voice behind him said, "I put them back on...after your tip-off."

Bandu spun around feeling naked, exposed and angry.

Uncle Sunna was leaning against the camera cabinet, sipping his coffee, studying him through his thick lenses. "Why, Bandu?"

Suddenly, Bandu was the angry young man he had been when they first met. "You know why! How else can you earn a decent living in this country?"

"I mean, why did you change your mind and try to blow the job?"

"I didn't want you involved."

The old man nodded. "I suspected so. Thank you for your consideration, but I thought you did not like losers? Backing out is admitting defeat."

"How did the thief get away?"

"I let Lennox out. Made it look like he overpowered me in the washroom."

"Just a minute...You know his name? You know Lennox?"

"Yes. We had to switch to Plan B, even though it was more painful for me personally...because of your change of heart."

"Plan B?"

"Yes. And even plans C and D, if things did not go as anticipated."

As Bandu's mouth gaped, Uncle Sunna continued, "I instructed Lennox to break in to Zenith Jewellers *once more*, in full view of the cameras this time, and to be clumsy about it. I also asked him to break the lock on the north doors while leaving. But first, I got him to answer your call. I didn't want you losing sleep."

"You were behind all this!"

Uncle Sunna shrugged, "I told you, you've got to show them that you are smarter. I came in last night because Lennox is shaky, though loyal. But he remembered the instructions I gave him on Plan B. He's making progress, that lad."

"And Guna?"

"Oh, I left him to deal with those drunks. Knowing him, he probably sat back in his chair and watched their antics through the window, hoping it would keep him awake."

"What about the cops?"

Uncle Sunna chuckled. "They think our burglar is a smash and grab artist who hid in the washrooms just before the mall closed and then got surprised by me just as he was getting ready to make his move. The mall is even trying to give me a citation for grappling with the burglar. I was knocked out for about fifteen minutes. At least, that was my statement to the cops." Then he turned serious again. "But you have a lot to learn, Bandu, like Lennox does. You are both too impulsive."

Bandu avoided the old man's gaze as he edged past him into the office. It hurt him to be classed in the same lot as the Ox. "I'm sorry for screwing up."

Uncle Sunna came back to the desk picked up his bag and put on his jacket. "Well, I'm off for a good nap. I need to put some ice where Lennox walloped me. Are you still coming to the wedding?"

"I'm sure it's going to be a good wedding." Bandu forced a grin. *Two hundred and fifty thousand dollars worth!*

"Oh, by the way, not a word of this to anyone, okay? Not even Sumana. Remember recruitment day?" The old man's benign face had altered into an inscrutable mask and Bandu shivered.

"Okay."

Settling down to his morning shift, Bandu tried to keep his spirits up. He kept telling himself, "Yah, it's great. We pulled off this job after all." But a sinking feeling predominated; one of being in a viper pit, where even the ladder out had just been yanked up. He could never belong in the world of Martin James. His actions over the last 24 hours had probably brought harm to his friend's ordered and civilized world. Somewhere along the way Bandu realized that his life had taken a different turn, and now there was no road back.

17. **Splitsville**

"Goddammit!" Vigo fumed, flinging the newspaper across his desk. "They're snooping everywhere now."

Martin sat across from him, nursing his first coffee of the day, wondering why he had been summoned so early in the morning. "What are you afraid of? They're investigating a jewellery heist in a shopping mall. So the store happens to be in Garibaldi's mall, so what? Robberies take place in this city all the time."

"It's an excuse, Martin. The robbery is an excuse for those stinking cops to hound us. How can an honest man make a decent living in this country?"

"Why did you want to see me?"

Vigo rose from his chair, straightened his grey silk vest and loosened his tie. He walked over to the window and opened the shades, looking out cautiously, as if suspicious of being under surveillance. Vigo's dramatics often amused Martin, though they would disturb him later. Vigo turned to pace in front of his desk, his chin on his chest. Suddenly, he looked up at Martin.

"Do you have any records of the companies of Enrico's associates?"

Martin remembered his meeting with Garibaldi on the golf course. "Only the usual, leaseholder forms and so on. The first year's lease was paid as cash transactions."

"That's it, that's it. No cash. Cash makes people suspicious. We need to have post-dated cheques from a company account. I will phone Enrico and tell him why you insist on it."

"I'll get my associate Marnie to contact them and ask for cheques instead. Their cash is sitting in our trust account waiting for the building to open and the tenants to move in."

"This robbery is not good for publicity."

"I wouldn't worry too much about it. It should give Garibaldi a chance to increase his perimeter security."

"All that costs money, Martin."

Martin pursed his lips but said nothing. "Is that all we have on this emergency agenda today?"

"Oh, one more thing..."

Martin paused on his way to the door. "Yes?"

"Do you have your own money in the building?"

"About a hundred grand."

Vigo grimaced. "You still think it is a good deal then, eh?"

"Hey, you were the guy who was full of thrusting instead of parrying. There's half a million of your own money in this too. Are you having second thoughts?" Behind his bravado, Martin had a sinking feeling in his stomach.

Vigo resumed his pacing. "No, no...I was just thinking aloud...thank you for coming here today, Martin. You will attend to that other matter we talked about just now, yah?"

"I can't get them," Marnie said, sitting in his office. "Their voice mail says they are out of town on business."

"They have no cell phones or hotel addresses?" Martin paced across his desk. Over the last two months Marnie and he had perfected the art of resuming boss-employee roles in this fishbowl. To anyone looking at them from outside of his glass office, they were all business.

"It's the voice mail on their cell phones that I was referring to."

He shook his head. "Keep trying them." The companies listed in the lease forms stated that their nature of business was "trading." Right now, given Vigo's uneasiness, this description sounded fishy.

Marnie spoke cautiously, "I started checking them out when they first offered cash, but you asked me to back off, remember?"

"I was persuaded that it wasn't worth the effort. Have you had any other clients sign up?"

"None since the robbery last week."

"Then the heist is having an effect. Are we slipping behind target?"

"We have signed commitments for forty percent occupancy and a dozen others pending. I'll follow up."

"Please do. And let me know how our prospects are feeling about this jewellery store incident. Heck, this is not another Jane-Finch area; it's an isolated incident unlikely to happen again."

Marnie laid her papers aside and crossed her legs. "You're kind of uptight lately, Martin. How's the home front?"

He shook his head. "Same old. I guess I am a bit paranoid with the building activity coming to a head. And now this robbery..."

"Would you like to come over tonight?"

"Ginny asked me to get my own dinner today. She has a committee meeting and Jamie has gone to a friend's for a sleepover."

"I can make you dinner."

"I'd like that."

That was the night that Marnie told him she was pregnant. It was after he had drunk couple of glasses of wine and eaten her homemade meal of prime-rib, roast potatoes and sautéed vegetables.

"What?" he exploded. "When?"

His outburst did not dampen her optimistic demeanor. "I've been meaning to tell you, but you've been pre-occupied."

He got up and started pacing. "What are you going to do about it?"

"What do you mean?"

"Marnie, we can't have this baby. It will blow the lid off everything."

She flushed, and for the first time he saw her lose her cool. "You're thinking only of yourself."

"No. I'm thinking...of us. Do you want to be a single mother?"

"Martin, I'm thirty-six. I won't be getting another chance. I'm keeping this baby."

"I thought you were...using protection."

"Does it matter anymore?"

He gaped at her. He felt betrayed. He had walked into this one. The sense of betrayal by yet another woman in his life slapped him in the face.

"This is all about you, isn't it?" he said in a measured tone. The shock was seeping in, and he was groping for options. "You will not be able to work at the brokerage, when it starts to show. There will be all those questions. Some of the guys already know about us, even though they don't say so. I see it on Vinod's face every time he sees us together."

She looked like she had been kicked. And he could not control the rational justification spilling out of him at that moment. After a pregnant pause, she sighed, looking forlorn. "I am not looking forward to coming into the office."

"That's why we've got to have this...issue...attended to, quickly." He felt a glimmer of hope appear. Maybe she would become rational now. That seemed to be the only way out.

Her next words rocked him.

"And that is why I am leaving my job at the end of next week. I will have the building leases wrapped up by then to hand over."

"Leaving? What's this about? Where will you go?"

"My mother in Vancouver has asked me to come over and live with her until the baby is able to go to day-care."

"You're moving to Vancouver?" he felt his legs wobble.

"Your attitude gives me no choice. I thought you'd be stronger. But men are like this, I guess—they fuck up and leave us to clean up the mess."

He had slept poorly the last week. Marnie had handed in her resignation and he had gone through the motions of accepting it and announcing her departure to the rest of the staff. The official explanation was that she was going to BC to care for an ailing parent. They had held a farewell wine and cheese party and a couple of the juniors had jovially commented that Marnie was already adopting the west coast tree-hugger mentality by not drinking alcohol. Vinod had raised his eyebrows and said nothing.

Martin stumbled to the breakfast table that Friday morning, still drowsy. He had found sleep impossible since early dawn. He had heard Ginny get up, slip into her dressing gown and pad downstairs as he kept his eyes shut and searched for an elusive sleep. He had stayed away from visiting Marnie since she had given him the news about her pregnancy. He replayed his final parting with Marnie as she packed her things in the office the previous day.

"Do you need help hauling your things to the car?" he had enquired, coming over to her cube. At that point he didn't really care who was in earshot.

"No," she replied, subdued. "Vinod has already taken care of that."

He held out a cheque, all his personal savings. "This is for you."

She looked at his offering, worth $25,000. "What's this for?"

"For the expenses you will incur in the months ahead."

"I don't want your money, Martin—now or in the future. You've already given me the best gift I can ever have."

"Keep it. For...whatever."

He left it on her desk. "Goodbye. Thanks for all the long conversations. They helped. And please do stay in touch."

She merely nodded, reaching for the box of tissues.

After Vinod had returned from helping Marnie to her car, he walked into Martin's office. "Mr. Martin, we lost a good colleague today."

"You don't have to tell me that, Vinod."

"Mr. Martin, I know this is none of my business, but let me give you some personal advice. I am older than you and treat you always as my younger brother, but also as my boss. Please do not live dangerously like this again. People get burned, you know—good people."

Martin looked down at his desk, nodding aimlessly. "I need some time to myself now, Vinod. If you will excuse me."

Vinod rose. "Of course, of course. Ah, one more thing..." He reached into his jacket pocket and handed Martin an envelope. "Marnie asked me to give this to you."

"Thank you." After Vinod left, Martin opened the envelope. It was his cheque, torn into two neat halves.

Now, as he entered the kitchen, he was surprised to see Ginny already at the table, poring over the newspaper, a cup of tea steaming beside her, toast crumbs dotting her plate. Her early morning habits, like all the others in her life, were timed: rise at 6:00 a.m.; Yoga till 6:45; 6:45 shower; 7:00—7:30 a.m., breakfast, and so on. It was 6:30 right now and she was already at breakfast, and had been for some time. Martin wondered if the change in routine was going to precede one of her mood swings.

"Good morning," he said, fixing himself coffee.

"You look like shit this morning," she said without lifting her head from the paper.

"Gee, thanks! Is it that obvious?"

"You tossed and turned last night."

"I guess I have been sleeping poorly."

"It's disturbing."

"Sorry to upset your rhythm."

She stabbed her finger at a newspaper article. "Do you still do business with this guy Vigo Matinsen?"

His reply was guarded. "Well, we sell some of his properties. It's at arm's length."

"Well, get ready for some flack." She tossed the relevant page towards him and resumed reading the rest of the newspaper with manic focus.

He looked at the article and nearly choked.

Italian Construction Mogul and Canadian entrepreneur arrested in daring midnight raid—mob dealings suspected, read the headline.

With mounting panic, Martin skimmed the article. "...a related investigation into the recent Northern Mall robbery owned by Mr. Garibaldi and managed by Mr. Matinsen's property management company led investigators to check out an "inside job" theory. This line of enquiry accidentally revealed 'accounting inconsistencies' within these companies and the Fraud Squad was brought in. A review was performed on both companies' books...various misallocations and transfers to numbered companies currently associated with drug smuggling were discovered... police are withholding statements on Mr. Garibaldi and Mr. Matinsen until further notice, except to say that the inside job theory on the mall robbery has since been abandoned for lack of evidence."

When he looked up from the article, Ginny had turned her piercing gaze on him. He knew that his face was giving him away. He looked back at the paper.

"You're screwed, aren't you? I saw the bust on TV last night, but you came in after I was asleep. Oh, Martin, how could you deal with these people?"

She dashed the rest of the paper on the table, eyes bursting with tears, and rushed out of the kitchen.

Breakfast took agonizingly long, even though all he did was down his coffee with shaking hands; he threw up in the bathroom afterwards, but managed to down a swig of scotch before setting out for the office. By the time he arrived, the phone was ringing incessantly and his assistant Tracey was telling everyone that "Mr. James was out of town." When he asked why, she said that the cops were asking for him too. So he told her to continue delivering her out-of-town message and he shut himself in his office.

The tumble came fast, even faster than the one in '87, even though the cops couldn't pin anything on him. They paid him a visit that morning and asked him all sorts of questions: they wanted to know, in particular, why the salesperson in charge of Garibaldi's office tower rentals, Miss Marnie Rogers, had suddenly quit her job and gone out of province.

"Ask her," was all Martin could offer.

They fished around in his trust account. Marnie had refunded the cash and deposited cheques from Enrico's three goons. They wanted to know why.

"Ask her," Martin replied.

By that afternoon, all Garibaldi and Matinsen assets were seized, including the near-complete building, which was to be re-sold at a distressed price by the Crown. Being a shareholder, Martin stood to lose half his personal investment. Mercifully they did not freeze his trust account, so he could continue to operate the brokerage, but he was advised that he could be summoned to court as a material witness.

Martin valiantly tried fighting back by going to his investors and asking for more money; the re-sale price was dirt cheap, he pleaded, if they could rustle up the extra cash, buy the building at its distressed price, and sit on it for a while, they could be in for an even bigger windfall in a few years. But no one throws more good money after the already tainted stuff and by the evening of that exhausting day, the last of his investors had decided to pull out.

The final blow came before he left the office for the day. His bank phoned; they were calling in his loan. The news was all around town. He had no real equity in his brokerage firm, it was only as good as its sales people, and he had just lost his star performer. If he did not come up with $100,000 by the following day, the family home in

Willowdale was on the block. How the heck could he even go to his trusted clients and business associates for a loan when they had all just bailed out on him? He had the 25 grand in his savings that Marnie had refused to accept, that was all. His only other asset was his half of the equity in the house in Willowdale.

He loosened his tie, went out to the main reception and closed the front door. Everyone else was gone for the day. He tried to separate the various disasters that were falling upon him at that moment: the house, Ginny, his money. And what about Marnie? Was all this a setup? Had she been in Garibaldi's pay in the end, signing up his crooked cronies so that they could flush their ill-gotten gains as lease payments, and had she skipped town the moment things got hot? Was there even a baby? He couldn't separate the facts from the fiction; there was no way to figure out which to tackle first.

He opened the office liquor cabinet and broke one of his principles of not drinking while at work, other than when celebrating a sale or entertaining clients. He poured himself a vodka and tonic.

If Marnie was telling me the truth—and I have to believe she was—then I never asked for her forgiveness. I guess I can start by asking Ginny and Jamie for forgiveness.

He slung his jacket over his shoulder and headed home to spill the beans, unburden and take whatever consequences he deserved. He was tired of fighting today.

Ginny took the news in silence; her face was fixed but swelling as he went into the details. Finally, she burst out. "And you did this under my nose? This is my home too."

"Slow down. It was with my half of the equity. Your share is safe."

"How? A mortgage is a mortgage. I don't have the money to pay it back. And I can't go to Mother for money."

"Don't."

She looked around her helplessly. "But our life is here. Jamie will have to re-adjust."

"We will all have to re-adjust. I'm sorry, Ginny. This jewellery store robbery was not supposed to happen. It triggered a domino effect."

"You should never have gotten in with Vigo Matinsen."

"It was a straight investment deal."

"So what happens now?" Arms folded tightly across her chest, face twitching, she was swinging from toe to toe as if ready to flee at whatever he told her.

"We will have to downscale to a smaller house, for awhile at least. I know of a few places in Pickering."

"Pickering. You want me to live in the boonies?"

"Not for long. Pickering is the next boom town on the real estate map. Once we have some equity built up, and this issue has blown over, we can return to the city."

She began flapping her hands, looking up at the ceiling, rotating her head from side to side. "I can't Martin; this is all too much. It's the concealed facts, the loss of this house, the changes to all of us—it's just too much to handle all at once. You even forged my signature."

"You were too pre-occupied, Ginny. I didn't want to bother you with the loan. It was such a small detail, I didn't think twice."

"That's not the point. My signature is my sacred right. And you violated it."

He bowed his head. "You're right. I'm sorry."

She started speaking to the wall. "And how can I ever trust you again?"

He pursed his lips. He had decided not to tell her about Marnie—that would put her over the edge.

"I'll go and tell Jamie, myself," he offered.

"I need to think this over. This is all too much," she said, going into the kitchen. He heard a glass fall and splinter, but decided not to go in and check. When he heard a plate follow the glass, he knew that Ginny was physically all right, that she was just venting. A few pieces of broken crockery were the least of his problems at this time.

"We have to leave here?" Jamie mulled the idea in his head. "Do I get to go to a new school?"

"I can take you fishing down by the lake more often," Martin said. They were sitting across from each other on the floor in Jamie's room.

Jamie's eyes lit up at that. "And I get to make new friends?"

"Yeah."

"Do they play music in this school?"

"Oh sure," he said, not knowing if this were true or not.

"Are you in trouble, Dad?" Jamie's blue eyes were probing Martin, like Ginny's used to when she wanted to gauge every reaction, visible and invisible in him.

"Some temporary issues that will blow away soon."

"Then we'll come back here again?"

"We can go wherever we want."

"But this house, we will never be able to come back to it, right?" Jamie was looking at the walls of his rooms, at the posters of his favourite comic book heroes and pop stars.

"We could create the same room for you in our new home."

"But it won't be the same, will it, Dad?"

Martin put his arm around the boy and drew him to his chest. He felt like his heart would burst. "No it won't be the exactly the same. I'm sorry about this, son."

"But I still got you, right, Dad? And Mum?"

"Sure buddy. You're stuck with us."

"Good." Jamie tightened his grip around Martin.

"Forgive me, son."

When he returned to the living room, Ginny was just placing the phone receiver back in its cradle.

"I've spoken to Mother. I'm taking Jamie and going to live with her until you sort things out. You got us into this mess; now you can get us out."

18. **In the Valley of Despair**

The next months saw Martin's descend and journey through a valley of despair. At night, as the alcohol deadened his pain, he drew strength from the old stories of Odysseus, for his hero had also endured the desperation of sinking hope as every bid for a return to his home in Ithaca resulted in him been blown even further away by the ill winds and machinations of the dreaded Poseidon.

Martin commenced his slide on the day that he bid a tearful goodbye to Ginny and Jamie, as they packed their things to leave for Rosedale.

"So I'm not going to a new school like you said, Dad?" Jamie asked, looking crestfallen.

"No," Martin said, packing Jamie's sweaters into the suitcase. "That was a bit premature on my part. But you will; trust me."

He pecked Ginny on the cold cheek she offered him. "I'll come and visit," he mumbled, lost for words.

After they had departed in her car, he walked the hollow house, letting the emptiness seep into his bones. He tidied the odd piece of furniture or the cushion that was out of place. He tried to focus on "doing;" after all, the house had to be in top condition for prospective buyers.

He called his bank and arranged for the property to go on the selling block. He went to the office and picked up the listings for Pickering. A detached bungalow in town that he'd had his eye on was still available. It was located on the waterfront at Frenchman's Bay, overlooking the nuclear plant. Unsubstantiated rumours about radiation pollution had kept prices depressed in that area. This was all he could afford now. When the environmental investigation turned up negative, as he was sure it would, he expected to recover some of his losses. He put in an offer, no conditions attached.

He called in his staff for an informal meeting at the end of the day. Given the news about the Garibaldi affair in the newspapers, even the two brokers who primarily operated out of their home offices showed up.

"Guys, I have some disappointing news. The Garibaldi project has fallen through, as you probably heard in the news already. But our pipeline is still solid and we can continue, and we will."

"Did you personally lose anything on the deal, Martin?" asked Tom, one of the younger sales representatives and a bit of an upstart.

"I lost some."

"Your house is up on power of sale," Tom continued, unfazed by the raised eyebrows around him. "One of my clients is interested."

"Ask him to buy it then," Martin said and turned to the rest of his staff. "My house is a hot deal right now. And that goes for any of you with clients out there. I need the best price you can get on that house."

"Do you have another place to move your family to, if we have an early closing?" Tom asked.

"That's my problem, Tom. You do the selling. That's all folks. I just wanted to let you know that it's business as usual. We've had a few setbacks these last few weeks, but that should motivate us to work harder."

He went back to his office and shut the door. There was a tap. Vinod stood outside smoothing his tie.

"Come on in," Martin held the door open for him. "I hope you're bringing me some good news."

"I wish I could, Mr. Martin. But this cannot wait, in light of today's news."

"Okay, spill it. I am in no mood for pleasantries."

"After Marnie left, those young bucks, led by Tom, have been talking."

"Saying what?"

"They think you are in trouble. They think this place is going bankrupt. Tom's already putting some of his deals through Bradley's who are still smarting because of the customers you took from them when you left. What goes around, comes around, Mr. Martin."

"Thanks for the tip, Vinod. I'll take the necessary action."

Vinod looked undecided. "You won't do anything stupid, eh boss?"

"Cancers need to be cut—fast."

After Vinod left, Martin called Tom on his extension. "Can you come in and see me?"

Tom bounced in, "Guess what, Martin, my client's just put in the offer for your house."

"Good. He'll have to bid really high. I hear that there's competition for it already."

"He's prepared to go as high as necessary."

"Very good. So we can keep that sale registered with James Realty and at least retain the commission."

"Sure. Where else would it be registered under?"

"You can register all other sales under whomever, Tom. I won't need your services after today."

Tom sat down. His face went red. "You...hah...you're firing me? Now?"

"Yes. I will not brook disloyalty, Tom. Not under any circumstances."

Tom was shaking his head, a look of insolence on his face. "Man, you are out of your mind. Your people are falling like flies. You can't afford to lose any more salespeople."

"But I don't need traitors. I'll ask Tracey to prepare the paperwork. Come along, let's go and announce it to the rest of the team since everyone is here today. They'd better hear the official version from me, before they get the tainted one from you." Martin gripped Tom firmly by the shoulder and propelled him out of his office.

That night he drank some more, alone in the empty house. He missed the patter of Jamie's feet as the child would dart downstairs to grab food from the fridge, or the strains of music that rushed out of his room whenever the door opened. Martin even missed Ginny's silences, her moods: things he had gotten used to over their years together. He wished the house goodbye. Another home to leave and move on from, for he was pretty sure that come tomorrow, the property would sell.

The next day in the office he was all focus again. He had to stanch the flow of departing staff. Even though it was going to cost him, he announced a premium commission split at the current top tier level of productivity. The team was thrilled; Martin also guessed that they were looking to put the unpleasantness of the past few days behind them. *Money talks in this country*. With one fell swoop he had cut that smart aleck

Tom out of the firm and stemmed the tide of others who may have been thinking of following. *Eat your heart out, Tom.*

The Willowdale property sold that afternoon, but not to Tom's clients; to one of Vinod's instead.

"How did you manage that?" Martin laughed as they celebrated the sale with coffee and cake.

"Maturity, boss, maturity," Vinod said, his face pumped with self-satisfaction. "You know that story about the tortoise and the hare, no? I let all those young bucks burn themselves out by outbidding each other. Then I put in one bid, with good financials. You know my clients from the sub-continent, no? They are coming loaded here. Minimum mortgage; high cash. The bank loved it—low risk, no? They accepted, *futta-fut.*"

Before Martin left home for the day he was also the proud owner of the Pickering property. Now he just had to stick handle the payments while waiting for the closing on his Willowdale home. He felt his problems were already beginning to ease.

He decided to celebrate down at the King Eddy that evening, by himself, and then to call Ginny and Jamie and give them the news. He missed them already. Maybe, he'd drop in and see them. Maybe Ginny had cooled down sufficiently to forgive him; maybe...

As he downed his third Vodka, it dawned on him how much he needed to drink, a dependancy that had started in earnest when the Garibaldi deal had kicked off, and had by now developed into a daily ritual. But today he should be feeling happy, yet he was drinking more. He tried to ogle the woman behind the bar, but she did not interest him. He wasn't emotionally free to let his lust loose.

He pulled out his cell phone and called Rosedale. Jamie answered the phone. "Daddy, where are you?"

"I bought the house in Pickering, son."

"Hooray! Then we can be moving soon?"

"You fed up with your grandma's place already?"

Jamie's voice fell to a whisper, "It's b.o.r.i.n.g."

"Yeah?"

"Mummy doesn't talk much, and Grandma has been going to the hospital all the time for her check-ups."

"Well, listen buddy; you stay upbeat, okay? I'm counting on you keeping those two ladies in good spirits, and me as well."

"Do you want to speak to Mum?"

"How did you guess? Put her on. And you take care, okay? I'm going to come and see you sometime this week. I'll arrange it with Mum."

Ginny was restrained, mumbling a strained, "Hello."

"I miss you, honey."

"Sure."

"Honest."

"Tell me something else. We have moved into the east wing of the house. Jamie is driving me nuts; he wants all his posters up in the same place and the walls don't work the same way as in our old house."

"Well, they'll work when he comes to Pickering. I bought the house today. And Willowdale sold too."

There was a sob in her voice at his last words. "Sold? Gone. Just like everything I've had to part with since we met."

"Oh come on, honey. This is change. I know you are not very good with change. But it's happening more and more in this crazy world. Dozens of houses go up for sale every day, and lifestyles change hands all the time. I see it at the office, over and over."

"Don't sell me any more of your crap today, Martin."

"I'm not selling anything. But I will need your signature on the purchase forms, honey."

Her voice got steely. "I have decided not to sign anything anymore from you without a lawyer's approval. I want Tim to look over the papers."

"Tim?"

"Yes. He is my brother, and although I love to hate him, he has always been trustworthy. If you need my signature, let him review the papers first."

Martin swallowed the retort bubbling in his throat and said. "Very well, I'll get them ready for him. Goodnight, Ginny. I'll call you again tomorrow."

The phone clicked abruptly at the other end.

Tim Summers' offices were immaculate, with an elegant reception area of gleaming marble, located on the 25th floor of a large office tower. Jim Duffield had retired, and Tim, who was senior partner now, had moved his office to this new downtown location. The overlarge sign behind the manicured and coiffured receptionist read "Summers & Associates."

Martin was ushered into Tim's enormous office after waiting 15 minutes past the appointed time. Tim was on the phone and did not even look up when Martin entered. In fact, on seeing Martin enter, Tim swivelled his chair to face the wall and kept talking for another five minutes. All Martin could see was the expanding pink bald crown protruding over the high-backed leather chair. Martin amused himself by walking about the office and poking into the various bookcases holding legal texts. He took some of the books out and piled them on the conference table in domino fashion, the last heavy tome leaning at the edge of the table. Then he tipped the first book in the line and watched them tumble, the last one falling off the edge and crashing to the floor, breaking its old binding and spilling pages on the marble floor.

Tim swung around at the noise, the phone automatically falling back in its cradle as if he had tired of the caller, or because this sudden disturbance had become a higher priority. "Hey, hey...what are you doing?" The look of annoyance on his face was tinged with apprehension.

Martin picked up the loose leaves of the damaged book from the floor and tossed them in an untidy heap on the conference table along with the others. "I get tired of being kept waiting in sterile offices."

Tim picked up a file on his desk and waved it. "I could delay this whole deal, you know."

"Quit playing games with me, Tim. Your sister wants this house as much as I do. Don't piss her off. You know what she's like when she's pissed off."

Tim scowled and went over the papers.

Martin paced the office slowly. "Since when did you become a real estate lawyer, Tim?"

Tim remained silent. The leaves rustled in the file. He made some notes on a pad.

"I have one real estate lawyer on staff. He reviewed the file."

"Then why don't I see him and not waste your time."

"This deal closes in two months and you have to vacate Willowdale in two weeks. Where will you be staying?"

"None of your business, but I thank you for your concern. Do you want to offer me a room at your swanky penthouse? I understand you have wild gay orgies up there."

Tim swore and rose from his chair, clenching the edges of his mahogany desk. His expensive suspenders could hardly contain his swelling girth as he lurched forward. "How dare you say that? That's pure hearsay."

"I've got my eyes and ears on the city, Tim. We sell properties in your building too, and we know things that go on in there. It's our job to know and to advise our clients appropriately. In fact, there are pictures that I can get hold of if you need to be reminded of what you and your friends have been up to. In fact, I'd advise you to put some extra air filters in your apartment. People on your floor complain of the marijuana fumes when you have those late-night soirées." Martin was beginning to enjoy this. "Don't worry, I won't tell Clarissa. And I won't show her the pictures and spoil her illusion that you'll still find a rich fat girl from Rosedale and marry into money. Even Ginny doesn't know, although she has strongly suspected your leanings since your teens."

Tim flung the file at Martin. "Take your file and your cheap rat-infested bungalow and get the fuck out of here."

Martin picked up the file, and retrieved its scattered contents from the floor. "I take it that we have your stamp of approval to proceed? Or would you want Ginny to call your real estate colleague?"

"Get out, Martin!" Tim picked up the phone and turned back to his imaginary caller. Martin left Summers & Associates with a jaunty spring in his step.

He received a letter from his father a week later that flung the satisfaction from Tim's discomfiture back in his own face. Victor rarely wrote, resorting to Christmas and birthday cards into which he crammed bits of information about what was happening back home. This time however, there was a dedicated letter, on foolscap paper, in shaky cursive handwriting from a time when handwriting was the principal method of communication, and clerks in Sri Lanka had walked around with fountain pens sticking out of their shirt pockets.

My Dear Martin,

The years go by and I lurch from one disappointment to another. I have been unable to maintain my room at the hostel—too many fights with the boarders. All bloody drunks, like me. But I can't drink anymore, too many cramps. Also, got the piles very badly now—bleeding all the time.

I have moved to my cousin Colin's home in Haputale. Colombo is too bloody polluted, hot and expensive. Colin and Mabel have a three-bedroom house they inherited from their parents, overlooking a tea plantation. It's nice to note that they still have colonial Dutch furniture and crockery in the house. Their six children are all in Australia, but Colin and Mabel are like me—we have only a few more years to live—so why not live in the best damned screwed-up country that we all like to curse but never want to leave?

The bad news I want to give you is about your blessed brother, Barney. What for going to the seminary and all, the disgraceful fellow got caught cupping the young seminarians there. What a damn shame! My youngest son—a homo! I wanted to go to the seminary and give him a bloody slap. We all committed indiscretions, but with the correct sex, no?

Anyway, if you can drive some sense into that bugger, please do. I have always looked up to you as my best son. I may not have given you much encouragement in my time, but you were my thoroughbred—the first press from the coconut as they say. All the other buggers were just weaker and weaker milk. I do not have Barney's address but you can try reaching him via the seminary.

Thank you and God Bless you for the money you send me monthly. My Provident Fund money is not worth shit. If you hadn't sent me anything, I would have been dead and gone long ago. Any news from your mother? I know I live closer to her than you, but I don't get any correspondence from that bloody asylum. Aney, if you have any news, please send it my way. I miss her so much. I keep her photo by my bedside and try to remember how she was when she was young, before all you children were born.

I have written too much and my hand is paining. The country is still going to the dogs, but now it's so bad, that we don't care anymore. We just laugh and take bets as to how much further it can go "down the pallam," as they say. Maybe we are in purgatory already. So when we close our eyes, straight to heaven we will go.

All the best to you, son!
Daddy

Martin drank more on receipt of the letter from his father. On those two pages of foolscap, Victor had unconsciously encapsulated the James family's decline, even though he was railing against the country's deterioration. This was the family that Martin had forsaken for moving up the social ladder in Canada. A family whose existence he would not acknowledge in his quest for upward mobility. And now, where the hell was he; forsaken by both.

And poor Barney, disgraced and in hiding. Sure, Martin would write to him care of the seminary, even send him some money if he needed it. But he doubted Barney would ever write back. *Barney, if you only knew that in this country, what you were accused of is a way of life, celebrated on the streets, and protected by legislation. How unfair the world is. Or maybe, the two of us need to switch countries.*

He moved out of Willowdale into a one-bedroom apartment in Scarborough, pending the closing on the Pickering house. Ginny had already taken the Ming vase, the Monet, the Persian rug and the Egyptian daggers when she left for Rosedale. Now he called her and asked if there was anything else she needed from the house before he donated the rest to the Salvation Army.

"I've taken everything that was mine," she told him.

"Thanks for signing those papers. I can get things moving now."

"Where will you be staying?" For once in a long time, he detected a note of concern in her voice.

"I've a bed-sitter for a couple of months in Scarborough." He gave her the address.

"You're back to your origins," she said, as if to herself.

"Not for long, Ginny. Not for long."

"You know Martin, I have been thinking. We both tried and failed at reaching greatness. I over-reacted to what happened with the Garibaldi business."

He remained silent, his palms sweaty. *She's coming around?*

"I've started to see a counsellor again. And he has helped me to make sense of things."

"Thank God, Ginny. Thank God, someone is able to make sense of this for us."

"Can I go out and see the Pickering house?"

"Sure. Can I drive you there? Let's make it a picnic with Jamie as well. It'll be our start all over."

"Slow down. No, I want to do this on my own, for now."

Dashed, but satisfied with these scraps, he gave her directions to the house and they hung up.

Despite Ginny's change of heart, he found himself drinking more at the end of every day. He tried walking the malls after work, to find some joy there, but that was an empty activity, and he preferred staying home to watch videos instead. He went on the golf course, as the first winds of fall started to blow fallen leaves over the fairways and hide the balls. He felt the stiffness in his back—not enough exercise—and had to ease up on the golf after a couple of rounds.

He spent a day with Jamie at the ROM and rounded it off with a viewing of the Toronto Symphony Orchestra's rendition of Wagner overtures at the Roy Thomson Hall. He did not understand this music, being weaned on Pop and Country & Western imports that had flooded the English radio channels back home. This music was a lot more technical and mathematical and, to his way of thinking, involved less soul. But he admired his son reaching this level of appreciation. The next generation was supposed to surpass the previous one in order for the human species to evolve: if Martin had been Victor's thoroughbred, was Jamie then Martin's thoroughbred?

During the performance's interval, he ordered a double scotch, while Jamie sucked on a Coke amidst a crush of people in evening gowns and dark suits, wafting waves of perfume and cologne in every direction.

"Dad, why are you drinking so much?" Jamie's voice was sharp above the chatter as he studied his father over the rim of his cup, sucking extra hard on the straw.

Martin put down his glass, as if stung. The bell for the close of the interval rang and lights fluttered in the foyer. "Let's go back," he said, leaving his unfinished drink behind, afraid to touch it under his son's intense gaze.

When he drove Jamie home that night, the boy was quiet most of the way, not displaying the ebullience that a performance such as the one they had just witnessed normally produced in him.

"Did you enjoy the concert?" Martin asked.

"Hmm, hmm."

"Hey, if it's only so-so, maybe we should do something else in the future."

"Like—let's all live together as a family?"

"Hey, where did that come from?"

"I'm sick of living at Grandma's, Dad. And I miss you. I miss us."

Martin swallowed hard. "Look, the house in Pickering is going to be ready in less than two months. Your mum has already gone to see it. We should be 'us' again in a very short time."

"Hmm." Jamie looked out of the window and lapsed back into silence for the rest of the drive home.

The apartment block in Scarborough was a depressing place to come home to at the end of the day. It reminded him so much of his early days in Canada. The elevator took an average of 15 minutes to navigate and was usually packed with humanity, dogs, bicycles, laundry and even garbage. The corridors smelt of stale cooking from assorted countries, and the carpets were old and musty.

One perk this apartment block with its heavy student population offered, was a satellite Internet connection. Martin had heard the noise about the Internet but had paid it scant attention. Now, on evenings, while at loose ends, he plugged in his laptop down in the rec room and surfed the Net, startled by the images that downloaded. He wondered whether he would one day sell real estate this way. Then he would not be limited to selling listings within driving distance; nor would his clients be loyal only to agents within their commuting area. Though yet a long way off, this phenomenon was interesting and threatening.

Martin found fleeting solace in the Sri Lankan restaurant on the adjacent block. He could go in there, even after a few drinks as there was no formality. He ordered comfort food: *thosais*, string hoppers, *idli*, *seeni sambol*—food he hadn't eaten in a long time and which took him back to fonder times. There was a cost to integration into Canada he realized: the bland 'meat 'n' potatoes' kind of food he had got accustomed to for instance, without realizing what he had given up. He relished the feeling of being able to sweat profusely again while eating, to burp and to blow from his mouth as the chillies found their spot. The hot and spicy food also sobered him up quickly.

Back in the apartment, when he was not surfing the Internet, he made sure there was always a video tape of the latest action movie, and a peg or two of Vodka in the bottle to help him ease into the quiet delirium that would eventually bring sleep. A photograph of the Pickering home stood on the TV so that he could visualize where he and his family were headed. One day he panicked as he sat down to his alcohol and video and found the picture missing. He felt throttled and confined in this hole with no way out, and charged around the living room looking for the picture until he found it behind the VCR, probably fallen during his vacuuming. He had an extra drink that night to calm his nerves.

"Martin, oh Martin...I don't know what to say!" Ginny was screaming on the other end of the line. Martin had just returned to the apartment at the end of the day, and was looking forward to more drudgery, booze and videos, when the phone had rung.

Trying to quell his rising panic, he tried calm words, "Ginny, please slow down. Take a deep breath...no not yet...there, now, exhale. Now tell me, what's happened? Is it Jamie?"

"No, it's Mother. She's been diagnosed, Martin."

Oh fuck! His relief was mixed with a new panic. Clarissa's emotional hold on her daughter was not to be underestimated. Although Ginny tried to show her independence, in times of trouble she had always defaulted to her mother.

"She got her results today. It's breast cancer and advancing rapidly. Oh, what shall we do, Martin?"

"Honey, I'm coming right over."

"No, no, Mother does not want to see anyone, least of all you."

"I was coming over to be with you and Jamie."

"That would be awkward in this house. And Mother needs me right now. But thanks for listening Martin. Maybe I'll call you later."

"Do you want me to speak to Jamie?"

"No, he is auditioning for a community opera performance. He doesn't know about Mother yet. I'll break it to him later."

"Community opera? That's new."

"Talk to him about it. Now I have to go. Oh, and I visited the property in Pickering."

"And—?"

"It's not what we're used to."

"It's just another change."

"There's so much change going around here, Martin, my head is spinning."

"Call me tonight, okay? I'll be here all evening."

He helped himself to a double vodka to steady his nerves. The house in Pickering was closing in a week and he had been busy getting ready for the move. Suddenly the house on top of the TV seemed to have moved several feet back, off its perch and into the next room.

Ginny did not call him that night and he drained the bottle and fell asleep in the armchair with the VCR running.

The next morning he downed several cups of coffee in order to focus on the transactional documents that were sitting for his signature back at the office. He cancelled two client appointments as he still looked and felt like shit. He hesitated calling Ginny because he did not want to throw her off the edge again, yet he felt that she must be close to it. He felt a black cloud hanging over him, pregnant with disaster, with unvoiced options that were intent on destroying his fragile family.

By two o'clock he could not hold back any longer and called Rosedale. No answer. He kept dialling every thirty minute; the act itself was a form of therapy. He got her at 4:30.

"We just returned from the hospital. She's going into surgery tomorrow. It's the whole works, Martin: surgery, chemo and radiation and it could take months. Poor mother."

"We can arrange nursing care for her, when she returns home," he said his heart sinking, not believing for a moment that his words were of any help.

"Nursing care? No way. She needs love and attention during this terrible time. I have to be there for her. Right through this experience."

"We're moving to Pickering in two weeks, Ginny. I hope you haven't forgotten?"

Her voice was flat, decisive for once. "Pickering will have to wait, Martin. You move. Jamie can spend weekends with you. I'm staying right here."

He moved to Pickering, all right, alone. He rented a U-Haul and drove it himself to the new house, a three-room bungalow with a finished basement, whose living room windows had a distant view of the bay, though for how long he did not know. He got gloriously drunk after the back-breaking work of unpacking. His boxes and un-stored belongings hung around for days until Jamie came for his first weekend visit and helped him put things away. One thing he did order was an Internet connection; there were so many wild thoughts swirling in his head about this phenomenon. The Internet looked like a lifeline out of the dreary and boozy existence he had trapped himself in.

He stowed his liquor bottles during Jamie's visit, but had to yield to the temptation of stealing away occasionally to take a swig from a bottle of Vodka stored under his bed. He also carried a hip flask to work now and found a tot at mid-morning, lunch, and mid-afternoon to be invigorating. He had become like his dead father in law—a tippler.

He walked with Jamie along the road leading to Frenchman's Bay one evening, but the late fall winds were gusting and the place looked desolate. The birds had gone south and the boats were tethered somewhere out of sight.

"We'll fish next summer," was all Martin could offer lamely.

Instead, they began to decorate the third bedroom, which was allocated to Jamie. Perhaps giving the boy his stamp on this house would make him return, despite having only the company of his boozy father. They shopped for new posters of Jamie's favourite musicians and put them up on the walls. Jamie was pleased; they hung exactly where he was used to seeing them in Willowdale.

As Christmas neared, Martin bought Jamie and Ginny presents: a small amplifier for Jamie's guitar and music sheets of Eric Clapton, Elvis Presley and Neil Diamond—hopefully the little guy could learn to play this stuff for when he visited—and a pair of gold earrings for Ginny.

He called Ginny and asked if she could find the time to spend the Christmas weekend with him and Jamie in Pickering.

She hesitated. "I'll come for a meal, but I can't stay over. Mother needs constant attention. Besides I don't want to leave her alone at Christmas. She gets depressed very easily these days. The chemo is taking its toll on her."

He bit the bitter pill of disappointment and said that he would look forward to their coming and that he would cook.

Their visit was pleasant, but strained and they came only on December 21st as it was between Clarissa's sessions of chemotherapy when she was at her strongest and could spend a few hours unsupervised.

Martin outdid himself on the meal: turkey, scalloped potatoes, garlic shrimp, rice, and assorted sautéed vegetables, along with a bottle of Californian chardonnay and liberal refills of root beer for Jamie. Ginny had baked a fruit cake for the occasion. He had taken several swigs of Vodka from his secret stash during the cooking before they arrived, so he was in good spirits. Even though Vodka was mild on after-breath, he brushed his teeth several times just to make sure.

After the meal, they opened their gifts and Jamie's eyes widened when he saw the amplifier. "Now I know why you asked me to bring along my guitar today."

"You could try playing me some of those Clapton songs," Martin said.

Ginny and Jamie had bought him a gift too: navy sports jacket with a wingtip collar.

"So you can sell more houses, Dad." Jamie grinned impishly. Ginny pursed her lips, a trace of a smile on her face.

After the dishes were cleared and Jamie had retired to his room to experiment with the new amplifier, Martin and Ginny settled in the living room. They each sat at either end of the sofa, the barrier of time and space still palpable between them.

Ginny looked around the room, at the ill-fitting arrangement of furniture. "The dining room table needs to be replaced. And this sofa set too," she said. "This isn't the Willowdale house. They don't fit here."

"I need you back here, overseeing stuff like that. I can't do this alone," he said. His hand reached over the sofa towards her.

She leaned away from him. "This has been hard for both of us, Martin. Please don't make it any harder."

"We don't have a relationship anymore, Ginny. We're just the parents of Jamie."

"This is my last chance to prove my worth to my family. Why are you denying me that opportunity?"

"But I am your family too."

"But you have had your way of coping. You are stronger. Don't tell me that there has been no other woman in your life since we...since we stopped having sex."

He looked away. There was no point in lying. Perhaps the truth might be a motivator. "I have my needs and my weaknesses too. Do you believe in testing me until I break?"

"I should have told you about my emotional problems before we got married. I guess I was in a state of bliss and thought everything would be okay."

"I have read up on clinical depression. I should have seen the symptoms in you: those shopping sprees, your sudden changes in image, and your moods. But I was a naive guy from the third world, where people acting out of pattern were simply classified as mad and shut away."

She got up and started pacing. "I'm better now, Martin, a lot better. The counselling and the meds have helped immensely. But I can only take disruption in small doses. I have to finish 'Project Mother,' and see that she's in a good space. Then I'll come back here and try to make our lives better again. I promise."

On Christmas Day he wrote to his father:

Dear Dad,

Thanks for your letter. I hope Christmas was good this year in your new digs. Sorry I did not send you a Christmas card—a very busy period, this season, as I also moved house. Please take a note of my new address. I am glad that you have moved in with Uncle Colin and Aunty Mabel. You need some looking after, and your cousins, if I remember, are God-fearing souls.

As for Barney, I will try to establish contact. But please do not be hard on him. After all, he is still your son. And he put up with a lot of shit in his formative years that you and Mum dished out, not that it was your fault either. There were worse predators attacking us as boys in Sri Lanka and scarring our lives than the likes of Barney—and they were never found out.

And talking of sons, I never told you this before, as I tried to partition this side of my life from you and from others back home, but I also have a son. His name is Jamie; he is seven years old and a wizard at music. He plays the piano like a young Mozart. I am attaching a recent photograph. Why didn't I tell you about him all these years? Because I was ashamed of my family, ashamed of how they had turned out. I am sorry. That's all I can say to explain things.

And I have also caught the "Burgher Curse" that you and my other relatives succumbed to. I think I am fast becoming an alcoholic. Taking a drink several times a day is now a comfort. I remember seeing you in that state and getting angry. Now I have followed in your footsteps. But you mentioned in your letter that you have stopped drinking and I wondered how you had managed that. Any secrets you can share with me will be welcome. I need help, I know that.

Sorry for destroying your illusion that I was your thoroughbred. I feel like a lame horse as I limp into the New Year.

Take care and write when you can. I will send you some news about Mum when I receive it.

Your son,
Martin

19. **Reclaiming Ground**

The chemo was followed by radiation, and from reports that Martin received during frequent calls with Ginny, Clarissa was responding well to her treatments, though devastated by the bombardment of her body by these invasions. Ginny had also upped her own anti-depressants as coping was becoming difficult, she said. She had increased her visits to the psychotherapist from once to twice a week. But she was "hanging in" she said, with a chirpiness that bothered him. Martin was her other outlet; she would sometimes stay on the phone for over an hour, unburdening. Then he wouldn't hear from her for an entire week.

One day when Martin drove over to pick up Jamie for the weekend, the boy was not at his customary perch by the front window. Martin checked his watch; he was five minutes early for once. On impulse, he got out of the car and walked up the winding driveway to the neo-classical-style house with its white columns and pillars. When the yard bloomed again in spring, there would be another chore for Ginny to manage, now that the gardener had been given notice. He tried the front door; it was unlocked. He swung it open gently and stepped inside. He was sure Clarissa was in bed somewhere in this yawning house and was hoping he'd get a chance to meet and talk to Ginny alone.

A figure stirred on the couch in the living room. Martin peered through the diffused light, trying to focus on who was there. The air was musty for once, none of the sterile cleanliness of his past visits; even the fish tank was in darkness. Suddenly a gasp came from the couch and a pile of clothing on it straightened up. A haggard figure with short-cropped hair was holding several blankets to her chin, eyes darting in panic.

"Who told you to come in unannounced?" Clarissa hissed, her voice dry and cracked.

"The door was open. I've come for Jamie."

"He's in his room."

"I'll wait outside, if I make you uncomfortable."

She sighed and began to deflate into the blankets. "It's all right. Take a seat. I was just resting."

Martin sat on the armchair across from her. A glass of water and several bottles of pills sat on a table within her reach.

"Where's Ginny?" he asked, looking for something to keep the uncomfortable silence at bay.

"Gone to get the car serviced. The poor thing has so much on her plate."

"She believes she has to meet family expectations."

"Yes, but she is not a strong child herself."

Martin was surprised at the softer tone, the acknowledgement of human frailty he once thought this woman could never be capable of comprehending.

"How are you doing?" he asked. "Ginny tells me you are responding well to your treatments."

"That is the official message. I feel like my body has been through the wringer—cut, burned and poisoned."

"I am sorry to hear that."

She let the blanket down slightly as she shifted position and he saw a sagging empty blouse underneath. Self consciously, she pulled the covers around her again.

"And I should ask, how *you* are doing?" she said. This surprised him even more. When had she ever been interested in him?

"I'm coping, as well as I can."

"You don't look well." Her eyes were boring into him. "You've lost weight."

"Yes, it's been busy at the office."

"No, that's not the reason. It's something else. Have you had your regular medical check-up?"

"I can't remember when I last saw a doctor."

A look of triumph illuminated her face. "Ah—there! You see? We think we are invincible until—bang, it gets you. George was taken by surprise too."

Jamie came running down the stairs and paused when he saw his father talking to Clarissa. "Sorry I'm late, Dad."

Martin rose. "That's okay. I was early. Come along, got all your things?"

Clarissa reached out two bony hands from underneath her covers, letting the blankets fall, this time, it seemed, without embarassment. "Come here, young man. Give your grandma a kiss before you head off on your adventures."

Jamie kissed his grandmother formally on the cheek, while she embraced him, her emaciated face creasing and her frame shuddering. There seemed to be a fleeting joy coursing through her with that embrace. Martin saw the gaps in her yellowed teeth as she opened her mouth to whisper to her tense grandson.

Breaking away from his grandmother when it was discreet to do so, Jamie picked up his knapsack and guitar and rushed out the door. As Martin made to follow him, Clarissa cackled, "Now remember, go and see your doctor before it is too late."

He attended two court sessions that spring to testify in the Garibaldi/Matinsen trial. On both occasions he was grilled by a Crown Attorney who seemed intent, not so much on extracting evidence to indict Enrico Garibaldi and Vigo Matinsen, as on dumping Martin in with them as well. Once, during the questioning, the prosecutor got close to very dangerous ground.

"Mr. James, did you have any personal investments with Mr. Matinsen or Mr. Garibaldi?" The beady-eyed, bald lawyer who stood just over five feet gesticulated as he spoke as if he was practising on an imaginary punching bag.

Martin looked across at the two accused. Garibaldi sat next to his lawyer, dressed in a dark suit, his features set, looking off into the distance as if he was above the enquiries of mere mortals. Vigo had gone through the biggest transformation: his once-fat cheeks drooped on either side of his jaw, and he had tried unsuccessfully to grow a beard—straggly grey hairs spouted unevenly on his face instead. Dressed in a cream suit and hunched next to a smartly trim young lawyer, Vigo looked like a man who was dying, slowly. When he looked at Martin, there was a plea in his face that seemed to say, "Don't rat on me, Martin, for old time's sake."

"Mr. James, will you answer the question?" the judge ordered.

"Ah yes," A drink would have been welcome before stepping into this witness box, but he had suppressed the urge in case he should say the wrong thing. "I played golf once with Mr. Garibaldi."

There was a titter in the court. Even Garibaldi came down momentarily from his Olympian heights to smile.

Martin continued, "My firm represented Matinsen Properties. I have other personal investments in mutual funds, savings bonds, and select commercial properties."

"Were any of those other investments with either of these two gentlemen or their companies?"

"I had some money with Garibaldi Construction."

"And that was in the Northern Tower?"

"Yes."

"You mortgaged your house to invest in this venture?"

"Yes."

"Very risky, wouldn't you say? Did your wife concur?"

Martin felt the sweat drain down his sides. He did not want the judge to see his face so he looked down at his shoes.

"It looked like a sure shot at the time. I guess we were wrong."

The judge intervened and asked the lawyer to keep the questions on Garibaldi's and Matinsen's investments and not the witness's. Martin breathed a sigh of relief; he had evaded that last question and now he didn't have to answer it.

He drank that day after being let out of the witness box; from three o'clock in the afternoon until a taxi deposited him in Pickering and he staggered indoors, fell on the couch and passed out.

The next day he was back on the stand, revealing transactions that had moved through the trust accounts of James Realty with regard to leases in the Northern Tower. He was dressed in a crumpled shirt that he had not had the time to iron, and his eyes were puffy and red. He was exhausted and hungover, and made many slips during his testimony, having to retract his statements many times. He was losing the thread of this trial and of the prosecution's line of questioning. His guage was the level of anxiety on Vigo's face: when the man blanched, Martin knew he had said something he shouldn't have, and revoked his words by saying, "Your Honour, I think what I meant to say was..."

Vigo's lawyer tore his testimony to shreds, and frankly Martin could not care less. He needed to get out of the courtroom and have a drink. He did not know whose side he was on any more; both the prosecution and the defence seemed to have it in for him; yet it was two other men who were on trial here. Vigo looked gleeful with every hole the defence made in Martin's testimony. At one point, Martin loosened his tie and put his hand up. "Your Honour, I do not feel well, can we postpone this to another date? Please?"

The young defence lawyer pounced on his chance to triumph. "I have no further questions your Honour. It appears our witness would be more comfortable sitting in a bar having a tall beer. I will excuse him to pursue that option if he so desires."

As Martin left the courtroom, he saw a large "thumbs up" coming from Vigo, why he did not know. He staggered out for fresh air and a drink.

A few days later, Vinod stood outside his office, smoothing his tie.

"What do you want?" Martin asked. He realized that the hip flask now stood permanently on his desk. It was more convenient there, as he used it more often.

"Boss, this can't go on anymore." Vinod stood just inside the door, quivering.

"Sit down. What's bugging you?"

"*You* are bugging me."

Martin looked up. Vinod seemed to be standing inside a cloud. "What? Have a seat."

"Look at you," Vinod hissed. "You are drunk by midday. Do you think I can bring any clients in to see you?"

Martin reached for the flask but saw it spin out of sight and into Vinod's cloud.

"Give that here, man," Martin said weakly. The whole room was spinning; like it did daily around four o'clock on most days now. He looked at his watch. "Is it four yet?"

"It's one o'clock. Everyone is at lunch. I thought I would take this moment to talk to you."

"Ah, one o'clock—that's early. Do you want to go for lunch? With me?"

Then Vinod was shaking him by both shoulders. "Listen boss, you need help. Something is wrong with you. Please get help before it is too late. We will lose everything—our staff, our clients, everything."

Martin stood up. The room swayed. "Okay. I'll go home then."

"Yes, and don't come back until you are better. We will manage. It is better if you are not here like this. It is bad for business."

He took a taxi home. There was a letter from Sri Lanka waiting for him.

He stood in the shower for half an hour until his head was clearer.

My Dear Martin,

I am so sorry to hear that you have the "Burgher Curse." Usually, we don't realize we have it until it is too late, or the doctor says, "Stop drinking or you will die,"—which is what happened to me.

There is a saying in Buddhism that "desire is the cause of suffering." There were a lot of things I wanted as a young man and I failed in everything: as a father, as an employee, as a husband, as a provider, as an immigrant. You know how many times I tried. It was like knocking my head against the prison bars. That is why I drank. I knew I couldn't, or didn't need to do these things any more, only after you left Sri Lanka. Then the need to drink also started to weaken, and when the doctor finally warned me, I just gave it up, willingly. It was like giving up a big burden.

I am not sure if I can give you any magic advice on how to stop. I can only tell you why I drank and how I gave it up. Maybe there is a lesson there.

You don't have to ask for my forgiveness about denying your family. I was a useless bugger anyway. But I am sorry that you denied your mother. She is a saint. Please don't deny her.

As for Barney, I will try to forgive him in my heart. By we were brought up to honour certain traditions. And for me, a man always made love to a woman. It is in the Bible and in every religious text that was drilled into our heads at St. Bernard's by those brothers with their canes and rosaries. I can only change so much. But I will try to accept him before I shut my eyes one of these days. This one is very hard for me.

I will pray for you, son. Ask for help from experts if you can, because that was another thing I did not do. We guys were macho men, no? Never wanted any help, never cried, never said "sorry." We bottled up and bottled up and when the pain got so intense we drank and drank and ran amok.

Please send me more pictures of my grandson—aney, they are so precious to have. I am showing everyone in Haputale the picture you sent me and they have fingered and fingered it and the poor picture is also crumbling now. Tell me about your wife and give her my love.
You are still my thoroughbred.
Love!
Daddy

Martin went on the Internet that evening and looked up Alcoholics Anonymous. The next day he registered with the local chapter.

They sat in a circle once a week. Many of them in their prime income-earning and childrearing years; mostly professionals, with a common look of deep shame and hurt lurking behind eyes that had lost their lustre from the constant onslaught of alcohol.

For Martin, this therapy, if this could indeed be called therapy, was more like a confession of sins. He had never confessed his trespasses; the priests in his day had committed more transgressions than he had done, and according to his father, they were still at it—so why bother going to a priest?

The conversations, after comfort levels for unburdening had been established, typically ran like this:

- Hi I'm Carl. I am an engineer, but I wanted to be a musician. I followed what my parents always wanted for me. I started drinking when I entered university. I passed every exam with distinction. You see I was good at engineering, but music was the holy grail for me...

- I'm Jenna. My father raped me when I was twelve. My mother was dead and I was the eldest who had to look after two younger siblings, and my father. When I was sixteen, he threw me out of the house as he had met my stepmother. I flunked college and started drinking, working in bars and hooking on the side. I really wanted to be an interior designer.

- I'm Garth. I don't know what I want to be. My family is rich and I had everything I possibly wanted. I was bored and drinking was an out. I still don't know what I want. But I do know that if I keep drinking, I will die.

And on they went…"Hi I'm Martin. I am looking to be acknowledged for who I am. Everyone whom I have loved seems to be living out of reach; everything I aspire to be is also out of reach. I don't know what home is. I guess I have never really had one, although I have lived in many." It was nice unburdening, letting some anonymous fellow-sufferer know about his tenuous journey, and to feel that he was not alone.

Al, the bearded chubby leader who believed in hugs and hand-holding prayers, was kind. He spent time with Martin before and after his first few sessions, giving him the lay of the land, the expectations, explaining the twelve steps, and yes—it happened even here—the politics of the group, what hot buttons not to press.

"You are not in as bad a shape because you've only fallen into this recently. Some of the others have been going on for years. Your best chance to kick it is now. It gets harder when you keep falling off the wagon repeatedly," Al said.

Martin had quit the booze with a passion: gone into every room, peered under the bed, couch and laundry cabinet, and pulled out all liquor bottles that he had stashed away, emptied them down the sink, then stuck the bottles in a garbage bag and thrown them in the nearby quarry. The withdrawal pangs gnawed at him incessantly. He drank Coke, prayed, put on his jogging gear in the middle of the night and went out running. He showed up for work daily, drank strong coffee and looked for approval in Vinod's face to give him the encouragement to go on. He surfed the Internet all day, reading success stories of kids out of high-school becoming millionaires overnight, while he just sat there and let others take care of his brokerage whose fortunes ebbed and flowed with every deal made and every one lost. Why could he not be one of these newly-minted millionaires?

The Garibaldi/Matinsen trial concluded: Enrico Garibaldi was convicted of money laundering and Vigo Matinsen was acquited due to insufficient evidence. Vigo phoned Martin one day in the office.

"Martin, I wanted to thank you."

"For what?"

"For playing the unreliable witness. You put on such a convincing performance. And you did it for your old pal Vigo."

"I'm an alcoholic Vigo. That's why I was unreliable. I wasn't doing you any favours."

A pause on the line as Vigo digested this new information. "I see. Well I am sorry to hear that."

"Me too."

"I am going back to Finland for a while."

"To parry again?" Martin couldn't resist a smile.

"Exactly. And to make sure that the people I deal with are not as unreliable as Enrico. I learned a good lesson with him."

"And I learned a good lesson working with a bunch of losers like you too. Vigo, I wish you luck with whatever you end up in next. But I don't want to hear or see you again, capiche?" And with that, not even waiting for an answer, he slammed down the phone.

Attending his fifth AA session, Martin was restless and wondering what the hell he was doing there. Although the cravings for alcohol had decreased, he knew that he had not got to the root of the problem. It was one thing to unburden and hug fellow sufferers. But deep down alcoholics had one thing in common: they were running away from who they were. From whom they should be. They were trapped in obligations and burdens that they had wittingly or unwittingly acquired. Today, he was waiting for someone to trigger that confirmation. And as Al had said, his best chance of kicking this ball and chain was now, before he failed again.

Affirmation came when Al asked Carl the engineer what would stop him from enrolling in music lessons while keeping his day job. Carl, who had been wallowing in self-pity up to that point, and who revelled in the audience he garnered each time he so indulged, looked surprised, and started coming up with flimsy excuses. *That's it. Al has said it. Why can't I go and yank Ginny and Jamie out of Rosedale? Why am I being a wimp, not wanting to hurt feelings or ruffle feathers, and taking all this pain on myself?*

Martin got up in the middle of the meeting, muttered an excuse that he had to attend to something urgent, and walked away. He never returned to AA.

That night, Martin showered, put on his best suit and went over to Rosedale without an appointment. He peeped through the tall windows that fronted the driveway. Ginny was playing Scrabble with a heavily blanketed Clarissa in the living room. Jamie was nowhere to be seen, but Martin spied a light in the direction of his son's bedroom.

He tapped on the front door. After some time, it opened a crack and Ginny looked at him surprised. "Martin, what brings you at this time of the evening?"

"I've come to take you and Jamie home."

A hand went to her mouth and she tried to suppress an amused but troubled smile.

"Aren't you going to invite me in?" he asked.

Seeing his determined look that was not going to take "no" for an answer, she backed into the hallway. "Sure, come in. We've just finished dinner. Mother will be going to bed soon. Jamie's on his computer."

"That's all right. Clarissa needs to hear what I have to say."

He walked into the dim living room. The fireplace was lit and it threw eerie shadows of the hunched figure leaning over the Scrabble board.

"Good evening, Clarissa."

A hand rose faintly and fell, acknowledging him.

"I've come to take Ginny and Jamie home."

Behind him, Ginny started to make excuses, "Martin, it's only two weeks after Mother's treatments ended. She needs more time to recover."

He swung back on her with clenched teeth. "And then it will be something else, Ginny. Always something that keeps you and me apart."

Silence descended like a knell on the room. Martin walked into the centre. He spoke loudly and clearly, keeping them both in view. He hoped Jamie was also listening from his perch upstairs.

"Ginny, we have not had the chance to make our marriage work. I did not know that marrying above one's class was such an uphill task." Turning to Clarissa, he said, "I do have a father—a former alcoholic; a mother who languishes in a mental home because there is no other place to treat her in Sri Lanka; and a brother who is gay. We have a lot in common as far as families go." He saw Clarissa push away her Scrabble tiles and turn to him.

"And what is more, I am steadily following in the footsteps of my ancestors. I joined Alcoholics Anonymous to try and get out of my hell."

Ginny's voice broke. She had a hand to her mouth, her features crumpling. "Oh Martin, so what Jamie told me was true? About your drinking?"

"I've tried to shield him as much as I can. I need you back, Ginny. I hope I have paid enough for my mistakes. You've looked after your mother and you have done an excellent job. My father advised me to ask for help. I am asking you now—will you come home and be with me? That is all the healing I need."

Ginny stood transfixed, uncertain where to move. Then Clarissa spoke, her voice calm and reedy. "Ginny, go back to Martin. I will manage."

"Hooray! We are going home." A voice came from behind them, on the stairs. Jamie's arms were thrown wide-open in exultation.

In full view of everyone, Martin walked up to Ginny, took her in his arms and crushed his lips down on hers. What shocked him was the way in which she yielded, for as his tongue circled hers, the taste of her was one of fright and uncertainty. The Ginny of old, the one he was trying to recover, was hidden somewhere out of reach. He knew that he would be taking her home tonight. But would she be really coming home?

20. **The Visionary CEO**

Martin stood by the window of his 38th floor office in the new landmark Gordon Tower in downtown Toronto and looked out across Lake Ontario. It was a hazy, sweaty day and the water danced in sluggish swirls out by the islands. Traffic roared on the Gardiner prompting him to wonder whether his career was zooming by faster than the speeding cars.

He turned towards his ebony desk and fingered the folder for the morning's investors meeting. He had sweated over this presentation the last couple of days and thought he now had it buttoned down. The investors were hungry for good news—the Internet had been only a good-news story to date—and he worried about being too cautious with his projections.

He looked across his plush office: thick beige carpets, ebony and mahogany furniture, an ornate glass cabinet containing awards and trophies, many from his real estate career. His navy blue suit was from Pierre Cardin and his shoes were Italian. None of this dot-com jeans, tee-shirt and messy office appearance for him. He could be a banker or a securities trader from the look of his office or from his get-up. He even had the clichéd golf putter and a handful of balls with a cup to practise upon the plush carpet while strategizing or when conducting an interview with a magazine journalist. Yes, here he was, Martin James, president and CEO of Jamestown.com, a man who had finally arrived.

He looked at his personal investment file, a daily activity he indulged in for his own ego stroking. His stock options were now worth five times their strike price based on the valuation he had received from an analyst yesterday. When they went public, hopefully next year, he would finally be in the millionaire class, outstripping the Summers family and its fortunes by a clean head. He felt vindicated.

He kept a maverick IT team in an old renovated factory in Scarborough, where real estate was cheap, and the dot-com rebellious streak could spark originality and creativity. This city office with its large boardroom and reception area was for customers and investors only.

He checked the news on his desktop monitor. Internet stocks were still growing, but not by as much as they had been last month. He wished he had entered this game a year earlier. By now his marketplace would have launched, gained traction and acquired customers. But he'd had his reasons for getting in late. Until Ginny and Jamie were back with him and his drifting life had stabilized, it had not been possible to embark on a venture requiring such dedicated focus.

A critical event that had triggered this new venture had been the sale of the old Garibaldi building—Northern Towers—for twice its fire-sale price, just as Martin had predicted. Two days after the sale, Martin received a call from Peter Bledsoe, one of his original investors in Garibaldi. After some small talk on how each had done professionally in the intervening four years, Bledsoe got down to business.

"Martin, we should have listened to you on Garibaldi. We should have hung in."

"Well, what goes down has to come up sometime."

"I know, I know. We were rather...hasty."

"Yes, it caused me a lot of personal grief too."

"I'm sorry to hear that. Listen, some of my colleagues and me are looking at a new venture on the Internet. People are making money left right and centre these days and we seem to be left behind. No one wants to bet on a traditional stock that has no Internet component in it any more."

"I've been exploring some ideas too. This marketplace concept looks promising—aggregate buyers and sellers into a single virtual website, give them all the information to make an informed decision, and help speed up the transaction with no intermediaries except the platform owner."

"What will we sell?"

"Real estate for one thing. Other services. Physical goods."

"It's going to be tough breaking through the established distribution gatekeepers in these industries."

"The Internet is about giving people choice. We're not going to shut down those other channels, but offer an alternative to them."

"And if we build it, do you think they will come?" Bledsoe was already using the term "we" too many times and Martin pricked up his ears.

Taking a deep breath, Martin said, "Right now, everyone is just building in cyberspace. Acquiring real estate, if you will. They must have some intuition that customers will eventually come. It is a better, faster and cheaper way. It democratizes the marketplace."

"We too have been talking about a marketplace concept. In fact, we have a technical architect who can develop the site. We need to ensure that we can collect enough buyers and sellers."

"It's a double-edged sword isn't it? You only get buyers if you have enough sellers, and the sellers won't come if there is no promise of more buyers."

"Exactly."

"I've thought about it. We need five or six anchor tenant suppliers and these we should bring on for free. The buyer end should also be free. Once we have the first set of customers on board and gain traction we can charge subscriber fees to new sellers, and over time, premiumize our offerings to buyers and sellers so they will find value in paying subscriptions at both ends of the spectrum."

"Sounds interesting. Make money on both sides? Wow!"

If this conversation was to go anywhere, Martin had to make his pitch at this point. "But we will need seed funding to keep the platform afloat until fees from buyers and sellers make it self-supporting."

Bledsoe changed his tone and got conspiratorial. "We *have* the seed money. We need the person who can realize the vision. Shall I set up a meeting with some of my colleagues?"

One thing had led to another. Unlike on the previous occasion, when Martin had pursued investors for money, this time they were all over him to come up with the right business model in order to *give* him the money.

Within weeks, a team of developers—young wannabes fresh out of university—were assembled under Gordon Marchal, the technical architect. The facility in Scarborough became operational, and Martin leased the downtown office, with its full corporate makeover, and set himself up as President and CEO of Jamestown.com. The name was Martin's negotiating gambit with the investors; if they wanted him to drive the vision, then he needed his name on the helm, identified as the guy who took the highest risk in this venture.

He picked up the folder, checked his watch—10 minutes before the meeting—time to put in his appearance, smile and shake hands.

He had left home at six o'clock this morning, dressing in the dark, not wanting to wake Ginny. He had decided against a tie today for he had to portray the image of the dot.commer. He slicked his hair back; thanks to the dye, he had managed to hide the grey streaks.

"You're looking dapper today." Her voice, thin and accusing in the stillness of dawn, jolted him.

"It's the big meeting today. Either we get the money for six more months or we don't."

"And do we have to sell up and move this time too if you do not get the approval?"

"Oh come on Ginny. I've got no money in this venture; just my salary and a bunch of stock options. Hopefully, the options will take off into the stratosphere after we go public. Vinod's got the brokerage well in-hand."

She was sitting up in bed now; he could see her angular frame propped against the headboard, the sheet pulled up to her neck.

"You just have to do this, don't you?"

He looked at her helplessly. He did not want another argument today. "Ginny this is important to me. I've stood by you during your big battles. I need you in on this one."

"For what? To stand around as the trophy wife of the dynamic dot-com CEO?"

"You're sounding jealous."

"Perhaps I am. Perhaps I don't the like the uncertainty you're plunging us back into."

"Ginny, my chance, our chance, to get out of this house and back to Toronto, is based on this deal. This is our only chance."

She got out of bed and put on her dressing gown. "I know, Martin. I have been a useless wife, unworthy of my family and of you."

"Oh come on, Ginny—let's not go there today."

She went downstairs and he heard the cups and saucers clack, water pour into the kettle and the fridge open.

When he descended the stairs a few minutes later, she was buried in the newspaper but had made him a steaming cup of tea.

At the last minute, he decided to take the laptop along with him even though he would not use it in the high-tech equipped boardroom; but the laptop, like his other accoutrements, symbolized what he was trying to project. He took a deep breath and stepped out of his office.

Jill, his red-headed (for today) assistant, flashed a toothy grin and thrust out her bosom at him. A tall double latte and a half-eaten donut decorated her marble-topped table. Martin took in his daily dose of overt cleavage; Jill always wore plunging necklines and a thick gold chain that disappeared between her breasts, accentuating their abundance. She even had the habit of sucking the cross on the end of the chain and letting it drop out of her mouth and plunge back into her bosom to get lost in its depths, several times a day. He chastised himself for falling for this idle pastime; perhaps if he was getting better sex at home he might be more circumspect.

"The boardroom is set up, boss," she chirped and dove for the ringing phone, cooing sweetly, "Jamestown.com, the marketplace of the future, can I help you?"

Martin walked past mostly empty, but fully equipped cubicles. The sales force was only partially hired; scaling up would take place only when business picked up. The plush carpeted aisle led to the double doors of the boardroom.

He pushed through into the room with extra vigour in his step and paused to assess the group assembled inside: dark-suited grey-haired men, no different from his real estate investors. People with money all looked the same, he observed: inscrutable, conservative, thrifty. The Internet was just a new place to multiply their wealth, or so they believed, else they would not be here.

Peter Bledsoe, a steel grey-haired man in his early fifties, a former hockey player, came over and shook Martin's hand energetically. "Good morning, Martin! Hope you have good news for us today. Before we start, there is a gentleman I want you to meet. He is new to our circle, but I'm told that he has made a lot of money in Eastern Europe after the fall of Communism. He is talking a lot of dollars here."

Bledsoe led Martin over to a small group clustered around the coffee and muffins. Martin nodded and shook hands with everyone in turn, as he knew them well. The newcomer was hunched and had well-combed grey hair trailing down to his shoulders, a beaked nose, a balding pate and a nervous tic in his left lip. His handshake was limp but his blue eyes were piercing.

"Ach, how good to meet you. Muller, is my name." When he spoke, Martin saw how stained and irregular the man's teeth were. He seemed out of place in a room full of well-groomed people.

"Martin James—pleasure to meet you." Martin pumped Muller's limp hand, reserving comment. *Wealth hides in strange quarters.*

The meeting kicked off and Martin presented the status of the project: the website and the back-office procurement engine were completely integrated and testing was in progress. Three of the five anchor tenants had signed up. The other two were holding out for concessions: they wanted to be paid for coming on board as they felt that they were providing more value than they were receiving from this unknown start-up. "The bottom line is, we need another six months of funding until we gain traction. I suggest we soft-launch next month with our three anchor tenants, before they change their mind. I am personally involved in bringing the two holdouts on board. In fact, I have a meeting in Calgary tomorrow with Godfrey's CEO."

Morrie Gluckstein, one of the older investors, a self-made man who had started life running a hardware shop on Bathurst Street, raised his hand. "Martin, you're burning half a million dollars a month. That's another three million you're asking for without a single customer on board."

Martin was ready for this question. "Morrie, the Internet economics are a bit different. Everyone is trying to capture share of eyeballs in cyberspace. The profits are expected to follow. If we don't snap up the opportunities now, there is no point in even playing."

"I agree," Peter Bledsoe said. "We got into this thing with our eyes open. This is either nirvana or skid row, there is nothing in between. Three million, though—that's a lot."

Martin quickly interjected before indecision spread among the group. "It's not quite three million. Our development work is done and testing should conclude by the end of this month. I think we will need to cover just fixed expenses and advertising at around three hundred thousand a month, plus contingencies. I am asking for two million dollars over the next six months."

Heads bowed, hushed whispers began and Martin let them digest his request. The only person looking directly at him was Muller, with a gleam in his eye.

"We are obviously going to need some time to discuss this Martin," Bledsoe said, looking at the fragmented conversations going on around him.

"I need to have an answer today, Peter. This business moves too fast."

"Why don't you leave us to work through this issue in private for the next thirty minutes or so? Come back into the boardroom after that. I think you have provided enough information to help us make a decision."

"That won't be necessary," an accented voice suddenly spoke out above the tittering. It was Muller, standing up and pointing a finger at the presentation screen. The room hushed and everyone turned towards him.

Muller straightened his hunched frame. "Gentlemen, we have to look at history when we make these investments, ja? What does history tell us? Look at the East European block: they did not go where progress was leading the world after the Second World War. See how far back they were when the Berlin Wall fell? This Internet thing is the new frontier; we must follow it."

"But you can't recklessly throw money away, when nothing is proven yet," Morrie Gluckstein interjected. "We've had the South Sea Bubble, the Tokyo real estate bubble and other lessons from history too."

Muller straightened up even more. "If I invest a million dollars in this venture, do I see any support from you gentlemen for the other half?"

Martin was taken aback. This type of confidence was frightening. But he said nothing, grateful to this unseemly angel who had mysteriously arrived on the scene.

Bledsoe put his arm on Martin's shoulder and moved him towards the door. "Give us some time, Martin. As you can see, we have a few things to discuss here."

Martin wished he was a fly on the wall in that boardroom, as he practised putting back in his office. Every ball missed the cup. He looked at the minutes tumble by on his large digital clock.

Lining the golf balls for the umpteenth time, he was about to resume putting when Jill stuck her head around the door. "They want you back inside."

The walk back to the boardroom was the longest one he had ever taken. He was reluctant to push open the door, fearing this would be his last time, having flash-forwards of packing his bags, winding down the operation and heading back to his brokerage to pursue the same old work he had got bored with over the years.

The door swung open to a smiling Peter Bledsoe. "Congratulations, Martin! The investors have approved your request."

A wave of relief, mixed with shock, coursed through Martin. He saw Morrie Gluckstein shaking his head and picking up his papers, while Muller, encircled by a trio of other investors, seemed absorbed in recounting a story.

"Thanks, Peter. This is just what we need. I'll get word out to the team in Scarborough right away."

Martin stood outside the boardroom doorway and shook hands with each of the investors again as they filed out, thanking them for their trust and belief in him.

Gluckstein neared and dropped his voice to a whisper. "You'll be interested to note, Martin, that I was the only dissenter. Everyone overruled me, led by that *nishtikeit*, Muller. This Internet thing—*Oy Vey*—it's got everyone by the balls, I'm afraid."

"Thanks for supporting us this far, Morrie. And it's good that you are acting as our voice of conscience."

"What can I do? We have now crossed the point of no return. I just hope this thing pans out. Good luck, Martin." The old financier shuffled out.

The last to depart was Muller. He ambled towards the door, as if in no hurry to leave, but his eyes were on Martin all the time.

"Thank you, Mr. Muller. I am glad you are on board and see the vision of where we're heading."

Muller's eyes were like balls of fire. "When the Wall fell, we were also very confused. But then we saw unlimited opportunities to bring capitalism to Eastern Europe and we took it."

"Why did you leave?"

"It was getting too crowded. Too many Mafia were...'getting in on the act,' as you say? So I decided to come to North America, to diversify my interests. I think the Internet is going to be big. Europe and the rest will only be followers."

"I'm surprised you are not in the USA, in Silicon Valley, for example."

Muller looked at him with his piercing eyes. "I like to be a big fish in a small pond, ja? Canada works well for me."

"Got it. Well, we'll try not to disappoint you. You do however know that this is a risky venture?"

Muller surprised him even more by reaching out and pinching Martin on the cheek. "Ach, I know all about risk, Martin. But you are a smart businessman yourself. Like me, you do not like to fail. I can see that."

As Muller passed, Martin got a whiff of stale garlic and cigarettes hidden beneath his cologne; a hint of danger, of edge, a scent that makes one shudder involuntarily.

Martin stirred in the soft king bed; someone next to him was snoring contentedly. With eyes closed he nudged a naked leg, his hand encircled a large breast, and the snore turned into a contented sigh. He suddenly sat up. He was still in that woman's suite in Calgary, not at home in Pickering.

Memory rushed back: the night flight out, the business class cabin and the woman in her early forties, in a blue power suit, including a tie, sitting next to him. They had traded business cards. She was a bank vice president on one of those boring office visits out West. After a couple of glasses of wine (for her; he stuck to Coke) on the four-hour flight, their talk had turned to personal lives. She was divorced with two teenage sons who alternated visits between her and her ex. When describing his wife, Martin had been guarded; he just said that he wished there was something more in the relationship, that the years together, and circumstances, had sucked the romance out of his marriage. After her third glass of wine, the vice president didn't seem to care about propriety. Her hotel was three blocks down the road from his, she told him. Equally boldly he asked her if she would like to get together for a drink after they landed, as he slid his hand into hers. The rest had followed.

How many times had he done this before? It was becoming routine. He had developed a knack for spotting lonely women on planes or in bars. It had started soon after Ginny returned with Jamie to live in Pickering. Martin should have guessed that the gallant rescue of his wife and son from Rosedale would only be a hollow victory.

Soon after she arrived in Pickering, Ginny began marking down their personal belongings and entering them in a spreadsheet in her PC. Martin discovered this when she gave him a printout of the items and asked him to check if she had missed anything. When he asked her what the list was for she never gave him an answer. He ignored the issue, thinking it was probably not a bad idea after all, should there ever be an insurance claim. Then she opened a separate bank account for herself and started depositing any money that she received into it. She did not bring over the Ming vase, the Monet or the Egyptian daggers, preferring to keep them at Rosedale, although the Persian rug did arrive. Martin did not pressure her on these items, even though he considered them mutual property. She opened a dry goods cupboard down in the basement and stocked it with tins of beans, bags of pasta, rice, sugar, tea, jams, dried fruit and other canned food, until the cupboards were near overflowing. He chuckled at this effort and labelled it her "disaster-recovery planning," like they did in the software business. Even though Martin was receiving two incomes—one from the residues of the brokerage and a full salary from Jamestown.com—Ginny established a monthly grocery budget and never wavered from it, chastising him every time he took Jamie out for ice-cream or fast food. A winter coat now had to last three years; gone were the rapid-fire changes when she would go out and splurge on clothes. She cut out movies, the Stratford and Niagara-on-the-Lake theatre festivals and dinners at their once favourite hangout, the King Eddy.

How people changed! But after what had happened to his mother, Martin was resigned to changes, especially in those one idolized and at one time had held beyond human frailty.

Ginny's home exercise routine slimmed and hardened her physically. Her breasts flattened out until they were tight little mounds. There were times when he reached out for her at night and wondered if he was sleeping with a man. There was no yielding on her part either. Sex, which had dried up before she left him for Rosedale, returned with the same dutiful mechanical precision: twice a week, on Tuesdays and Fridays, and nothing in between. She slept on her side of the bed, not with her hand in his as they had done in the very early days of their marriage.

He sensed that she resented coming to live with him in Pickering, entering the confines of this small cookie-cutter style house, something she had never been accustomed to.

One day, in a fit of remorse, he had put his arms around her.

"I'm sorry, Ginny. I guess I brought us to this. How do we start again? I mean, properly?"

She took his hands firmly from her neck and eased out of his embrace. She walked over to the opposite end of the room and busied herself in putting the old newspapers into recycling bags, another of her recent "green" habits.

"We'll survive," she said.

"Surviving isn't enough. You are not used to mere survival. You have always had a good life."

"Mum told me that we come from good farm stock. They slaved away on the farms a hundred and fifty years ago. That ethic is bred in me. It surfaces in tough times."

"I'll get us out of this—soon. Jamestown is our ticket back."

She looked up immediately from her work. A look of panic crossed her face. "You are not jumping into another risky scheme, are you?"

"No. This one is carefully planned and funded."

She bit her lip and stepped away. "Martin, I can't go through another one of those…those…flops."

"Don't worry, honey." But his words fell into empty air as she had already stumbled out of the room; the bag of papers was on the floor, its contents spilling out.

There had been many similar "cut and run" episodes whenever he had broached the touchy subject of their relationship. He had even suggested couples counselling, given that she was so in favour of that form of therapy for herself and still paid regular visits to her shrink. But she put him off saying that she was not ready.

Eventually he stopped trying. She was a faithful wife and a good mother—that he had to grant her, erratic and mixed up though she was. In that sense, he had done better than Victor. With ancestral stoicism he had accepted his lot and focussed his energy on Jamestown.com. And when transient one-nighters, like this one in Calgary, presented themselves, he helped himself to the opportunity.

Now, in this stranger's hotel room, he dressed in the dark and hoped that the concierge or the bell boy would not look at him suspiciously. He had to get back to his hotel and shower for the meeting with Godfrey's CEO at ten o'clock.

"What time will I see you tonight?" The tousled and yawning vice president asked from the bed, swinging a naked leg over the bed sheets. She clicked on the side-table light.

"I'm flying back this afternoon."

She sat up. The sheets fell off her and her large breasts hung heavily down her chest. What fit of lust had made him draw on them so vigorously last night? He wished she would put out the light and go back to sleep. "I thought you told me you were here for a few days. What happened to our plan to visit the Saddle Dome tonight?"

He remembered that he had made fictitious plans last night, just to make sure she wouldn't think of him as the one-night stand he was.

"I'm sorry," he said, turning his face away from her. "I got this voice mail saying that they need me back ASAP. So all I have time for is my meeting this morning."

She sank back in the bed. She looked crushed, but kept a straight face. After all, she was a vice president and accustomed to weathering unexpected changes in plan. "Why is it always like this? Snatches of life amidst a dreary, mind-draining job?"

"Tell me about it," he said, looking sympathetically at her.

She held out her arms. "Will you at least give me a hug before you go?"

He walked up to her, took a deep breath and pecked her on the cheek, stepping out of her reach before she demanded anything more. "I really have to go. Thanks for everything."

"Will I see you again, in Toronto?" She looked plaintive, her vice presidential air slipping momentarily.

"I'll call you," he said as he slipped out the door. In the elevator he tore up her business card and deposited the fragments in a waste basket in the lobby while the night clerk stared at him.

Ginny lay back on the psychiatrist's couch and stared at the ceiling. She was upset for two reasons today: Jamie, who was eleven, had been skipping his homework and experimenting with what he called "Blue Rodeo derivatives" on his guitar, and Dr. Baird, her psychiatrist of many years, had retired last month and referred her to a new shrink, Dr. Brian McDonald, whom she knew nothing about. Now she was in this unfamiliar office of Dr. McDonald, waiting for him to enter. And unlike Dr. Baird, Dr. McDonald was late. She heard papers shuffling in the outer office. If the new doctor was going through her file only now, he had a lot of catching up to do; the first entries dated back to the early eighties when she had first overdosed and brought about the chemical imbalance.

She was restless and rose from the couch, checking out the oak-paneled office. The dark wood made the atmosphere sombre and gloomy. Photographs adorned the mantelpiece. A distinguished bearded man, tall, athletically built, with salt and pepper hair and light eyes embraced two teenage children—a boy and a girl—on a sailboat, while the wife in dark glasses, sunhat and striped nautical outfit managed the steering. In another picture of the foursome—a portrait, this time—the boy had freckles and ginger hair, the girl, slightly younger, wore braces; the wife was a redhead and had small pointed eyes, a forceful chin, and a bored expression compared to her husband's eyes that were alight with an inner fire.

For a moment, Ginny wondered if she was looking at a picture of her own family when she was a child—the stereotypical WASP unit. A feeling of regret coursed through her; the stereotype might have been much more manageable than what she had ended up with.

A door opened behind her and the bearded man entered. "Virginia?"

"Dr. McDonald. Pleased to meet you." She extended a dry hand. His grip was warm, comforting. She liked it immediately.

"Please call me Brian. Sorry I am a bit late. I was reading your file. We can go an extra ten minutes if you wish."

She nodded and took her place on the couch. She was used to this routine. She wondered how she would cope if unable to have this weekly visit.

"So where would you like to go today?" he said, pulling his armchair closer to the couch. She smelled his aftershave. His easygoing manner relaxed her; there were no schedules, he just let her run with things, giving her the sense of control she needed.

"What did you gather from my file?" she asked.

"That you are not alone. One in five people suffer from some form of anxiety in our society."

"I feel I carry my family's expectations. They are too much to handle sometimes."

"You have a complex family, with some very gifted and talented individuals. There is sometimes a price to pay for that. Hopefully, the price is worth it."

She was starting to feel better already. He was giving her the boost her ego needed. She began to talk. She talked about growing up, of her early feelings of inadequacy, about the drugs that helped dull those feelings, about that one wild party when things had gone overboard. The tranquilizers that had followed to keep the mood swings in check. Meeting Martin and trying to keep balanced while they dated. The crash of '87, her father's illness, taking over the firm and the relapse into inadequacy as the demands had overwhelmed her once more...and on and on she rambled, well past the allotted hour.

Now she felt good about Dr. Baird's retirement. He was a time freak, specific to the "issue of the week." This Dr. Brian McDonald was fluid, prodding her with only an "and-what-happened-then" to launch her into another stream of recollections.

Her conditioned times on the couch over the years told her that they had exceeded the hour and soon she heard him clearing his throat politely.

"Are we out of time?" she asked, anticipating his answer.

He surprised her again. "We are, but I don't have another client for an hour, so you can have a few more minutes to wrap up. I hope this has been as good for you as it has been for me. It has brought me up to speed very quickly."

"I looked at your family's pictures on the mantelpiece before you came in and wondered why I couldn't have gone the route that you did."

He cleared his throat gently again. "Pictures are staged events and one should not draw too many inferences from them." She sensed a hint of regret in his voice.

She looked at him, but he was turned towards the photographs. "But you are successful and happy," she insisted.

"Happiness is a state of mind. That's where we have to take you. My wife is a paediatric surgeon and is rarely home. But we grab moments—like in those pictures—as testaments of happy times."

She did not want to continue. The thread of unburdening had been broken. She rose from the couch. "I think I am done for today."

"Good." He rose too. "Next week, I'd like to delve into your family relationships. I think we may want to start to uncover some blocks there."

"You have remarkable insight."

"I think today was a good prelude. But we were skirmishing around the issues that you are currently facing. Let's try to get to them fairly soon."

As she passed him in the doorway, she shuddered, wondering if it was because of all the unburdening, or his aftershave, or the masculinity of his body—aspects of men that had failed to arouse her for a long time. She was already looking forward to her next visit.

Martin was driving home. He had dropped in on the IT group in Scarborough en-route. Gordon Marchal's progress report was not encouraging; there were more bugs in the testing than anticipated.

"These wunderkinds are hard to manage," Marchal said sotto voce, stroking his beard, as they walked past the booths of young programmers and testers hunched over their work with empty pizza boxes and pop cans littering the floor, and heavy metal music blasting in the background. Marchal was a 30-year veteran of the computer industry and had project-managed some major software developments in his time. Martin had hired him as the voice of reason in an otherwise delirious world of dreams and hype. As if to re-emphasise that fact, two of the programmers were taking their break by shooting hoops in a temporarily rigged basketball ring in the empty reception area. Marchal flushed and shrugged.

When they were back at Marchal's cube, Martin reviewed the bug report; they were still uncovering an average of five bugs a day.

"We were hoping to advance our launch date by a week," Martin said.

Marchal furrowed his brows. "I didn't know that."

"We discussed it only this morning with the investors. With Godfrey's still holding out despite my personal interventions, we are thinking of pre-empting matters by launching without them. Hopefully, Godfrey's will not want to be left out for too long."

"That may be the strategy, but the practical experience will be a horde of dissatisfied customers walking into too many blind spots if we don't fix these bugs."

"Well, cut out the pizza parties and the basketball, and get these guys working evenings and weekends if necessary to make it happen. If you need me to speak to them, I will."

He had left Marchal looking crestfallen. Now, in the car, he felt bad for the way he had handled his legitimate concerns. Gordon Marchal was an old-school guy who delivered perfect products, but the Internet was full of launch-now, fix-later applications, and nobody really cared about functionality. Only hype and first-to-market mattered.

When he got home, Jamie was waiting for him in the front yard, dressed in a track suit, bouncing a basketball.

"Want to shoot hoops with me, Dad?"

"Sure." His son was always a pleasant diversion from the day's pressures.

They walked out to the park, a few blocks away. Given the cooling weather, no one was on the outdoor court, littered now with fallen leaves from the park's massive poplars. Jamie shot and missed quite a bit. Martin knew that his son would never excel on the court as he did with his music. Still he helped recycle the ball for Jamie standing at the foul line. When it was his own turn, Martin shot and scored a few, but he had never played this game as a kid and felt little enthusiasm for it.

"Why do you play this game, when it's harder for you than playing the guitar?" Martin asked.

Jamie laughed and ran after one of Martin's errant shots that had bounced off the rim.

"You're the one who told me, Dad, that I should always try to reach higher than what's comfortable."

Martin laughed. He had forgotten his old advice. "I told you that?"

"Yeah, the night you set up your new Internet company."

"Oh, yeah." He had been so high with having his own dot-com name that he had forgotten all the free advice he doled out that night.

"Are you practising hard for the provincials?" Martin asked.

"Yeah. But the piano is starting to get boring. I like the spontaneous stuff that comes off the guitar."

"The provincials are no joke, buddy. There is a lot of hard work involved."

"Yeah, yeah." It was now Jamie's turn to shoot and he looked relieved at having something to do. He paused after his second shot and looked Martin straight in the eye.

"Dad, you are not like the rest of our family. You're different."

"What do you mean?"

"I mean, you're not loud like Uncle Tim, or so certain about things like Grandma. But you look like you know a lot. Is that because you are a Burgher?"

Martin laughed. "Well, I don't take the day for granted. Anything could happen tomorrow."

"Mum says that you never relax."

"I guess I was brought up in a country during a time when one could never sit back, even if one wanted to."

"But you live in Canada now."

"Yes but it's bred in my bones. Just like your mother's family's material comforts are bred in yours."

"Will you take me to Sri Lanka, one day?"

"Maybe. I have never gone back. I'm not sure I would ever see the country I once knew."

"Maybe if you go, you'll relax there?"

"It's difficult when you feel you don't belong. That's the same here, Canada may be my home; I've even got the passport now to prove it, but there are times when I feel like the outsider looking in."

Jamie nodded, pondering that information. They shot more hoops, in silence this time.

Suddenly Jamie looked at his watch. "Oh geeze, we're late for dinner. Mom said only 'til 6.30."

Martin laughed. "That puts us both in the dog house. Come on, grab the ball. Let's go home."

Dear Martin,

I thought I'd write you at this e-mail address now that you are advertised for the whole world to see as <u>martin.james@jamestown.com</u>. I am sorry for the silence over the last few years, but I thought you needed your space (and we needed ours). The reason for this e-mail is to let you know that I am moving back east, to Port Hope, a small town just east of Oshawa. I am rather burned out in Vancouver and Julia (yes, I picked that name as I remember how enamoured you were with it) will be starting grade school soon. My mother passed away last year too, hence there is nothing keeping me in BC.

A colleague of mine who moved east has started a real estate brokerage and has invited me to join her. I get to set my hours of work and Port Hope is not as frenetic as Vancouver, I presume.

I am not sure if you would want to see Julia and build a relationship with her. I am not even sure if your family knows about her existence. However, I thought it prudent I should tell you about this move, just in case we bump into each other in the street one day.

I am still single, if you are interested to know. I met a bunch of losers in Vancouver and have now decided to focus on our daughter.

Hope you are well. I read great things about Jamestown.com—hope it helps you realize your immigrant dream.

Regards!
Marnie.

Martin printed out the e-mail and read it several times over. He filed the original electronic copy in his personal folder and stared at the hard copy again. A lump sat in his throat. This was one of life's gifts he had ignored. Julia—what kind of girl would she be? There had always been a Julia that had evaded him. Would he be lucky enough to see her this time? Was he worthy of this little Julia, a child he had abandoned so casually while all the time moving heaven and earth to get Jamie back into his reach? Would Julia grow to love him or did she already hate him? Did she even know that he existed? Did she even care? And what of Marnie? He had even suspected her once of being in cahoots with Garibaldi, while she had been bearing and rearing his child. He hurriedly tucked the printout into his jacket pocket as the phone rang.

"Martin...?" the snaky voice of Muller sent a shiver down his spine. The German had called him daily since he had come on board with his million dollars. Martin felt as if he was maintaining a separate line of reporting to this investor compared to the others whom he met with as a group weekly.

"How is the project coming along, Martin?"

Martin sighed, hoping his displeasure echoed over the phone line. "Much the same. I will be reporting to the investors on Monday. I hope you'll be there."

"Martin, I am reading some bad news these days. Is it true?"

"Herr Muller, you can't believe everything you read. If you read the Internet magazines, cyberspace is going gangbusters. If you read the conservative financial newspapers, the journalists—who are out of their league in this space—tear it to pieces as a big joke. What I know is that companies are still signing up to do business and investors like you are putting forward the money to develop this space."

"What about Godfrey's? Why didn't they sign?"

"It's in my report for next Monday. But if you must know, Godfrey's is a traditional office equipment store with established commercial accounts. Perhaps they were the wrong player to bring on board. The more I think about it, the more we need an upstart with good supply chain links to come in and unseat Godfrey's from their comfy perch. That's what this Internet thing is all about, unseating comfortable and complacent players."

"Ah, your words make me feel good, Martin," Muller cooed on the other side. Martin still felt uneasy about this guy. He had checked out Muller's company; it was a sole-proprietorship involved in import/export with Eastern Europe, which meant nothing; it was similar to the outfit of those goons who had finally dragged Garibaldi down. Muller's million-dollar investment in Jamestown.com seemed to have come from his personal funds. Perhaps he was trying to get his Canadian immigrant status formalized via the Investor category.

"How is the testing?" Muller caught him off-guard again with this direct question.

"It's progressing. We are working through the bugs. We are still going to launch a week early."

"Gut, gut. But why so many...what do you say...bugs? I am German, Martin. We have zero defects in whatever we do. You North Americans seem to sell only buggy products, ja?"

"There is more forgiveness in the Internet space, Herr Muller."

"Okay. Okay. I believe you. But it is nice talking with you Martin. It is very re-assuring."

"Good day, Herr Muller. I'll see you on Monday."

"Yes, Martin. I will be there."

21. **Three Strikes and You're Out!**

"Let's talk about your husband," Dr. McDonald said gently from behind. During Ginny's recounting, he had risen from his chair and commenced pacing quietly. This was her third session with him and she had become very comfortable.

"He is a risk taker. He lives on the edge," she began.

"As in gambling?"

"Not the Vegas stuff. He gambles with our lives. His whole life has been a gamble."

"Tell me more."

From the corner of her eye she noticed Brian McDonald resume his seat and lean forward. She wanted to be fair; after all, Martin was still her husband: the man she had been wild about not so many years ago, the exotic pet in her WASP bastion of Dr. McDonald-like men. She talked about his life overseas; the forces which she believed had shaped him to be what he was today. She talked about Jamestown.com.

"Your husband is ambitious," Dr. McDonald summed up when she paused.

"He feels that he is not worthy of me. That he has to scale these heights all the time to prove himself."

"And you feel the same unworthiness?"

"Yes. What can we do about it? Our sex life is routine now, non-existent even, and not worth talking about. I know he has other lovers."

"How do you know that for certain?"

She leaned over the couch and pulled out a crushed note from her handbag. "I found this in his jacket pocket the other day. I made a copy."

He read Marnie's note and nodded. "You go through his things regularly, I take it?"

She blushed. "I don't trust him anymore. Not after he forged my signature on a loan that nearly sank us five years ago. He does not tell me a lot of about his business dealings now. I don't even know how he came into this country. He never talks about it. Jamestown.com is all he talks about."

"Perhaps that is all he is involved in." Dr. McDonald waved the note in his hand. "Besides, this affair, if you can call it that, took place some time ago, when you yourself were not...settled."

"What are you suggesting?" she snapped.

"I am suggesting that you can try forgiveness. If there is no forgiveness there is no progress."

She slumped back in the couch and exhaled loudly. His words sat on her chest like a 50 pound weight, suffocating.

"What do you feel when you touch him?"

She jerked upright, as if electrocuted. "What?"

He held her gaze with his gentle but uncompromising eyes. "You said your sex life is in shambles. What do you feel when you touch him?"

"We don't touch anymore."

"Ah." He let the pause hang. She was beginning to sweat and wanted to end the session. Just then he said, "I'd like your permission to touch you. It's purely clinical, I assure you."

She closed her eyes in silent acquiescence, though she felt challenged and wanted to respond aggressively. His warm hands touched her cheek and slid down her neck to end just above her breast. Her anger melted. She felt her nipples hardening and knew she could not hide it from him through the flimsy cotton dress. He let his fingers remain on her, gathering heat, kneading slowly until she was bursting with desire. Then he removed his hand abruptly.

"You are a normal woman with normal and healthy emotional responses."

She was angry at both his intrusion, and his sudden withdrawal from touching. A flood of emotions clogged up inside her. "That was a huge professional risk you took."

His eyes were smiling, gently. "Sometimes we have to take risks to get to the heart of the matter. I have two homework exercises for you: forgive your husband for his trespasses, and respond to his touches. See me again if you face any difficulties."

She got off the couch and stalked out of the office, leaving the copy of Marnie's letter still in his hands.

She was waiting for Martin when he got home that evening, late as usual. He dropped his laptop bag in the hall and plunked himself in front of the TV. She had most of dinner still on the table while the roast kept warm in the oven. Jamie was at his final week of performances at the provincials. She would go and pick her son up after dinner. She poured Martin a glass of ginger ale and brought it out to him. He raised his eyes at this gesture; normally he got his own drinks, but he looked grateful for the offer.

"Sorry, I'm late for dinner, again," he said. He was watching the business news on CNN.

"I waited for you," she said, looking for a reaction. The slow raising of his eyebrows signalled that he had heard and was digesting her new behaviour pattern, although his main attention was captive to what was happening on the television screen. She too was drawn to it. A major dot.com company had collapsed and another two were merging. Her resolve slipped and the old panic returned momentarily.

"They were over-leveraged and over-hyped anyway," he said, pointing at the screen.

"And Jamestown isn't?" she bit her lip after the words came out. This was not how she wanted the evening to go. *Watch it, that old pattern is slipping back.*

He sighed. "We've got committed suppliers. And we launch on Monday. We'll know very soon after that if we have any buyers." He slumped back in his armchair and switched off the TV.

"How are Jamie's performances coming along?" he asked.

"He's in the semis today. I'll find out when I see his coach later this evening. I do not want to talk about Jamie tonight."

He looked at the clock. "Then let's have dinner. Thanks for waiting for me."

He served himself with a generous helping of roast beef and vegetables, while she pondered if this was the right time to broach the subject. She decided it wasn't. When he had eaten his last morsel and pushed the plate away, she began, "Martin..."

"Hmm"

She paused, her palms clammy, a light-headedness taking over. "Never mind."

He noticed her unease. "What's on your mind?"

She had to go on now or lose the opportunity forever. "Who are Julia and Marnie?" The words slipped out of her.

His face clouded over but he remained silent. He gripped the glass of water tightly in his hand and she could see his brain working.

"Is it the same Marnie you used to work with at the brokerage?" she pressed.

His hands instinctively went towards his pockets. "You've been going through my things."

She felt defensive, this was not the position she had wanted to end up in. She tried to claw herself back. "Answer my question. Please, Martin."

He sighed and looked down at his plate with its crumbs and traces of gravy. "Yes, I worked with Marnie. Julia is my daughter."

His words cut her like a knife. She had half expected this news, but still couldn't handle it when it was delivered. A protest immediately poured out of her. *Protesting is easier than forgiveness, Dr. McDonald. I am not as strong as you think.*

"You betrayed me—again, Martin."

"We were going through a bad patch, Ginny. I'm sorry." He rose and tossed his napkin on the table. He hesitated in the doorway as if uncertain whether to stay or flee. Then he shrugged his shoulders in a beaten way and walked out of the house.

"No, wait," she shouted into the empty air. She rushed to the door and called after him, but his receding footsteps on the sidewalk indicated he was almost out of earshot. She leaned in the doorway and spoke to an empty street, "I was supposed to say 'I forgive you'. I want to forgive you. But I can't. I want you to touch me. But I don't think you will, especially now."

She returned to the living room and crumpled to her knees in the middle of the floor, her body shaking, tears streaming down her cheeks. "Damn you Brian McDonald—you have no idea how hard this is."

He had spent the previous night in a motel after driving around the city aimlessly with just his thoughts for company, not wanting to go home to face an unforgiving Ginny, wrapped in her own sense of betrayal.

Today he sat in his office with a coffee. It was 7:30, and no one was in yet. He had several e-mails, many still requiring response. The one from Marnie was one of these; it had been two weeks now and he still did not know what to say to her. Finally, he decided to put the matter to rest.

Dear Marnie,

I am sorry for the delay in responding. There are too many things going on in my life right now. You and Julia are only tipping it over the edge. I am glad that you are returning to Ontario. And yes, I would like to meet my daughter and begin to build a relationship with her. But I can't do that just yet. I am not ready for her or for you.

Please give me some time and I will get down to it.

Give my love to Julia. And take care.

Martin

There was another e-mail waiting, from Sri Lanka; one he had dreaded receiving all these years:

Mr. James, your mother has taken a sudden turn for the worse. Pneumonia this time. She may not survive beyond the week. Please advise if you need any changes made to the funeral arrangements.

The news on Internet stocks was all bad. Money was the biggest coward and investors followed a herd mentality. There was no stampede yet, just some selective failures, mergers and exits. He would have to set aside a couple of hours to assuage his nervous investors again. And make a call to Gordon Marchal to have him step on the gas even more.

The phone rang. It was his home. He picked it up tentatively. Jamie was on the line.

"Dad, where were you last night? I was so worried."

"I had a late meeting. I decided to sleep over." He did not like lying to his son, but just now he couldn't go into explanations.

"Are you coming to the finals this evening?"

"Oh, shoot, I forgot. You made it?"

"Yes, I did."

"Congratulations, buddy! Sorry, I've been a bit distracted."

"Yeah, yeah, Jamestown again, eh? So, are you coming tonight?"

"Yes, for sure. I'll order the tickets right away."

"Don't forget to buy tickets for Mom and Grandma too."

"Sure, sure. I won't forget. You do well today, okay, buddy?'
"I will. I have to go to school now. Bye, Dad."

That afternoon he drove to the municipal park near his home in Pickering. The normally well-groomed flower beds looked desolate as fall embraced the grounds with its dead leaves, scattered petals and muddy earth.

Mama, finally at 68, outliving most of his family; mentally ill but determined to fight it to the end. Resilience, she had had, and that's what she had bestowed on him. Should he drop everything now and go to her side? It would be a nice escape from the troubles at home. Would she even recognize him? No, he concluded, going back to Sri Lanka at this stage was not going to help.

He had pried the wedding photograph of his parents from the frame sitting on his credenza in the office, and torn off his mother's half of it. He dug a small hole in the park grounds by the flower beds, and buried the scrap of photograph. This park would outlive the number of places he would live in over his lifetime. The regional municipality poured a lot of money into keeping their parks beautiful, and every summer this place sprang to life; it was a fitting, permanent place to store her memory. She would be in a special graveyard, not among rows of undistinguishable gravestones in the General Cemetery in Colombo. Every time he came to this park in the future he would remember Mama and the happy times they had walking among the flower gardens in a distant Kelaniya and reading the adventures of Ulysses.

He sat down on a park bench, answers coming in waves. He spoke out aloud to his mother, hoping she would hear him in some strange way. "Mum, Canada is a lovely country, despite the bumps we have had to navigate from time to time. I wish you were here with me. There is no difference between those who move and those who stay. You were a stayer, like Ginny. I am a mover. Call it karma that makes us stayers or movers. Those who stay and those who move are both on journeys that are entirely of their own destiny. The journey is not negotiable; everything else is. That's why Homer was so important to you. Thank you for helping me to understand Ginny."

He returned to the office and replied the e-mail from Sri Lanka:

There is no change. Please follow the instructions I laid out for my mother's last rites when she first came to your institution. And please send a telegram to my father and place an obituary notice in the newspaper so that my brother, wherever he is, may read it. Send all expenses to me. And please pray for my mother's soul.

He phoned Jill and asked her to use his credit card and buy three tickets for the provincial music finals in Toronto that evening and then put everything out of his mind to focus on his work. His mother would have expected that of him.

"I couldn't do it!" Ginny paced Brian McDonald's office, wringing her hands. The doctor was sitting calmly in the armchair as if expecting his patient to return to the couch after her outburst. "There is too much hurt and disappointment between us. I can feel it when I get near him."

"It appears so," the doctor said, appraising her closely. She had taken off her sweater which had concealed a thin stretch-top underneath, accentuating her figure and giving curvature even to her small breasts.

"It is so much easier to start fresh than to cover all this old ground. I don't know where to even start."

"Are you suggesting a divorce?" he asked cautiously.

"I'm not sure what else to suggest. It would destroy Jamie, of course."

"Kids usually bounce back. Kids are not a reason to remain in a marriage."

She turned back on him angrily. "Why do you stay in yours? It's pretty obvious that your wife and you are merely going through the motions." As the doctor gulped and tried to regain his composure, she pointed to the photographs on the mantelpiece. "Those pictures speak a thousand words. All my friends have pictures like that. Yet they cheat on each other on the side."

Brian McDonald rose and approached her. His figure was suddenly larger than normal. "Perhaps, your friends have found a middle way to keep their marriages intact while finding sexual and emotional balance."

"Are you suggesting I have an affair?"

He was very close and she could smell his luring perfume again. He asked her in very deliberate words. "Would you like me to touch you once more?"

She felt herself being overcome by his presence and by the years of deprivation, much of it self-imposed. Now all she wanted to do was let go.

"Yes," she replied, and closed her eyes.

The performance had been spectacular, at least Martin thought so later. Somewhere out there, his mother was dying tonight, but up on a stage, the new life he had created was reaching heights of achievement. Tears clouded his eyes as he had watched Jamie move through Chopin's Etude in E Major with grace, a piece he had only heard as "No Other Love" by Perry Como back in the old country.

Next to him, Ginny had been all tears throughout the performance and he did not want to say anything to her. On the other seat, Clarissa sat contentedly, a half-smile on her face, clapping delicately between numbers.

When the winners were announced, Jamie was among the top three who would go to the nationals. Martin rose with a hoot, stunning the normally reserved audience, and shouted, "Attaboy, Jamie—yo da man!" Even Clarissa allowed herself an embarrassed grin.

He returned home that night after taking the family out to dinner at the King Eddy to celebrate Jamie's success. It was nice to dine in the familiar heavy dining room with its polite waiting staff, a place that had been the scene of so many momentous occasions in his life in Canada. Ginny had been polite and had focused her comments and attention on Jamie who was basking in a fleeting moment of adulation when all three of his significant elders were in his camp. As Martin downed a final espresso, a mist of premonition enveloped him that this might be the last meal they would all have together. He did not know where it came from but the feeling got stronger as the meal progressed, clouding his ebullience. As much as there was joy around Jamie tonight, something was dying and it was not just his dear mother back in her nursing home.

After dropping Clarissa at home, they drove back to Pickering. Jamie wanted to stay up and play his guitar, and Martin took the opportunity to spend some time with him in his room, as Ginny settled in the living room at her computer.

"Dad, you want me to win at the nationals, don't you?"

"Sure I do. Why the heck have you tried so hard up to now?"

"Is winning so important to you?"

"When I was growing up, nobody noticed the guy who came in second. The doorway to success was very narrow. Only the guy in front got out before they plugged the loophole again."

Jamie plucked at the strings of his guitar, his long blonde hair falling across his forehead. The Adagio from the Concierto de Aranjuez trickled off his fingers. In many respects this child was old for his age, in his prowess at music, at his ability to digest information, and for his incisive questioning. Martin wondered if Jamie was a re-incarnation of an old master sent to teach him life lessons. In Buddhist Sri Lanka that theory would have gone down well. Or was he one of those gods, like those from Olympus who visited Odysseus so many times in the guise of mortals, to help him on his journey?

"I have to go to bed," Martin said rising, even though he would have liked to linger and listen to the ending of the adagio that played so flawlessly." You've had a good day, and I'm proud of you."

"Thanks, Dad."

"Listen buddy, there is something I want to tell you. Over the next few days, things are going to happen that will be very disruptive. But I want you to stay focussed on the nationals, okay? We all get distracted by outside noise. Champions don't. And you are a champion."

Jamie looked up frowning. He stopped playing. "What kind of things?"

"All kinds of things. The launch of Jamestown.com for instance, and others. It's just a hunch I have. You know the old saying, 'when trouble comes, it comes in legions'? These troubles pick cycles in which to occur. I think we are coming up on one. We've just been too quiet for a long time. That's when you have to be alert—in the quiet times."

"Is that why you never relax?"

"Probably. Goodnight, son."

As he shut Jamie's door, the adagio resumed, at a slower tempo this time.

Ginny had switched off her computer and gone to bed when Martin came downstairs. He knocked off the house lights, poured himself a glass of water from the fridge and headed upstairs to the master bedroom. He found her rolled over to the edge of her side of the bed, the lights out. He changed into his pyjamas aided by the light trickling in from the street and slipped beneath the covers.

Something is dying tonight. The feeling was stronger now. Was it because his mother was breathing her last breath? Was it because he was unable to share that fact with this woman who was his wife, a woman wrapped up in her own problems?

He reached over and held her. She was tense and unyielding. Then he sensed it, palpable and clear: the sense of betrayal. He sensed how she must have felt the number of times he had come home after sleeping with someone else. Now it came from her side of the bed and lay like a heavy foam barrier between them, like those bolsters they had used when guys in the cricket team had to share a double bed while travelling outstation for "away" games. This time it was like the bolster had reared its head and hit him squarely in the face.

Years ago, even as recently as last year, he would have fought against this force, but now he was spent. *Something is dying tonight, and it is not just my mother.*

As if in response to his thoughts, Ginny rolled over and took his hand tightly. "Please let me go, Martin. I cannot handle this anymore."

He eased his hand from her grip and lay back on his side of the bed, staring at the ceiling. There was no more need for words.

The following morning, the Friday before the launch, thoughts of his mother and Ginny lingered only on the periphery of his mind which was now a ferment of pre-launch hyperactivity. He had left the house while Ginny was still asleep. He had deliberately switched the radio off on his way to work as he did not want to be distracted. The newspapers had more bad news for dot-coms. Even Godfrey's had come out with a communiqué dismissing the Internet marketplace and saying that they would be opening their own site in the future, when the market for e-commerce had matured. When asked by the reporter when that would be, Godfrey's CEO was quoted as saying "in about five years."

Martin's took his first call at 7:30 from Morrie Gluckstein.

"Have you heard the news, Martin?" Gluckstein sounded agitated.

"It's a blip. A pause," Martin countered.

"It's no bloody pause. People are pulling money out of the dot-coms. We've caught the US bug. Europe is no better this morning."

"I'll prepare a communiqué to our investors, suppliers and customers immediately. I'll calm them down."

"They are not going to believe you. You'll be the only marketplace standing with others folding down south and in Toronto as well. You should have seen this coming, Martin."

Fuck, when the going gets tough—blame me! Martin bit his tongue and continued as evenly as he could manage.

"Can I count on you to keep us going, Morrie?"

"I don't know, Martin. If the others vote to pull out, you know where my vote was all along."

Peter Bledsoe called at eight. "It's not good Martin. We cannot pour any more money into this."

"But the launch is on Monday. We'll be pulling in customers soon after that. The sales team is out in full force on the streets and on the phones."

"You'll get blasted in the press for being a suicidal net junkie for opening now, when everyone else is shutting down. I'm calling an emergency conference with the rest of the investors at 10:00 a.m. I'll let you know what we decide."

Martin spent the next two hours writing and re-writing press releases, sending personal e-mails and making phone calls to shore up the paranoid behaviour of investors. *Capital, you are a fucking coward!*

At 10:15 Peter called back. "Martin—it's over. We're shutting down. It was a unanimous vote except for Muller who is still in shock after seeing his money go down the drain."

Martin swallowed hard. He was groping for a line. "Well, he's not going to lose all of it; if we shut down now, probably fifty percent may be lost, when all the severances are accounted for. Are you sure you guys want to do this? We are so close."

"Martin, the board has decided and is resigned to the consequences. They stepped out of their comfort zone on this one. They have now paid the price. I'm sorry. Can you start the wind-down?"

At two o'clock Martin issued his last communiqué:

Dear Investors and Customers,

Due to the downturn in the climate for Internet investment and the lowering of expectations, we have decided to postpone the launch of Jamestown.com. This was not an easy decision but we feel that now is not the time to launch this futuristic venture, whose potential is immense, as we are heading into a period of adjustment and stock-taking. We are very confident that this is only a temporary pause in an otherwise relentless journey towards the boundless rewards of electronic commerce. We request your patience until the dawn of this new era becomes a reality.

We wish to thank each of you for having the confidence to support us and ask for your patience and courage to stay the course while we weather the next few turbulent months together.

Sincerely,
Martin James
President and CEO
Jamestown.com—the marketplace of the future

Thus ended the still-born life of Jamestown.com, just like his sister Julia's those many years ago. After hitting "send", Martin pushed back his chair and rubbed his eyes, waiting to see the reaction he would get. He did not have to wait long. First came the staff, and he had to listen to Gordon Marchall and team vent to him on the phone. Then followed the three anchor suppliers who had signed up and participated in co-development of the site; they even threatened to sue, but Martin ignored their threats. By 4:00 p.m. he was thinking of calling it a day. But he realized that he had to keep the doors open until after five today, just for credibility's sake. What was that thing about the captain staying on the deck of his sinking ship? Jill brought him a double espresso latte and bid him a tearful goodbye, her tears mingling with the spit from her soother cross, leaving a wet gloss over her half open bosom.

At four-thirty Martin received a call from his brother-in-law Tim Summers.

"So, how's life Martin?" Tim's nasal voice came over the phone like a slow moving stream of slime.

"Have you been sent to pick my bones clean?"

"I told you I'd get you one day, Martin. I've been retained by your investors to liquidate your company."

"Why did you take so long to call?"

"You happen to be married to my sister, in case you forgot. I was being sensitive."

"But you aren't holding back now. And I am still married to your sister."

"You've outlived your stay, Martin. Ginny's fortunes have gone downhill ever since she met you. My sister deserves better."

"Yeah? Like a better brother?"

The intake of air on the other side of the phone was undisguised. Then, "See you in court—Paki."

"Listen, asshole, I've had a tough day. So let me lay this on the line for you. Stick to the liquidation business, okay? If you pull any shit about my background, your party pictures will be plastered all over the Internet. And the Law Society will be very embarrassed to explain how one of its members went snooping inside a colleague's client files."

The line went dead.

At 6:00 p.m. the phone rang again. Martin was about to ignore it when he recognized Muller's number. He sighed and picked up the receiver.

"Martin, we are ruined." The voice did not sound desperate but had a venomous snarl in it.

"You could have tried to rein the investors in like you did the last time," Martin said.

"You have failed me, Martin."

"Hey, I failed nobody. The launch was on target for Monday, if you guys hadn't chickened out. I kept my part of the bargain."

"Never mind. How do I get my money back?"

"You're gonna lose some, that's what liquidation means."

"Martin, I do not like to lose. I placed my trust in you."

"You placed your trust in the Internet, and it let you down."

"Martin, I expect you to get me my money back."

That's when he lost it. After all, it had been a hard day, a hard couple of days.

"Herr Muller, with all due respect, why don't you go take a flying fuck? I have to go now and close down our company. Good day." He slammed the phone down and did not pick it up when it rang several times afterwards.

Martin worked late in the office, wrapping things up, dreading going home, dreading facing his staff who would come in on Monday to receive pink slips instead of celebrating the launch that they had worked so hard for. He took out his personal finances file and tore up the stock options table; they were worthless now. At 9:00 p.m., running only on automatic pilot and adrenaline, he called long distance, sensing the reception he was about to get. The nursing home was just opening for the morning in Colombo. After many, please-hold-the-lines, he got through to the ward matron.

"Mr. James, ah yes. Calling from Canada? Ah yes. Yes, so sorry to inform you, Mr. James. Your mother, she passed away last night. She was a very good soul. *Aney,* all our nurses and inmates were so fond of her. She…" He let the receiver drop from his hands.

He picked up the remaining wedding photograph from his credenza, the one of him and Ginny, and dropped it into his briefcase.

It was time to go home and face his wife for the third strike. Many things had died today: his company, his mother, and his marriage. He had just been avoiding accepting these facts until now.

22. **Christo's Secret**

The man in the bed reached for his wallet on the side table. The bandages around his head and neck barely allowed him to move and it hurt like crazy. But he needed something from his wallet badly. *I need a friend.*

He stared at the clipping and at the smiling face of the real estate agent: Martin James. He had collected many clips about his friend, even the ones about his failed dot-com company of last year. Now he carried only this most recent one in his wallet. His sketchy contact with Bandu had broken off completely; understandably, with the type of work Bandu was involved in. Martin was the only one left. *How can I contact him after all these years? Never a word since that last parting at the airport in Sri Lanka. What would he think of me? A failure?*

At that last thought, he began to sweat under his bandages. He stuffed the clipping back into his wallet and buried it under his pillow.

But now the flood of memories that he had tried so hard to stanch broke loose. *Oh, for God's sake, let 'em come.* He settled back in the bed and let them wash over him…

That dinner was like all the others they'd had at Christmas in the old country, or so he thought. Daddy and Uncle Bunty at the table, talking politics, amidst opened bottles of arrack and soda. Mummy frying more "taste" in the kitchen, while the main meal simmered on the kerosene stove. She was perspiring and tired, but her men had to be provisioned. Ever since Christo could remember, Mummy looked tired and he felt sorry and helpless towards her. Daddy was in his "jolly" mood today, the alcohol expanding his spirits; tomorrow he would sulk for hours once the effects wore off.

Christo was under the table, his usual safe place, driving imaginary race cars and sneaking up occasionally to catch a devilled sprat from the fried taste bowl between the men. The conversation had turned towards that dream place all Sri Lankan Burghers wanted to eventually "burgher-off" to: Australia, the land of milk and honey. That is, if you brought your own cows and bees, as Daddy's brother David, who had migrated ten years ago, had written back to emphasise.

Australia, where one could afford to buy a house, a car and other luxuries like TVs, stereos, washing machines, dryers and stuff that would "make life easier for Mummy," Daddy had said in his jollier moments.

"Someone still has to cook. You bet I'll still be cooking over there." Mummy could be heard through the wafting smells of beef curry and crackling fish.

"Yah, we'll all go together," Uncle Bunty said. "I'll go first. Then I'll sponsor all of you."

"You've been saying that for ten years," Mummy said. "When are you going to get off your arse and do it?"

"All in good time. All in good time." Uncle Bunty said. Christo saw his legs begin to twitch under the table. Uncle Bunty usually got that way when the neighbours' servant boy raided their mango tree, the one Uncle Bunty had planted and still tended with loving care. He had come to live with them after his wife died giving birth to their only child, strangled in its umbilical cord. Left him scared of marrying again, Mummy had explained.

The first bottle of arrack was nearly empty and Uncle Bunty was rhapsodizing over the TV he would buy so that he could watch the test cricket. "Imagine, they have wide-screen colour sets over there and we don't even have bloody TV in this country. The international test cricketers won't even stop here on their way to India or Pakistan."

Daddy drained the arrack bottle into their two glasses and shouted to Mummy, the edge returning to his voice. "Bring the other bottle. What about the sprats? This bowl is almost empty."

"Christo boy is eating them under the table." Uncle Bunty said, appeasingly and swooping down playfully to grab his nephew. Christo smelled his uncle's alcohol laden breath. Luckily, Uncle Bunty was tipsy by now, so Christo could dodge him easily. When he was sober, Uncle Bunty read stories and played with Christo in the garden; when he was drunk, Uncle Bunty only felt sorry for himself.

"Christopher, come and help, child," Mummy called again, her voice breaking slightly.

Christo parked his imaginary car, got out from under the table and went to her aid. She looked washed out: seven months pregnant and all. This was supposed to be Christmas Eve and soon the neighbours would begin lighting firecrackers. Uncle Bunty and Daddy would be too far gone by then to worry about fireworks. However, he knew that each had bought him a toy, to be revealed when he opened the gifts tomorrow. But this was Mummy's Christmas too, and all she did was work. Christo started to empty the potato and onion skins into the garbage.

"You know, you men should all bugger off to Australia. Then I can be at peace," Mummy said. "Bunty, you may be my elder brother, but you have no balls either."

"What the hell are you talking about?" Daddy was slurping about her in the kitchen, trying to hang on to his jollity. "You will live like a queen, honey. None of this shit. This country is fucked up—at least, for minorities like us." Now, these many years later, Christo had figured out his father's motivations. Daddy wanted to give Mummy a good life despite his mood swings. Coming from a fast-disappearing minority and working as a clerk in a mercantile firm in the city, he could never rise in rank despite his best efforts. Daddy had never realized his ambitions; and with the national language switching over from English to Sinhala—which he had never studied—his aspirations had finally flamed out. Daddy only thought of getting out, like many Burghers were doing at the time, but he wasn't successful at that either.

Australia was very attractive because of its accommodation of Asians of mixed European ancestry. Burghers, with their Dutch and Portuguese roots, fitted the bill perfectly. But all of Daddy's applications had been turned down because of his erratic performances at immigration interviews, Mummy had said.

"Bloody Jansz up the road got passed. The bugger has not even got a grade six education. His welding is more recognized than my clerking!" And so Daddy would rail against his misfortunes. He irritated Mummy a lot. Daddy drank particularly hard when he was feeling depressed and sad, and on those occasions, if Uncle Bunty wasn't around, he drank alone.

Mummy slapped his hands off the pan. "Wait till it's served. I put a lot of effort behind it—not for you to go fingering it."

"I'm hungry, no?" Daddy had that look in his eyes when he came home after a drink with the office crowd, and Christo heard the bed bonk and Mummy cry afterwards.

"All you men do is drink, eat, fuck and dream. You can't *do*."

"Don't talk to me like that you ungrateful woman. I have tried. There is nothing else to do but eat, drink and fuck in this shit-hole."

"You can try by not being so smart at those interviews."

"Those white embassy bastards, they are prejudiced."

"And you want to go and live there?"

"Don't double talk me woman. I put bread on the table."

"And I bake it!"

"Sammy..." Uncle Bunty's voice came nervously from the hall. "What size TV will you buy when we get to Australia?"

"You're an ungrateful bitch," Daddy said, taking a handful of beef from the pan and shoving it in his mouth.

The scene disolved to a hospital bed, his hospital bed; a TV monitor hung down from the ceiling and the walls were light green. There were other beds on either side, with people in them and screens drawn around, shutting him from human contact. The Maple Leafs were playing the Flyers on television but he was not interested. A thickset middle-aged man in a trench coat walked in; his face was set kindly, but he looked like he had seen a lot of trouble in his time.

"Inspector Benoit." He pronounced his name French-style. He offered Christo his card. "Can I ask you a few questions?"

Christo nodded and the pain shot through him again. The inspector pulled out a notebook and pen.

"Your name is Chris Martenstyn?"

"Yes," Christo replied in a croaky voice.

"That's a Dutch name. It says that you were born in Sri Lanka."

He's just like the others.Canadians have no clue of our mixed up culture. They see a pile of Tamil immigrants in Toronto and think all Sri Lankans are dark skinned Dravidians.

"Yes. I'm not Dutch—my ancestors were.

"Employed?"

"Unemployed. Last two years."

"It says here on the report that there was a domestic dispute. Your spouse—"

"Common-law—"

"Your companion, then. Ms. Bonnie Bagley. She assaulted you with a baseball bat?"

"Yes."

"Want to tell me about it?"

"No."

"This is a criminal investigation, Mr. Martenstyn."

"She called me a failure."

"Why?"

"I'm not a failure. Never was."

"Was it your unemployed status? No money coming into the family coffers? I've seen it before, Mr. Martenstyn."

"So we were backed up on the mortgage. And they reclaimed the car. So what?"

"Things must have been tight, financially."

"Well, UI ran out and I had a few odd jobs while she waited tables. It wasn't that bad."

"It says here that you were both under the influence."

"It was Christmas Eve, I think. It's not illegal to take a drink, is it?"

"No. So you had both been celebrating?"

Christo felt as if his head was about to explode. *I have to keep going.* "She was drinking to pluck up the courage to say that she was leaving me."

"Oh."

"She had it good when I had the government job. Then they downsized. No one hires a government employee, you know."

"I should know. That's why I'll retire a cop."

"She called me a failure. I'm no failure. I came to this country on my own steam. Built my life here these past fifteen years. Even got a good job. I'm not a failure."

"Do you have any family? Children?"

"No, I didn't want kids in this dangerous screwed-up world. She wanted kids. That was another reason she gave for leaving."

"Any siblings? Someone who can help you at this time?"

"No. I am an only child. My parents are dead back in Sri Lanka. There was a still-born younger brother, and my old uncle Bunty, who is an alcoholic back home. No, I've got no one."

"No friends?"

"I have a couple of school friends from Sri Lanka living here. But I have lost contact with them." *That's not quite true*: the realtor's advertisement was burning a hole in his wallet and pulsing under his pillow.

"How did you come to Canada?" Inspector Benoit asked.

"After my mother died, I worked as a seaman on board a freighter. That was the only way out of Sri Lanka for a kid with only a grade ten education. I left the ship in Halifax. Your system is so generous, they gave me asylum. I really wanted to go to Australia. But what does it matter—Australia, Canada, America, England—its freedom that we wanted. Any port in a storm. I wish my mother was alive to know that I took the plunge, unlike my father and uncle. Don't call me a failure."

"Do you want to tell me the rest of the story? Or do you want a lawyer present."

"No. I'm glad it's over. I'll take whatever is to come."

"Why did Ms. Bagley hit you?"

"Because she wanted me to react to her leaving, expecting me to try and hold on to her—but I didn't. Then she called me a failure. That's when I lost it. I slapped her. She went at me with the bat."

"Has she been violent before?"

"I was attracted to her *because* she was violent. We first met in a pub ten years ago when she was brawling with another woman who'd been sleeping with her boyfriend at the time. Her boyfriend left her that night, despite her brave performance. She was devastated. She reminded me of my father, who always wanted to go some place but no one would allow him or believe in him. I took her back to my apartment and cleaned her wounds. We stuck together after that."

"You've had other violent incidents on record with Ms. Bagley?"

"Several. We kept it to ourselves. She's a manic depressive, like my father. I took her beatings and ranting and stood it. I'd promised my mother, I wouldn't lift a finger to a woman. Bonnie was my test."

"What did you do after she hit you with the baseball bat?"

"Violence makes you lose your grip in the end, I guess—that much, I know now. This time, I broke my promise to my mother. That's what I'm sorry about. But we all have our limits."

"What's your mother's connection to all this?"

"Leave her out of it!"

"Okay. Then what did you do?"

"I was bleeding. From my head, where she hit me. It was all woozy. I remember the kitchen knife in my hand. My father flashed before me. Then I woke up in hospital."

"Bonnie's throat was slit and you had her blood all over the knife and you."

"I see. I guess, I killed her then."

"You may get a sympathetic hearing. Self-defence would get you off. Manslaughter could get you a lighter sentence. You'll still make a second go of your life. If you survive prison."

"I've been in prison for a long time, Inspector. I'm just starting to be free."

The Inspector looked at Christo quizzically, still making notes in his book.

"Well, that's all we'll cover today. Get well soon. We'll need a formal statement tomorrow."

"Whenever... Thanks."

As the inspector left the room that scene played back again for Christo. It had replayed too much lately. Perhaps Bonnie's blow from the baseball bat had shaken his memory loose ...

"You bastard... I told you not to eat that food." Mummy took the pan of beef curry and threw the hot contents at Daddy. It missed him and splashed all over the kitchen wall. "Eat bloody scraps tonight. I'm taking Christopher and going to my mother's place. You can celebrate Christmas with your bottles of arrack."

"You fucking bitch!" Daddy howled, slapping her across the face.

"Sammy, Sammy..." Uncle Bunty came in pleading.

"You stay out of it, you son-of-a-bitch," Daddy said.

Daddy continued to pummel Mummy on the head and Christo felt sick to his stomach. This was the worst he'd seen him beat her. He ran across, caught Daddy, trying to pull him away from her. "Don't…leave her alone." Daddy swung his wrist and the action sent Christo flying, knocking over the newly-opened bottle of arrack and spilling its strong contents over the floor. Daddy turned back to maul Mummy again, when he stopped in his tracks like he was skewered. Mummy was holding the knife that had plunged into his throat and emerged from the other side, the blood spurting all over, like water from the garden hose. The last thing Christo remembered before blacking out was Daddy falling like a pole-axed animal amidst the blood, arrack and beef curry, Uncle Bunty crawling all over him saying, "Sammy, don't die. I'm really sorry," and Mummy standing there remorselessly, holding her big belly and saying, "You don't have balls!"

He wished she were alive today, so he could write her one more letter, like the many he wrote while she languished in prison until her death.

"Mummy, I understand how you felt that day. I *had* balls, and got out of the shit-hole. I wanted to break the cycle. But I guess I am my father's boy too. I carry both of you in me."

His hand reached under the pillow and grasped his wallet but he knew it would be a long time before he made that phone call.

23. **Payoff**

"Something is wrong. You are not so sure this time," Sumana said, looking directly at Bandu, her dark eyes sad from so many departures. Bandu was glad for the gathering dusk.

"It's insurance for you and Ravi. Mistakes happen." Bandu tried not to return her gaze. Instead, he looked towards the basketball court in the community park, floodlit in the deepening gloom. Ravi was playing guard; his height did not allow him any other position. But the kid was fast; get a ball into his hands and he would move, focusing on nothing else, weaving in and out of opponents while heading determinedly towards the net. Perhaps it was the child's way of blocking out the family's problems. A feeling of pride filled Bandu as he gazed after his son. *The boy will do well in this country, no doubt.*

Sumana placed the package Bandu had given her in Ravi's gym bag. Bandu frowned.

"Don't worry. Ravi will not see it," she said quickly. "I have shielded him from your activities so far."

"Do you need money?"

"No. We are managing. Take care of yourself."

"Tell Ravi that I will come and see him again. When this is over. We can meet down in the ravine, after dark."

"Let us know if you have to cancel. He was disappointed the last time."

"Does he suspect?"

"He knows, I'm sure, although he doesn't talk about it. When he cannot go out with you in the daytime, see a movie, ride his bike—like he used to—I'm sure he knows."

Bandu's throat constricted. He did not like this part. "Goodbye," he said, embracing her and quickly letting go. "You will do the translation then?"

She nodded. "Only if something happens..." She left the rest unsaid. He fished out a crumpled business card from his wallet. "If you need help, contact this man."

She scrutinized the card holding it up to catch the lights from the court. "Who is this Martin James? Another one like Muller?"

"No. He is a good man. One of the few I trust. I met him today."

She thrust the card into the pocket of her blouse, picked up the bag and walked into the glare of the floodlights, something he could not do these days. He wondered whether she would react differently to him upon reading the manuscript.

He exited the playground, crossed the road, skirted two side streets and leaped over the fence into the strip mall where the Toyota was parked. The brown van that had been on his tail was nowhere to be seen. They must have tired of him.

He drove a zigzag route towards Muller's apartment, looking constantly in the rear view mirror for telltale signs. Things looked okay.

Muller. How does one summon enough hate to kill a man? Bandu had to focus on this or he would start feeling sorry for the bastard and blow the job.

It was easy to hate Muller. The man resembled the sexual predators that had descended on Sri Lanka back in the seventies to "adopt" pubescent boys. Bandu had played that game well in those days, allowing himself to be used as he stole from them and disappeared just as they were about to get serious. He hated what he had done, hated the economic conditions that forced him into that business and, most of all, hated those animals who had forced themselves on him and filled him not only with their filthy seed but with anger and remorse that started him on this life-path.

Uncle Sunna, his Toronto contact and benefactor, and the only man who had shown him any compassion, had taken him under his wing and introduced him to those "side jobs." Bandu became very good at side jobs. One thing had led to another and soon after that mall heist he had gravitated from Uncle Sunna's gang to bigger bosses. He met Muller through Uncle Sunna. Muller said that his boss was into the people smuggling business. Shuttling illegals into Canada and down to the USA and vice versa was good business. Bandu felt good when he started doing it: giving poor souls—like he had been once—a second chance.

Then one of the guys he had dropped off south of the border was caught in New York and found to be associated with a terrorist ring. When he asked Muller about it, the man shrugged, "Ach Bandu, what to do? It's still better doing business with these guys. They have money and are more organized."

"They are murderers."

Muller grinned, showing his gold fillings. "You want to quit now, eh Bandu?"

Bandu had thought of quitting then, but the money was good. He had just bought a house in Pickering and upgraded from the battered old Crown Victoria that Uncle Sunna had sold him, to a Range Rover. He had also bought a small Mazda for Sumana. Things were just starting to look good after years of scraping the bottom.

When he had seen those images of the buildings collapsing on the day called 9/11 he knew that his world was going to change. Sumana called him from a neighbour's house a couple of days later to say that the police had been enquiring after him. He decided not to go home that day. In fact, he never returned home again. A warrant for his arrest was issued shortly thereafter.

But the boss came to the rescue and found him a safe house, safe houses, more appropriately. Bandu moved every few days after that, all over the province and into neighbouring Quebec. However, there were no more drives across the border into the States. Muller drove him around now. Sometimes the old German was accompanied by his boyfriend Marc, an effeminate young man who always had a scowl on his face and whose hair colour was different every time Bandu met him.

But bosses aren't philanthropists; there is always a payoff.

Muller visited alone one day, while Bandu was holed up in a farm house in Cobourg. "Got a job, Bandu. The boss says, got to ah…rub out someone," he said unloading the food parcels that would suffice for a few days.

"I don't do those jobs."

"My gutte friend, you cannot choose these days, eh?"

Muller pulled out a gun from the bag. "Here, it's untraceable. Use it. There are pictures and location inside the bag. Tomorrow. Don't worry, it's what they say—a piece of cake." The man seemed to enjoy watching Bandu squirm. "You have a young family, my friend—the boss takes good care of them—but you must obey, ja?"

The target was a witness about to testify against suspects in a recently busted drug smuggling ring. Could put the finger on the boss,

Muller said, and bring them all down in the process. Bandu was disappointed to hear that the boss was into narcotics smuggling; he had thought it had only been illegal immigrants.

Bandu drank that night, not enough to slow down or make mistakes but enough to blunt feelings. He tapped at the front door of the witness's bungalow on a suburban street. The man who opened the door was about his age. Behind the man, two teenage children were having supper in the kitchen, while a woman was busy at the sink. Bandu would always remember the smell of roasting meat that gushed out of that front door as he emptied the gun into the witness and staggered down the porch steps. There was screaming and yelling as he ran down the lane, hoping like hell that Muller was still parked in the adjoining street. He was. The old German smirked as Bandu shivered and threw up in the car before it even got onto the highway.

"It is always like that the first time, my friend. Don't worry, I bring you Sumana."

"Leave her out of this!" Bandu gasped for air.

"No, no, you need some comforting, no? Like my Marc does for me, ja?"

Bandu knew that he *did* need Sumana just then, even though he did not betray his need and looked out of the window, remaining silent all the way to Trenton, his hideout for the next few days.

He went vegetarian after that, and Muller kept his word. The next day, the German drove up to the nondescript bungalow on a side-street and Sumana descended from the car. She ran up to Bandu and he embraced her in sheer desperation. He hadn't seen her in months. They made frantic love and he did not care if Muller was watching. Later, he held her close and smelled the German's cigar smoke filtering in from the hall. There was a knock on the bedroom door. "You are finished? It is time for Sumana to go back." Muller was not only efficient, he was frugal with time.

As Sumana dressed, Bandu asked, "How is Ravi?"

"He misses you. He got on the school basketball team."

That night all he dreamt of was Ravi shooting baskets. Ravi running circles around all the white, black and yellow kids of his neighbourhood and shooting baskets. That was a good mental picture to build on each night as he moved from place to place.

There were more "jobs" after that. Always, well organized and supported. It got easier but he still threw-up afterwards. As a reward, Muller smuggled Sumana in to see him and offered a small cash bonus with every hit, which Bandu immediately turned over to his wife. Muller even arranged clandestine meetings at night with Ravi, but Bandu was leery of letting the boy travel alone with the German and insisted that Sumana come along too. When his son asked him why he was in hiding, he replied that it was only going to be for a short time, but he would never say when it would end. They scrimmaged in the dark, in empty parking lots and on deserted driveways under moonlight while Sumana watched, and he knew that there were tears in her eyes but he never told them about what happened during those jobs.

Slowly he came to the realization that he had become a killing machine with no end in sight. He was killing in order to survive. He wasn't getting any richer for it either. Perhaps the boss was. His only connection with the boss was Muller. How had he let himself fall into this situation?

"I want to see the boss," he said one day.

"That's not possible. You know he does not want to be connected."

"There will be no more jobs then."

"Bandu, Bandu…please do not talk like that. You have a young family. You want them safe, ja?"

Trapped. How did one escape? One morning, in the deepest of those dark moods that were his constant companions, he started to write. He had never written anything in his life. He could not write in English either; it had never been a familiar tongue although he had trained himself to speak it—barely. He always communicated with Sumana and Ravi in his native language; that way, Ravi could stay connected to the mother country. He wrote therefore, in his local language: long lyrical sentences, like the ones written in school, before his mother had prostituted herself just to live from day to day, before the sexual predators came and he in turn had prostituted himself in order to survive. Before all that had happened.

He wrote of being faceless in his new home. About rejection upon rejection as he looked for jobs. "No Canadian experience, eh?" He wrote about Uncle Sunna and the little jobs on the fringe that had given him a taste for bigger ones, about that feeling of descending into the snake pit and finally finding that there really was no way out. Writing helped purge some of the blackness that had surrounded him. Finally he dropped the manuscript in an envelope and decided to get it published. He included a self addressed envelope just to make sure the package did not go astray and put the return address of the place he was in at the time, an apartment in downtown Toronto. Even though he had written everything in his native language, barring the addresse on the envelope that was in English, he figured that this multi-cultural city should have someone at the newspaper who would be able to translate it and uncover that this was not the prattling of a mad man, but the plea of someone in torment looking to be free of his yoke. That way, the truth would be out and he would be discovered, arrested, sentenced, serve his time and come out and still have time to enjoy his family. Ravi would be proud of him. Bandu slipped down to the post office one day when Muller was out and mailed the package to the national newspaper. *Why not just give myself up to the cops? No, this way was better—more dramatic.* He imagined a serialized news story running for days: "Confessions of a Reluctant Assassin…" Perhaps the serial would also get down to Sri Lanka via the news channels, and atonement would be complete.

He looked in the papers daily to see the story break. The only ones that did were reports of deaths: a shooting in the Jane/Finch area, a man jumping off the subway platform in front of a moving train, a kidnapped child's body parts discovered in Lake Ontario. There was even one of his own hits, "…suspected underworld member shot in mall parking lot in gangland style slaying…" Dead people made news, not living fugitives like him with rich stories to tell and future slayings to avoid.

Three months later, he was back at the apartment in Toronto as part of his schedule of house hopping. The package had been in the mailbox for some time, under all the other junk mail. Muller picked it up and barked.

"Are you crazy? What is it?"

Bandu was excited and ignored the old man's venting. He ripped open the parcel. The story lay intact. There was a note in English from an editorial assistant "…we don't publish foreign language news stories…"

"What is it?" Muller was almost apoplectic. "Who knows you are here?"

"It's from Sumana," he lied. *What the hell—they do not care to understand my native language. Do they have to see it spelled out in bloody English to even pay attention?*

His explanation was good enough for Muller. The old German eased on the controls after that. He offered Bandu a car and said that he should get out more.

"Go to the mall, maybe a movie once in a while, ja? You spend too much time on your own."

The offered car was a beat up Toyota—nondescript.

"But stay away from Sumana and your son, ja? No more mail. I bring them to you."

Bandu knew better than to attract attention to his family. He got out and it was nice walking in the malls and becoming faceless in crowds, or standing in the shadows watching his son play basketball under floodlights at the community centre. He also followed Muller. He had to get to the source of his problems. Many years as a taxi driver in Toronto had trained him to be faceless in traffic too.

He followed Muller to the big house in Richmond Hill, the one with the pool, where Marc languished all day, tanning his beautiful body, where Muller would fawn over his young companion and even shamelessly lick his toes; and to the apartment on Isabella Street that Muller went to regularly on Thursdays. Muller always used public transit to get there after parking his car in front of the theatres at the Yorkdale Shopping Centre. Bandu would park down on the street opposite the apartment block on Isabella. Promptly three minutes after Muller entered, a light went on in the southeast corner apartment on the fourth floor. As he followed Muller on his excursions, a pattern began to emerge that made Bandu even more convinced of what he had to do next.

But he was also being followed now: the brown van became a constant companion, and despite his many attempts to shake it off, it always showed up in his rear view mirror during those evening excursions. When it appeared opposite the half-way house in Toronto one day, Bandu took that location off his list of overnight homes. Maybe the newspaper folks were not as dumb as he had taken them to be.

When he met Sumana next (it was always after a "job" and it was almost as if he would never get to see her unless he acquiesced to one), she told him about the progress with her ESL classes.

"You can write good English now?" They were lying in a cramped bed in the house in Trenton.

"Yes. My instructor says I should apply for a desk job at the ministry."

He was happy for her. Finally, an office job, and a chance to get out of that cafeteria.

That was when he told her about his manuscript.

"Translate it? What is it?" she asked.

"My story."

"They will arrest you."

"And then I can pay my dues finally. My story protects you and Ravi, so you will never be involved."

"But we *are* involved, whether you mention it or not. Why do I get to see you only in filthy rooms like this? And your son only meets you under cover of night."

"Will you please translate it?"

She had always obeyed him; that was the virtue of women from back home. "If you insist," she said. "And only if you get arrested." She snuggled closer to him and his shoulder was wet with her tears. "I'm still hoping and praying that all this will go away and you will come back home soon."

How could he bring himself to tell her that he was not hiding merely from suspicion of smuggling a few people over the border? That he had graduated now? Having her read the manuscript was easier. That was another reason why he wanted her to have it.

Muller returned to the safe house after dropping Sumana at the train station the next morning.

"We have another job, Bandu. A different one."

Bandu ignored him, reading the newspaper, drinking his coffee.

Muller tossed the usual brown envelope across the table. Bandu ignored it.

Muller snapped. "You'd better look at it, my gute friend. There is no killing this time. What is the matter with you? I try to make things easy for you and you ignore me."

No killing this time. Bandu opened the envelope. A handsome teenage boy stared back at him, jogging a forgotten memory. The boy looked familiar.

"We need to take this boy, ja, and keep him with us for awhile. His father owes the boss some money. Perhaps he will pay when we have his son, ja?"

"And after he pays?"

"Then we 'return' the boy. No problem."

And reveal our identities to the cops. Not likely. Bandu laughed cynically. Two smaller photographs fell out of the envelope.

"The boy's parents," Muller said, reaching for the coffee. "Just in case you bump into them when we take the boy."

The blonde woman had fading beautiful looks, but it was the man that made Bandu sweat. The same real estate agent's photograph, smiling back at him was Martin James.

"What's the matter, Bandu? This is too much for you?" Muller's voice was steady, cold.

If I don't do this, someone else will. "I need to check it out first. I'll start tomorrow morning," Bandu said.

Muller smiled, a trickle of coffee spilled out of the side his mouth. "Ach, I knew you would do this job, Bandu. You da man!"

He sat in the Toyota at noon opposite the house in Pickering, summoning his courage to knock on the door. His own home was barely a subdivision away. *You could live in this country for years and never know who your neighbour is.* He reviewed his actions over the last three days.

At 7:00 a.m. on the day after Muller gave him the assignment, Bandu had checked out the sprawling house in Rosedale first; he had to park his car on the top of the road and walk past the house, the Toyota would have stood out a mile in this fancy neighbourhood. He spotted a red BMW and a silver Cadillac in the driveway. When the Cadillac exited the giant gates of the house, he tailed the mother, the blonde woman who was driving, and his target—the son—to the latter's private school, Trinians College. *Martin has definitely made it.*

Bandu spent that first morning timing the activities in the school: noting when the kids broke for recess and lunch, and if they went outside during those breaks, what time they went home. He tried to establish patterns. This also gave him the time to keep Muller off his back and figure out how he was going to handle this job. For the next three days of his surveillance, the boy never left the confines of the school, and the blonde woman dropped and picked her son up daily. On the third day, realizing that the school was too well protected, Bandu was about to drive away, when a Lexus pulled up opposite the school and a man got out, buttoning his jacket against the chill wind. Bandu's pulse quickened when he recognized his old friend. Martin walked through the gates of the school. He came out half an hour later with some papers in his hand and his son by his side. Bandu's heart skipped beats with envy and loss; he couldn't do this in public with Ravi. But all did not seem well between Martin and the boy; they were arguing. After what looked like a heated exchange, the boy kicked the dust with his foot, turned on his heel and walked indoors. Martin shrugged wearily, returned to the car, and drove away. Bandu put the Toyota in gear and followed the Lexus.

Now he was parked outside the house in Pickering where Martin had returned after visiting his son. *Martin has two houses? Or is he visiting a mistress?* The parking garage doors had activated the moment Martin turned into the driveway and the Lexus was quickly swallowed up inside and had remained so for the last three hours.

Bandu got out of the Toyota, stretched his cramped muscles and walked up the driveway of the house. When he tapped on the door, he said to himself that he was doing this to prove that his friend was up to legitimate business. Martin was his last hope of redemption in this country. Bandu needed to believe that, or everything would be lost.

The man inside the house opened the door, cautiously. First Bandu heard shuffling behind the door and the peephole darkened for a whole minute. Then the door opened a crack and a pair of eyes stared at him on the doorstep, before opening wider. Martin had changed into a golf shirt and slacks and was wearing loafers. He squinted at Bandu, a frown on his face.

Hope he also doesn't mistake me for a crank caller.

"Hello, Martin." There was a lump in Bandu's throat, the years were slipping way. Martin had broadened and carried a slight paunch; his features were still intelligent, energetic and his skin was tanned; the wavy salt-and-pepper hair was luxuriant and combed.

Martin's eyes started to widen and his mouth fell open. "Bandu!" he exclaimed.

In a flash, Martin had yanked him indoors and was embracing him tightly. "Bandu, oh Bandu, it's great to see you, man!"

When they broke away, Bandu hesitated on the threshold staring at the insides of the house, sparsely furnished with a few paintings and ornaments making discreet appearances. Martin's ebullience was contagious and Bandu felt his spirits rise despite being almost rocked off his feet.

"Come into my office," Martin ushered him into an adjoining room. This room was well furnished: a heavy desk and executive chair, a computer on the desk, a sofa and coffee table, files and family pictures on a book case nearby, potted indoor plants, a water cooler, certificates on the wall.

"I've just put the tea on. How about a cuppa?" Martin was gone before even waiting for a response and Bandu heard his voice from what must be the kitchen amidst the clinking of crockery. "How did you find me?"

Bandu groped for words as he wandered around the room looking at the certificates—many real estate awards: "Salesman of the Year," "Rookie of the Year," "Regional Sales Person of the year." Bandu felt a sense of pride for his friend. He tiptoed into the living-dining room around the corner. A stereo set lay on the floor, its wires trailing to two speakers on either side, a large-screen TV stood at the other end facing a solitary wing-backed armchair. There was no dining table, no sideboard with fancy crockery that these houses usually boasted. He gingerly stepped back into the office room.

When Martin returned with two steaming mugs of tea, Bandu spoke for the first time, "You work from this house?"

"Yes."

Bandu felt a sense of relief. He sipped his tea. "I live close by here. That's how I found you."

"Really! Goes to show doesn't it! Well, what have you been up to all these years?"

"I am in… business," was all Bandu could manage and hoped that Martin would not pursue it.

Martin was studying him and merely nodded, changing the subject. "Have you found Christo?"

"He is in jail. In Kingston," Bandu replied flatly.

"What?"

"I have some contacts who gave me the news. A fight with his wife. I don't know the details." Bandu decided to change the subject too. "You are very successful in Canada I can see."

Martin waved his hand dismissively at the certificates. "Oh, those things. They accumulate like flotsam in a river. Things are not as solid as they look." He snapped his fingers. "It could all disappear tomorrow in this country."

"I know. Still, you are successful. Your wife and son are very beautiful in these pictures."

Martin sighed. "Thank you! I suppose they are. It's nice when others see it."

"Have you been back to Sri Lanka?" Bandu asked.

"No, but I'm thinking about it, as my father is not in the best of health. I never got a chance to see my mother before she died. I don't want to miss out again."

"Yes, it is good to see them and make amends. I went to Sri Lanka and made my peace with my mother just before she died. I am happy that you are going back."

Bandu wanted to say that he had seen the big house in Rosedale, the blonde wife, the son, and Trinians College, but decided against it. Martin was not ever to know his role in this seedy venture. Instead he asked the question that was burning inside him. "Do you know a man called Muller? A German with crooked teeth?"

Bandu saw the confident air of the salesman in Martin slip. A look of caution took over. His friend sipped his tea warily. "How do you know Muller?" Martin asked, hedging.

"I have contacts."

"Are you involved with the mob or something?" Martin's gaze was direct.

"What do *you* know about Muller?"

Martin exhaled and paced the room. "I wish we had met not just to talk about Muller. But since you asked, he was a friend of a friend who financed one of my business ventures that failed. I told you, things are not as great as they look. Even though he was cautioned, Muller poured money into the deal, which was risky at best. It's nearly two years on, and he's still pestering me for his money. In fact, his requests have become more threatening of late." Martin waved his hands around the room. "As you can see, I don't have any money to give him."

"Okay," Bandu was starting to see things clearly now. "I have to go. But for the next few days tell your family not to go outside alone. That includes you."

He could see the look of alarm spread on Martin's face.

"How are you involved in this?"

Bandu shook his head. "It's a long story. But one day it will be told."

"I wished I had never taken his money. The man does not understand business risk. What do I do?" Martin stopped his pacing and swirled the contents inside his mug, splashing a few drops on the floor.

Bandu rose. "Don't worry. Remember, I am your friend. Soon everything will be all right. And then I will come again. And then we can talk about the old days."

At the door, Martin held him by the shoulder. "Give me some more information, Bandu. You can't just show up, give me this news about Muller and leave. Can I, at least, have your phone number?"

"No. Not at this stage. Please be patient. And trust me. I am still your old friend."

Bandu broke away the moment he saw Martin nod reluctantly and step back.

A wave of regret enveloped Bandu as he returned to the car. This was not how he had wanted their meeting to have gone, not after all these years. There had been so many good things to talk about: Sumana and Ravi for starters, to enquire about Martin's wonderfully generous mother back home. It would have been so good to have boasted about their sons and their respective talents. But life never happened the way you planned it.

Bandu sat in his car for a long time, staring at the house across the road. Then he smiled as he started the engine. Despite his lowly circumstances, he felt that he had something Martin did not have. Ravi respected him more than Martin's son respected his father. And that barren house across the road had not radiated the warmth of a woman's presence: Martin was living alone.

Bandu pulled the Toyota into an empty parking spot alongside the curb on Isabella Street. It was about 7:00 pm. Soon Muller would be making his appearance. There were a couple of passengers in a silver coupe parked in front of him, closer to the walkway of Muller's apartment. The brown van was nowhere in sight. His meeting with Martin the day before and handing the manuscript to Sumana later that evening had only reconciled him to what must now be done.

He lit a cigarette and waited. Muller got off the bus and hurried up the walkway. People went in and out the building's entrance constantly; visitors used a house phone to be let in while residents flashed a key fob that opened the front doors. Muller belonged to the latter category. Three minutes later, the light went on in the fourth-floor apartment.

When he saw the two male residents head indoors from the grassy patch opposite the building, Bandu got out of the car and made for the entrance. One of the men was in a wheelchair, with his companion pushing him gently. The former's emaciated body looked to be in the last stages of AIDS. The two men were going in after their regular bout of fresh air. Bandu had watched their routine every Thursday. He strolled after them, as they neared the front entrance. He passed the parked silver car and caught a glimpse of its occupants: two young lovers wrapped in an embrace: a flash of a red-headed woman and a man wearing a beret and leather jacket, slobbering over each other. *Oh, to be young in this country.* These were many hidden pleasures that he had been denied in his life. He'd had old foreign men panting over him in Sri Lanka instead.

The man pushing the wheelchair used his key fob and then wrestled to keep the front door open as he pushed his companion through. Bandu reached out from behind and held the door open. "Please…"

"Oh, thank you." The man sounded harried but relieved for the help. The dying man in the wheelchair raised his head and smiled; he looked more cheerful, resolved. "Thank you very much," he said. "You have a nice day." Smiling and nodding, Bandu slipped inside behind them.

He took the stairs, two at a time and was panting by the time he got to the fourth floor. He ran to the end of the corridor and banged on the door of the corner apartment. He hefted the gun out of his jacket pocket and kept it behind his back.

Muller looked tousled, half-dressed and shocked when he peered through the chain lock.

"Bandu—what are you doing here?" Muller dragged Bandu inside the apartment.

"There is *no* boss," Bandu said, bringing the gun up and training it on the German. Out of the corner of his eye he saw the bedroom door open and a young man came out gasping.

"Bruce, go inside" Muller said. "This is private business."

"Marc will be jealous," Bandu said. He was beginning to feel good. *It does get more cheerful near the end.*

The bedroom door slammed.

"There is no boss," Bandu repeated. "Ja, Muller?"

The old man sat down. He was dressed only in his underpants. This scene was so familiar. Hotel rooms with elderly tourists offering money for sex from underage boys—Bandu's training ground in the '70s. There hadn't been visible signs of AIDS then; that was the only difference.

"I shouldn't have given you the car," Muller said.

"*You* are the boss. I was a bloody fool."

"Bandu," Muller was pleading now. "We can work something out."

"I'm going to kill you first. Let's see if 'boss' will come after me."

"But you earned good money with me."

"And lost what was most important to me. You shouldn't have messed with terrorists."

"Mein Gott! Don't think this is about causes. It is business. It's all about money."

"Getting people like me into this country was good enough, if you wanted to make money. And you shouldn't have messed with my friend, Martin James."

"Your friend? What are you talking about? Have you gone crazy?"

"My friend from many years ago. In another country. In another lifetime."

There was a sound by the door and it crashed open. Muller grabbed his head and sank to the floor crying, "Ach, please help! This man is trying to kill me."

Bandu spun around, his gun still trained on the German. He caught sight of a red headed woman and a man in a beret and leather jacket, badges upheld in one hand and guns aimed squarely at him in the other.

"Freeze—police!" The red-head did not look so amorous anymore, her jaw was set squarely and her eyes pierced him. It looked like she'd done this before.

Bandu turned slowly towards Muller, the gun unwavering in his hand. He laughed at the irony: the cops will take him away and Muller will be free to carry on. Suddenly, the old German, kneeling with his hands on his head, begging, represented all that had gone awry in Bandu's life: Muller represented the snake charmers who had lured him into the pit. Weed them out, and the rest of humanity would survive. Ravi and Martin's son would survive.

And they will tell my story only if there are dead people!
Bandu pulled the trigger.

Part 3 – Finding Home

"Even his griefs are a joy long after to one that remembers all that he wrought and endured" – Homer

24. **Back Home**

Martin sits inside the air-conditioned restaurant at mid-morning and watches the traffic clog the Galle Road, the main artery that once supported most commercial life in Colombo. The semi-cooled sherbet is refreshing but even in this oasis of comfort flies have crept in off the street and buzz over anything sweet or sticky, which is everything and everybody inside. He arrived in Sri Lanka three days ago and is still acclimatizing to the heat, time change and congestion. He has spent his time lounging around the pool of his city hotel, sleeping at odd times of the day to combat jet lag and making short trishaw trips to visit selected old haunts, places that have changed completely in appearance and whose former inhabitants have either relocated, gone overseas, or died.

August 2005 is a tough time to visit the country: the ceasefire which had spread so much optimism and fuelled reconstruction, is all but dead, and the giant tsunami that hit the southern and eastern coast of the country six months ago has killed hundreds of thousands. But it was the tsunami that has led Martin to discover the whereabouts of his brother Barney and write to him after all these years.

He swipes at a fly that has settled on the lip of his glass. He needs to go out into the street again, but the sheer roar of traffic, the black exhaust fumes and the indiscriminate blaring of horns make him hesitate.

Procrastination had driven him crazy back in Canada. Victor, based on recent correspondence, could pass away any day now, and Martin felt that he had left their meeting as late as he possibly could. That, and the discovery of Barney's whereabouts, had pushed him to finally call a travel agent.

He shakes aside his lethargy and tosses some cash on the table; the Sri Lankan rupee is down to a tenth of its value from when he was last in the country, and he gets confused with the quantity of notes he has to carry in his wallet. Outside, the blast of humid air grips and oppresses him. The shape of the Galle Road has changed; it is now a one-way street; reverse traffic flows along with its fully built-up parallel cousin, Duplication Road. The pollution is intense, and his throat has been raw with a permanent itch since his arrival. Newer buildings sprout on top of older structures which hug narrow city roads built by the

British during colonial times, hemming in the once-broader vista and adding to the feel of congestion. Yet the newer construction seems to have hit a pause, evidenced in many unfinished buildings left vacant; they seem to be waiting for the resumption of peace talks.

Armed policemen patrol the sidewalks at regular intervals. Someone must have made a huge windfall selling all these guns to the security forces. When Martin was a kid, the only armed personnel he had seen were two sentries outside the Prime Minister's residence in Temple Trees. Now, that same property looks like a military camp, heavily fortified with pill boxes, sandbags, tanks and snipers.

He hails a trishaw and three of them screech to a halt around him, one cutting across traffic to heed his summons. "Sorry, guys, I only need one of you." He shrugs and dives into the first one, and gives the driver instructions, hoping that today's excursion will be better than previous ones.

Yesterday, he had visited Kelaniya and Kotte, places he had lived in. The old homes of the James family were so drastically altered that he couldn't recognize them, surrounded by ten-foot tall shuttered gates with only their new upper storeys visible to the street. The open fields he had roamed as a boy were concrete roadways lined with apartment buildings on either side, the sins of the old *kirakotuwa* buried forever under this new construction. He had asked his driver to keep driving and hadn't even stopped to take a picture of those old homes. What was the use? He would be photographing an unfamiliar place. The old way of life was dead for sure, and he was glad that he had not harboured illusions about "back home," a crutch held by many Sri Lankans returning from overseas.

Today, he has instructed his driver to take him to Peter's Lane, where his grandmother had lived until her death in the late '80s. Peter's Lane is wider now and many of the once-residential houses have been converted into office buildings, but the lack of zoning in the city strikes him: one can pass a hospital, a factory, a restaurant, a bank, a private residence, and a book store operating right next to each other.

He almost misses the address because he is looking for the familiar bend in the road just ahead of Grandma's old house, his only landmark. He is not counting on recognizing any of the buildings, for they are all new. But no, the old house still stands, dwarfed by newer structures. He tells the driver to wait and rushes to the gate of the old two-storey house, badly in need of a coat of paint, the sandy garden still visible in patches where recent asphalt paving has not encroached. The old gate is chained and locked and a dog barks inside. He takes pictures through the metal bars, of places in the garden where he and his cousin Jenny had once played and created paint butterflies. His camera moves up to the apartment above the garage where Mahinda had preyed on him. How ominous and scary those scenes had been to him then; how innocuous they seem now, except perhaps for the frantic dog.

A middle-aged woman in a housecoat comes out and stares at him. He waves to her.

She shouts across to him in Tamil. He talks back in English. She does not understand. He tries his broken Sinhala which has been coming back to him in spurts during these first days in the country. She still does not understand and continues to speak in Tamil. She looks scared.

The taxi driver, spits a stream of betel juice onto the sidewalk, sidles up and offers to translate. He speaks Sinhala and Tamil, but very broken English.

"Tell her," Martin says to him in halting Sinhala, "That my grandmother used to live here. I'd like to walk around the garden and take pictures if I could."

The driver translates. The woman shakes her head.

"Her employer is a doctor. He does not allow visitors on the grounds," the driver says.

The driver converses some more. Their exchange becomes animated, then the woman smiles.

The driver spits out more betel. "Sir, she wants to know if you have dollars."

Martin grins. "Sure. Tell her to open this gate and I've got ten dollars for her."

The woman's eyes come alive when the driver informs her of the reward. Then the driver turns to Martin, "Sir, five dollars is enough for her. You can give me the other five, for my trouble."

Martin laughs aloud. "Lead on, Macduff," he says.

He takes photographs of every strip of the back garden: the stairway leading up to the back door, the steps leading to Mahinda's apartment, the wooded area that he used to wander when he wanted to be alone, still miraculously preserved by the same shade trees, the temple compound next door having a school added to its property. As a cool breeze flits in and swishes the coconut palms, he closes his eyes and feels the heat on his face and hears the crows caw overhead; he is being transported back to his childhood and he holds onto that moment for as long as he can. He knows that flashes like this will be hard to come by. The voices of the caretaker and the taxi driver eventually drift into his consciousness and break the spell.

He decides not to ask the woman whether he can see inside the house, in case this leads to more financial wrangling or gets her into trouble with her employer. The taxi driver and the woman have struck up a conversation and Martin wonders whether this will lead to a future clandestine meeting between the two for mutual benefit.

He pays the woman ten dollars in the end, and as the driver opens his mouth in puzzlement, Martin winks at him that everything is under control. Back in the taxi, he tells the driver, "I think I know one of the reasons for this country's problems—when we were growing up, we were not taught to talk to each other in all our three national languages. We were only given the choice of picking any two. So now we need interpreters and the truth gets lost in the translation."

The driver ignores Martin's epiphany and is uncommunicative on the return journey. But his eyes light up when Martin gives him a ten dollar tip on top of the four-dollar cab ride as they pull up at the hotel. Martin feels that he has paid well for seeing, photographing and experiencing a fragment of his past, preserved from change by some fluke of fortune. The feeling of "back home" had returned to him unexpectedly.

Martin walks into the hotel bar after dinner. The place is nearly empty, except for a few patrons sitting at the counter. The season is over, and with rumblings about the ceasefire breaking down and the post-tsunami reconstruction being so far behind schedule, the local papers are speculating whether tourists will return in the same numbers this year.

A lounge band is playing '70s favourites as Martin orders a Coke and mellows to the tunes of "Sweet Caroline" and "Snowbird." Like at the house in Peter's Lane earlier that day, moments like this still bring back the comfortable, the old, familiar world he had once been ensconced in. Part of his reason for coming to Sri Lanka, apart from wanting to meet his father and brother, was to capture this essence, if that was at all possible. He closes his eyes, leans back on his bar stool and lets the music transport him back.

He wonders what Ginny must be doing now. He still thinks of her, although it's been four years since the divorce. The flashbacks of their life together come less frequently now. Last he'd heard, she was re-enrolled in university, completing an MBA; she apparently wanted to teach, or so Jamie had informed him on one of his bi-weekly visits. Ginny represented the world Martin had once set out to conquer, a world that had finally vanquished him and set him adrift, scarred and wounded. Now, sitting on this stool, he is back in his old world, and even though this bar scene is making him dreamy, he still feels like an outsider, and is being treated like one everywhere he goes, especially when he doles out foreign money or flashes his Canadian passport as ID. The locals are shocked whenever he opens up a conversation in Sinhala, as they take him for a foreigner with his fair skin and touristy dress. He wonders where home for him really is.

Today's visit to Peter's Lane has triggered off a deeper question in his mind: can he make a new start in Sri Lanka? Can he close off Canada as a chapter in his life that is over, and start again in the land of his origins? Many had done that over the years, despite the country's obvious flaws. He also knows that one of the prime reasons for his coming here, apart from Victor and Barney and capuring that "back home" feeling, is to make a new start. Does one make new starts in old countries? Does the actor come back on stage after curtain call? Who does he play to? An empty playhouse? He mulls over the question, with the music only helping to bias his decision in favour of playing empty playhouses by keeping him in a time warp of pleasant memories.

"Nice music?" the voice is feminine, foreign—English, he thinks. He opens his eyes. The woman is sitting beside him at the bar. She must have arrived when he was lost in thought. She is black-haired, late thirties, slim and attractive with cat-like eyes. She is overly tanned and sports freckles on her arms that stick out of a safari shirt. From the olives floating in her drink he can tell that she is imbibing his once-favourite drink: vodka martini.

"Yes, it is nice." He feels that old rush go through him: desire. Lonely women in hotels had been one of his pursuits and lust rises in him, switched on by the proximity of this woman and her openly inviting talk. "Hi, I'm Martin James."

"Louise Fletcher." She is studying him curiously. "You sound...colonial. Your accent..."

"Yes. I get asked about that all the time. I was born here. I'm back after twenty years."

She is a freelance reporter, covering the peace process, she tells him.

"I'm a freelancer too, real estate. I thought you folks were just about wrapped up here. The peace talks seem to be all but dead."

"There's always hope. I'm sticking around just in case there is a last-minute breakthrough."

"It's not safe in these parts for a woman travelling alone."

"I've been in worse places. Cut my teeth in Rwanda ten years ago, and did my tour of duty in Afghanistan." She downs her drink and orders another.

He is starting to get excited. This woman intrigues him. Danger hovers about her. He can't remember how long it has been since he has been with a woman, especially one as experienced as Louise.

They talk about local politics, about the debacle over tsunami charity contributions, the potential of a fresh election and the opposition party being elected to resume the peace process. She finishes three vodka martinis and orders Spanish coffee during their conversation.

"I like the beaches here. I get to walk about nude and nobody bothers me." She looks at him and laughs.

He laughs too. This should be easy. Suddenly, he is on the hunt again, tired of the dance.

"I'd like to view your nude body," he says looking straight into her face.

She returns his look. "Sure. I'd like that too."

They go up to her room. It is tidy: an unruffled bed, a few papers and a laptop on the desk, a knapsack on the floor. She strips quickly as if she is late for an appointment, tossing her clothes on the armchair. "Take yours off," she says as he ogles her tanned breasts, the tautness of her belly muscles and the full bush of pubic hair, as if she were a throwback to the '70s, like those songs in the lounge.

As he takes off his underpants she pushes him onto the bed, grabs his swollen cock and starts to stroke, playfully at first, then harder and deliberately.

"Hey, go slow," he mumbles, enjoying the stroking. It certainly has been a long drought, he reminds himself.

He wishes she would take him in her mouth, lubricate him, but she goes on rubbing almost maniacally until he comes in a gush.

"Shit, I hoped you wouldn't have done that."

But she is oblivious to his complaint. She grabs his hand and places it between her legs. "Now me, please." He obliges, wading through tufts of hair to find her. She bucks and groans and he is obliged to keep the pressure on. He brings her to climax within minutes.

They lie side by side, naked and he thinks that this was an opportunity squandered. This woman is either kinky or stupid. He wonders what her next move will be, whether he will have the stamina for another erection. He rises and heads for the washroom.

"Where are you going?" her voice sounds anxious despite her euphoria.

He doesn't answer, still angry about the abruptness and incompleteness of their sex act.

She sinks back in the bed with a sigh.

As he switches on the washroom light, he immediately catches sight of the row of medications lined up on the counter. He shivers involuntarily as he reads the labels. He steps into the shower and lets the hot water scald him as he furiously rubs himself clean. He dries himself and steps out angry and betrayed. She is sitting up in bed, wearing a dressing gown.

"You should have told me," he says.

"I told you, I've been around. Don't worry. I was careful."

He begins to put his clothes on. "Why do you travel to these hot spots? You should be getting medical care."

"I'm on a mission in the limited time I have. And I do get lonely from time to time."

He pauses in the doorway, ashamed of himself, of the beast in him that had overridden logic. "I hope I've been of some service."

"Yes, you have. Thank you."

The next morning he takes the bus to Galle. He is still kicking himself for being so...so juvenile the night before. The bus station in Colombo is teeming with people while stray dogs hunt for scraps of food between the sweating, swearing and sweltering commuters. No one trusts line-ups and everyone stands as far away as possible from each other around the adobe and metal shelters and then rush through the narrow doors of the buses even before the vehicles come to a full halt. Disembarking passengers have to battle their way through the crush of new entrants. Martin wonders why he did not hire a car; but he has wanted to recapture his youth, recapture the struggle of living in this country, of performing day-to-day errands that vex and tire one out and leave energy for little else at the end of the day but to sleep, until the cycle resumes early the next morning. Now he understands why the standard response to a person greeting another with a "How are you?" is a plain and simple, "Existing!"

He manages to get a seat at the rear of the bus; in order to be by a window he has to take the one over the wheel. His knees hunch up and his sling bag reaches up to his nose. Travellers bunch up in the aisle, arms raised to hold the support bar on the roof, exuding armpit odours in varying degrees of staleness; in the packed confines men press crotches onto women's backsides with impunity; the women endure the rubbing and even the odd leak, having no other option but to wait for the next bus with no guarantee of avoiding a re-occurrence. Martin suppresses a smile—nothing has changed riding the buses—another touch of "back home."

The coast still bears flooded stretches on either side of the road and its parallel railway track, where the tsunami waters have yet to recede, lingering, tormenting the residents of battered broken houses along the bus route. Flood water lingers, like the arguments still going on between the politicians about how the relief money that has poured in from around the world should be divided up. Even here the rival ethnic groups have a reason to quarrel: the other side appears to always get more aid. Yet the broken houses, the new graveyards, the people living in tents, the bolder ones reconstructing their abodes with whatever shelter material they can lay their hands on without waiting for government assistance, are testaments to bureaucratic breakdowns along this stretch that had once been a tourist paradise of endless pristine beaches.

In Galle, he takes a trishaw and gives the driver the address to the orphanage. They leave the town with its distinguished stone Dutch fort, the teeming jumble of colonial-era buildings and temporary shops of corrugated steel, and traffic mingling with pedestrians who in turn are navigating puddled stretches of asphalt. They turn off the coast road and head down a broken gravel lane, through coconut palms and banana shoots until the driver turns in through the gateposts—the gate itself is missing—of an old colonial mansion with half of its roof under construction.

Paying off the driver, Martin lugs his bag to the front door. A stream of half-dressed children interrupt a game of volleyball in the large garden and run towards him, to encircle and look curiously, smiling shyly, reluctant to communicate.

"Is Mr. James here?" he asks in Sinhala.

The children are taken in awe at this foreigner's command of their language, and titter among themselves. Then one child, a boy of about ten years, asks, "You mean, the headmaster?"

Martin shrugs. "Yes, I would like to meet him."

The boy points at the house.

"Thanks." Martin heads towards the house with the children following on his heels; some are giggling between themselves as this man does not appear to be such a stranger after all.

A slight-built male in his late twenties or early thirties, effeminate in his gait, comes out of the house and bows graciously as Martin ascends the verandah steps. The man is dressed in a bush shirt and a sarong, and is bare-footed. The children stand back at the bottom of the steps, until the man gesticulates kindly, ushering them back to their interrupted game.

"You are Martin?" the man asks in halting, accented English. "Barney *aiyah* is at the back of house, repairing. Come."

Martin walks through the high-ceilinged living room with its rusted, stilled ceiling fans and water-marked walls. There is a mustiness inside that the open windows on either side with a steady breeze blowing through cannot dispel. A set of wooden doors lead to the rear of the house and a man, in his early forties, dressed in shorts and a tee shirt wet with sweat, is on a ladder by the side of the house laying tiles on the sloping, exposed roof frame. He turns and Martin recognizes the weak chin, the watery eyes, the child, now grown, who formerly shat in his pants whenever their father was in one of his alcoholic rages.

"Hello Barney," Martin says, tears welling in his eyes.

"Hello, Martin." Barney's chin pouts as if something is irritating his nose. Then he descends the ladder, jumping off the last two rungs and runs up to his elder brother and embraces him. "I am so happy you have come, brother."

They hug each other for a long while, the years melting in their warm embrace, taking them back to the days when they were children, before life had intervened to pull them apart. In his arms, Barney is still his baby brother, Martin realizes, fragile, vulnerable, caring.

"Come, you must be thirsty and hungry." Barney breaks free, wiping his dripping nose and taking Martin by the hand to lead him back into the house. "Sena has prepared a feast for us."

Sena, the young man who had met Martin earlier, brings out a tray of rice and dry-fish curry, with a *mallum* on the side. He also brings out a clay pot of water and three glasses.

"This is a feast, trust me," Barney says, pulling three chairs around the small wooden table on the back steps. "I saved the dry fish for your coming."

Martin slakes his thirst first; the water from the clay pot is cool. He serves a small portion of the food, realizing how little there is to go around for the three of them. He notes the absence of cutlery; it is time to go local, and to use his fingers. He runs water over his right hand from the finger bowl that Sena next places on the table.

"What about the children?" Martin enquires before tucking in.

"They eat out in the open kitchen on the other side of the house. The older children supervise the meal," Barney explains, then says a silent prayer, accompanied by Sena, before taking the first morsel of food.

During their meal Barney gives Martin a description of the origins of the orphanage.

"This was an abandoned coconut estate. The owner went bankrupt twenty years ago and took off for Australia without paying his staff. The estate was acquired by the local government and parcelled off to the unpaid workers. Each labourer got an acre to plant on. The Church requested the estate building, this one we are in, and a few surrounding acres to build an orphanage. Then some internal politics got into the picture and plans for the orphanage were abandoned as the funding got diverted elsewhere."

Barney pauses, and looks at Sena, as if seeking permission to continue. The younger man nods and focuses on his food, his head aslant.

"When Sena and I were asked to leave the seminary—I think Daddy already wrote to you about that incident—I asked the Director if I could come here and revive the orphanage. The Director was a kind and caring man, even though he was caught in a public-relations scandal over us. My request was granted, as it killed two birds with one stone: it got rid of their embarrassment—us—and passed off a financial headache just as the local authorities were pressing for action on the original orphanage proposal. By the grace of God, Sena and I have been running this place these last ten years, with contributions from the community. We started with thirty children. Our numbers doubled after the tsunami. We had no room to accommodate all of the orphans and we took as many as this house could hold. The building also suffered water damage in the flood. Our supporters in the area built us a website and I launched an appeal to private donors over the Internet and we were surprised at how much support we received, especially from overseas, despite the many scams that were going on."

"I know," Martin replies. "That is how I found you. I saw your picture as I was trolling the Internet in search of where to make my donation towards tsunami relief. My anonymous donation ended up with you. Not with the 'official' ones, that I understand, are still awaiting distribution."

"We have fared well. Our international donors are very supportive. In the tourist season, many are coming to visit and help build more facilities for us."

"You have done well indeed, Barney. I am proud of you."

Barney nods in acknowledgement but a frown remains on his brow. "I wish Daddy would say the same."

"He is an old, sick man, living out his last days in regret. I am going to see him next."

"When you do, please ask him to allow me to visit him, or ask him to come down here. He will see, and hopefully appreciate, the work we are doing for these children. More than what he did for us as kids."

"I will. That was one of my reasons for coming. To reconcile the remnants of family I have left."

"I was sorry to hear about your marriage. And about the loss of your business."

"They were dreams I pursued."

"Still you were able to get out and see the world and follow your dream."

"You know, Barney, when I look around this place, I think you have done more than I have ever managed in all my ramblings. Sometimes 'stayers' achieve more than 'leavers'. I learned that lesson from Mum."

After lunch, Barney shows him around the property. A section of the grounds has been cleared for a large vegetable patch. Two giant aquariums, like miniature swimming pools, are dug into the grounds on the other side to rear tropical fish; several young men (volunteers from the nearby village, Barney explains) are working the tanks: cleaning, feeding and packing some of the catch into water-filled clear plastic bags for transport in a battered lorry. A pen houses chickens, and two large pigs waddle about the backyard. A long shed, with a corrugated metal roof and open sides, stands at the back of the house; this is the school. Children are at classes as they walk by; one class for older kids and another for younger ones, led by women dressed in saris.

"The fish exports keep us afloat financially and we try to grow our food on the grounds, supplemented of course, by donations. The teachers are volunteers who lost their families in the tsunami. Teaching the children has been the best therapy for them," Barney explains.

In the fading daylight, Martin sits on the porch and watches his brother and Sena go about their duties in the orphanage. There is a fluid co-ordination between them: whether it is in the instruction of the volunteers at the aquarium as they wind down their work for the day, or when leading the children in a game of soccer after their classes, or when instructing the older children who will cook dinner and serve it to the others in the open-kitchen mess hall. There is an instinctive rhythm in the gentle movements of these two men, lovers and pariahs of the church they once offered their lives to. And always, there is a smile of appreciation in one's eyes for the other.

The children mirror the headmaster and his assistant's behaviour. Martin observes a girl of about ten, combing the long hair of a younger child, both seated in the shade of a coconut tree; an older boy is demonstrating to a group of younger peers how to dodge an opponent with a football; a group of boys and girls are singing as they wash clothes by the well, and from the quantity it looks as if the clothes belong to the entire orphanage, a motley collection of rags in all shapes, sizes and faded colours.

Martin's mind drifts back to where he has journeyed from: his little cottage by the lake, now his permanent workplace and home after the house in Pickering had gone on the block to settle his divorce. Instinct had made him pick the little town near Port Hope, even though he had yet not made contact with Marnie or Julia. Something had told him that he needed to locate nearby.

On one of his early real estate sales in the area, Marnie had represented the buyer. She had looked as beautiful as ever: dark hair cut short, body still curvy in the right places, mature, engaging. There was calmness about her now, gone was the bouncy ebullience, replaced with a sense of knowing. They had worked well together on that deal, still recognizing each other's pressure points and playing to their strengths, just like Barney and Sena are doing here in the orphanage. On the subject of Julia, he had remained silent, and she had respected that. When the sale concluded to everyone's satisfaction, he had invited her out to a drink in a bar in town.

They talked about old times, being polite again. He told her about how he had sold the old brokerage to Vinod Sharma, and relocated as a realtor to the lake area.

"Good for Vinod," Marnie said, a smile of fond remembrance on her face. "He was your most loyal employee."

Then he decided to get to the point that they had both been skirting around. "I'm not ignoring you, or our daughter."

"I know," she said. "You're 'not ready.'" There was no sarcasm, just cold acknowledgement on her part.

"I'm still not through the changes in my life. My son is still coming to terms with the effects of the divorce. We all are, in varying degrees."

"We never really get through everything. There are just pauses between changes, Martin."

"I'm going back to Sri Lanka, for awhile."

He saw the momentary look of disappointment on her face. She shrugged it off and focussed on her drink, professional once again. "Do you plan to come back?"

"I need to go back to my roots to find out who I am. Find out what and who I have become. I hope the visit helps me to deal with my unresolved issues."

"I wish you luck. My time with Mom in Vancouver helped me deal with some of my issues too. But at the end of the day, we need to face reality and live our lives."

He had not associated with her since.

He knew where she lived and had driven by her house a few times. Once, he even followed the 10-year-old dark-haired girl back from school. He snapped a quick picture of her as she turned into the driveway, took a key from the chain around her neck, unlocked the door and entered the house. But he did not have the courage to tap on that same door afterwards. In fact, he panicked soon after taking the picture, thinking that the neighbours would peg him as a pedophile, and had never returned to Marnie's street again. He kept the pictures of his son and the little girl on the desk of his home office to remind himself of whom he needs to be worthy.

Looking across the yard of the orphanage at his brother freely giving of himself to the 60 children who have no parents, he feels inadequate at his own lack of courage to face the two children he has sired and abandoned.

After dinner, eaten by lamplight as the building still lacks electricity, Barney throws a mat on the floor in the master bedroom.

"You can sleep on our bed and use its mosquito net," he says matter-of-factly. "I will sleep on the floor, and Sena will sleep in the hall."

Martin protests saying that he will bunk down in the hall instead. He does not want to put anyone out.

"Brother—," Barney smiles firmly, "You have slept in too many soft beds over your years abroad. You will not survive on the floor. And the mosquitoes don't take kindly to full-blooded foreigners."

Martin concedes the point without further argument, feeling grateful for the bed.

The children are accommodated at night in the eastern section of the house where the walls have been knocked down to create a large dormitory with beds and mats lining both sides of the long room. As the lights go out in the house, and the moon shines through the window, Martin hears a chant coming from the dormitory.

"The children are singing a hymn before bed. It helps them to sleep," Barney explains softly from his mat.

"And I used to read you stories—remember? After Paul died?"

"Yes, that's where I got the idea from. Your stories took me to another place, away from death. That's why I started the hymns with the children, and it seems to help."

"Barney, there is something I need to ask you. How are you and Sena viewed in this community? This is not Canada, where your lifestyle is legal and commonplace. People were tough on homosexuality when I was growing up here. I hope you don't mind me asking, but I still see this prejudice in Dad, for example. How do you get by?"

Barney's answer cuts like a knife in the dark. "The people of this country have lost too much, Martin. They have gone to hell and back several times: in the civil wars, both in the north and the south, in the tsunami, in just the daily grind of living and watching their earnings shrink between morning and evening. What they need is love, compassion and inclusiveness, and the banishment of greed. They have no time to look at our lives and find fault with us—in idle times, perhaps; but not now. Sena and I cannot alter our nature but we give of ourselves.

We stand for the values this country needs. Even in the seminary, we offered nothing else. The priests may not have seen it that way, but I think these people do, and appreciate it in these dark times."

"Thank you, brother. I am really glad I came to see you."

"Me too."

25. **Reckoning**

Martin is on the bus again, but this time he is heading into the central hills. The vehicle is less crowded and he has the space to let his mind wander over the events of the last week.

He has spent three soul-satisfying days at the orphanage. Donning a sarong and tee-shirt he mingled barefoot with the children during their class breaks, talking to them in Sinhala, listening to their stories, all pathetic but the new-normal to them. They stared at his missing toes, and that gave him entrance to their club of the scarred. The children he conversed with were happy to live in the orphanage; it was the bright spot in their lives, a place where they did not feel threatened. They revered the headmaster and his assistant.

Martin helped with the re-construction of the roof, and by the time of his departure, most of the new tiles were in place. Food was meagre: he had eaten dhall curry and bread three times in a row, and on his last night, Barney had treated him to string hoppers and *seeni-sambol*, purchased in the village. The feeling that had enveloped him on the day he visited Peter's Lane returned: despite the hardships in this country, Barney and his partner were engaged in the struggle for life. Struggle provided purpose. Even Louise Fletcher had found her purpose here. That feeling, more than an impulse, moved Martin even more strongly now, making him want to write off everything in Canada, and take up work in this country again; follow in Barney's footsteps, if he dared. If peace in the country held by some chance, financial optimism would return, and the economy would blossom. All the construction that seemed to be in a sort of a limbo in Colombo, would resume with unstoppable ferocity, fuelled by the dreams of returning emigrants and guest workers. This place could be the next Singapore. The paradise beaches would be re-built and Sri Lanka would re-claim its tourists who had fled to the nearby Maldives.

Then practicality took over. There were lots of loose ends back in Canada, the home and native land that he had taken an oath of allegiance to when he unhesitatingly accepted citizenship and promptly destroyed his Sri Lankan passport for all the bad memories it evoked in him. And now he was considering returning to Sri Lanka permanently? Is this the eternal conundrum of the immigrant: to have his feet splayed between two countries but not have a permanent home?

He bid a tearful farewell to Barney before boarding his trishaw. Sena was standing a couple of paces behind.

"I'll do my darndest with Dad, Barney. I've taken lots of pictures to show him."

"Thank you."

"And don't you go AWOL on me again."

Barney smiled shyly, that old smile, after which, as a child, he would put his head down and mutter to himself quietly. Barney reached for Sena's hand. "No, not now that I know how you respect my situation."

"You are my hero, brother. One day if you ever visit Canada, you will find that your life is quite normal. Bye, for now."

As the bus strains up the mountain road in Belihuloya, Martin raises his head to the mist coming in through the window and lets it dampen the heat and sweat of the low country. It is cooler here than in Colombo or Galle, but not cold enough for a sweater or a jacket which he used to wear whenever visiting "up-country" in the old days. The unguarded mountain road is under construction and in some stretches, the bus inches past oncoming traffic. A lorry has gone off the road at one turn and lies in the ditch; the driver is sitting on his haunches smoking a *beedie*, sarong drawn over his knees, waiting for help that may take hours, even days, to arrive.

He gets off in Haputale, a town of old buildings perched on a mountain ledge, looking down on a beautiful vista of tea plantations that fall down precipitous rock. Giant Mara trees spread their shade in all directions and swaths of mist like cotton wool blot out the lush greenery of the valley. He hears gunfire and is told by a fellow passenger that it is coming from the army camp at nearby Diyatalawa. Sound carries across the valley, someone is playing a flute on the opposite mountain and the mournful tune plays a sad counterpoint to the crack of rifles.

He takes a trishaw to his Uncle Colin and Aunt Mabel's house that is midway to the next town of Bandarawela. Colin was a planter who retired after spending his career in the estates and discovered at the end of his active working life that he was good for no other occupation. His children immigrated to Australia, but that country had no need for an ex-planter. So he and Mabel moved into the old walauwe-style house that had been in the family for several generations. They are now ably supported by remittances from their six children in Melbourne. Victor was given a room in the sprawling house as he was Colin's only living relative left in Sri Lanka.

The trishaw stops by a chained and padlocked gate on the main road. The driver advises Martin that he cannot proceed further. Martin pays him, takes his sling bag, jumps over the fence and starts walking.

The path winds its way through giant pine trees. And he thought that pine trees only grew in Canada! He remembers coming here once when he was about 12, when Victor had taken the entire family on an outing, saying "we have to see this country before we immigrate to Canada. Let's go to my cousin's place up-country." They had travelled by train via Kandy and Nuwara Eliya on that occasion, and it took a day and a half to arrive at their destination.

He walks through two moss-covered pillars with globular crests; they were formerly gateposts. Their empty hinges once held spiked gates which, as children, they had been forbidden to climb. He enters a large front yard with grass growing in patches. A wide verandah wraps around the bungalow-house. Wing-armed, rattan-backed chairs and accompanying side tables are spread out about the verandah. The doors leading inside the house are wooden and hinged and fold into each other when left open.

Martin pauses on the steps leading to the folding front doors and senses a stirring on one of the wing-tipped chairs to his left. There is someone sprawled on it: an emaciated old man wearing thick lenses. He has streaky grey hair grown long, and his bony legs stick out from under a faded blanket and spread out on the two winged arms of the chair. Martin studies the man who is chewing on toothless gums, struggling to speak, but only managing a hollow cough. Recognition dawns even as he tries to shake it off. *This can't be... This shrunken bag of bones is not my father?*

"Martin?" the man croaks hesitantly.

"Dad?" Now he knows why in the twenty years that he has been away, he has never received a single photograph of Victor. Pity swells in him as he looks down at this man who was once the strong guy who would bicycle three hours each way, with an infected foot and all, to get a dog's head analysed by the lab.

Victor is reaching out with quivering talon-like hands and Martin drops his bag and rushes over. He takes his father's light frame in his arm and rocks him gently. "So nice to see you, Dad."

"Bullshit," Victor croaks in his ear and Martin catches the pungency of his father's breath—a combination of pyorrhoea, garlic and some kind of medication. "I've been waiting 'til you came. Now I can close my eyes."

Martin holds Victor at arm length. "Not yet. I just got here."

"And you damn well took your time."

"He's still full of shit, isn't he?" a voice says from behind. Martin turns and recognizes Aunty Mabel. Dressed in a faded floral dress and rubber slippers, she too has lost weight; her grey hair is tousled and there are missing teeth in her smile. She is wearing glasses that magnify her eyes disproportionately. She embraces Martin and then points towards Victor. "He has been talking only about you ever since we got your letter."

"Shut up, Mabel," Victor croaks. He turns to Martin and shrugs. "Women have always been the death of me. This one will see me to my grave."

"And feed you until you go." Mabel straightens Victor's blanket that is trailing on the floor. "Have you drunk your *thambili* water?"

Victor reaches for the half empty glass of milky white liquid. "No, I've had enough, thank you. Get some for our sonna boy here, will you?"

"Yes, yes, I will get. You rest. Don't get too excited now."

As she heads indoors she whispers to Martin. "Don't let him get agitated. He has coughing fits that are very hard to stop."

Martin pulls up a chair and sits next to his father.

"Have you brought the photographs?" Victor asks, sitting up.

Martin reaches inside his bag. "Yes, and I brought some others that I would like you to see as well."

He hands Victor pictures of Jamie, not the more recent ones after the boy had his ears pierced and had grown his hair out, but ones from the earlier concerts: dressed in a suit, playing the piano with style and confidence.

"Shah! What a nice looking boy. You have more recent pictures?"

"Er, no. I forgot to pack them. I'll mail you some. Here's another picture I want you to see." He hands Victor the sideways shot of the little girl unlocking her door and entering the house in Port Hope.

Victor looks intently at the picture and then up at Martin, waiting for the explanation.

"That's my daughter."

Victor moves his head up and down several times. "You never told me. Do you have other children I don't know about?"

"Her name is Julia."

"Julia... Julia..." Tears start pouring down the old man's face as he chews harder on his gums. Martin takes Victor's quivering hand. The photograph falls on the outspread blanket. "So we have our Julia, after all."

"Yes, Dad—we do."

Mabel interrupts by bringing Martin a tall glass of King Coconut water. "I'm serving lunch in about half an hour. You must be famished, no? Colin is in the back garden tending the vegetables. *Aney*, child, that's all our Colin does these days, gardening, gardening, gardening... Ah. I'll let you catch up with your father. Now, remember, don't get him too excited. I can see he is already starting with the waterworks."

"Don't worry, Aunty, I'll make sure." Despite his reassurances Martin is not confident that he can actually deliver on his promise. There is too much emotional ground to cover.

Victor shoos her off. "Go, go and get the lunch ready. And let me talk to my son in peace."

Martin downs half a glass of the refreshing cool liquid. He sits back in his chair and closes his eyes, letting the King Coconut water course through him, basking in memories it evokes.

"Why did you divorce your wife?" Victor's incisive and reedy voice interrupts his reverie.

"That was a long time ago, Dad."

"Yes, but you never told me why."

"It was mutual. We had reached the end of a road we both thought was going to be longer."

"I never believed in divorce."

"And you don't believe in same-sex unions, either."

Victor coughs. "Don't talk to me about that. I have tried, believe me. If we compromise everything we believe in, what will be left holding us together? Nothing. We will go bloody mad."

"Take a look at these pictures," Martin pulls out the more recent digital photographs that he has got printed soon after returning to Colombo from Galle. And he had them made in high gloss, extra large size, so that the old man can see clearly.

Victor fingers the pictures cautiously. Uncertainty crosses his face.

Martin explains, "He is giving sixty kids a new life, Dad. Without any church or government assistance. Something you and I cannot do and have never even attempted."

Victor lets the pictures fall on the blanket as he views them. The enthusiasm seems to be going out of him.

Martin presses on. "And how do I compare? My talented son is a dropout of his music program, and we worry whether he will even make it through high school. And I am so scared to face her that I have not spoken to Julia in my life. She does not even know who her father is, and if she does, I am sure she will be pretty disappointed in him."

Victor's cough increases and Mabel shouts from inside the house, "Victor, take it easy now!"

Martin picks up the fallen photographs. "I'm sorry, I had to put it to you this way, Dad. All Barney wants is for you to recognize him. In Canada, gay people—homosexuals—can even legally marry. It's a change of mindset that is needed here. Perhaps if people start accepting each other's differences there will be peace in this country."

Victor slumps back in his chair. He waits until his coughing eases. Martin remains silent too, not wanting to push the old man over the edge.

"There can be no peace in this country, until there is peace in our hearts." The words seem to come from a distance. Victor is uttering them staring at the ceiling. "There has been so much hurt in our lives, that it is very difficult to find peace. It is easier to hurt and to hate."

"Mum did not hate."

"Your mum was a saint."

"That is a cop-out, Dad. We both need to find that peace. Barney has already beaten us to it."

Mabel arrives on the verandah again. "It's time for lunch. Victor, you look like a wreck. No more deep discussions today, okay? Come along, let's eat."

Lunch is served in the large dining room with its intrusive grandfather clock ticking away as if it is counting down everyone's life. The teak and glass wall cabinet contains authentic Dutch crockery handed down through Uncle Colin's family line. Unlike the meagre pickings at the orphanage, Mabel has put on quite a spread: rice and beef curry, devilled potato, fried *watakulu* from the garden and okra in white coconut gravy; *seeni sambol* and mango chutney round off the offering. Mabel fusses to ensure that Martin fills his plate again every time he finishes his food. The servant woman keeps bringing more steaming plates from the kitchen.

Colin himself is in an ebullient mood. Unlike his wife, he has put on weight since retirement. "Not like the old days, son, when we were mustered at six in the morning and did not go home till after sundown, six days a week. Now, even with my gardening and all the walking up and down these hills, I still can't put down the weight."

"You are too bloody happy—that's what." Victor grumbles, chewing slowly and deliberately on a piece of meat, his lack of teeth not helping any.

Colin laughs and burps. "What to do? Must be happy in this place no? Otherwise we will all be dead. My children are doing well in Australia. Ten grandchildren also, and more on the way now that our youngest, Cecilia, has married." He turns to Martin and says, "Victor and I have had this argument several times. Must forgive, I say; it's easier on the heart. He keeps it all inside."

After lunch, Mabel shows Martin to the guest bedroom, next to his father's. Martin has planned on staying only a few days.

Victor takes his afternoon nap that lasts until 5:00 p.m., after which Martin accompanies him on a short walk around the property. The mist has come down from the mountains and the air is chill. Victor is bundled up in two sweaters and wears woollen pants. He walks very slowly, limping, and has to take frequent breaks.

"I can't handle the pollution in Colombo. That's where my lungs gave way."

That, and smoking. But Martin holds his tongue, content to let the old man ramble on, recalling old memories.

"What happened to your two friends Bandu and Christopher? I remember they went to Canada also, no?"

Martin tells him, and the old man shakes his head. 'It's karma. Your lives were bound to each other, no matter where you went. That's why I think I will be born with your mother in the next life too. The next time she will be the husband and I the wife, and she will make my life a misery. I deserve it."

They reach the boundary of the property and Victor has to rest, while Martin talks to Colin who is uprooting manioc on the fence line. "Tomorrow's lunch," Colin announces breezily, pulling out a new tuber.

On their way back to the house, Victor suddenly asks Martin, "And what will you do about Jamie?"

"The divorce hurt him. He was right in the middle of the national music championships and had to drop out. Couldn't get out of bed most mornings. We fought over how much custody each of us could have of him and that hurt him even more. I guess Ginny and I let him down."

"Do you see him?"

"Every other week. But that is not enough attention for me to give him. He sees a counsellor and a psychiatrist to help him deal with his issues. He is also a teenager, facing that age's problems. I guess he has a lot on his plate at the same time."

"I don't believe in psychiatrists."

"Me neither. But his mother does."

"And your daughter. Julia..."

"I meet her mother on the other side of real estate deals from time to time. But we maintain a professional, arms-length relationship. Marnie, Julia's mother, would like me to get back with her now that Ginny is out of the picture. She has let that slip on a number of occasions. I guess I am scared of screwing things up again."

"Hah. You people live complicated lives in Canada. I wonder what would have happened to our family if your mother and I had emigrated when you boys were small."

"The grass sure isn't greener on the other side."

"No. But it's dying over here."

Victor's prophetic statement rings through the following morning when they read the newspaper. The foreign minister, a well respected figure in the international community has been assassinated by a sniper outside his home in Colombo.

"That's the last straw in the peace process," Victor says glumly, discarding the paper. "Now there will be all-out war again."

Martin tries to bring some brevity to his father's pessimism. "But others have been assassinated before."

"We've had about two years of peace. But it was like the balm you pour over a wound to mask it. I told you, there is no peace in our hearts, son. That's where all wars start."

The following day, threats and incriminations on both sides of the ethnic conflict are reported in the newspaper. No one is claiming responsibility for the assassination.

At dinner the following evening, Colin has a profound observation to counter Victor's prattling on the state of the nation. "We have all got to recognize that this country now has a war-based economy. We have been fighting for over a generation and we have forgotten how to run a peace-time economy. How will one survive without kickbacks, influence peddling and backstabbing? No, we have to cut the bull and get on with surviving under these circumstances and forget about trying to return to peace. For example, how dare we blame only the Tigers for assassinating this minister? What about all the others fellows who profit from keeping this conflict going? The arms merchants, the religious zealots, the politicians—the list goes on."

They take regular walks each afternoon, father and son. It is a time for letting go, for sharing each other's trials in life, particularly for Martin, as he realizes there is a lot of stuff he has not shared with anyone. Victor points out various landmarks on their walks, as if all this unburdening bores him or makes him uncomfortable.

"See that fire over there," he points to a pall of white smoke drifting from the opposite mountain. "They are burning their garbage. In the dry season, it starts forest fires."

Another time, when Martin has just finished giving Victor the inside story on the failure of the Garibaldi deal, Victor suddenly jerks up and points to an outcrop of pine trees. "They are cutting down those trees now. Pine trees drink too much water, so people are ordered to cut them down. Bloody fools don't see we'll have even more drought then."

Martin wonders whether his father is trying to block out details of his eldest son's life in Canada and whether he does not to wish talk about events in the Frozen North anymore. On the last evening of Martin's stay, there is a spot of rain and they don raincoats and carry umbrellas.

"Are you sure you want to go out in this weather?" Martin asks.

"Wouldn't miss it for the world. Besides this rain is a fluke, we won't get any more for the rest of the year."

They walk to the southern edge of the property, Victor's favourite spot. There is a stone bench where they can sit and look out across the valley, at the nearby tea plantation that Colin once worked in.

"Best thing they did with those tea plantations—privatizing them. Governments should stick to governing. Even that they can't do very well." Victor says, blowing his nose into a handkerchief.

"Yes, I am impressed when I see statistics that say Sri Lanka has regained its number one spot in the world in tea."

Victor abruptly interrupts Martin's musings. "You had a company once, did you not? The one that was on the Internet? Tell me about it."

"Nothing much to tell. It went belly-up."

"Tell me anyway."

Martin looks askance at his father. Victor's rekindled curiosity in his fortunes piques him. "I thought you weren't much interested in my business dealings in Canada. You kept changing subjects on me."

"I am very interested. I feel your pain when you tell me about them. I was trying to make it better for you by showing you some distractions around this property. Tell me about your company. We don't have much time left together. It will be good for you to talk."

And so Martin talks. Taking his father from concept to closure of Jamestown.com, reliving the joy, the rush, the uncertainty and finally the pain of liquidation.

The thin drizzle has ceased by the time he finishes and the sun is coming out from behind low-hanging cloud. The trees droop under the burden of moisture; birds shake water from the branches as they resume their hunt for food.

Victor nods his head as Martin winds down his recounting. "I am so glad you came to see me. These walks have been a gift."

"It's helped get things off my chest too."

"You know, Martin, we are similar in many ways. We didn't learn how to cry. We only did so when it drove us crazy."

They rise from their wet perch and set off back for the house. "You know what you have left to do, don't you?" Victor says suddenly.

"There are moments when I think of returning back here, despite all its chaos. It would give me a chance to start with a clean slate."

"Bullshit!" Victor's explosion shocks Martin. The old man relapses into a bout of coughing and Martin thinks his father is about to collapse.

"Hey, we'd better get you inside." Martin takes Victor's arm and half carries him towards the house. Victor jerks, coughing uncontrollably.

"Lay me down here," Victor says weakly, pointing to a wingback chair when they near the verandah of the house.

Mabel comes out and surveys them with hands on her hips. "Why the devil did you go out in this rain, Victor? Do you want an early grave?"

"I'm sorry. He insisted on going out," Martin explains.

Victor raises his hand weakly at Mabel. "Leave me alone, Mabel, darling. I'm not going to my grave today. There are a few things I have to attend to yet."

She takes his off his raincoat and places a thick blanket over him.

Victor winks at Martin. "I told you your mother was a saint; here is another one."

"Oh, shush, Victor," Mabel says tucking him in warmly. "Now stay there. I'll bring you a warm cider." She goes indoors shaking her head.

"She's an angel," Victor says, chuckling, after his coughing has subsided. "Sent to a cruel old man in his last days."

"Maybe all that emotional talk was not a good idea."

"Maybe your thinking of coming back to Sri Lanka to live is *not* a good idea. Now you listen to me while I have the energy to talk. Do you know *why* I have not made my peace with Barney? It's not the homo thing, although I have my opinions about that too. It's because I'm bloody scared, that's why. I did nothing for that boy. I was already drinking like a fish when he was born. I only saw him scurry about the house whenever I was there, like a mouse, not a human. And it angered me when I saw him wet his pants every time I looked at him. And then you show me those pictures: he has made it, in spite of me. I am not bloody worthy to kiss his toes—that's *why*." Victor slumps back in his chair, exhausted.

Martin rises and paces the verandah. Mabel arrives with a mug of steaming cider and places it on the table beside Victor. She looks at both men and decides that she is better gone from there.

When they are alone again, Victor sips his cider. "That business about returning here— that is just a dream, like my dream to immigrate to Canada. 'The grass is always greener' stuff. You have two beautiful kids whom you've got to raise, and I don't care how screwed up they are, you still got to raise them and be a part of their lives, the lives they will make for themselves in this world. So don't you end up like me, scared to face the son I abandoned."

Victor places his cup on the table and leans back in the chair. "I'm tired and I need another nap. Come and wake me when it's dinner time."

26. **Suicide Bombers**

Dear Barney,
I did my best with the old man. Victor is a stubborn mule, and scared too. One thing:
he respects what you have done and feels unworthy due to his neglect of you while you
were growing up. I have given him your address. Now it's his turn to reach out. My
stay with him was pleasant, though emotionally draining for we dredged up a lot of old
stuff.
I leave Haputale for Colombo today, and my flight departs for Canada in
two days.
I am enclosing e-mail addresses, postal addresses, phone numbers, fax
numbers etc., for you to find me in Canada. Please call me collect, if you have to, the
moment Dad gets in touch with you. This is very important to me and one of the main
reasons why I came to Sri Lanka.
All the very best to you and Sena in your heroic attempts to give those
children a chance in life.
I am proud of you!
Martin

Martin places a stamp on the letter and drops it in the old red colonial mailbox in town and heads for the bus station.

The pull of home is strong in Sri Lanka, especially when looking and walking among surroundings that are familiar: crowds in the bus station, the bullock cart pulling a load of cement and being steered by an emaciated ebony skinned carter wearing a white turban, the man making tea outside his little *the-kade,* streaming the steaming brew from one glass to another like a juggler. And yet, Victor has given him some inescapable facts to ponder. What would be good is a gigantic blow that will render choice useless and push him in only one direction, the right one.

He has been told that he could get a seat on the mid-day bus. He has toyed with hiring a car to drive back to Colombo, but nixed the idea: this is going to be his last bus ride in Sri Lanka for a long while, so why not enjoy it?

The passenger next to him in the window seat is in his sixties, with long grey hair; he wears a thin black tie over a white shirt, the pocket of which is lined with fountain pens. He keeps screwing his features every time he looks up from the thick wad of papers on his lap, as if trying to balance the heavy lenses on his nose. Martin nods politely and takes a seat next to the man, hoping that he will not be disturbed during the ride.

The passenger in front of him however, looks like she will not let him sleep in peace. She is about five years old, standing on the seat and looking back at him: dark curls framing a round face, long earrings dangling, kohl accentuating eyebrows, giving shade to her sparkling eyes. She is bouncing on her seat beside a woman who must be her mother, a woman in a sari, who looks too young for motherhood and is trying valiantly to get the child to settle down. The girl keeps waving a lollipop in Martin's face.

"Ah, the ebullience of youth," the grey haired man on Martin's left says, raising his head from his papers and screwing up his face again as he observes the little girl.

Martin smiles. "Refreshing in a land of conflict, isn't it?"

"Are you a tourist here?" the man asks.

"No. Visiting my family after many years."

"From Australia?"

"Canada."

"Ah. Nice country. I went there on a study exchange once. My sister lives in Vancouver."

"I see." Martin realizes that between the man and the little girl he is going to be kept awake for the trip.

Just as the bus is about to pull out, a young woman in her early twenties, who has been hesitating at the bus stop, jumps on board, and receives a rude telling-off from the conductor. She pulls herself slowly down the gyrating bus and sits across from Martin on the right side of the aisle. She is dressed in a long loose dress, a thin sweater thrown over, and carries a heavy knapsack which she stows under the seat. Martin smiles at her, but she looks down instantly. She is tired and pre-occupied. From her dark complexion, white pottu and short oily haircut like a boy's, Martin makes her out to be Tamil. He idly wonders how long it will be before the bouncing five-year-old in the seat in front will end up cowed and beaten by life like this young woman.

"Professor Achibald Silva." The grey haired man extends a bony hand. "And you are?"

"Martin James."

"Burgher?"

"Uh huh."

"Not many of them left. First, we drove them out with the language issue, now this civil war has put the lid on it."

"I guess that's one way of describing it. You can add Standardization, Nationalization, Catholic Action, the '71 Insurrection, and a few others to your list of drivers."

"Yes, yes we are good at marginalizing people. In fact, that is the subject of my dissertation," Prof. Silva says pointing at his jumble of papers.

"Marginalization is your subject?"

"No—suicide bombers."

Martin leans over. This man is beginning to sound interesting. "What do you mean?"

Prof. Silva puffs his chest and launches into his theory with authority. "I have studied these cases extensively. Suicide bombing is now an integral part of our culture. We lead the world in it."

Martin sighs. "And I thought we led the world in tea."

Prof. Silva smiles. "I wish it had only been in tea."

"But there are suicide bombers everywhere. Those guys who blew up the towers in America were promised virgins in heaven."

"Ours is a unique conditioning. Children, usually orphans, are plucked from refugee camps and 'prepared' in jungles under a leader. The leader shuts them away from all human contact and demands absolute obedience. This is an extreme form of marginalization. When the children are in their late teens, they know no other life but obedience to this leader. Disobedience results in shame and ostracism from the tribe."

"Is that when they get their orders to kill?"

"Precisely."

"And why are you writing this paper now? Isn't this a hackneyed subject that hit its peak after 9/11?"

"My theory is that we are going to see a spate of these bombings again, now that our ceasefire is in tatters."

"Very reassuring."

"Yes. I am preparing a profile of how one could identify a suicide bomber. This will be a benefit to our security forces."

"I see." *I'm sure they have plenty of profiles already.* Martin is beginning to lose interest the more Prof. Silva gets fired up on his subject. "Just to reassure me, did you see any suicide bomber types board this bus?"

Prof. Silva screws up his face, looking to see if he is being played the fool. When re-assured that Martin is serious, he looks around. "I don't see any on cursory inspection. You see it in their eyes—they are dead eyes, without expression. The suicide bomber is dead long before he, or she, kills others."

Martin suppresses a shiver. "Thanks for letting me know. I'll keep a lookout." He slumps back in his seat and closes his eyes, signalling that he wants some peace. The professor returns to his papers. The child in front is now on her mother's lap singing a song. Martin glances to his right: the young girl is reading what resembles a prayer book. She senses his glance and looks up momentarily. She looks distracted, far away; there is no life in her gaze. *She has dead eyes.* A chill runs down Martin's spine. He tries to shrug off his misgiving.

Bandu had been a suicide bomber of a kind, Martin rationalizes. In his friend's case, everything he had possessed was deliberately taken away from him before he turned into a killing machine without concern for his own life. Christo was a suicide bomber of sorts too, when he shot Maha in the open without any consideration for the consequences. And those 60 children in the orphanage under the care of a charismatic leader like his brother, whom they would literally die for; do they fit the profiles of future suicide bombers? *Are all marginalized people potential suicide bombers? Am I one?* He has difficulty with Prof. Silva's narrow definition of the model. And yet he cannot shrug off the feeling of impending doom when he glances over at the young woman with dead eyes sitting across the aisle from him.

The rocking bus must have put him to sleep. He is trying to board a flight, rushing through the airport, but they have closed the gate, and a little girl with kohl on her eyebrows and a key around her neck is waving to him from a window in the plane. He is chasing the aircraft down the tarmac but it explodes at the point of take off and he falls on his knees and wails, "Why did I leave it so late?"

He is jolted awake as the bus hits a bump. Next to him, Prof. Silva swears under his breath as his papers spill on the floor. "Potholes," the older man says and bends to pick them up, bumping his head against the seat in front. The little girl is asleep on her mother's lap; the mother has fallen into an exhausted sleep too, both their heads rocking in unison. The young woman on his right has her eyes closed, but a nervous tic plays over her left eye. *She is awake.*

"You see, my dilemma is this," Prof. Silva says, now that his companion is awake. "What solution do I give the forces even if I help them to identify a suicide bomber? The moment one of them is stopped at a checkpoint, everyone gets blown to bits, because the bomber never turns back. Failure is not an option for them."

Martin ignores his companion and his problem and focuses his attention on the little girl, who has woken up and is back at her perch staring at him. The kohl in her eyes has become smudged with sleep. She is not in her bouncy mood, being still half asleep. Martin hunts in his shoulder bag and finds a piece of candy, a remnant of the stash he bought over from Canada. He holds it out to the girl. Her eyes widen. She looks at her mother then quickly grabs the offering, a hushed "thank you" in Tamil coming from her lips. Martin wonders if Julia was like this when she was five years old. Somehow, he has missed all that growing up; an experience never to be re-captured. He realizes why he is so uneasy. Something tells him that he will not leave this bus. That he has missed the opportunity for fixing things back home. The aircraft dream was telling him that. He has to get off this bus.

"Where are we?" he asks Prof. Silva.

"Nearing Kollonawa. Very soon we will be in Borella."

"Kollonawa? The big hydro station, right?" They are entering the outskirts of Colombo.

"Yes. And we will have to get off at the checkpoint soon," Prof. Silva says sliding his untidy papers into a briefcase that he fishes out from under his seat.

As if in answer to the professor's statement, the bus begins to slow down.

"They check ID and bags and things, sometimes on a random basis, sometimes on all vehicles—it depends on their mood. After the foreign minister's assassination I don't know how they will be reacting. You should be all right if you show them your Canadian passport." Prof. Silva seems accustomed to these inconveniences. "This is also now part of our culture—checkpoints."

Martin swallows hard and tries to remain calm, but he feels the sweat trickling down the sides of his arms.

"Main thing is to keep calm. They shoot people who try to run," Prof. Silva says.

The bus takes an eternity to get to the checkpoint, and Martin figures today is a check-all-vehicles day.

He decides to face his fear and confront the young woman, even though he is pretty sure that she does not speak English or Sinhala. He tries Sinhala first and is surprised when she answers him in accented English.

"I am going back to my novitiate in Colombo," she says in answer to his question. "I was attending my mother's funeral in Haputale."

Martin exhales. He feels like an idiot. A paranoid idiot. An English-speaking nun-to-be. Certainly not the profile of a suicide bomber. He has let himself get into a funk, when all he had to do was to simply talk to another human being. He lets the relief wash over him as the bus keeps inching forward. "I'm sorry to hear about your mother," he says more ebulliently than he should.

Now he can relax, let the damn bus take as long as it needs to get past this checkpoint.

A soldier gets on board and walks down the aisle ordering the passengers to disembark, from the front door only. When the man gets to the row ahead of Martin, he blocks the aisle.

"Stop!" he orders, as Martin begins to rise.

"They don't want to crowd the checkpoint," Prof. Silva whispers.

The woman in front sighs and asks the soldier if she can leave the child on board while she goes through the checks. Her Sinhala is Tamil accented. The soldier nods with a bored expression. The woman kisses the child, mutters something in her ear, and props her up on the seat. She then takes her bag and with a quick look at the child, follows the rest of the disembarking passengers. The child immediately stands up and sticks her hand out at Martin. He shrugs, looks at the soldier, and reaches inside his bag.

"No bag!" the soldier's gun falls heavily across Martin's knuckles making him squirm in pain. The child screams in fear. The young novice reaches out across the aisle and pats the sobbing child.

"I was only searching for a bar of candy," Martin shouts at the soldier in Sinhala.

The man is surprised at this "foreigner" speaking the local language, but continues with his reprimand, "No bags are to be touched," in a softer tone this time.

"They are very scared and nervous," Prof. Silva explains. "Don't do anything suspicious."

"Take your seat," the soldier orders the novice. She carries the child back to her own seat, places the little girl on her lap, and talks to her gently in Tamil.

The bus inches closer to the checkpoint and Martin sees the tail-end of the line-up of travellers waiting to get their ID and belongings checked. The child's mother, in her red sari draped in the style that widows use to cover their midriff, is lurching forward with her heavy bag in hand.

Martin turns to the nun-to-be. "What is the girl's name?"

"Kamini."

"Does she have any brothers or sisters?"

The novice talks to the girl in Tamil. Kamini shakes her head several times.

The novice says, "She does not know her family. I think she is an orphan. She is travelling with that woman, who she says is an aunt."

The soldier interrupts by ordering the rest of the passengers to disembark.

As he rises, Martin sees the woman in the red sari, Kamini's aunt, talking to a soldier, as another soldier roughly tugs at the bag in her hand.

Then the world explodes.

There is a ringing in his ears and a body is pressing down on him, smelling of sweat, fear and blood. Martin is having difficulty breathing as all he can inhale is smoke, acrid cordite that burns his nostrils. He pushes the body away from him and gropes towards the light on his right. It is a window ringed with shards of glass that cut him. He sticks his head out and a cleaner burst of air fills his lungs. He stays there until the ringing is partially replaced by moans, screams and sounds of rushing, panicked people.

The smoke clears and he sees bystanders on the street taking pictures with video cameras, cell phones, camcorders and any other photographic device available. Some of the onlookers are staring at him, others are pointing to a spot just out of his sight. He gets his bearings: he is staring out of one of the bus' windows. Then he remembers the explosion; it went off on the other side of the vehicle. He slides back into the bus. The last of the passengers are scrambling towards the door in the thinning smoke. He has lost sight of the novice, Kamini and Prof. Silva. The soldier lies on the aisle, groaning, his back a mess of splintered glass and round holes seeping with blood; he has taken the bulk of the explosion for all of them. Martin grabs the soldier by his feet and pulls him towards the door, but his own feet have no life left in them. He tries again. After several attempts he makes it to the door. He calls for help but no one responds. Ambulances are blaring sirens.

He stumbles down the steps and his knees give way at the bottom. "There is a man who needs help in there," he gasps. Still no response. "A soldier," he shouts at the top of his lungs. Then someone pays attention and two policemen enter the bus cautiously.

The novice is by his side, helping him to stand up. With her help, he rises, and the strength slowly returns to his legs. "Where is Kamini?"

"She is okay. You and the soldier blocked us from the blast. She is being checked in the ambulance."

"And the professor? The man sitting next to me?"

"I don't know. But there are many people being treated at a portable unit down the road."

Martin checks himself. The ringing in his ears is ceasing. He has surface cuts on his neck and arms, and his back is stiff. But he is okay and decides that he does not need medical treatment.

"Walk this way," the novice says, still holding his hand. And he sees why. The road between the obliterated checkpoint and the bus is strewn with blood, body parts, mangled machinery, a bloody boot, an exploded sand bag with its contents mingling with oil, blood, grease and garbage. Strands of a red sari are scattered over the debris. The bile rises in him and he retches involuntarily. The novice holds his forehead as he vomits. He thinks she is an angel sent to him from heaven.

"Thank you," he says as he lets her lead him toward a police barricade, with ambulances lined up beside it. Volunteers are running, bearing stretchers and mangled bodies. He realizes that he cannot get back to the bus even though his camera and all the photographs taken on this trip are still inside.

The novice leaves him momentarily; when she returns, she is leading Kamini by the hand. She speaks in English so that the child will not understand. "Kamini does not need to know the truth. I have told her that her aunt died in the explosion. She is used to losing family members. We all are."

Martin embraces Kamini. She is rigid with fright, but after a few moments she starts to tremble. Then she begins to cry. He holds her until her crying trails off. He fishes in his wallet and pulls out all his cash, local and Canadian. "Here, take this," he says to the novice. "And look after this child."

The novice shakes her head. "It's okay. I will take her to the novitiate with me. We will try to find her a home."

He gets her to accept some money. "Here's my card. Let me know if there is anything you need to help her, okay?"

She takes the card. "Thank you. And God Bless you."

She puts her arms around the child and they retreat behind the barricade, waving briefly to him.

"Wait, I don't even know your name," he calls after her. But they are gone amidst the babble of voices, sirens, loudspeakers and onlookers.

He staggers away, limping, leaving this site of death. No one notices him; after all, he is one of the survivors. Everyone who walks these streets is a survivor of a harsh life. Only the dead warrant any attention; and then too only until they are buried, forgotten, and replaced by others. His romantic illusions of ever returning to Sri Lanka are buried in that bus. He has been waiting for a push, and has received a kick. He knows now what he must do. Victor was right.

As he clears the barricades, he sees a man with his head in a bandage sitting in a bus shelter, clutching a battered briefcase.

"Prof. Silva..."

The man's eyes light up. "I forgot to put it in my thesis: the use of decoys and diversions. I have it now." He looks triumphant; as if the mortality strewn around him is inconsequential, because he, Professor Archibald Silva, has found another nugget for his research. He is even oblivious to his own injuries.

Martin passes the professor and makes for the main road. Trishaws descend like mosquitoes. He gets into one.

"Where to, sir?" the driver asks.

"Home," he says and slumps back in the seat.

27. **Atonement**

Martin stands outside the house in Port Hope. A brook runs behind the shaded garden at the back where several children are playing. A sugar maple in the front yard is trying to turn colour even though this is the first week of September. He rings the front door bell. It is Saturday and Marnie's car is in the driveway. He checks the gift box in his hand for the fifth time.

The door swings open and Marnie is standing there dressed in a V-necked halter top, shorts and sandals. Desire wells in him as he sees her so revealingly dressed even though the hot summer is beginning to slip. He tries to suppress his blush. She holds onto the door, a smile on her face. She has slimmed down over the years but is still attractive, the go-getter in her matured to a quiet determination; the only sign of aging are the crow's feet hovering at the corners of her eyes.

"So you've finally decided to make an appearance," she says.

He nods. He has a lump in his throat and just wants to step inside. She holds the door wide for him. He passes her, absorbing the faint whiff of shampoo in her hair.

"Julia is playing with her friends. I'll get her."

"Not yet," he says, standing in the living room, one that he is unaccustomed to, a feminine living room, with dolls and girls colouring books and pincushions and multi-hued paintings of stick people and school portraits of Julia.

"Have a seat then. I heard you had quite a trip to Sri Lanka. Can I get you a cup of tea?"

"Yes, that would be fine, thanks."

She comes up to him and frowns when she sees the scars on his neck and arms. "You've been in the wars?"

"You could say that." The scent of her hair, the warmth of her smile draws him in and he resists cradling her in his arms. He realizes why she is so desirable. She has never held herself back from him. It was he who has withdrawn, for various reasons, like Ginny had withdrawn from him. He curbs his desire by sheer will power and walks away from her, not wanting it to show in his face. *Not yet, not yet. I want to get this right.*

He places the gift box on the sofa and sits on the other end of it, studying the room further, trying to get a sense of the people who inhabit it, people whose lives he had abandoned ten years ago. Marnie puts on a CD and goes into the kitchenette to make the tea. Barry Manilow sings.

He sees a bible and some religious magazines on the coffee table within reach. He picks up the black book.

"I didn't know you had gone all religious," he says, trying to sound playful.

"My mother took me back to church. She found God in a big way after she was diagnosed."

He remembers his ex mother-in-law. "Funny things happen to people when they are diagnosed. And you...did you find God?"

"I'm still seeking, but going to church and spending some time with that person called 'Me' was very revealing."

He places the bible reluctantly back on the table. "I envy you. My religious teachers were a bunch of perverts. I guess I fell by the way."

"It's not the humans claiming to interpret the message that matters, but the message itself."

He decides to switch subjects before he gets in too deep. "How did you know about my adventures in Sri Lanka?"

"The real estate community is incestuous in small towns."

"So everyone knows who everyone else is sleeping with?"

"Pretty much."

"Who am I supposed to be sleeping with?"

"No one knows yet."

"I'm surprised that an attractive woman like you does not have a steady man in her life."

"When you have drunk a good vintage, it is hard to be satisfied with cheap table wine."

He chuckles. "I've been thinking of inviting you and Julia over to my place some time."

"You haven't met her yet. She may not like you," Marnie says.

He gulps. That is true; he has assumed too much. Julia may hate him, and that would blow his visualizing of this auspicious moment to pieces.

"What have you told her about me?"

"I've told her that she has a father, whom she will meet one day."

"And has she asked you why this father has been avoiding her all these years?"

"Yes, she has. And I have said that he has been asleep. And that when he wakes up, he will give her his full attention. Like the fairy tale, *The Sleeping Prince.*"

He gets up and goes into the kitchen. "You told her that?"

She looks up from pouring the tea. "No. I have asked her to be patient, and that one day you will appear. Girls of this age are used to having absentee parents. It's no longer an anomaly. But I will never forgive you if you leave her this time."

The back door opens and four screaming girls dash in and head down the steps to the basement.

"It's time for the day's re-run of *The Gilmore Girls.*" Marnie shrugs. "You'd better get used to girls' TV programs." She hands him a steaming mug of tea. "If I remember right, you used to take one sugar and bit of milk, right?"

"Right."

Another girl comes inside from the backyard, laden with Hula-hoops and Frisbees. Martin sucks in his breath when he recognizes Julia.

"Honey," Marnie turns to the girl. "Before you go downstairs, come here for a moment."

"But I'll be late for my show, Mom." Julia says, stashing the toys in a corner of the living room.

"There is someone I'd like you to meet."

Julia catches sight of Martin for the first time. She has my chin, he realizes, and the way she tosses back her head.

"This is your father, Julia," Marnie says in a soft voice.

Julia stares at him. She puts her hands behind her back and assumes a pose one takes in front of the principal. There is a long silence, interminable to Martin, punctuated only by the creak of the floorboards as she rocks absently on her feet. Then she tosses her hair back again. "I thought you would be taller," she says in a small, measured voice.

Martin gropes for the right words to say. He looks towards Marnie for help, but she is letting him fight this one alone. *Serves me damn right too.*

"Hi Julia," he finally croaks. "I... I brought you something." He staggers out into the living room for the gift, as if in search of a prop.

Behind him he hears Marnie saying, "We are going to have to manage him carefully, honey, in case he gets scared and runs away again."

When he returns, the gift extended in his hand, Marnie has her arm over Julia's shoulder. "I'll take the gift for now, Martin. I think your daughter would like to talk to you first."

He struggles for words. "There is no excuse...for my absence."

Julia remains silent. She looks confused.

"I'm sorry," Martin says again. "I'm really, really sorry."

That's when he breaks down and goes on his knees in front of this 10-year-old and asks her to forgive him, declaiming once again that there is no excuse for his absence and that he would like to spend the rest of his days involved in her life. There is no coherence to his words, they just stream out amidst his tears, and Julia looks at him with wide-open eyes, tears lurking on the sides, nodding for lack of words. Marnie too is now sobbing behind him, while in the hall, Manilow sings the remix of *I'm Your Man* with no one listening.

Finally, Julia takes the situation in control. "You're quite pathetic," she says. "I thought my father would be a strong man."

"He is strong, honey," Marnie advises, wiping her eyes with a tissue. "It takes a strong man to cry."

Julia extends her arms to Martin. "If I give you a hug, like Mom does to me, will you stop crying?"

Martin scoops her up in his arms and they embrace. She is open and warm in his arms, defenceless, and it shames him that he has not let her be a part of his life all these years. He knows that he will never let her go now.

Martin and Julia move into the living room and sit on the couch, while Marnie disappears into her bedroom. Julia brings him a box of tissues and he wipes his tears. She watches concernedly as he blows his nose.

"Why do you cry so much?" Julia asks.

Martin laughs between snorting. "My dad said that I did not cry enough. You've given me a reason to catch up."

There are so many questions to answer, so many holes to fill. He tells her about his life in Canada for starters. Julia's eyes open wide every time he gives her a new piece of information.

"How did you meet Mom?"

"We worked together."

"Why didn't you marry her?"

"I was married already."

She chews on this information, looking down at the beige carpet. He feels good for laying this information on the line. It lightens his heart. After a few seconds of contemplation, Julia nods. "My friend Cecilia's dad and mom were like that. But they got married in the end."

He talks about Jamie, leaving Ginny out as best as he can.

"I've got an older brother? Gee, that's cool."

"Sure. I didn't think older brothers would be interesting to you. Guess I've got a lot to learn."

"Is he handsome? Or is he a real jerk, like Sandy's brother?"

"Well, he plays the piano and the guitar."

"Cool! That's really cool."

He is still talking to Julia with his tea long gone cold, when her four friends come upstairs again.

"What happened to you?" the blonde short one who seems to be the ring leader, says. "The show's over. Logan's becoming a bigger and bigger jerk."

Julia reaches out and takes Martin's hand. "This is my father. And Sandy, I've got a cool brother who plays piano and guitar."

The friends display looks of surprise, envy and shock, and start to edge in embarrassment toward the door when Marnie comes out of her bedroom, freshened and dressed in pants and blouse, and suggests that it would be better if they come back later in the afternoon as Julia is dealing with a lot of new information and needs time to soak it all in.

Marnie asks Martin if he will stay for lunch and he accepts the invitation gratefully.

"It's not anything special. Spaghetti and meatballs. And I'll throw in a garden salad," she says.

"I was in Sri Lanka recently—remember? This is a welcome break from curries."

"Tell me about Sri Lanka," Julia says. She is smiling now and more comfortable in his presence.

Martin exhales and the lump in his throat is all but gone. "We'll have to set aside a few days for that. Even Jamie has not heard all the stories. I'll promise to have several fireside chats with you and your brother this winter, and tell you both about my life back there. There are many stories to tell. But they need to be told slowly."

After lunch they open her gift. Martin is nervous, thinking that he has chosen incorrectly despite the research he has done. Julia is thrilled with the Barbie video game and console, and the DVD series of the Olson Twins.

Marnie nods neutrally. "You are learning fast, Martin James, but you still have a way to go. I'll have to check to make sure you don't spoil her. I would prefer you buy her outdoor games in future. Kids don't get much exercise these days."

"I'll make a note of that in my how-to-raise-young-girls scrapbook," he replies.

Before he knows it, it is four o'clock and Julia's friends are back, curious as ever to find out all the news about this dark stranger who has crossed their friend's threshold. As Julia goes downstairs to proudly display her gifts and talk about "Dad," Martin takes the opportunity to make his exit.

"This has been one of the happiest days of my life, Marnie," he says standing in the doorway. "Thank you, for your patience."

"Thanks for coming. I'm sure it took some courage." There is a question in her eyes and he knows he has to address it.

"I've got to take this slow. I've just moved into Julia's life. I'm not going to rush back into yours. I can't screw it up again."

A look of mild disappointment crosses her face very briefly. "I understand. I feel the same way. But don't test my patience again."

"You have raised a great daughter. You deserve all the credit."

She cocks a wise eye. "You're going through the honeymoon stage with her right now. Make sure you're there for her during her tough times. And she does have bad days."

He leans over and kisses Marnie on the cheek and she closes her eyes. "I will be there, I promise. Thank you again," he whispers in her ear.

Then he turns and walks out to his car before he does anything foolish.

Politicians suspected in scam to divert tsunami aid into offshore accounts, the headline of a tucked-away article on Sri Lanka in the local newspaper proclaims. Not many will read it here in Canada, given its obscure positioning amidst advertisements for luxury cars and new condominiums. Not many will care. Martin sighs and finishes his coffee. *Same old rackets—bigger stakes these days.*

It's time to go to the railway station to pick up Jamie. It is Martin's weekend with his son, the first since his return from Sri Lanka, as the boy has been vacationing with his mother and grandmother in PEI over the summer. This weekend is special.

His second-hand Honda—a trade-down after the lease on the Lexus had run out—chugs through the sleepy streets of the small town on Lake Ontario east of Oshawa; a place once relegated to retirees, farmers and derelicts, until city professionals discovered it a few years ago and the ninety-minute commute got embedded into the national psyche. Martin is glad that he was able to buy this tiny bungalow before prices skyrocketed. This is all he has left now. The old Honda has only enough oomph to ferry clients around the county to view houses and to transport him on the 45-minute monthly excursion to the municipal park in Pickering for his ritualized commune with his mother.

The VIA train glides into the station; the lonely chime of its bell reminds him of temple bells in Sri Lanka. Dishevelled passengers disembark: office workers from downtown Toronto, the well-heeled ones—consultants, bankers and software engineers—the ones who endure working in the Big Smoke so that they can enjoy their weekends in the country.

Jamie has his suitcase in one hand, and a guitar strapped over his back. He never comes to visit his father without at least one musical instrument, as Martin has none in the house—well, until now. Sixteen, Jamie wears his customary frown, something he developed soon after his parents separated. Martin winces at the earring in the lad's ear. *For all my youthful angst, I never pierced my body.* But times are different now, he accepts. Two years of counselling has still not cured the angry kid. *Well, it's going to end soon, and this time I'm doing it my way.*

Martin swallows a welling of emotion as his son walks over to the car, gazing upon the long hair falling over the boy's eyes, his 6'2" height that has already made Martin "the short old-man," and the designer-label clothes that Jamie got used to at a young age.

Jamie tosses his bag into the trunk. "I'll keep the guitar with me," he says, getting into the back seat.

"What's bugging you?" Martin asks casually, pulling out of the station and heading for the waterfront to take the coast road home.

"School. And Mum."

"Quite a load. Care to talk about them? One at a time?"

"It's the same crap. Mum wants me to sign up for business studies in grade twelve. Grandma's encouraging her, of course."

"And you want to pursue…a music career, perhaps?"

"How did you guess? Don't be cute, Dad. I want to play in a rock band. How many times do I have to say it to you guys?"

"Perhaps you'll feel better when you get home," Martin says. The road curves inland and there is construction to navigate, a new subdivision coming up, bungalows. Jamie strums his guitar in the back, a mellow Elvis Presley tune from the sixties.

"That song came out way before you were born," Martin says, surprised at the choice.

"And you used to hum it in the bathroom all the time. I looked it up online."

The song, *I can't help falling in love with you*, is comforting. It reassures Martin that things are yet familiar in a changing world.

At home, Jamie takes his bag down to the basement, his room whenever he visits. Martin waits for the exclamation. Instead, he hears Jamie running back up the stairs, excitement, shock and that youthful vibrancy back on his face. "Dad, are you crazy? They're Boses, man. I mean, that's top of the line!"

"You are going to need the best," Martin says.

"You bought that...for me?"

"Yes. You are not a two-bit rock star. If that's what you choose to be, then you might as well be THE rock star."

"But...but..."

"There are no 'buts' anymore, Jamie. I'm tired of psychiatrists, counsellors and other bull-shitters who grab your money and coax you to 'find yourself,' but not too fast, because they don't want their revenue streams to dry up. You were born a musical prodigy, in case you forgot.

Just because you missed a national championship doesn't mean that you don't have it *in* you."

"I don't have any formal qualifications. I dropped out of music lessons entirely after that, in case you don't remember, Dad."

"Formal qualifications be damned! That's what your mother, grandmother and uncle put into your head. You have music in your blood. You never come up here without your guitar and your songs are nostalgic yearnings. Listen up, buddy, I don't have a lot of money, but I just made the biggest damned investment in my life. In *you*."

Jamie bows his head as if burdened.

Martin closes in."What happened between your mother and me has nothing to do with you. Don't hide behind that event as a cop-out. I hid behind booze, and so did my father before me, just like your mother hides behind counsellors and anti-depressants, and now wants you to do the same. They're all nothing but cop-outs, band-aids, props, call them what you like. So you missed a national championship—so bloody what?"

"What do you want me to do?" Jamie is shouting back now, the anger a form of release for the scolding he is receiving.

"I want you to follow your star, even if it leads you to penury."

Jamie puts his hands up. "Okay, okay. I've had enough of this lecture." He goes downstairs again.

Martin gives him five minutes and follows. Jamie is seated at the new keyboard, loaded and programmed with every possible instrument and beat; the synthesizer; the giant speakers. He glides his hands over the keys and the room fills with deep sound. In moments, he is lost to the world, rolling out a jumble of Beethoven, Hendrix and Nirvana. Martin sits on the couch and closes his eyes; the familiar sound of Jamie's old room in Pickering has returned. It's time to let his son reconnect with his lost past.

That evening, after a dinner of rice and curry, which he has become adept at cooking, and which Jamie perspiringly relishes, Martin retires to the outside deck. Jamie is still experimenting with his new musical equipment. Elegant strains punctuate the air, interspersed with sounds that Martin has never heard before. He takes a deep breath and feels content.

He cannot see the lake from here, but he can make out the dark buildings rising up between his property and the water, soon to shut the waterfront completely from view—giant luxury condos. When Jamie had asked him at dinner how business was, Martin had pointed to those works-in-progress. "This is where the puck is going to land, buddy. All those buildings, being snapped up by people escaping the city. Immigrants from the class of the eighties, established and looking to move. I'm their man, a guy like them. I speak their language."

"Mum's right in calling you the 'Ulysses Man'. You keep coming back."

Martin threw his head back and laughed, loudly. "And my mum would have called it resilience. She told me that there was no other choice but to come back."

There is a sound on the deck and Martin realizes that the music has stopped playing in the basement. Jamie is surveying him in the dark.

"How's the equipment?" Martin asks.

"It's great, Dad. You must have spent a long time shopping for the right pieces and setting them up."

"I bought them online. It was a piece of cake to source and install."

"Wasn't that what Jamestown.com was supposed to be about?"

"Yes sir, it was. But we were ahead of the puck there, I guess."

"I really like the system, Dad. It's fantastic. Thanks!"

"Good. Sit down. There is something else I want to tell you."

Jamie sits on the balustrade of the deck and waits patiently.

"You have a sister."

Silence.

"She's ten years old. And she is beautiful."

"Does Mom know?"

"Yes."

"Is she Sri Lankan? A Burgher?"

"She is just like you. And she is looking forward to meeting you. Julia thinks that having an older brother is cool."

Jamie remains silent in the dark. Then he laughs nervously. "I think having a sister is pretty cool too."

"I know. I found my missing brother Barney in Sri Lanka recently. It's a great feeling."

"Are you, and your brother, the last of the Burghers in your family line then, Dad?"

Martin ponders this one. "It's hard to say. In a sense, you are a Burgher too. So is Julia. I think the line lives on, enriching other cultures."

Jamie rises to go indoors again. "It's been a great day for me, Dad. Thanks. I got two gifts today. I'm not used to having so much all at once."

28. **Homecoming**

The man, dressed in a faded blue sweatshirt, jeans and sneakers, and carrying a khaki knapsack, pauses and squints against the glare of an early fall afternoon. Leaves sweep against the neo-classical columns of the facade he has just come through. A Canadian flag blows forlornly in the dying wind from the bell tower above his head. He looks undecided, craning his neck from side to side. A vehicle bearing the insignia of the Ministry of Correctional Services turns off the road and heads through the gates beneath the facade that the man has just come through. The man steps quickly aside from the path of the vehicle, as if he wants nothing more to do with that institution.

Martin gets out of the Honda parked across the road and waves. The man hesitates, looks hard at Martin and holds his ground.

"Christo, it's me, Martin."

The man breaks into a relieved smile and hurries over. They meet in the middle of the road and embrace. Martin smells Christo's cheap aftershave and carbolic soap. A scar runs from his ear and disappears into his long grey hair.

"Thank you for coming." Christo's voice is measured, cautious as he surveys Martin from head to foot. He nods several times as he talks. They move off the road and walk towards the Honda as a motorist impatiently toots his horn. Christo pushes Martin along, as if scared that he will be locked up again for another offence.

"I'm glad you called," Martin says.

"I have nowhere to go. I thought you might be able to help."

"I came to take you to my place. I live about ninety minutes from here."

Christo's eyes immediately hood over. "No...no...that would not be okay. Your family..."

"You are part of my family too. I've been gathering members of my lost tribe these last few months."

"But... I'm a killer."

"I think they called it manslaughter. And you've paid your dues. Come on, get in the car. The family is waiting to meet you."

Christo stands by the passenger door, reluctant to get in, clutching his knapsack in both hands. "Martin, this is too soon."

Martin leans over. "What would you rather have me do? Drive you to a whorehouse and let you get it off after all these years? Or would you prefer a bar to drown your sorrows in?"

Christo leans forward and grabs Martin's hand. "No, it's not that. Getting out after five years is so sudden. I didn't think it would be like this. Shit, I'm still getting used to breathing the air on the outside."

"Well how about a barbecue and some human company?"

Christo pauses. After a long minute, he cautiously opens the passenger door. "I guess that sounds okay."

"May I smoke?" he asks as they pull out.

"With the window down," Martin says. "I take customers around in this car."

"Sure. Thanks." Christo rolls the window down, lights a cigarette with shaking hands and inhales greedily. "Picked up this habit in prison. There was a lot of time on my hands. I quit the alcohol though."

"Me too. How did you get hold of me?"

"Your real estate ads. You were famous with your Internet business too, I remember. You've done well, Martin."

Martin laughs slowly. "I can get my marketing messages to say anything I want. Don't believe half of it." During the ninety minute ride they bring each other up to speed on the highlights and lowlights of their lives.

"And I am starting again," Martin concludes. "Just like you."

"I thought I was all washed up," Christo says tossing his third cigarette out of the car and rolling up the window. "I'd like to read Bandu's manuscript. Maybe I can write *my* story. Write all our stories."

"That will be a huge relief. I haven't done anything with the translation since Sumana mailed it to me six months ago. Except read it and feel guilty each time. Bandu took the ultimate fall for me."

"Shooting it out with the cops! He sure outdid us all. Yes, I'd like to write the stories. It will be a fitting way to get back. By getting it all out."

"You can stay with me for awhile if you like, until you get your bearings. Marnie and I still maintain separate homes."

"You think you'll ever get together with her. Get hitched?"

"I don't know. We've made a start. I am not going to force things anymore."

"Let karma take its course, eh?" Christo says, a smile lurking in his eyes.

"Yes."

When they get to Martin's house, the children are in the backyard. Jamie is teaching Julia chords on the guitar. Not bad, Martin thinks, for just their third meeting.

Julia breaks away and runs towards Martin. He hugs her. "Daddy, Jamie is teaching me to play," she says excitedly.

"Make sure he teaches you some happy songs," he says ruffling her hair as Jamie makes a face.

"Kids, I'd like you to meet an old friend of mine who goes back to my childhood in Sri Lanka—Chris Martensteyn."

Christo shakes a tentative hand with each of them.

"Are you a Burgher?" Jamie asks.

"Yes," Chris replies.

"Oh good," Jamie relaxes. "I thought we were the last ones on earth."

"Who's a Burgher?" Julia asks. "Isn't that something you eat?"

"Come along, I'll tell you about them," Jamie pulls her away, back to the guitar. "At least, I'll tell you what Dad's told me, if you play your chords right."

"They have your eyes," Christo says as the children return to their interrupted exercise.

"Salad's ready," Marnie says, coming out on the back deck. She is dressed in a black turtleneck sweater and pants. She descends the steps to the garden, extending her hand. "Hi Chris; Martin's told me about you. Nice to meet you."

Martin watches Christo suck in his breath as he shakes Marnie's hand, taking in her shapely body, contoured with the sweater. Poor bugger, I need to get him out into society soon, Martin muses.

"Glad to meet you too," Christo stammers, holding onto Marnie's hand as if it is a fragile wafer. "Thank you for inviting me into your family."

Martin fishes in the ice box and pulls out two cans of Coke. He tosses one to Christo and pops the other. "Time to put the barbecue on."

"The steaks are marinated and ready," Marnie says. "I'll bring them out." She heads back indoors.

As Martin fires up the barbecue, Christo sits in a garden chair, leans back and closes his eyes, inhaling deeply. "I could get used to this, you know. That smell of open-air fire reminds me of old times."

"And so you should. Now is pay-back time."

"In prison, I learned to stay in my box and not tread on other people's turf."

"It's the same on the outside. And every time you step out, you face retaliation. The question is how much turf do you want and how much are you willing to risk for it?"

Marnie walks out on to the deck, laden with a large platter held in both hands. "I'll get these going, there's a phone call for you, Martin. It's from overseas. From Sri Lanka."

Martin bounds through the open screen door to the kitchen, to the phone lying off its cradle. His heart is beating fast. A wave of expectation and fear is colliding inside him; he remembers the last time he had a phone conversation with Sri Lanka, the time his mother passed away. He picks up the phone. The crackly-voiced operator enquires, "Martin James?"

"Yes."

"You have a collect call from Sri Lanka. Do you accept charges?"

"Yes."

"Ah, go ahead then." She puts the caller through.

"Martin?" The voice is faint and even cracklier.

"Barney! Yes, it's me."

"I got some news for you. Won't take too much of your time. It's Daddy."

A vice grips Martin's heart. "Yes?"

"He's written to me and asked that Sena and I come out to see him. He says he cannot trust his lungs to make the trip himself. He's made sure by sending us a postal order for the bus fare."

Martin starts laughing uncontrollably. He jumps around in the kitchen.

"Martin, are you all right?" Barney is sounding confused at the other end.

"Yes, yes... I'm fine. I'm fantastic! This is the best goddamn piece of news I've had in years."

When he puts down the phone a few minutes later, Martin is beaming. He looks through the kitchen window out into the backyard. Marnie is turning the steaks over a blazing fire, Julia is straining her fingers to reach the chords Jamie is teaching her—it seems only yesterday that her older brother had been in the same "stretch" position; Christo is walking idly among the tall maples that have turned their fieriest red, Coke can in one hand, a cigarette in the other, stealing the occasional surreptitious look at a glowing Marnie. A new family, a fragile one, one that could be easily destroyed again. But Martin has worked with less before.

He smiles and walks through the door leading into the garden.

Acknowledgements

I would like to thank the many people who read and critiqued earlier versions or sections of the manuscript, notably: Ben Antao, Sharon Crawford, Deborah Stiff, Brian Mullally, Pat Calder, Felicity Sidnell-Reid, George Boycott, Shelagh Watkins, Drew Cameron and Sam Perera.

To the Humber School of Writers who gave me valuable feedback on the first draft.

To my editors Anushka Pereira and Jake Hogeterp—a big thank-you—for looking after the Sri Lankan and Canadian sections of this novel from your diverse perspectives. And to Lizz Jacob for her brilliant nit-picking of the proof copy. Thanks to Joanna Joseph for the cover design and to Blue Denim Press for taking a chance on "another immigrant novel."

Shane Joseph
2011

Biography

Shane Joseph began writing as a teenager living in Sri Lanka and has never stopped. From an early surge of short stories and radio play scripts, to humorous corporate skits, travelogues, case studies and technical papers, then novels, more short stories and essays, he continues to pursue the three pages-a-day maxim and keeps writer's block at bay.

His career stints include: stage and radio actor, pop musician, encyclopaedia salesman, lathe machine operator, airline executive, travel agency manager, vice president of a global financial services company, software services salesperson, project manager and management consultant.

Self-taught, with four degrees under his belt obtained through distance education, Shane is an avid traveller and has visited one country for every year of his life. He fondly recalls incidents during his travels as real lessons he could never have learned in school: husky driving in Finland with no training, trekking the Inca Trail in Peru through an unending rainstorm, hitch-hiking in Australia without a map, escaping a wild elephant in Zambia, and being stranded without money in Denmark, are some of his memories.

Shane is a graduate of the Humber School for Writers in Toronto and studied under the mentorship of Giller Prize and Canadian Governor General's Award winning author David Adams Richards.

Redemption in Paradise, his first novel, was published in 2004. *Fringe Dwellers*, his first collection of short stories, was released in 2008, and is now in its second edition. Shane's third work of fiction, *After the Flood*, a dystopian novel of hope, was released in 2009 and won the Canadian Christian Writing Awards best novel in the futuristic/fantasy category in 2010. His short fiction has appeared in literary journals and anthologies internationally. His blog at www.shanejoseph.com/blog is widely syndicated.

After immigrating (twice), raising a family, building a career, and experiencing life's many highs and lows, Shane has carved out a niche in Cobourg, Ontario with his wife, Sarah, where he continues to work, write stories, and sing and play guitar in a dance band.

More details on Shane's work can be found on his website at www.shanejoseph.com